A
CURIOUS
DAUGHTER

Jules Van Mil is passionate about being creative. Her career spans education, fashion design, styling and writing. Her debut adult novel *A Remarkable Woman* was published in 2022. In her spare time she loves to paint mixed medium abstracts and to kayak. She lives in Sydney with her husband.

You can find Jules at www.julesvanmil.com
or on Instagram @jules_vanmil

ALSO BY JULES VAN MIL

A Remarkable Woman

For children

Gemma Riley and the Fashion Fiasco

A
CURIOUS
DAUGHTER

Jules Van Mil

MACMILLAN
Pan Macmillan Australia

Pan Macmillan acknowledges the Traditional Custodians of country throughout Australia and their connections to lands, waters and communities. We pay our respect to Elders past and present and extend that respect to all Aboriginal and Torres Strait Islander peoples today. We honour more than sixty thousand years of storytelling, art and culture.

First published 2023 in Macmillan by Pan Macmillan Australia Pty Ltd
1 Market Street, Sydney, New South Wales, Australia, 2000

A catalogue record for this book is available from the National Library of Australia

Typeset in 12.5/16 pt Sabon LT Pro by Post Pre-press Group

Printed by IVE

The excerpt on page 18 is from the poem 'The Fire at Ross's Farm' by Henry Lawson, first published in 1894.
The excerpt on page 63 is from the poem 'Clancy of the Overflow' by A.B. 'Banjo' Paterson, first published in 1889.
The excerpt on pages 88–89 is from the poem 'My Country' by Dorothea Mackellar, first published in 1908.

The paper in this book is FSC® certified. FSC® promotes environmentally responsible, socially beneficial and economically viable management of the world's forests.

In memory of my mother – DJC
For all the love and encouragement you gave me

PROLOGUE

Melbourne, August 1994

The heavy rain from the late-afternoon storm had eased when the black BMW pulled up outside the legal practice of Carmody Meredith Partners on Collins Street. The driver held up his umbrella as Avril Montdidier-Meredith stepped from the car. She touched his forearm.

'Thank you, Ron. It's been a very emotional fortnight for both of us. I should be about an hour; I'll call you ten minutes before I'm ready to leave. The traffic will still be heavy so please pick me up in the laneway behind the building.'

Ron gave a courteous nod before he retreated to the car and edged his way into the line of peak-hour traffic.

How many times have I walked through these doors over the last forty-three years? Avril thought as she made her way slowly to the shelter of the canopy above the revolving glass door. She stared over the tops of the cars towards the Block Arcade, recalling the day she'd opened her first le Chic boutique in 1951.

What if I'd stayed in Paris after the war? What if I hadn't meet Henry Meredith on the train?

A cold gust of wind encouraged her inside and, as the elevator doors closed, she glanced at her reflection in the mirrored walls. Dressed in black from head to toe, her tired eyes stared back at her through the lightweight netting across her face. At seventy years of age, time had not diminished any of her poise and elegance, but today she felt weary. How she longed for some decent sleep.

It had taken all her energy to stay composed during the memorial service earlier that day, as six hundred people had gathered in the State Room at City Hall to pay their respects. Somehow, it had been even more difficult to deal with than the funeral ten days earlier. The finality of it all. The realisation that he was truly gone.

The doors opened on the seventeenth floor and a receptionist moved swiftly towards Avril, greeting her halfway across the carpeted foyer.

'Good afternoon, Mrs Montdidier-Meredith,' she said. 'He's waiting for you.'

'Thank you. I know the way,' Avril replied as she continued past a large modern sculpture and down the corridor to Reece Meredith's corner office. She knocked lightly and upon entering saw her brother-in-law place his whisky glass on the coffee table next to a pile of documents.

'Please, don't get up,' she said, greeting Reece with a kiss before taking a seat beside him.

'I'm sorry I took off like that,' he said, stretching his arm along the back of the sofa. 'I couldn't do any more chatter. What time did everyone leave?'

'Most had gone by three o'clock. You should have gone straight home, Reece. You look exhausted. I'd have been perfectly happy for one of your partners to witness my signature.'

'No, no,' said Reece with a dismissive wave of his hand, 'I wanted to. If I'd been able to change the execution dates for this sale, believe me, I would have. Besides, after all these years, well,' he hesitated, 'this is our final deal. The last big transaction I'll carry out on your behalf. Strange, isn't it? Today of all days.'

Avril opened her handbag and took out her reading glasses and fountain pen. Reece sighed as he leant forward, drew his hands together and rested his elbows on his knees. Avril suddenly pictured him sitting beside the campfire at Monaghan Station, the Meredith family's cattle property, laughter echoing over the flames as he and his two brothers traded stories. A familiar scenario through the years.

Reece tapped the pile of documents with his fingers. 'You realise once everything's signed, you'll have no recourse should you change your mind? All contracts are absolute.'

Avril unscrewed the lid of her pen and opened the first file of documents. Without looking up, she began signing the designated pages. 'When have you ever known me to change my mind once I've made a business decision?' she asked.

'True,' he said, finishing the last of his whisky.

Within a few minutes, Avril had signed all the necessary papers and sold her entire fashion empire, a conglomerate of manufacturing, fabric wholesaling, retail businesses and commercial property that had taken her more than forty years to build.

Sixty-four le Chic retail clothing outlets and fifty-two Jive Jeans stores, along with a large parcel of retail premises, had been bought by a private equity company. Monash Garment Manufacturing and Lewmont Fabrics, two enterprises Avril had started in Melbourne in 1953 with her business partner Joshua Lewin, had been acquired by another Australian consortium. Her bridal business would be taken over by the assistant designer who'd worked with Avril since the stores first opened. *That's in safe hands,* she mused.

With the formalities completed, Avril placed the pen in her handbag, removed her reading glasses, and sighed. 'To think it all started with one small shop, twenty buckram hats and sixty dresses. The strange thing is, it feels like only yesterday.'

'I never thought you'd do it. This really is the end of an era,' said Reece as he gathered up the folders and stacked them neatly on his desk.

Night had fallen and the sparkle of the city lights drew him over to the window. He stared at the heavy traffic below, the cars and buses bumper to bumper, clogging the rain-soaked street.

'I'm pleased your companies have been acquired by entities who want to continue the businesses as they are. Having two large consortiums snapping at your heels for the last year certainly made the sale easier than normal.'

Avril nodded. 'My heart wasn't in it anymore. Not once he was diagnosed.' Avril couldn't bring herself to say his name or the word *leukaemia*. So unexpected. All those weeks she'd spent at his bedside, waiting, hoping the treatment would work.

'It's the end of an era for me as well,' said Reece, turning towards Avril and sitting on the wide window ledge. 'I wanted you to be the first to know that I've decided to retire. And this time, I mean it.' He smiled.

'I'll oversee these final transactions for you and then I'm done.'

'I don't blame you. Especially considering everything that's happened. Caroline must be thrilled.'

'Oh, she's over the moon. She wants us to spend more time with the grandkids and do some of that travelling we're always talking about.'

Avril pulled a long cream envelope from her handbag, and sat beside Reece on the ledge.

'There is, however, one more transaction I'd like you to carry out, then you really can retire.'

'What's this?' he said as she handed him the unsealed envelope.

Reece sat motionless as he read the contents. When he'd finished, he re-read the two-page document, his expression leaving Avril in no doubt as to how astonished he was. Avril placed her hand gently on his shoulder.

'You can't be serious,' he said eventually. 'Tim would never agree to this.'

'I am serious, and he did agree. We talked about it at great length. It's what we both wanted to see happen. And when *you've* had time to think about it, I think you'll agree that this is the best decision.'

'You've totally surprised me,' said Reece. 'Both of you.'

He was still looking at her in disbelief as she gathered up her belongings and called her driver.

Reece refolded the pages, slipping the envelope into the inside pocket of his jacket. His brother and sister-in-law of thirty-four years had every right to make this call. And as Reece started to think about the ramifications of that decision, he struggled to find a downside to what the future would hold.

He embraced Avril.

'There's a time for everything in life,' she said.

'After all these years, Avril, you still amaze me. You've always been one step ahead of all of us. If this is really what you want, then I'll proceed as you've instructed. But I'd be lying if I said I saw this coming.'

Avril looked around the room, recalling the countless deals that had been orchestrated and signed within these walls.

'Do you remember what your father used to say? "We're here for only the flick of an eyelid. Just the flick of an eyelid."'

PART 1

Love sought, is good; but given unsought, is better.

William Shakespeare

CHAPTER 1

Monaghan Station, Queensland, 1979

J oy Meredith had regretted making the phone call the moment she put down the receiver.

She'd sat in her father's leather chair for half an hour, swivelling distractedly from side to side as she twisted the telephone cord around her finger. Eventually, hesitantly, she'd dialled the number.

Now, as she repositioned herself in the saddle in preparation for the next jump, she replayed the telephone conversation over and over, turning her face away from the early-morning sunlight that was already nudging the horizon to the east.

When he'd answered, her attempt at sounding relaxed and confident had only made her feel embarrassed and foolish. Even her joke about getting older was met with awkward silence. *He probably thinks he's a last-minute invitation*, she realised as she'd waited for his response. And he had been, but not entirely.

Sure, they'd danced together at a couple of Bachelor

and Spinster balls last year. Even shared a spontaneous New Year's Eve kiss the previous month as he'd swept up her hand in his and, along with a dozen other school leavers and uni students, staggered up the hill on a neighbouring property to watch the first sunrise of 1979. But he hadn't asked her out or called a few days later as she'd hoped. Wasn't that what boys were supposed to do if they liked you? *Why would he be interested in me anyway?* she berated herself, pulling angrily on the reins. *I'm probably just another country girl to him.*

A feeling of loneliness suddenly overwhelmed her. She circled her horse back around to the first jump and tried not to think about Hugo Lombardi and the complete idiot she'd made of herself by trying to invite him to her eighteenth birthday party.

Joy had never wanted to celebrate with a big hooray. At least, not the kind her parents liked to throw. Parties hosted by Avril and Tim Meredith were legendary, a show of hospitality that harked back to her great-great-grandfather's day, when graziers and pastoralists travelled hundreds of miles by horse and carriage to attend a gathering at Monaghan Station, two hours north of Toowoomba on Queensland's Darling Downs. What Joy would have preferred for her eighteenth was a small family dinner with her uncles, cousin Ben and her best friend, Scarlet. But once *The Planning Committee* – as Joy often referred to her mother – had suggested a party and a recovery lunch the following day, the festivities had gathered momentum like an unstoppable force. There'd been little room for negotiation. There rarely was where Avril was concerned.

Joy spurred the gelding forward towards the final jump, but completely mistimed her take-off. Confused and startled, the horse reared back then lunged forward, his chest careering into the jump and sending the top two bars crashing to the ground. With an apologetic pat to the big grey's neck, Joy settled the horse and slowed to a walk. Only then did she notice her grandfather standing at the wooden fence of the jumping arena watching her performance, leaning casually over the top railing. In typical Henry Meredith fashion, he had ensured that horse and rider were perfectly proportioned and that the sixteen-hand gelding, his birthday gift to Joy, was the perfect partner for a young woman of above average height.

Always the tallest girl in her class, Joy had learnt to deflect the playground taunts and nicknames with quick retorts and funny comments. She'd realised at a very young age that humour made an excellent ally when no other could be found. But she'd have given anything to have blended in inconspicuously with the other girls. To have felt the same as them.

The four-year-old grey had exceptional athleticism and she'd fallen in love with him the instant he was led off the horse truck a week ago. 'There might be something in there for you,' Henry had said as the truck, which had been driven up from his horse stud outside Melbourne, stopped in front of the stables. It hadn't taken Joy long to name the striking gelding Calypso – a moniker that borrowed both from the sire's name, Trinidad Rhythm, and the dam's, Hidden Song.

The cackle of kookaburras from the gum trees lining the Condamine River rang out as the warm February sun rose higher, bathing the station in a warm glow. At its centre was the elegant Georgian-inspired, two-storey brick and stucco homestead known to the family as the 'big house', which the Meredith family had called home for almost one hundred and twenty years. The original holding of 350,000 acres purchased by their ancestor Samuel Meredith was still intact, and cattle and sheep grazed the lush plains as they'd done for decades.

Except for the installation of electricity and plumbing after the First World War, little had changed in the forty-six-room home over the years. The white wrought-iron railing that ringed the second-floor balcony and the sweeping columns lining the front veranda were original and meticulously cared for. The manicured lawns, hydrangea-filled garden beds and a swathe of jacaranda trees that ran the length of the driveway shaded the house on all sides.

It was just before six o'clock and, despite the regular late-night singsong around the piano with some of the family, Joy was always eager to ride early. Henry, too, was an early riser, rarely sleeping more than five hours a night and usually up and about even before Kevin Lowry, the station manager, emerged from his weatherboard house a hundred metres away.

Joy collected up her reins and walked over to greet her grandfather.

'I mucked up the last one,' she said, resting one hand on her thigh.

'Never take your anger out on your horse,' said Henry. 'I thought you'd know that by now.'

'Well, I'm pissed off,' she fired back, not bothering to mask her frustration.

Henry drew himself up, grinning, and placed his leathery hands on his hips. Even when she was angry, the set of Joy's facial features – her full lips and high cheek-bones – made it difficult to believe she was anything but upbeat and cheerful.

'Yes, I can see that,' he replied. 'Not too happy about all the fuss that's going on around the place, are you?'

'Oh, I'm loving it. It's just terrific.' Joy waved a fly from her face. 'My birthday the way Mum wants it. I can't think of anything better. Can you?'

Henry surmised there was more to his granddaughter's annoyance than simply Avril's overzealous event planning but he chose to let it go. He'd watched this moment coming – when the calf inevitably pulls away from the domination of its mother – a moment he'd experienced with his own three sons. Joy was no longer a child but not quite an adult in the fullest sense of the word. Station life, boarding school and a smattering of travel – that had been her world until now. But school was over and the next phase of Joy's life was about to begin.

Henry ducked through the fence, crossed the arena and repositioned the poles. He caught Joy's attention with a raised hand.

'Go around again,' he called. 'Take your time.'

In his eighty-eight years, Henry Meredith had ridden, bred and raced more horses than he cared to remember. It came with the territory of a life on the land. He loved nothing more than to study each new batch of spring foals, his discerning eye searching for any idiosyncrasy, any anomaly that made one stand out from the rest. People, he would often tell Joy, were a lot like horses. *No two are alike, and a horse with a mercurial nature is unlikely to change.* He'd recognised something special in the long-legged colt born to his Arabian mare and immediately earmarked the spirited youngster for his eldest grandchild, whose passion for horses matched, if not surpassed, his own.

With her last round completed, this time successfully, Joy slid from the saddle and released her chin strap.

'Nicely done,' said Henry. 'How did that feel?'

'He's a dream to ride. Did you see how easily he cleared that last jump?'

'So, he's a keeper then?' said Henry, the palm of his large, weathered hand caressing the horse's sweaty hindquarters. 'Up to the mark, you reckon?'

'Definitely. I thought I might jump him at the Toowoomba Show in April, if I can make it back. Do you think he'd be up to it?'

Joy's independent nature meant she rarely sought the opinions of others, but with Henry it was different. In many ways he was more friend than grandparent, her confidant and mentor. She loved him dearly. And in his nonchalant yet caring manner, he freely shared his knowledge of horses, livestock, and life in general with his only granddaughter.

'The Toowoomba Show,' Henry repeated, folding his arms and squinting his deep blue eyes. 'You won't have much time to train once university starts. You can't come home a few days before the show and expect your horse to be ready. That's the quickest way to end up with an injured animal.'

'I guess you're right.'

'No guessing about it,' he said, pulling a couple of sugar cubes from his pocket and allowing the gelding to suck them from his palm. 'So, what are you up to today?'

Joy flicked the reins against her side.

'Helping with the set-up. I'm sure Mum's got an itemised checklist prepared with your name on it somewhere, too, so watch out.'

'Ah, yes, the birthday,' said Henry. 'I'm getting older while adulthood's getting younger. It wasn't that long ago that all the fuss was made when you turned twenty-one. Key to the door and all that.'

'Well, it's eighteen now,' she said, sweeping her hand over the horse's mane.

'Eighteen,' he repeated. 'Geez, that's a worry. Voting, drinking. You can even get married without your parents' permission. Whatever will they think of next?'

Joy kissed her grandfather on the cheek.

'Thanks again, Grandpa. You couldn't have given me a better present.'

'I see you had a win – with the shed I mean,' said Henry, as they strolled towards the stables. 'Didn't fancy a big marquee on the lawn?'

'No way. What a complete waste of money,' Joy replied. 'I managed to get Dad onside with that one. But I still wish we weren't having any of it. Have you seen how many people have been invited?'

Henry placed his arm around Joy's shoulder without mentioning the final tally, which he was certain was now north of one hundred, with the majority of the guests being close friends of Avril and Tim and members of the Meredith clan.

'You're their only child and your mother and father love you more than life itself. You'll be fine,' he reassured her, well aware of his granddaughter's reluctance to be the centre of attention. A broad smile broke across his face. 'But remember, if you ever need to work something out, saddle up and take off for an hour or two across those paddocks.' He glanced towards the horizon. 'That's where you'll find your answers.'

Joy nodded. Her grandfather had a way of talking that neither lectured, criticised or pried.

As she tied her horse to the hitching rail, the sprinklers at the front of the big house sprang to life, and watery arcs leapt across the lawn. It appeared the rest of the family had not yet stirred. It wasn't like the old days, when a full-time staff of thirty-five had lived and worked on Monaghan Station. There were, however, still plenty of permanent inhabitants – the cook, housekeeper, yard man, stockmen and jackaroos – who'd soon be up and about as the constant cycle of checking stock and fences, maintaining pumps and windmills began. Joy's summer break was nearly over, and Henry wanted to make the most of their time alone. He grinned at her.

'Fancy a ride with me?' he said.

'But are you up to it, Grandpa? I thought you still had a problem with your back.'

'Well, my camp drafting days are over, but I think I can manage an easy ride out towards Bunker's Ridge and back before the work orders are shelled out for this shindig we're having.'

'Which horse do you want?' asked Joy, delighted at the thought of a ride together.

'Saddle up the black mare,' he said with a wink. 'I'll get my hat.'

Joy and Henry mounted up and walked their horses down the edge of the airstrip, crossed the river where the water ran hock-high, and headed in the direction of the Bunya Mountains. As they passed, a small mob of kangaroos jolted upright, frozen in the long grass like a cluster of grey anthills. To the northwest, the grazing cattle dotted the landscape, their rust-coloured coats illuminated in the early-morning light.

The pair rode in companionable silence, lost in their own thoughts.

Henry noted how easily and naturally Joy sat on her horse. There was an emotional camaraderie like no other that existed between horse and rider, a partnership conveyed by touch, feel, pressure, movement. He had often wondered if Joy's passion for riding ran deeper than simply her love of all things equine. When a rider is in the saddle, it can be difficult to gauge his or her height, and he knew that height had always been a sore point for Joy. The combination of Joy's statuesque physique, brunette curls and cool green eyes like her mother's often drew thoughtless remarks that weren't intended to wound, yet so often did. *Look how much you've grown*, he'd often heard some well-meaning person say, or, *Are you really six feet tall?* As if Joy was somehow blissfully unaware and needed reminding.

'Got your speech written?' asked Henry as they approached an arboretum of gum and wattle trees at the base of a rocky outcrop.

'Just about,' she said. 'I thought I'd give you all a roasting.'

'Deflect the attention away from yourself. Is that your tactic?'

'Something like that,' she replied. 'Anything Dad has to say will be short and sweet, but you and Mum will be hard acts to follow, so a laugh is better than getting all sentimental.'

'Is that so?' said Henry.

'You'll probably finish off with a poem, like you always do,' Joy said, recalling some of Henry's more spectacular performances.

'You don't like me reciting my beloved Henry Lawson or Banjo Paterson?' Henry asked in mock outrage. 'You take exception to my ardour?'

'No, Grandpa.' Joy chuckled. 'I love your speeches. Honestly. And your poems.'

With a natural spontaneity, they broke into the first

verse of Henry Lawson's 'The Fire at Ross's Farm', a poem
they both loved, reciting the words with enthusiasm. They
looked towards the low-lying hills as the sway of their
bodies and the stride of the horses kept pace with the
narrative.

> *The squatter saw his pastures wide*
> *Decrease, as one by one*
> *The farmers moving to the west*
> *Selected on his run.*

Henry pulled his mare to a stop and used a log to aid his
dismount.

'Are you okay there, Grandpa? Need a hand?'

'No, thank you. This old bushy can still get on and off
his own horse. Even if I need to canvas a little help in the
process.'

They tethered the horses to a hitching rail underneath
the bough of a large gum. Henry lifted the hinged lid of a
wooden box that sat beside a circle of rocks and retrieved
a well-used billycan and two enamel mugs.

'Let's see how quickly you can get a small fire going,'
he said, pulling a bottle of water from his saddlebag and
half-filling the billy.

The winter rains that had filled the dams and the
Condamine River had chased away any possibility of a
harsh brown summer. Instead, the thick lush grass clung
to the riverbank and hugged the base of the trees, fanning
out across the paddocks. Joy gathered small sticks and
branches and within a few minutes, tendrils of smoke
drifted through the kindling as the tiny fire took hold.

'Let me do that, Grandpa,' she said, taking the can
from Henry and sliding the handle onto the wire frame,

allowing the flames to lick the blackened base of the billy.

Henry drew what looked like a tobacco packet from his hip pocket, opened it and sprinkled the tea leaves into the water, stirring the brew with a stick. He placed the mugs on the ground then pulled some shortbread wrapped in greaseproof paper from his shirt pocket and placed it on the log between them.

'We haven't done this for a while,' said Joy.

'Too long,' said Henry.

As steam rose from the lid of the billy, Henry tapped the side of the can with a long thin stick.

'She's ready,' he said.

Joy removed the billy and placed the hot can on the edge of a rock, carefully filling the mugs. The sun had breached the hills to the east and the only sounds were the chortle of the magpies and the husky bellow of a lone calf.

'I see Hugo Lombardi's name has recently been added to the guest list,' said Henry, taking hold of his mug. 'Since you've invited him, I guess that means you must like him?'

Joy blushed. There was no way to dodge a reply, not that she ever did that with her grandfather. With Henry's penetrating gaze and straight talking, he had a way of drawing the truth from her.

She sipped her tea and thought about Henry's question. She *did* like Hugo. For one thing, he was five centimetres taller than she was – a scenario she rarely experienced. The number of school socials she'd spent in flat shoes looking at the top of her dance partner's head were too many to remember. *Why not ask him?* she'd decided a week ago. Besides, he'd already told her that they'd probably run into each other at university.

'Why do you ask?' she said, deciding she wouldn't give up her answer without a little jousting.

'Ha!' laughed Henry, throwing back his head with delight. 'Touché. Well played.'

'Some matters are no one else's business except yours. That's what you've always told me,' said Joy.

'I have indeed,' said Henry, stretching out his legs and crossing his ankles. 'I'm just interested. You don't think Hugo's a bit old for you? What is he now – twenty-four?'

'He'll be twenty-three this year,' she said. 'He's not too old for me. You're ten years older than Grandma and that wasn't a problem, was it?'

'Well, you've got me there,' said Henry, smiling down at the contents of his mug. 'What's he studying again? Engineering, isn't it?'

'Architecture.'

'I thought he'd end up in the family business, but there you go,' said Henry. 'Not everyone does.'

'And yes, Grandpa, I like him,' she replied easily. *More than like him*, she admitted to herself.

'Well, if my opinion still counts for anything, he seems to have grown into a likeable young man. I've known his mother and father for over thirty years. As long as he's good to you, that's all that matters.'

'Grandpa. He's just a friend.' She laughed. 'I'm not about to run off and get married.'

'Well, that's good to know. You're far too young for that sort of caper,' Henry said with a wave of his hand.

'Dad said you've known his parents about as long as you've known Mum.'

'I have,' said Henry, recalling the first time he met Avril in 1950. 'Not long after your mother arrived at the station to work as a governess, the Lombardis leased some land from us. Wanted to grow wheat and maize, if memory serves. And as your mother spoke Italian, she used to visit, helping Gina and Mario with their English. I remember thinking the night of the Winter Dance, the first one your mother attended, what good people they were. Salt of the earth. They lost everything in the big fire of 1959, but then so did a lot of folks.'

He fell silent, lost in a memory of sound and fury, and the roar of a fire raging across the land.

Joy knew about the horrendous fires that had happened two years before she was born. She'd seen the black-and-white images of smoke-filled skies and the utes and trucks loaded with men and firefighting equipment in her parents' photo album. The yellowed newspaper clippings in the back of the album left Joy in no doubt they were very fortunate the homestead hadn't been destroyed.

'But they picked up the pieces, started again,' said Henry, shaking the past away. 'These days, the Lombardi family owns one of the biggest heavy machine businesses in the state. It's strange what can come from carnage and misery.'

Henry poked at the fire, rearranging the collection of glowing coals. Joy knew he had something he wanted to say. She could see it on his face.

Henry placed his mug on the log, folded his arms across his chest and lifted his chin slightly.

'Did you ever think about having a career in the rag trade?' he asked. 'Any desire to be involved in your mother's fashion empire?'

Joy looked at Henry in surprise, and shook her head.

'It's not my thing, Grandpa. You know I've always wanted to be a vet.'

'Well, you'll have your work cut out for you. Five years at vet school,' he said.

Joy didn't need reminding. As far as she was concerned, school had been an endurance test, like a long and arduous cross-country race. She'd met the entrance requirement by the barest of margins – two marks – and credited her best friend Scarlet with getting her over the line, particularly where physics and chemistry were concerned.

Fortunately for Joy, when it came to her interview with the dean of the vet school, her rural background and extensive experience with horses played to her advantage and she managed to secure a place at the University of Queensland. Practical abilities, the dean informed Joy, were just as important as academic rigour.

'Which reminds me,' continued Henry. 'I want to visit the stud before the month is out. Got time to join me for a short trip? Two days down and back? Your father will fly us there.'

'I'd love to,' said Joy, sipping the last of her tea. 'I'm hoping I can do some of my equine prac work there, if that's okay with you?'

'Of course it is. You won't get to work with a better stud manager than Oliver Tonkin. What that man doesn't know about horses isn't worth knowing.'

He gestured to the land around them.

'As my oldest grandchild, all of this will be yours one day,' he said. 'You're young and there'll be many twists and turns in life, most of which you won't see coming, but I hope when your father passes this property on to you, you'll be able to make a go of it, keep it in the family.'

Joy looked confused. 'But I thought Monaghan Station belonged to you?'

'Oh, it does, from a legal point of view. But I've long

considered your parents the owners, and rightly so. In spite of all their other business interests, together they've steered this place safely through fire, flood and drought and kept everything ticking along since before you were born. The transfer of the title will simply be a formality.'

They sat quietly for a moment as the burning bark crackled and the woody smoke filled the air. Then, unexpectedly, Henry reached over and took Joy's hand.

'Never forget, Monaghan Station is more than just your home. It's a refuge, a safe place whenever you need it.' He paused. 'I know school's over and I can see you're ready to strike out on your own. Happens to us all. It's part of life.'

'Oh, Grandpa. You sound so sad when you say that.'

'No, darling. I'm not at all sad,' he said, patting her hand. 'I'm very happy. Very happy indeed. Now,' he added, changing stride. 'When do your mates arrive?'

'Scarlet and some girls from school will be here later today, but just about everyone else will arrive tomorrow.'

'You're all bunking down in the shearers' quarters, I take it?'

'And in tents and swags.'

'Mayhem, in other words,' said Henry as he downed the last of his tea. 'Reminds me of all the parties your father and uncles used to have. And don't get yourself worked up over your mother's enthusiasm for putting on a show. It's in the blood. You just make sure you enjoy yourself.'

At the thought of seeing Scarlet and her cousin, Ben, Joy smiled to herself. Henry was right. She would enjoy herself. *Why do I get so worked up about things?* she wondered. Joy had become an expert at appearing outwardly calm when she frequently felt anything but.

'I suppose we'd better put out this fire and head back

before they send out a search party,' said Joy, and she reached for the water bottle and doused the flames.

*

Joy and Henry pulled their horses to a standstill at the end of the airstrip as the homestead came into view. There was a coolness in the morning air that would not last much longer. The sun would climb relentlessly and by early afternoon the temperature would soar, sending anyone who could spare the time down to the deepest part of the river for a swim.

'We couldn't have picked a better morning for a ride,' said Joy. 'And thanks again for my horse, Grandpa. He's beautiful.'

A shiny orange sedan was rumbling to a stop in front of the stables. The station manager, Kevin Lowry, and his kelpie, Drummer, crossed the yard to greet the visitor.

'Who's that?' said Joy. 'It's not the new farrier, is it? Not in that sort of car.'

Henry turned to look at Joy as the driver's door opened and Hugo Lombardi climbed out, greeting Kevin with a handshake and Drummer with a pat.

'What's he doing here?' said Joy with surprise. Although she was delighted, he was the last person she was expecting to see.

'What's he doing here?' Henry echoed. 'He's come to see you, of course.'

Joy tried to suppress her smile, then shortened up her reins and pulled her shoulders back.

'He called yesterday when you were in town with your mother,' said Henry. 'Said he was staying with his parents for a couple of weeks. Wanted to know if you'd be around today. I told him we could use an extra pair of hands. Did I forget to mention it? Must have slipped my mind.'

'Sneaky more like,' said Joy.

'Just a friend then, is he?' said Henry, and he signalled to his mare with a click of his tongue, lifted his hand and moved forward into a slow canter, grinning.

CHAPTER 2

Joy put the black mare in the back paddock behind the stables then turned her attention to Calypso, all the while watching the interaction between Henry, Hugo and Kevin. Her grandfather had been right. It was better Joy hadn't known about Hugo's visit. She'd have worked herself up into an anxious mess, and for what? She focused on grooming the young grey. How well her grandfather knew her.

Hugo popped the bonnet of his Valiant Charger and the three men leant over the engine for a minute, Hugo trying to answer Henry and Kevin's rapid-fire questions. Then Kevin headed off to work and Henry strolled towards the big house, his gait a little slower than usual. He reached the edge of the lawn and the two pups that had been playing on the veranda – labradors, Henry's favourite breed – tumbled down the front steps to greet him. Joy couldn't remember a time when there wasn't one by his side.

'You little rascals,' she heard Henry say, then he crouched slightly, gently scooped up one of the pups and continued into the house.

Joy was still scraping the water off her horse when Hugo appeared and leant on the frame of the doorway. Lifting a towel off the rail, she began rubbing Calypso's neck, moving swiftly down his shoulders and along his back.

'If you're looking for work, you'll need to see the manager,' said Joy. 'But I'd watch out for the boss's daughter, if I were you. She's a bit of a handful.'

'I've heard that,' said Hugo, smiling. 'A real nightmare, apparently.'

Joy glanced at him as she continued to rub down her horse. He had a conservative short back and sides, and black-framed reading glasses intensified his dark brown eyes. This neat presentation seemed to clash with his fashionably flared jeans and fitted V-neck t-shirt – a contrast to the moleskins and chambray shirts worn by the stockmen and jackaroos who worked on the station. Hugo looked like a country boy who preferred city life, a sort of studious John Travolta, minus the white satin disco suit. Aware of her gaze, Hugo casually crossed his ankles and she saw he was clutching a copy of the latest Dire Straits album.

'I called yesterday to see if you'd be home. Didn't your grandfather tell you?'

'He must have forgotten,' said Joy.

She busied herself with the lead rope, removed the headstall and sent the big grey through the gate to join the mare. She hung the wet towel over the rail and gathered up the equipment she'd been using, glad of activities to keep her nerves at bay while she tried to appear unfazed by Hugo's presence.

'This is for you,' he said, giving her the record. 'You said you didn't have this one.'

He returned her smile as Joy wiped her hands on her jeans and took the album from him. 'No. I don't.' She turned the cover over, her eyes drawn to the image on the back. 'Oh, this is great. Thanks so much.'

Hugo nodded towards the yard.

'I've got a stack of records in the car – Fleetwood Mac, The Cars, The Stones – in case you need them for Saturday night.'

'That's really kind of you, thanks. My cousin, Ben, has volunteered to be DJ. My mother suggested a band but . . .' Joy rolled her eyes.

'Yeah. I agree. I reckon a DJ is a much better choice for an eighteenth.'

'I hear you've been roped in to help today. You really don't have to stay if you've got things to do. I mean –'

Hugo wedged his hands into the front pockets of his jeans.

'I'm more than happy to help. The truth is, I've come to see you, Joy. And in case you're wondering, I was hoping you'd ask me to your party when I saw you on New Year's Eve. When you didn't, well, I thought perhaps you had a steady. Then, when you called . . .'

Again, Joy dropped her gaze to the back of the album cover. Almost every girl she'd ever known seemed to have had a serious relationship at some point, except her. She'd dreaded the late-night talks in her dorm in her senior school years when the other girls would gossip about their boyfriends. Joy had always nodded and listened intently while saying nothing. What could she possibly contribute to the conversations? She knew nothing of dates at the drive-in or sneaking down the hall to call some boy when the house mistress wasn't around. It was simply a club she didn't belong to.

'I know I sounded like an idiot on the phone,' said Hugo. 'It wasn't anything to do with you, I promise.'

His candidness took Joy by surprise and she looked him straight in the eye.

'The thing is,' he went on, 'you called just after I'd had a massive argument with my old man. I should have explained then, but I was in a bit of a state. Anyway, even if you hadn't called, I was going to orchestrate an invitation one way or the other.'

Joy fiddled with the record as she rocked back on her heels. She could feel her face warm as they stood close to each other. She wasn't sure what she wanted to say next; this was uncharted social territory. Hugo laughed nervously. It was his turn to feel a little uncomfortable.

'I think the last time I was at Monaghan I was about seventeen. Do you remember? You and I played tennis and I'm pretty sure you beat me.'

'I did,' said Joy. 'And you couldn't ride a horse to save yourself.' She tapped Hugo playfully on his chest with the tip of the album cover.

'Not everyone who grows up in the country loves riding,' he said. 'I was that serious, quiet, arty kid who'd do anything to get out of sports day. Born and bred in the bush but, well, it's not for me. So, no. You'll never see me on a horse.'

Joy sensed an inner loneliness in Hugo, similar to the one she felt herself.

'Have you eaten?' she asked.

'I pulled in at the Temples Roadhouse on the way out and bought a pie, but it was pretty woeful.'

'Temples Roadhouse. You were game,' she said with a chuckle. 'Come on, we'll go in. Breakfast will be up by now.'

Hugo took a small step closer to Joy and gently lifted a long curly strand of hair that had fallen across her face. He tucked it carefully behind her ear.

'Happy eighteenth birthday,' he said softly.

'It's not until tomorrow,' she replied.

He brought his lips close to her ear. 'I know,' he whispered. 'I just wanted to be the first one to say it.'

*

Avril had been in Tim's downstairs office with the door closed for the last hour, re-reading the sales agreement for Regency Footwear, when the telephone rang. Certain it would be Reece, she lifted the receiver and instantly dispensed with any time-wasting pleasantries.

'The last two clauses on page eleven,' she said, hovering her pencil over the page. 'I can't agree to that. Not with inflation running at thirteen per cent.'

'I don't think you have much choice,' Reece replied. 'They're unlikely to budge.'

There's always a choice, thought Avril.

'I'm more than happy to renegotiate the leases and get them locked in place,' said Reece. 'Especially if it helps to get this sale over the line.'

'That was never our agreement. Star Capital said they wanted to handle the leasing side of the contract themselves. They're buying a business with twenty-five successful retail outlets, an exceptionally low staff turnover and a marketing campaign that has made Regency a profitable business.'

'Yes. But that aside, it's still a good deal, even if we have to present them with renegotiated lease agreements.'

'Perhaps,' she said, a little irritated. 'It's a good deal, but not a *great deal*.'

Over the past twenty-eight years, Avril had become the Commander-in-Chief of the *great deal*. She'd planned her business strategies like a chess grandmaster, intricately considering her every move. She'd had her fair share of disappointments, even losses on occasions, but she'd never been foolhardy or impulsive with her investment decisions, nor had she been content to play it too safe when it came to expanding her enterprises. In the years since Joy's birth, Avril's desire to succeed in business had only intensified. She wasn't sure why; perhaps it was merely the habits of a lifetime, and her belief that true freedom came with financial independence, especially for a woman.

She'd been quick to spot the active lifestyle trend in the early 1970s, long before Jane Fonda's workout video would become a world-wide phenomenon and women would be motivated to *feel the burn*. But as Avril diversified into gym and workout wear, so did many others. Her designs were frequently copied, and cheaper, inferior garments, almost identical to her own label, began to appear on the market.

With each passing year the fashion industry had become more and more challenging. And while Tim ran the station, Avril ran her business operations from Melbourne, trying to avoid being away from Monaghan for more than a fortnight, if only to return for a couple of days. On the odd occasion when Avril couldn't make it back, Tim would fly himself south to the city that was like a second home to both of them.

As the 1970s drew to a close, the uptake of the designer label, which had started in womenswear, soon spread to accessories. Sunglasses, shoes and handbags carrying international brands became the must-have pieces. Local designers and manufacturers, such as Avril, tried to keep pace with consumer trends and demands. And yet, with all its fickleness and uncertainty, the world of fashion was still Avril's great love. She relished every aspect of it: the shop-floor experiences, the interaction with people and the buzz of starting something from nothing; taking a designer's initial sketch right through to the moment a finished dress or jacket walked out the door of one of her stores; all the talented people who helped to turn the giant wheel that was the fashion industry. She likened it to watching a vase of tightly budded lilies burst into full bloom.

If she had no appointments for an hour or so, it wasn't unusual for Avril to leave her Melbourne office mid-morning and stroll through the Walk, Royal and Block arcades to look at the window displays. Then she'd dash across to the womenswear sections in Grace Bros. or David Jones, stopping by a couple of her own shops on her way back, to talk to the sales assistants. There were times when she simply couldn't help herself. She'd start tidying the racks or compliment a customer on their selection, then show them through to the change rooms, winking at a member of staff.

Rarely had her intuition let her down. At least, not until she decided to expand into manufacturing and retailing footwear. This was something she was beginning to regret – fervently.

Now, as she ran her eyes over the contract, she knew she'd been outmanoeuvred like never before. At the same time, she also knew this predicament was of her own making. She'd spread herself too thin; tried to take on the other footwear retailers. The amount of time and effort it took to run a shoe manufacturing business simply hadn't been worth it.

'Look,' said Reece on the other end of the phone. 'If you're really not happy with the deal, why not wait and sell next financial year? There'll be other buyers.'

Avril tapped her pen on the desk as she reassessed her

position. In the times when the station had seen financially lean years, due to drought or plummeting sheep and cattle prices, it was cash from Avril's businesses that had kept Monaghan afloat. Not once had it been the other way around.

But now the tables had turned.

It was so unlike her to become distracted, to let such financial fundamentals go unaddressed. But this time she had, and she knew it. She sensed the wolves circling, ensnaring her.

'Reece, I need this sale to go through. *We* need this sale to go through.'

'As in Tim and yourself?' he asked.

Avril paused, her mind thinking kaleidoscopically, trying to spy an alternative solution.

But she knew. There wasn't one.

'Yes.'

'Are you in some sort of financial trouble? If you are, please, Avril, let me advise you.'

'No. It hasn't come to that. Not yet, at any rate,' she said, exhaling. 'Give Star Capital what they want. Let's get this sale finalised before the month's out.'

'I'll contact them today and set up a meeting as soon as possible. Caroline and I will be up in the morning with Ben. We can talk about this over the weekend.'

At the sound of Joy's laughter in the outside hall, Avril glanced at the clock on the mantelpiece and closed the manila folder.

'I'd better get a move on,' she said. 'Lots to get sorted.'

She looked out the long French doors to the blue sky that stretched to the hills beyond.

'What sort of day have you got up there? Fine I hope,' said Reece, as if he knew exactly what she was doing.

'Not a cloud in sight. It should get to about thirty here today. You know, Tim and I might even head out for a ride this afternoon.'

And as Avril put down the receiver, the thought of the two of them alone and away from the busyness of the homestead for an hour or so reminded her that it might be the perfect time to talk about what she'd been putting off for months.

It couldn't wait any longer.

*

A hot breakfast was a tradition at the big house, with Patricia Lowry, Kevin's wife and the station cook, laying out the bain-maries on the oak sideboard in the dining room by eight o'clock each morning.

Patricia and Kevin Lowry had come to Monaghan as newlyweds on what was to be a one-year stint. Two sons and three kelpies later, they were now permanent fixtures. With breakfast served to the stockmen and jackaroos at seven o'clock in the staff kitchen, Patricia then took a short walk along the veranda to the main house, where she cooked for and served the family. For decades, this morning ritual had given the household a chance to come together to discuss the events of the day or say their farewells before heading out.

Henry, Tim and his younger brother, Jordy, were already seated at the table, a selection of eggs, bacon and tomato on their plates, when Joy and Hugo walked in. After exchanging greetings, Tim went back to his conversation while his daughter and Hugo helped themselves to what was on offer.

'Good morning, everyone,' said Avril, coming in behind them and pouring herself a long black coffee.

'Mum,' said Joy. 'You remember Hugo?'

'Of course I do. It's lovely to see you again,' said Avril. 'And very kind of you to help out.'

'Good morning, Mrs Meredith.'

'Oh no, please, call me Avril. I always look around for my mother-in-law whenever I hear someone call me Mrs Meredith.'

Avril bent down and kissed Tim on the cheek. 'Morning, darling,' she said softly.

Tim Meredith had his father's deep blue eyes and imposing stature. He had spent all of his adult life involved in the running of Monaghan Station, except for his years as a pilot in the Second World War flying missions over France and Belgium. During those years, in the solitary moments before dawn broke, he had often wondered if he'd ever see the vast open plains west of the Great Dividing Range again; if he'd return to climb the fern-covered slopes of the Bunya Mountains or swim in the Condamine River. But unlike so many of his countrymen and women, he did return, and although life on the land was not for the faint-hearted, he never took its pleasures and beauty for granted.

Henry's heart attack a few days before Christmas in 1959 had seen him willingly relinquish the reins to Tim, at the same time as the worst bushfire in fifty years devastated the southern part of Queensland.

The fire had changed them all forever.

Col, their head stockman, who'd been like an older brother to Tim, Jordy and Reece, had died in the blaze.

Tim had then worked like a man possessed to restock the herd and repair the damage, not only to rebuild the station but to come to terms with the death of his first wife Rachel and the ten years he'd spent in a loveless marriage.

Every major milestone in Tim's life had taken place on Monaghan Station. The day he'd met Avril – he could still see her riding towards him along the edge of the airstrip in the late afternoon, her smile warm and engaging as she introduced herself as the new governess.

He could also remember long lonely stretches in the intervening years that had kept them apart.

They'd been married in a marquee under the jacaranda trees.

Their daughter had been born here.

Tim could no more imagine his life without the station than the night sky without the Southern Cross.

'You were up early,' Tim said to his wife. 'I thought you were taking a few days off?'

Avril sat down and shrugged, distracted by the mental checklist of things that needed to be done that day. She turned to Joy.

'I'll leave you and Hugo to set up the shearing shed and the quarters for your friends,' said Avril. 'Both will need a good sweeping out. The ladders and the lights have already been taken down, but you'll need to get the trestle tables from behind the tack room.'

Talk about Saturday night's festivities and the recovery lunch planned for the Sunday continued throughout break-fast. Fires would be lit in the forty-four-gallon drums and the buffet tables would groan under the weight of roast lamb, salads and desserts, replenished as the night wore on. A couple of the young stockmen had offered to man the keg and bar, which Henry had remarked was like putting Dracula in charge of the blood bank. Tim had taken the lads up on their offer all the same.

While Tim and Avril were asking after Hugo's parents, Joy caught Jordy's eye and flicked her head in the direction of the sideboard. Jordy, who after years of working along-side Tim now spent much of his time living at his own property in the Sunshine Coast hinterland, sidled up to his niece as they refilled their plates.

'Your grandmother and I are going into Toowoomba this morning,' he said. 'So if there's anything you need, just let me know.'

'Can you take Mum with you as well?' Joy whispered. 'She's doing my head in. She's been walking around with a clipboard for days. Why does she have to turn this weekend into such a big production? I'm sure I could organise a few fairy lights and a couple of fire drums.'

'And you thought school was over, didn't you?' Jordy said, grinning. 'It comes naturally for her to organise things. And we haven't had a big bash like this for a while. Think of the weekend as one big Bachelor and Spinster ball and you'll be fine.'

Joy replaced the serving spoon as Jordy leant in closer.

'Speaking of taking charge, have you said anything to your folks about the house in Indooroopilly?'

Joy looked at Jordy and quickly shook her head.

'I'm sure Dad will be cool with it, but not Mum. She's convinced that living in residential halls while I'm at uni is the way to go. But I think it would be like boarding school all over again. Besides, Scarlet and I thought we'd tell them together.'

'Force in numbers, huh?' said Jordy. 'Duncan and I are happy to have you as our tenants. And if you need me to come in and bat for you, just say the word.'

'She's got to quit with the controlling,' Joy said. 'She doesn't let up.'

'Well, I'm here if you need some support. I've known your mother a long time. I know what makes her tick.'

He helped himself to some spinach. 'But wait until your party's over before you say anything. You don't want to have a showdown before the big night.'

Anna Meredith entered the dining room, greeted everyone and reached for the teapot.

'This is a lovely surprise,' said Henry as he pulled out a chair for his wife.

It wasn't often that Anna joined the family for breakfast anymore. Over the past six months as she recovered from a knee operation she preferred to have breakfast in her room. She'd rise late then spend the rest of the day in her studio, painting. But today, with the shopping trip to Toowoomba with Jordy on the cards, Anna had risen early.

She reached for the toast. 'I was watching you earlier, Joy,' she said. 'Ever since that old wattle was taken out I have a clear view of the arena. You were jumping so well.'

'Until I lost it at the last,' said Joy.

'What happened?' Avril asked.

'Timing,' Henry interrupted. 'Her stride was out.'

'He's a young horse and maybe the jump was too high,' Avril said.

'No, Mum,' Joy snapped. 'The jump wasn't too high. It was my own stupid fault. I mistimed my approach completely.'

Avril picked up her teaspoon and stirred her coffee in silence. Joy felt Hugo's hand on her arm and instantly regretted her childish outburst.

'Well, I'd better get moving,' said Tim, dropping his napkin on the table. 'Hugo, could you give me a hand? There's a stack of wine and champagne that needs to go into the coolroom.'

'Sure. No problem.'

After the two men left, silence settled over the dining table and lingered, even after Anna and Jordy said goodbye and Henry headed off to 'tinker around in the workshop'.

Joy turned to her mother. For a second she thought about speaking in French, knowing how much her mother loved it when they spoke in her native tongue. But that would be conceding too much ground, thought Joy, as she mentally composed her short yet sincere apology.

'I'm sorry, Mum, I didn't mean to speak to you like that.'

For the first time since Avril had arrived from Melbourne, Joy noticed how exhausted she looked. Her face was without makeup and the circles under her eyes were dark. Avril held her coffee cup to her lips and closed her eyes.

'Are you okay, Mum? You don't look that well. Is everything all right?'

'Everything's fine. I slept badly, that's all. Go and enjoy your day. I'll see you later on.'

Joy hesitated in the doorway and looked back at her mother. From Avril's pensive look and her subdued mood, Joy sensed everything wasn't fine. But in the past, whenever Joy had tried to talk to her mother about her business interests, Avril had always been reluctant to go into any detail. Why, exactly, Joy was never sure. Maybe it was because Joy hadn't spent much time with her mother over the past year. Or maybe her mother didn't want to talk business all the time. All Joy knew was that she'd given up asking. It was easier that way.

Joy stepped aside to allow Patricia and the large cane tray she had cradled on her hip through the doorway.

'Telephone for you, Avril,' Patricia said, picking up an empty bain-marie. 'It's Reece and he says it's urgent.'

Avril sighed and shook her head. *Once more unto the breach*, she thought.

*

The shearing shed and shearers' quarters, located at the bend in the river two kilometres from the homestead, had been built there over a century ago for the most practical of reasons. The distance created a barrier between the homestead and the army of flies that accompanied the mob at shearing time. It also meant the shearers had a mere thirty-metre walk to their accommodation at the end of long, back-breaking days.

Nineteen years previously, Anna had overhauled the shearers' quarters to use as guest accommodation for Avril and Tim's October wedding. Ceiling fans, flyscreens and new beds had been installed throughout and the place completely repainted. A wooden sign that read *The Monaghan Motel*, whipped up by one of the shearers years ago, still hung above the kitchen door at one end of the veranda.

Hugo reached up and tied the last of the fairy lights to a wooden beam, completing the criss-crossing geometrical pattern that spanned the shearing shed like an intricate spider's web. He took great care to ensure the lights hung at a uniform height. Once Joy flicked on the switch, even the daylight couldn't diminish the jewel-like spray of sparkling lights that hovered high above the floorboards. Hugo climbed down from the ladder and studied his handiwork.

'What's next?' he asked.

They ferried tables and chairs up the wooden steps, arguing the merits of rural versus city life, talking about friends, music and what they each wanted to do once they'd finished their degrees, even though Joy hadn't even

40

started hers. She listened with interest to Hugo's stories about his part-time bar work at the Crown and Anchor pub, a popular watering hole for the students who lived in the suburbs that surrounded the university in Saint Lucia. Keen to find a part-time job herself, the thought of working in a nearby pub seemed a no-brainer to Joy, and she quizzed Hugo a little more.

'It's a dive,' he assured her. 'But the live music on Friday and Saturday nights draws a pretty strong crowd. I think you'll like the place.'

With the shearers' quarters swept out, Joy and Hugo drove back up to the big house to collect the sheets and pillows. Then they hoisted the drums onto the back of the ute, delivering them to the area between the two sheds. When the heat of the day abated and the cooler night air settled in, the fires were sure to lure the revellers off the veranda to enjoy the crackle of the flames and the beauty of the night sky.

Hugo sat in the ute's passenger seat, his left elbow sticking out the window as they drove about the property collecting one thing or another. There was an honesty about Hugo that made Joy relax. He was, she'd ascertained in a very short period of time, not only easy to talk to but a good listener. Not content with superficial conversation, Hugo's questions were direct, even a little probing. Yet to Joy's surprise, she didn't hesitate to answer him. Most of the boys she'd ever come into contact with talked mainly about themselves, but Hugo didn't.

'That house in Indooroopilly you were telling me about. The big old Queenslander. Did you get it?' he asked.

'Oh, yes. I mean, it belongs to my uncle, but he doesn't use it anymore. Not since he and Duncan bought a place in Eumundi. So he's happy to rent it to me.'

'Who's Duncan again? Another uncle?'

'Duncan's just . . .' Joy hesitated. 'Duncan's just Duncan. He worked with Mum for years as her assistant, and then he started his own events management business. Jordy and Duncan have been together forever.'

'You mean, as a couple?' said Hugo.

Joy flicked him a sideways glance. 'Yes, as a couple. Is that a problem for you?'

Hugo laughed and stretched his hand out the window, feeling the rush of the wind through his fingers.

'Not at all. Why would it be? One of my flatmates is gay. He's a great guy. If I have a problem with anything, it's with the way they're treated. Wait till you get to uni. There's plenty of opportunity to get involved with gay rights if you want to. That and about a dozen other causes where social change is needed.'

'Jordy and Duncan can tell you all about people and their prejudice and discriminatory attitudes,' said Joy.

'I'm sure they could. So, have you found anyone else to share the house with you?'

'So far it's just Scarlet and me. We'll need to find two others.'

'I can put the word out at uni,' said Hugo. 'There's always someone looking for good accommodation.'

'Well, we don't care who it is. As long as the rent's paid on time, they're tidy – I hate mess – they buy their own food and are fun to live with, we'll consider them.'

Hugo chuckled, shaking his head. 'Ah, you've never lived in a share house before, have you?'

'No. Why?'

'You might want to aim for the "pay the rent on time and fun to live with" aspects before anything else. If you can find a couple of flatmates who do that, you'll be doing well.'

'Well, I'll have Scarlet around, anyway. Life won't be dull with her, that's for sure,' said Joy.

'Scarlet. Is she the friend I met on New Year's Eve?' said Hugo. 'The one with short blonde hair? The one who got really, really sick and threw up in the back of Rick's car?'

'That's her.'

'Man, she likes to party hard.'

'That's Scarlet.'

Hugo drummed his fingers on the seat.

'You and Scarlet. What do they say? Opposites attract.'

'What, you think we're opposites? In what way? Don't you like her?'

'Oh, no. Don't get me wrong,' said Hugo, staring ahead through the bug-smeared windscreen. 'She seems like a great girl. I just get the feeling that a little bit of Scarlet would go a long way. It's not a criticism. Just an observation.'

Joy changed down into second gear as they left the gravel track and headed across the paddock. She wasn't quite sure if Hugo had made a barb at her friend, or a sideways compliment to her. Or both. She pulled up in the shade of the trees. The water level of the river, the highest it had been in many years, had formed a wide circular pool at this particular spot. Joy scooped a towel up off the seat.

'So, what do your folks think about you having your own place?' Hugo asked.

'I haven't told them yet. I think I'll bring it up after the weekend's over. No matter what, I'm not living in residential halls. That was my mother's idea. Not mine.'

'Too much like boarding school,' said Hugo as he closed the car door.

'Exactly,' said Joy. 'And school's over.'

CHAPTER 3

Joy and Hugo took turns using the rope that hung from the bough of a tree to swing out from a short wooden jetty, dropping like heavy weights into the cloudy current below. The grassy bank sloped gently to the water's edge and the large gum trees that grew on each side of the river cast a lovely dappled shade. It was a typical lazy summer's afternoon, with a setting that was as picturesque as the water was refreshing.

Joy and Hugo raced each other to the far bank of the river and back again. Joy reached for Hugo's outstretched hand as they staggered from the water, falling onto their towels a little out of breath.

'So, are you all ready for tomorrow night?' said Hugo.

Joy broke off a long blade of grass and twisted it between her fingers, trying not to stare at Hugo's wet arms and torso.

'I think so. You might as well bring your gear for the recovery lunch. There's no point driving back to Toowoomba tomorrow night, only to turn around and come back on Sunday.'

'Thanks,' he said, slowly pulling the blade of grass from Joy's hand. 'I'm glad we got that sorted. I was planning on crashing here Saturday night anyway. I'm sure we're in for an all-nighter.'

'Well, there'll be plenty of room and a ton of food if my mother has anything to do with it – which she does, in spades – so the more the merrier, I say,' said Joy, rolling her eyes at the thought of Avril's meddlesome planning.

Hugo lay down on his side, propped up on his elbow, and shooed away a fly. He held up the green blade and closed one eye, using the makeshift apparatus to estimate the distance between himself and a point of reference further along the bank. Then he stroked Joy's calf with the tip of the grass.

'I know it's not my place to say, but maybe go easy on your mum with the whole finishing school and starting uni thing. Not to mention moving into a place of your own. You have to remember our parents never did what we're doing. They're from a different generation.'

'My dad was a boarder,' said Joy.

'Well, okay. Your father had the boarding school experience like both of us. But so much has changed in the last twenty years. And life at uni is a world away from here, from country life.'

'My parents haven't lived under a rock,' said Joy. 'In fact, my mother was a bit of a trailblazer.'

'In what way?'

'Well, for one thing, she lived with James Carmody, my godfather, for many years before she married my father. And, remember, that was the 1950s when women simply didn't do that sort of thing. At twenty-six she started her own fashion business when most women had almost no financial independence. And she set up a charity, supporting women and children experiencing domestic violence.'

'That's pretty impressive,' said Hugo. 'Even so, most parents find it hard to let go.'

'I know my mother doesn't mean to make me feel like I'm ten years old. But she does. All the time. She's been so consumed with running her businesses and managing staff that I think she's forgotten I've grown up. Most school holidays I was here, at the station, hanging out with Dad and Grandpa. I spent hours riding by myself. Mum would flit in for a few days and then she'd be off again.'

Joy rolled over onto her stomach and rested her head on her forearms.

'My cousin, Ben – he's a year younger than me – would come up for some of the holidays, but most of the time I was here on my own, although there were usually a few kids around whose parents worked here. Lucky I like my own company, I guess.'

'Did that bother you?' Hugo asked. 'Spending so much time here without your mum?'

'Sometimes. Maybe. I mean, I always knew my mother wasn't a stay-at-home mum like a lot of my friends' mothers are. You know what holidays are like when you're a boarder. All anyone wants to do is go home, so there was no point asking any of the girls from school if they wanted to come and stay. They wanted to see their own families. Scarlet ended up spending a fair bit of time here last year while we were studying for our finals. If it wasn't for her help I don't think I would have passed a couple of my subjects.'

The cackling cry of a kookaburra rang out from a nearby tree and further along the river, another bird joined its call.

'Every family has its nuances,' said Hugo. 'Try being

an only son who doesn't want to go into the family business.'

'Did your parents want you to go to uni?' said Joy.

'Not at first. But I was determined to go. They came around in the end, but we certainly had many heated discussions about it. Dad was convinced I'd be turned into a radical communist. "No protest marches,"' said Hugo, shaking his finger as he imitated his father's Italian accent. He smiled, and then looked more serious. 'If I can give you a bit of advice,' he said, 'stand your ground about what you want to do but try not to get into any big arguments. It's not worth it.'

'This birthday fiasco. I didn't want any of it. It's what my mother wanted, and to a lesser extent, Dad.'

'Why didn't you want a party?' asked Hugo.

Joy shrugged. She wasn't ready to give a truthful answer to his question, which was that parties were a slow form of social torture for her. That she hated being the girl no boy asked to dance because she was so tall. Those feelings weren't that easy to explain. Besides, if Hugo liked her as much as she liked him, then for 'No-Boyfriend Joy', as one of the girls in her year had called her, things might be about to change. Joy sat up as a breeze skimmed across the surface of the river, and looked across to the gums on the other side.

'Most girls I know would love all the fuss,' said Hugo, sitting up beside her. 'Hey, I'm from an Italian family with three older sisters. They do this sort of thing all the time – over-the-top dinners and parties with everyone piling in.'

Joy sighed. 'I know. I know. I probably sound like some ungrateful brat. It's just that –' She turned and looked at Hugo. 'I'm happy to be involved, but I prefer to be on the edge of things.'

'As opposed to being at the centre?' he said.

'I sometimes think I'm a bit weird. I mean, I like my friends but I guess I also like being on my own, if that makes sense. I don't need a big birthday production, that's all.'

Hugo took Joy's hand, leant over and kissed her. Their foreheads touched as they both started to laugh, then he kissed her again. Being with Hugo was effortless, easy, thought Joy. As natural as walking and talking.

'You've got an amazing family. You're turning eighteen and you're about to start uni. What are you afraid of?'

'I'm not sure.' She slid her hand from his and pulled at the grass again. 'Life. Growing up. Making mistakes. All of it. Maybe, deep down, I'm still that little ten-year-old girl.'

'We're all ten years old in some ways. When you called to invite me to your party . . . Well, that fight I told you I'd had with my father? It was my fault, if I'm being honest.' Hugo rested back on the palms of his hands. 'There's always pressure for me to work in one of Dad's businesses during the uni breaks. But I prefer not to. That's the main reason I work at the pub, so I'm not relying on my father for money. It comes with too many conditions. I should know by now how to avoid the arguments but I guess we're all flawed. It's okay to feel uncertain. To feel vulnerable.'

Joy twisted her long wet hair into a ponytail at the back of her neck. She'd never opened up and spoken to any boy like this before. For the first time, she didn't feel the need to disguise her feelings with throw-away lines and a joke. Sitting in the dappled light, just the two of them, this wasn't worthless chatter. It was a proper conversation and she wished they could lie by the river and talk all afternoon.

'Is it?' Joy finally said. 'I feel like I have no idea about anything at all.'

Hugo tilted his head back and smiled.

'You and the rest of us, birthday girl,' he said. Then he leant forward and kissed Joy again.

From beyond the crest of the hill came the sound of a car horn tooting, shattering the moment. They jumped up and watched as a lime-green Torana bumped its way across the paddock, streamers flowing from the aerial, David Bowie blasting from the tape deck.

This could only mean only one thing: Scarlet Nelson and her entourage had arrived.

*

Avril and Tim didn't go out riding that afternoon as Avril had hoped they might. Instead, they were sitting in the cane chairs at one end of the veranda – deep in a tense conversation – when Scarlet's car flew down the driveway and skidded to a halt at the front of the house. It was a welcome distraction and they walked across to say hello, then sent Scarlet and her passengers off in the direction of the river where Avril was sure Joy and Hugo had headed.

As Scarlet drove away, Avril took in the garden beds and the pillars that lined the front of the grand old house with fresh eyes, and recalled the day she'd first arrived, twenty-nine years earlier. She could still see the house-keeper, Mrs Carmichael, bustling down the steps, shooing away the dogs as Jordy unloaded her two suitcases – her worldly possessions – from the back of his ute.

For the young French immigrant, Monaghan Station had been an unforeseen oasis, an island in the storm of events she'd left behind in Melbourne. She had only intended to be away for a handful of months. How could she have known that eleven years later, on a warm October afternoon, she'd walk down those very steps behind her to marry Tim? *How much of life is fate?* she asked herself.

Avril thought about her own eighteenth birthday. In 1942, life in Tours, France, had been beset by constant fear, hunger and senseless destruction. Month after month, year after year, the Second World War had raged on. Joy's childhood experiences could not have been more different from her own. Perhaps for that reason, Avril often felt torn between two worlds: the comfortable world of Monaghan Station where she was a wife and mother, and the ruthless business landscape in which she was a self-sufficient entrepreneur, driven by a determination born of hardship.

While she loved Joy and she knew Joy loved her, Avril could not ignore that there was a disconnect, a distance in their relationship. Somehow the closeness Avril had expected had not developed between them, not in the way it had between Joy and Tim, or Joy and Henry.

It saddened her.

'But why didn't you tell me about this sooner?' Tim said, picking up where they had left off with Scarlet's arrival. 'I didn't think we kept secrets from each other.'

'I wasn't keeping any secrets from you. What I was doing was running my businesses.'

'Your businesses!' said Tim, surprised. 'Don't you mean *our* businesses? I thought we were a team.'

Avril sighed. 'Don't be pedantic, Tim. Of course we're a team. We've always been a team. But the manufacturing, the retail shops, the commercial property, those are my businesses, just as buying and selling cattle is yours.'

Tim drummed his fingers on the arm of the chair.

'How much does Reece know?'

'Well, obviously he knows the sale of Regency Footwear has fallen through. He called me this morning the moment he found out,' she replied. 'That deal is dead in the water so now I have to find another buyer.'

The thumping headache Avril had had since that morning had not eased and her normally objective approach to discussions such as these was beginning to fray.

'Reece does the majority of my legal work, but he's not privy to any of my financial records, unless they're needed for some sort of transaction. He's my lawyer, not my accountant.'

'*Your* legal work. *Your* financial records. *Your* accountant. Can you even hear yourself?' said Tim, his voice rising in frustration.

'For god's sake, Tim,' Avril said. 'Don't pick me up on every word I say. You don't seem to get it. Business is tough and getting tougher. Competition from new labels is fierce. My wage bill alone has doubled in the last ten years, and this sale falling through is a real complication.'

'A complication in what way?'

She hesitated for a moment, sipped some water and returned her glass to the small side table. Her head was pounding at every word.

'Avril. How is this a complication?' he repeated.

'I guess this all started a while ago,' she finally said. 'Years ago, really. And yes, I should have spoken to you before now. If there's anyone to blame, and blame is not a word I like, it's me. Certainly not Henry and definitely not you,' she said.

Tim stared at Avril with a look of bewilderment. He had never heard her talk like this before. She sounded weary and defeated.

'Blame. About what exactly? Darling, what are you talking about?'

Avril knew she could not put this off any longer and it saddened her.

'I've been wrestling with two issues for a while now,' she said. 'The first is that this family's been living well beyond its means for some time and it's no longer sustainable.'

'Who exactly do you mean when you say "this family"?'

'Us, Tim. Monaghan Station. This whole situation,' she said, and for the first time her voice wavered. 'I know you de-stocked when the bottom fell out of the wool trade over ten years ago, and that was the right decision to make. But that also meant a substantial loss of income.'

'Income that you were only too happy to supplement with funds from your company, AY Holdings, as I remember,' Tim said.

'That's true. However, I don't have to tell you what it's been like these past four years since the beef price crashed. Look how many farmers have simply walked off their land or had the banks foreclose on them. When you had the chance to sell the other two stations up north, you didn't. I told you and Henry at the time that I thought interest rates would hit ten per cent or more, but you both dismissed my concerns as being alarmist.'

'Do you think I've mismanaged things? Is that what you're saying?'

Avril looked at Tim. She knew he was angry but she did not want to get into a heated debate, not this weekend.

'No. I'm saying that we have some serious decisions to make. It's not about mismanagement. It's about being realistic. And if anyone's mismanaged anything, it's me. The income from my fashion businesses and commercial property have been bankrolling the station for ten, probably twelve years at least. But it can't go on.'

Tim leant back in his chair and closed his eyes. A southerly breeze whispered through the jacaranda trees and tempered the silence between them.

'For starters, I have a massive tax bill to pay,' Avril said. 'That's why I needed the Regency sale to go through. In hindsight, I should never have bought that business. It's been nothing but trouble from the start. That's one regret I'll just have to live with.'

'Can the payment be delayed, or a part-payment made? You must have spoken to the accountant you've been dealing with at Parkers. What's his name? Don Whitby? The new chap that's bought into the partnership. What did he say?'

Avril hesitated. The very sound of the man's name made her skin crawl. She knew what she had to say next would crush Tim, let alone Henry, who had been a loyal client and close friend of the firm's founder, Eric Parker, for over half a century. But Eric had long retired, and what had started out as a one-man show was now a large company offering multiple financial services. Avril had hoped to save this part of the conversation for another time, preferably after Joy's party, but perhaps it was better to get it over with.

'My tax bill's the first issue I mentioned, and this is the second.' Avril stood and picked up her water glass.

'You'd better come into the office,' she said. 'There's something I need to show you.'

*

Hugo didn't stay long once the girls arrived. He glanced at Scarlet's car, which was now hurtling towards the shearers' quarters.

'I can't wait to see you tomorrow. I think we're in for a big night,' he said, then kissed Joy before driving away.

Joy had no idea where she and Hugo were headed but she didn't care. He'd left her in no doubt that he liked her, a lot. As far as she was concerned, that was a good place to start.

Joy headed over to the shearers' quarters, where the girls had claimed a bedroom and were busy unloading their gear, hooking their flared jeans and floral dresses over the rail of the bunk beds, depositing bags of chips and biscuits on the kitchen bench along with Scarlet's cassette player and a box of cassette tapes.

By late afternoon, they were all up in 'the yard', a haphazard collection of sheds and outbuildings covering an area the size of a football field where most of the station's activity began and ended. Scarlet and Joy were heading to the big house while the girls from the city had piled onto the back of Jordy's ute for a guided tour of the homestead and surrounding area. Chris, the station's full-time mechanic, was filling the ute with fuel.

If employees made it to their third year at Monaghan, they tended to stay. Sometimes for years. Chris Kennedy was one of them. Nine years earlier, Tim had just left Dubbo and the sun was not quite up when he caught sight of a hitchhiker. A duffel bag swung across his shoulder, his stride was brisk and purposeful.

'Where're you headed, mate?' Tim had called.

The lanky lad with a mop of fair curls bent over to the level of the car. The bluish-purple shiner around his right eye was plain to see.

'Anywhere my old man isn't.' He smiled.

Chris was only too happy to say he was dug in for the

long haul at Monaghan Station and wasn't going anywhere. He'd been dating one of the local dental nurses for the last year and had his eye on some land. When asked how he was, he would give his usual reply: *Happy and getting happier all the time.*

Chris replaced the petrol cap on the ute, pulled a cloth from his back pocket and wiped his hands. The girls looked back at him, laughing and waving as Jordy drove off, bumping along the edge of the airstrip.

Scarlet and Joy headed up to Joy's bedroom, where Scarlet made herself at home on the bed, pulling the latest issue of *Cosmopolitan* magazine from the bottom of her tote bag.

Joy slid the Dire Straits record from its cover and placed it on the turntable.

'I've been wanting to play this album since Hugo gave it to me.' She turned up the volume before opening her wardrobe doors.

'This dress is on my shortlist for tomorrow night. What do you think? In or out?' asked Joy.

Scarlet blew a smoke ring as she glanced up from the page.

'Definitely out. It's your eighteenth, not a school dance.'

Joy had to agree. As much as she liked the pale green floral dress, it was not party material.

'So, what's going on with you and Hugo?' Scarlet asked, pleased they were finally alone. 'I think he's a dish. You know, the strong silent type.'

'He's really nice. I like him,' said Joy, holding a pair of denim flares up to her waist.

'Oh, come on. *He's really nice. I like him,*' Scarlet repeated, tapping her cigarette on the edge of the ashtray. 'What does that mean?'

'It means exactly that,' said Joy, and she turned back to flicking through her clothes.

'Well, I think he's hot, even if he's a bit conservative. And he's smart which makes him *really* hot. It's pretty obvious that he more than likes you.'

She could feel Scarlet's stare drilling into her back. There was nothing Scarlet could say that would induce Joy to talk about anything she didn't want to. It was Joy's nature to keep things she considered personal to herself and yet, she was pleased with the decision she'd recently made. *Now would be the perfect time to tell her.*

'I made that appointment we talked about,' said Joy. 'The one with Family Planning. I went at the beginning of December. I'm on the pill.'

'That's a great move. How do you feel? Any nausea?'

'None at all, but I've gone up a full cup size in two months,' said Joy. 'I just feel . . . relieved. Like I've taken control of my life somehow.'

'Aren't we the lucky ones. Having a choice,' said Scarlet, closing the magazine and stubbing out her cigarette. 'That reminds me . . .' She reached into her bag and tossed a tattered paperback across the bed.

Joy picked up the book and looked at the front.

'*A gynaecological guide for life,*' she said, reading the subtitle on the cover that was held together with sticky tape.

'I can't think of anyone else I'd rather give one of my most treasured possessions to,' said Scarlet. 'I probably should have bought you a new copy, but –'

'No. I'd much rather have this one,' said Joy as she sat on the end of the bed. 'Thank you. Do you remember how all the girls in our dorm used to read this book under the covers after lights out?'

'And someone covered the book with a dust jacket from a copy of *War and Peace*, so it wouldn't get confiscated. And all that boy talk,' said Scarlet. 'I don't know why I used to go into so much detail.'

'Don't worry,' said Joy, and she grabbed hold of Scarlet's foot playfully. 'You were just as informative as you were entertaining. You were an educational resource for all of us.'

Unlike Joy, Scarlet never held back when it came to sharing the details of any of her romantic encounters. At parties, she had always been confident when it came to chatting up guys, even fearless. Teetering in her high platform shoes, she'd sashay her way into a group and instantly hold court. She'd had two serious boyfriends while Joy had had none, though neither ever made an issue of it.

'Hey. What about those jeans and that top for the big night,' Scarlet suggested, jumping off the bed, taking the hanger and holding the shirt in front of Joy.

'I've got something else,' said Joy. 'I'll show you,' and she opened the other side of the wardrobe, lifted a hanger and unzipped a long white garment bag.

'Oh, that's wild,' said Scarlet. 'I love it. Go on, put it on,' and she jumped back on the bed and lit another cigarette.

Ever since Joy had known her, Scarlet had been in a hurry. A hurry to learn, a hurry to grow up, a hurry to have fun. Joy knew that people wondered how she and Scarlet could be friends, as they seemed diametrically opposed in almost every way. Classically petite at 162 centimetres when wearing her favourite orange platform wedges, there was an elfin quality to Scarlet that made her appear younger than she was. While long hair with Farrah Fawcett side-flicks was all the rage, Scarlet preferred to wear her hair short with a long fringe swept to one side of her face.

In quiet moments over the years, Scarlet had told Joy about her childhood: a glimpse into a world so different from the one Joy knew. Everything Scarlet didn't want in life was contained within the four walls of her parents' seaside milk bar and the pale blue weatherboard shack at the back that they called home. Thanks to the foresight and perseverance of Miss Jankovic, her year six teacher, Scarlet's father had begrudgingly signed a scholarship application form, conscious of the unpaid labour he could potentially lose. He'd leant on the front counter on a customer-less Saturday afternoon, one ear tuned to the radio as he listened out for the next race at Doomben, picked up a red Bic biro and scrawled his signature across the bottom of the page. 'She'll never get it, Shirl,' was all he'd said before tossing the pen aside and returning to the sports page of the *Courier-Mail*.

When Scarlet recounted this story, Joy could see how much her father's low opinion of her had hurt. But she had won the scholarship, and she'd left for bigger and brighter things.

It was through Scarlet that Joy had first heard about the book Scarlet had just given her. On the day she'd left for school, Scarlet had waited until the Greyhound bus pulled away before taking her mother's well-worn copy of Derek Llewellyn-Jones's *Everywoman* from her canvas backpack. By the time the coach had turned onto the Burnett Highway, she was leaning against the window, already halfway through the chapter on reproduction. Scarlet didn't look back.

And now they'd both been accepted into university. Joy was to study vet science and Scarlet, medicine.

'No more scooping ice-cream, making milkshakes and frying onions,' Scarlet had said to Joy the morning she received her year twelve results. 'Watch out, world. Here we come.'

*

By Saturday lunchtime the shearing shed and 'The Monaghan Motel' had morphed into Party Central as the rest of Joy's cohort began to arrive. The paddock behind the shearing shed soon resembled a used car lot as a fleet of well-travelled Ford Falcon sedans and utes, Holden Geminis, Toranas and a couple of hotted-up Monaros rolled in. Those first to arrive claimed a bed in the shearers' quarters while others pitched tents or dumped their swags on the veranda. The eclectic mix of country and city kids, some of whom had never been much beyond the outer suburban limits, had carpooled to make the five-hour trip from Brisbane to the property, an hour northeast of Dalby. Most had recently finished year twelve, some were already at uni, while a few had full-time jobs. Some local friends from Joy's primary school and pony club days arrived and headed to the river for a swim. With the invitation being 'guest plus one', many of Joy's friends had brought either their boyfriend or girlfriend, some of whom Joy had never met. But no one was going to stand too much on cere-mony when it came to who showed up to an eighteenth birthday bash in the bush. And like any weekend celebra-tion where spirits are high and the anticipation of a good time is prevalent, promises would be made on the dance floor or out the back of the shed, and a few hearts would be broken before the weekend was over.

CHAPTER 4

By nightfall, the shearing shed at Monaghan Station had come to life. A delectable aroma drifted from the barbeque as Tim and Avril stood at the entrance to the shed greeting friends and family.

Joy and Hugo, who were standing on the veranda, turned in unison at the sound of a voice calling Joy's name.

'Cousie!' Ben shouted. 'Happy birthday. Wow, doesn't this place look amazing?'

Joy grinned. 'Hugo, this is my cousin Ben, or BJ.'

'Great to meet you,' said Hugo.

Hugo, who hadn't left Joy's side since he'd arrived, scooped up a few glasses of champagne from a nearby table.

'Cheers,' he said, handing out the drinks.

'I'd better get the music pumping,' said Ben. 'Nice to meet you, mate,' and he slapped Hugo on the back and winked at Joy, spinning on the heels of his boots and heading towards the turntable.

When Hugo had first arrived, Joy had been surprised to see that he wasn't wearing his glasses. She hadn't said anything, but he must have read her mind.

'I'm giving contact lenses a try. So far so good.'

'I don't know,' said Joy. 'I kind of like those glasses of yours.'

Just as a song by the Bee Gees began to blast from the speakers, Scarlet appeared and whipped the flutes from Joy and Hugo's hands.

'Come on, you two,' she said. 'This is no time for talking.'

On the dance floor, Joy's soft pink jumpsuit shimmered beneath the intricate maze of fairy lights. Ben, who was revelling in his self-appointed role as DJ, kept the turntable in overdrive as he quickly changed records, flicking through boxes of albums to locate the perfect tracks for his captivated audience.

'Where's my goddaughter?' Joy heard a voice shout over the music.

With a glass of red wine in one hand and arms spread wide, James Carmody greeted Joy with a loving hug. James's life had been so intertwined with Avril and the Meredith family that it was often assumed he was a relation.

Joy introduced Hugo to James who turned and called to his wife, 'Margot, come and meet Joy's boyfriend.'

Joy was instantly taken aback but she needn't have worried. Hugo took her hand and gave it a gentle squeeze.

'I knew we'd get there sooner or later,' he whispered in her ear. 'Now that your godfather's declared it, I guess that makes us official, if that's what you want.'

'I think that's a great idea,' said Joy with a smile.

*

Just as Joy had predicted, her father's speech was short, her mother's somewhat longer. Both were full of praise and love for their only child. Joy's friends whooped and howled at each entertaining detail when Scarlet recounted anecdotes from their school days. Assisted by the rum and Cokes she'd been knocking back, Scarlet tried to contain her tears when she spoke about how much Joy's friendship meant to her.

As much as she had dreaded standing up in front of everyone, Joy responded with some well-chosen sentiments, thanking her friends and family for making the trek to Monaghan for the night. She then launched into a well-thought-out yet seemingly spontaneous one-woman comedy routine, where she jokingly lambasted her parents and other members of her family.

The last speech of the night was made by Henry. As he stepped forward, a respectful hush settled throughout the shearing shed.

Henry didn't recount events from Joy's childhood or wax lyrical about her equestrian talents. Nor did he mention the countless hours they'd spent together on Monaghan Station since she was born. Instead, he talked of friendship and trust, of dreams and possibilities, and the ebb and flow that is life. He spoke not only to Joy, but to every person in the shearing shed that night, casting his gaze around the room, lowering his smooth baritone voice, forcing his audience to a complete, enthralled silence as they listened.

'Before I finish up,' said Henry, 'and let you all get back to the bar and the dance floor, there is one thing I wish to say. To my darling granddaughter, I gift you these words from "Clancy of the Overflow", by A.B. Paterson.' He paused and took Joy's hand in his. 'For we are all poets. May your life be filled with beautiful verse.'

In my wild erratic fancy visions come to me of Clancy
Gone a-droving "down the Cooper" where the western
*   drovers go;*
As the stock are slowly stringing, Clancy rides behind
*   them singing,*
For the drover's life has pleasures that the townsfolk
*   never know.*
And the bush hath friends to meet him, and their kindly
*   voices greet him*
In the murmur of the breezes and the river on its bars,
And he sees the vision splendid of the sunlit plains
*   extended,*
And at night the wond'rous glory of the everlasting
*   stars.*

*

As the night wore on revellers gathered around the fire drums as sparks of illuminated gold spun up into the cool night sky. It was after midnight and Joy had just sat down on the veranda to catch her breath when she felt a hand upon her shoulder. She passed her drink to Scarlet and stood as Henry put his arm around her. They both laughed as a chorus of 'Mamma Mia' rang out from the conga line that was weaving its way around the dance floor.

'Anna seems to have snuck back up to the house,' said Henry. 'I think I'll call it a night as well. It's been a lovely gathering, Joy. I'll get Jordy to run me up.'

'I'll take you, Grandpa. I want to change my shoes anyway. These ones are giving me blisters.'

They walked arm in arm along the veranda.

'So, you and Hugo are girlfriend and boyfriend, I hear? What did I say about parties and romance?'

'Nothing's private in this family,' said Joy.

'Oh, you'd be surprised,' said Henry, and he chuckled, remembering youthful dalliances long past.

Henry stopped and patted Joy on her arm. She thought he seemed out of breath and a little unsteady on his feet.

'Are you okay, Grandpa?' she said, feeling a tremor run through him.

'I think I'll just sit for a moment,' he said, lowering himself into the closest chair. 'I might have overdone it a bit today. Keep forgetting I'm not fifty anymore.'

'Let me get you a glass of water,' Joy said.

'No, no. I'll be fine in a minute. Don't fuss or you'll have your mother summoning a doctor from town.'

They sat for a few minutes, watching the party-goers, content in their silence.

When Henry was ready Joy drove him up to the big house and escorted him upstairs. Anna was still awake, sitting up in bed reading. Even in her pale blue nightie, Anna Meredith looked composed and elegant. Her silver-grey hair was swept back off her face, falling in waves to her shoulders. She peered over the top of her tortoiseshell reading glasses.

'Here I am, my love. Back from the muster,' Henry joked, then turned to Joy and hugged her. 'Thank you for seeing me home, sweetheart. Now you go back and *party on*, as you youngsters say.'

''Night, Grandpa. Thank you for your lovely speech.' She bent down and kissed his forehead. Joy stopped halfway across the room and looked back. 'Sweet dreams. See you in the morning.' Then she closed the door quietly.

Pleased to have a moment to herself, Joy sat on the top step of the front veranda and looked up into the starry sky. It had been a wonderful night, far better than she'd imagined. She pulled her knees into her chest and folded her arms around her legs. She was in no rush to head back to the shed. Scarlet would be leading the partying, probably until sunrise.

She saw Hugo walking towards her, his silhouette clearly visible in the light of the full moon. They sat facing each other with their backs against the pillars.

'What a night,' said Hugo. 'Tired?'

'I'm exhausted. But it's been fantastic,' replied Joy.

'I hear BJ has organised a mini-Olympics for tomorrow,' Hugo said. 'Tennis, swimming, croquet, and a run of some description.'

Joy chuckled. 'That sounds like a sure way to cure a hangover.'

Hugo offered her his hand.

'Come with me,' he said. 'Let's look at the stars.'

Hand in hand they walked across the gravel driveway and lay down next to one another in the middle of the lawn in front of the house, staring up at the inky sky ablaze with stars. Joy's head rested on Hugo's shoulder as he playfully looped his leg over her ankle. He twirled a strand of Joy's hair between his fingers.

'When do you head down to Brisbane?' asked Joy.

'Not until uni goes back. I've got a christening to attend and my sister's engagement party next weekend. So I'm around for the next couple of weeks. How about you?'

Joy was about to reply when she heard her name. She sat up and turned back to the house. Anna was standing on the veranda near the front stairs, holding on to a pillar.

'Joy?' Her voice wavered. 'Can you hear me? Are you still here?'

Joy jumped to her feet and sprinted across the lawn as Anna's legs gave way and she folded onto the floor.

'What is it, Grandma? What's the matter?'

Anna tried to speak but the words would not form. Her breathing was laboured as she closed her eyes.

'Quick,' Joy called to Hugo. 'Take the ute and get my mother and father. Don't make a scene. She might be having a stroke. I don't know.'

Joy cradled Anna's body into hers.

'I'm here, Grandma. I'm with you. Hugo's gone to get Mum and Dad. Everything's going to be all right. Everything's going to be fine.'

A short while later a vehicle skidded to a halt in front of them and Tim and Avril leapt from the car and charged up the steps. Anna reached out and took Tim's hand as Joy supported her. Avril put her arms around Anna's shoulders.

'Mum, what's happened?' said Tim. 'Do you feel unwell?'

Anna's head lolled to one side as she tried to speak.

'It's . . . it's not me. He . . . he – he's gone, Tim.'

'Who's gone, Mum?'

A crushing weight descended on Joy as Anna took another deep breath.

'It's Henry. He's gone.'

*

Joy would later say she'd somehow known what had happened the moment she'd seen Anna standing on the veranda. In the days that followed she recalled over and over, in a series of film-like fragments, the last days she'd spent with her grandfather and the signs that might have warned them – his quietness, his tiredness, his growing unsteadiness.

While Hugo had gone back to the party to find Jordy,

Reece, Caroline and Ben, Tim and Avril brought Anna into the living room and laid her down on the sofa. At the same time, Joy walked calmly to her grandparents' bedroom and stopped in the doorway. Her grandfather was lying on his back, still in the clothes he'd worn that night, his eyes closed. He looked as if he were asleep. Surely he would wake at any moment. And yet his stillness was undeniable, irreversible. Joy lowered herself onto the edge of the bed and gently stroked his hand. Whether her composure was the result of shock she wasn't sure. Whatever the case, a feeling of serenity overtook her and though her eyes were burning, there were no tears.

Tim crossed the room slowly and looked down at his father in disbelief.

'Dad, it's me,' he said, as if to wake him.

Joy guided her father to where she'd been sitting. Tim grasped his father's hand and began to sob. His sob became a howl as his head fell to the bed. Without a word, Joy walked to the door and closed it behind her, leaving her father and grandfather together. Jordy and Reece would also need time alone with their father, and time alone as brothers. Joy found her mother in the main entrance, sitting at the bottom of the staircase.

'This is such a shock,' said Avril. 'I can't quite believe it. He was only talking to us all this evening and . . .' Avril began to weep uncontrollably in her daughter's arms.

'Dad's with him. Go on in there, Mum. He needs you.'

In the heartache of the moment, the normally formidable Avril seemed bewildered, lost.

'All our guests. Your party,' said Avril.

'Don't worry about any of that right now, Mum. I'll sort things out.'

Joy surprised herself with her own clear thinking, and went to join the other family members, now gathered in the living room.

Anna was sitting up, Jordy and Reece beside her.

'Dr Maynard's been called. He's on his way,' said Caroline, Joy's aunt.

Anna's eyes met Joy's, and Joy knelt in front of her grandmother and placed her hands gently on her knees.

'You left and he took off his shoes and lay down on the bed,' said Anna. 'He said, "I'm so tired, darling, I feel so very tired. But what a lovely evening we've all had." I was agreeing with him when I saw he'd closed his eyes. I thought he was asleep so I went back to my book. About twenty minutes later when he hadn't stirred I got up and went around to his side of the bed to turn off his lamp.' Her voice drained away. 'That's when I realised he wasn't just sleeping.'

Joy hugged her grandmother as Anna began to sob.

*

As a quiet descended over the big house, the party was still raging on two kilometres from the homestead. Joy sent Hugo to find Kevin and Patricia. Once they were up at the house and had been told about Henry's death, Kevin put up his hands to stop Joy mid-sentence.

'Leave it to us, Joy. We'll keep an eye on everyone and everything down at the shed. You just focus on your family.'

Gratefully, Joy joined her grandmother, parents, uncles, aunt and cousin by Henry's bedside. This moment had come upon them so suddenly and unexpectedly that it didn't seem real. Yet they knew it was. Birth and death were the alchemy of life on the land.

Anna was sitting on the bed, holding her husband's hand, while her sons surrounded her. When Joy entered the bedroom she lit the cluster of candles that were on Anna's dressing table. The faint scent of gardenia drifted in the air.

'We're all here, my darling,' said Anna, her voice breaking. 'You're not alone.'

No one spoke except for Anna. Joy pulled her gaze away from her grandfather as the full moon caught her eye through the window, a perfect ball of light hovering in the darkness. The moonlight fell through the glass like a soft voile curtain, and in the moment, that unchangeable, irreversible moment, Joy closed her eyes.

She could see her grandfather lifting his reins, his silhouette becoming smaller and smaller as he cantered effortlessly across the paddock to the hills beyond as he'd done so many times before.

*

The following afternoon Joy went in search of the station manager. A steady stream of cars had been exiting since mid-morning and she wanted to know what had been said to all the guests. Joy and Kevin sat on the veranda at the Lowrys' cottage with Drummer at their feet. The flyscreen door swung open and Patricia appeared with tea and sandwiches.

'Try to eat something if you can, love,' she said to Joy. 'It'll do you good.' She patted Joy on her shoulder, stepped around the kelpie and went back inside.

'I have to tell you, you've got a couple of good mates in Hugo and Scarlet,' said Kevin as he poured the tea. 'Not only have they packed away all the equipment from the shearing shed and quarters, but they've cleaned up as well.

Despite her filthy hangover, Scarlet rallied everyone at first light as soon as Hugo told her what had happened. She got everyone into the shearing shed and Hugo did the talking. I wasn't there at the time but Chris said Hugo handled the situation brilliantly. *Spoke eloquently*, he said. Christ, I didn't even know Kennedy had that word in his vocabulary! In a nutshell, Hugo said it would be appreciated if everyone could make tracks as respectfully as possible, by midday.'

'Do you know where Hugo and Scarlet are now?' asked Joy.

'They both said they'd wait for you to call them. They headed off about an hour ago.'

Joy reached down and scratched Drummer behind his ear. She took a small bite of a sandwich even though she wasn't the least bit hungry and gave the rest to the grateful kelpie.

'Doesn't seem real, does it?' said Kevin.

'Not in the slightest,' said Joy. 'I can't seem to cry. Is that normal?'

The chair creaked as Kevin leant back and ran his hand down his thigh.

'There's nothin' normal about death, if you ask me. No matter what they say. You loved ya grandfather and that's all that counts. Plenty cry tears for those they don't care about. I wouldn't worry if I were you. You'll grieve in your own time and in your own way.'

'Will I?' she said.

'You're stronger than you think, Joy. You'll get through this.'

He pulled a packet of Woodbines from his shirt pocket and offered them to Joy. She took one and leant forward as Kevin struck the match and lit their cigarettes.

'I'm not really a smoker,' said Joy. 'Mum hates it, but Grandpa and I sometimes had a smoke together on the quiet.'

Kevin chuckled and lifted his mug of tea. 'To Henry. And the smokes we shared.'

'To Grandpa,' Joy replied. 'And the cigarettes Mum never knew about.'

*

Henry Meredith was buried in the cemetery at Monaghan Station five days later. The local minister and immediate family members walked behind Tim as he led Henry's favourite black mare to where the ceremony was to take place. Tim's eulogy was as moving as it was humorous as he recalled moments from his father's diverse and interesting life, but as he came to the end of his words, Tim found it hard to hold it together. Jordy and Reece moved closer and each placed a hand on Tim's shoulder. He took a deep breath.

'When I see a newborn foal I'll think of you, Dad. When I hear the music of Vivaldi or pour myself a whisky you'll be right there with me. No ice, of course,' said Tim, and there was a slight ripple of laughter. 'You were the best of men and the kindest of fathers. May the stars of the night sky guide you and your campfire warm you, until we meet again.'

For February, the day was surprisingly cool. As the family members walked back along the river, a large flock of black cockatoos swooped over the gum trees and landed in a jacaranda at the edge of the drive, their underwings alive with flashes of crimson.

'He's watching us, Mum,' said Tim as he looped his arm through Anna's. 'I know he is.'

Henry's memorial, which was held the following Monday, was one of the largest services the district had seen in many years. Jordy told the gathering how Henry had suffered a heart attack shortly after midnight, and had died immediately. To the best of their knowledge, Henry had not mentioned any chest discomfort in the weeks prior. Jordy, like Reece, struggled to stay composed as he spoke.

'To leave this life, lying in your own bed with the love of your life at your side,' said Jordy, 'and after a night of laughter and good cheer with your family and those you hold dear – well, I don't think you can ask for fairer than that, as Dad used to say.'

Reece read one of Henry's favourite poems and as the congregation left the auditorium, the local choir sang 'Amazing Grace', a song he'd loved since he was a boy.

*

The day after Henry's memorial service, Avril threw herself back into work, having negotiated a payment system with the Tax Department until her footwear business was sold. More pressing were the suspicions she had regarding Parkers, and the discrepancy in the accounts overseen by Don Whitby. The documents Avril had shown Tim the day before Joy's birthday were a labyrinthine paper trail that only the expertise of a good lawyer and a forensic accountancy team could guide them through.

When Avril looked up from her desk, Tim was stretched out on the leather sofa, his hands behind his head. He was staring at the bookcase then suddenly sat up and swung his feet to the floor, resting his forearms on his knees.

'We'll need to spend some serious money to sort this mess out, won't we?' he said.

'Tim, we don't have to talk about this now. Let's leave it a day or two.'

'No, it's all right. Gives me something else to think about. The funny thing is, I keep thinking I can hear his voice in the other room or his footsteps through the front door.'

Avril sat beside Tim and he took her hand.

'I have an understanding of what you must have gone through when you lost your mother all those years ago. You were so young.'

'Those were very different times. I'd just turned twenty and the war was still going.'

Tim nodded. 'I'm so lucky to have had Dad with me for almost sixty years. And he wouldn't want us sitting around doing bugger-all, so come on, how are we going to deal with your suspicions about Don Whitby?'

'Reece, James and I will work out a strategy. I'm guessing it will involve a full examination of all our dealings with Parkers. James has suggested we go in hard and fast to show we mean business.'

'Good. Once Reece and James get the bit between their teeth, there'll be no stopping them,' said Tim. 'And I'll be right by your side. We'll get this sorted, my darling. We're a team and always will be.'

*

Joy tapped on the door of her father's office, a door that was normally open but so often closed of late. There was never going to be a perfect time to speak to her parents, she reasoned, so finding them together like this swayed her hand. She couldn't put off this discussion any longer.

'Ah! There you are,' said Tim. 'How's the packing going?'

73

'Oh, I'm getting there,' said Joy as she wandered over to the other side of the room. She took a seat on the wide window ledge and crossed her legs. Henry's labrador pups were curled up on a tartan rug in one corner of the room. Joy watched their bellies rise and fall as she wondered how to begin. *Straight in*, she thought.

'There's something I want to tell you both. I've decided not to live on campus. I'm going to share a house with Scarlet and two others. I know I've got a place at the Women's College, but it's not for me.'

'But it's all arranged,' said Avril. 'We talked about this and it's what you wanted.'

'No, Mum. Actually it's not what I wanted. It's what you wanted, and I –'

Avril raised her hand, cutting Joy off.

'We've all been through a lot since your grandfather's death. Your father and I think that living at Women's College, at least for the first year, will work best for you. At least you won't have to cook for yourself.'

Joy looked at her father as he stretched his arm along the back of the leather sofa.

'Well, I don't know,' said Tim. 'Let's hear Joy out. Where are you thinking of living?'

'Tim!' said Avril, but he kept his attention on their daughter.

'We're going to rent Jordy and Duncan's place in Indooroopilly. It's fully furnished and it works out cheaper than living on campus. I'd have to move out of college during the uni break anyway. This makes much more sense.'

'So, you've worked all of this out with Jordy and Duncan already,' said Avril, frowning. 'I'm disappointed that you didn't talk to your father and me first.'

'For goodness' sake, Mum. Don't be so dramatic. It's not a conspiracy.'

'Well, it seems like it's all been decided,' said Avril.

Joy looked at her father and rolled her eyes. She didn't want to get into a slanging match with her mother.

'You're right,' said Joy. 'It has been decided. By me. I'm not at school anymore and I'm not a child.'

'I'm very fond of Scarlet,' said Avril, 'but she's a bit of a . . .'

'Party animal?' said Joy. 'No more or no less than most people I know. There's more to life than work, you know, Mum.'

Avril was silent. Stung by the comment. Hurt by the truth of it.

'I'll be sharing a house with friends. Anyway, I've made up my mind. Scarlet and I are moving in this coming weekend.'

'And are you planning on getting a part-time job? Or do you expect your father and I to pick up all the bills?'

Tim looked at Avril in surprise while Joy shook her head.

'Nope. You'll be pleased to hear I won't be a drain on your resources,' she said. 'It looks like I can get a bar job where Hugo works. It's in one of the grungiest pubs in Brisbane, not far from uni.'

Tim threw his head back and laughed, thinking Joy was merely baiting her mother.

Joy glared at him. 'I'm not joking. Friday happy hour and the Sunday session. Hugo and I will be working together.'

'Well, that's something, I suppose,' Avril murmured.

'Good for you, darling,' said Tim. 'And if you're talking

about the Crown and Anchor, I know exactly where to find you. Grungy – that's being complimentary.'

*

Avril walked along the bank of the river, following the line of ghost gums until her eyes came to rest on the bend in the river where the Condamine traversed south. After the emotional roller-coaster of the last ten days, every member of the family had disappeared into one room or another at some point, needing time alone. Nobody seemed to be able to talk anymore. Even the normally busy yard and work-shop were unusually quiet. A horse whinnied from behind the stables and Avril turned towards the sound. *Why not?* she said to herself, and in less than twenty minutes, she was cantering down the edge of the airstrip.

Walking the bay gelding out of the water on the other side of the river, Avril pulled her mount to a standstill and looked across the paddock, deciding on her course. With at least another couple of hours of good light and only a light breeze against them, she tapped her heels against the horse's side, turned his head slightly and headed for Bunker's Ridge.

Up the steep incline, through the saplings and over fallen branches, they reached the clearing and the open plateau. In the twenty-nine years since Jordy had first shown Avril the view from the ridge, the landscape had changed very little, if at all. Once again, she considered all the turns her life had taken. *I could have easily settled in Sydney instead of Melbourne. What if I'd never phoned Henry and asked for a job?*

'Did you change my life, Henry Meredith, the day I met you on the train? Or did I do that myself?' she said to the wind.

And in that moment, she was overwhelmed by a memory from long ago. She was running through the vineyard at the Chateau de Vinieres, hand in hand with Guy Leon, her first love. The war had taken her mother, her fiancé and her one-day-old son. There'd been nothing left in France for her, except her dear friend Madame Leon and her beautiful chateau. Avril berated herself for not having visited Madame Leon for four years. *After everything she did for me.* But she knew she'd made the right choice. She had to leave.

No, Avril decided. *I changed my life the day I stepped onto the* Harmony Prince *and set sail for Melbourne. But you, dear Henry. You gave me Monaghan and your son.*

'Tim.' She said his name out loud. *Should I have done more with Joy over the years? Did I push too hard? Did I spend too much time working?* she wondered. It had never seemed like work. It had seemed like freedom.

A tiredness overtook her as she walked her horse down the steepest part of the descent. At the bottom of the hill she swung back up into the saddle and saw Tim riding towards her. With the reins in one hand, he slowed his bay mare to a trot.

'I feel like I don't know my own daughter,' said Avril without preamble. 'How do I get close to her?'

'By letting go,' he said. 'Come on. Let's walk back together.'

As usual, they stopped beside the river. The days were beginning to shorten and the sky had turned a pale shade of pink and golden honey.

'Do you remember our first camp?' he said. 'Our first nights alone under the stars?'

'Of course I do,' said Avril. 'Sometimes those days feel like yesterday.'

'Give her time, give her space, and most of all, let her fall off the horse if need be. Metaphorically speaking, that is.'

'Am I really as controlling as she says I am? I know what Joy calls me.'

Tim turned away, trying to hide his grin.

'You don't achieve what you've achieved, my love, without having a touch of the sergeant major about you.'

'So I haven't lost her then? And I haven't lost you?'

'No, my darling, you haven't lost either of us, and you never will.'

Tim circled his horse around and shortened his reins.

'Let's gallop back like we used to when we were out with Henry.'

And they took off across the water, up the bank and down the tree line with the wind willing them on.

CHAPTER 5

The day after Joy and Scarlet moved into the house in Indooroopilly, they started interviewing possible housemates. Some contenders came via friends, others from the ad they'd placed in the *Courier-Mail* and posted on the noticeboard at the Student Central Office.

In the end the decision was unanimous. Tony Drakos, who was studying architecture and in his final year like Hugo, won them over with his self-professed love of cooking and the fact that Hugo had said what a great guy he was. Vivienne Lucas arrived for the interview with an unexpected yet delightful surprise. Her five-year-old son Leo climbed the front steps carrying a plate of fairy bread and proudly announced, 'We're here for the intra-viewed and did you know, I made this?' He offered up the sugary treats. 'I go to big school,' he added as an afterthought.

Joy felt an instant warmth for single mother Vivienne and her son, remembering a kitchenhand and her daughter who'd lived at Monaghan for many of Joy's primary school years. *How many times have I seen this scenario?* she thought, watching Leo play at his mother's feet. Growing up on the station, Joy had seen many different relationships – relationships that most people might not consider the norm. She could hear Henry's voice in her head reminding her, *Character. That's what counts. People find themselves in tricky circumstances for all sorts of reasons.* The stockmen, jackaroos and itinerant workers all arrived with their own backstory and family dynamics, and a woman with a child or two in search of work was frequently among them.

It turned out that not only did Vivienne and Leo share the same olive skin and dark curls, they were both determined and forthright – attributes Joy admired. Studying education part-time while working in the typing pool at the Channel Nine television station, Vivienne's story, they discovered, was similar to Scarlet's in some respects. Her hometown, along with Leo's father, was a distant memory she had no desire to revisit. At twenty-four, Vivienne's prime consideration was keeping herself and her son housed, fed and happy.

'I always wanted to be a teacher,' she explained. 'And this way I'll be with Leo in the school holidays. It seems like the perfect fit for us.'

And so the lazy weatherboard Queenslander came to life as boxes of books, clothing and Tony's twelve-string Gibson were carried up the wide wooden stairs that graced the front of the grand old house.

Joy decided that Vivienne should have the corner bedroom, which was the largest. At some stage, part of the wooden veranda had been glassed in, creating a small room that was perfect for Leo's play table and toys. The other three bedrooms, which ran the length of one side of the house, were protected from the summer sun by a row of Norfolk Island pines that grew on the adjoining property. And over time, the open-plan kitchen and lounge room that dominated the centre of the house would come to be the communal hub at number sixteen.

The one luxury Joy had all to herself was a small en suite that Jordy and Duncan had installed when they'd carried out the renovations.

It didn't take long for them to meet the neighbours, either. Two days after Tony, Vivienne and Leo moved in, Joy and Hugo were busy unloading groceries from her dusty red Suzuki four-wheel drive when the front gate swung open and up the path bustled a woman carrying a wicker basket. The smell of freshly baked scones was unmistakable and for a moment, Joy was carried back to a childhood memory of the staff kitchen at the station and Patricia pulling a loaf from the hot oven for smoko.

'Welcome,' the woman said, her cheery smile beaming. 'You must be Joy. And you are?' she said to Hugo without any hesitation.

'I'm Hugo. Joy's boyfriend.'

Joy and Hugo replaced the shopping bags on the back car seat and shook the woman's extended hand.

'Oh, yes, I can see the resemblance. Tall, just like your uncle Jordy. I'm Mrs Banovic. I live next door,' and she pointed towards the pines. 'Have done for forty years. These are for you, dear.' She handed Joy the basket. Underneath the tartan linen tea towel was a pile of pumpkin scones and some jam and cream.

'That's so kind of you,' said Joy. 'They smell delicious.'

Sensing her neighbour was in no hurry to leave, Joy invited Mrs Banovic to share the scones.

Hugo shot Joy a smile as he unpacked the groceries. Joy was certain Hugo wasn't interested in being inter-rogated by Mrs Banovic at nine-thirty in the morning and suggested he go to her room to do his 'uni reading'. She would have to negotiate the neighbour's fact-finding mission on her own.

At the kitchen table, Joy refilled their cups as her guest reached once again for the cream.

'I've kept an eye on the place for Jordy and Duncan since they moved out. How I miss them. Such lovely neighbours.'

By the time Mrs B, as they quickly came to call her, had left an hour and a half later, both she and Joy had increased their respective knowledge. Joy had received a detailed historical tour of the suburb and surrounding area, as well as the first half-a-dozen chapters from the autobiography of the Croatian widow's life. For her part Mrs B had successfully used four cups of self-raising four, some butternut pumpkin and a hot oven to learn all she could about who would be living at number sixteen.

'And Leo, the little chap,' said Mrs B as they reached the bottom of the steps, 'I'm happy to help out if he needs minding anytime. I'm sure I still have a box of toys under the house. I'll pull them out and give them a scrub.'

They said goodbye at the front gate and Joy could hear the whistling right up until the screen door slammed behind Mrs B and she disappeared inside her pale pink chamferboard house, her mission accomplished.

In the kitchen, Hugo pulled Joy into his arms and kissed her on the neck, making her squeal.

'Thanks for the get-out-of-jail-free card, though I'll take one of those scones now,' said Hugo mischievously.

She locked her arms around his neck and kissed him passionately.

'I can't believe I finally have my own place,' said Joy. 'It seems like such luxury compared with living on campus.'

'You've got that right,' replied Hugo, looking around. 'So, Vivienne's at work, Leo's at school and Scarlet is . . .?' He raised an eyebrow.

'She's working at the bakery.'

With a grin Hugo took Joy's hand and they raced to her bedroom, pulling their t-shirts over their heads as they went.

Taking their relationship to the next level was something Joy had not only anticipated but wanted. She knew the right time would present itself and so it had. The day Joy and Scarlet moved in, Hugo was on hand to help in any way he could.

'What on earth have you got in these boxes?' he'd asked as he carried yet another load from the back of Joy's car to the lounge room.

Once dinner was over and the takeaway containers had been cleared, Scarlet said good night and disappeared into her room, leaving Joy and Hugo alone. The transition from sofa to Joy's bedroom that night had felt like a natural progression, the mutual passion that had been building since the afternoon by the river reaching a turning point. Their first night as lovers had been far more natural and uncomplicated than Joy had imagined it would be.

'Being with you feels so right. So normal,' she told Hugo afterwards as she lay with her head on his chest.

He ran his fingers slowly through her hair, picking up long tendrils of curls and stretching them skyward.

'I feel just the same,' he said. And they lay there listening to the sounds of the night until they both fell sleep.

*

With part-time jobs in short supply and every student within a twenty-kilometre radius trying to track one down, Joy headed off to meet the owner of the Crown and Anchor. The two-storey, one-hundred-year-old building had once served as a second home to the countless sailors whose ships docked along the Brisbane River. The wide wooden veranda encircled the building, capturing the breeze and expelling the heat of the day over its railings.

Hugo was waiting in the front bar, chatting to one of the staff.

'Barry's a character,' said Hugo as they climbed the stairs.

Hugo and Joy stood in the doorway of the first-floor office and waited for the publican to finish his phone conversation. Finally he replaced the receiver and waved them in. The mid-century grey ceiling fan oscillated reluctantly overhead but did little to alleviate the heavy humidity that clung to the walls.

'Hi, Barry,' said Hugo. 'This is my girlfriend, Joy Meredith. I take it the job's still available?'

Barry O'Brien's deep-set eyes travelled from Joy's face to her white Dunlop Volleys. There was just the hint of a smile behind his gaze and his eyes were shrewd but kindly. *I bet he never asks a question that he doesn't already know the answer to*, Joy thought.

'Ya can start this Friday at four.' He grinned. 'I take it ya can pour a beer, sweetheart?'

Joy nodded. 'I can pour a beer. And I make a pretty mean cocktail.'

'Cocktails,' he parroted. 'Do ya now?'

The big bear of a man rocked back in his seat, the springs beneath him groaning. Joy had the feeling that Barry O'Brien was the kind of person she'd either like or loathe. There'd be no in between, a bit like the stockmen and jackaroos she'd known.

'Well, we don't make a lot of fancy drinks in this pub, but who knows.'

Joy thought she could see his mind already calculating the profit margin on a Fluffy Duck or a Pina Colada.

'Might be worth a try.'

'I'll see you Friday then,' said Joy. She turned to leave.

'I was sorry to hear about yer loss,' said Barry, unexpectedly. 'Yer grandad was a good man and there aren't too many about.'

'Did you know my grandfather?' said Joy, taken aback.

Barry hesitated, as if to consider which memories to recall and which to forget.

'A long time ago,' he said dryly, holding Joy's stare. His hands were draped like mammoth paws over the arms of the old leather chair. 'I did a bit of shearin' back in the day. Jude's Creek, Minadarrie, Parry's Crossing. And Monaghan Station.'

Joy could visualise every one of these properties, especially Jude's Creek, which still belonged to her aunt Caroline's family.

'Wasn't half bad.'

Barry swung himself forward and scooped up a pen that was sitting on top of the newspaper. He twirled it between his fingers like a baton. 'Never cared for that Doug Stanley and the show he ran at Cathaway Downs, though. Burnt down, didn't it?'

Joy didn't reply. She was too busy digesting Barry's barrage of historical events. Doug and Mary Stanley and their late daughter Rachel, Tim's first wife, were a cheerless memory the Merediths rarely dredged back up, although Tim had told Joy the long sad tale one night around the campfire. Tim had held nothing back, saying half-truths weren't worth knowing. If Rachel hadn't died in the bushfire of '59, Tim had said he doubted they would have stayed together. *It was doomed from the start*, he'd said.

Barry turned and stared through the dirty sash window down at the Brisbane River below.

'But Henry Meredith,' he said. 'He was in a class all of his own.'

*

Later that night as Hugo lay sleeping next to Joy, a rising wind lifted the paisley curtains in her bedroom, a reprieve from the cloying humidity. While the household slept, Joy slipped from the white cotton sheets, picked up her pen and black leather journal from her bedside table and wandered onto the veranda. She slid into the wicker chair and placed a cushion on her lap. The furrowed weave of the cane pressed into the back of her head as she stared past the edge of the gutter. The rainfall strengthened, and the branches of the frangipani shook with the weight of it while shards of intermittent lightning seemed to accentuate the drumming on the corrugated-iron roof.

Joy closed her eyes and listened. In the days that had followed Henry's death she'd kept herself constantly busy – sorting out her clothes, packing up her belongings, riding her big grey each morning, avoiding her mother. With all the activity surrounding her move to Brisbane she felt she'd been in a whirlwind that was only now starting to abate.

Before she'd left Monaghan, Joy had discovered her collection of schoolgirl diaries – a dozen or so small books in various shades of pink and green – while emptying out the top of her wardrobe. She'd opened one and begun to read.

> *Tuesday, 20 March 1973*
> *I spoke to Dad tonight but had to wait ages to phone*
> *him because Sarah Bradley was hogging the phone*
> *(as always) and she made two calls and you're only*
> *supposed to make one. Dad said Mum is going to*
> *France. Duncan is going with her. They are looking at*
> *fashion. They are going to stay at the chateau where*
> *Mum used to live with Madame Leon. Dad said she*
> *might not be back by Easter but he'll come down and*
> *get me for the break. Dad said Grandpa has made me*
> *some new jumps and I will love them.*

She'd thumbed through a small white journal, laughing at the intermittent drawings. It was the diary she'd kept when her mother had returned to France with her fourteen-year-old daughter. In an attempt to improve her language skills, Joy had written all her entries in French. She'd laughed at some of the grammatical mistakes she'd made, the mishmash of masculine and feminine. Joy pulled three colour photos from the back of the book: shots she'd taken of the inside of the chateau. She remembered the fun she'd had exploring the rooms in the attic; armoires crammed with newspapers and magazines, a pram and nursery furniture from another era, all piled up in a corner. Her afternoon explorations had sparked her interest in asking Madame Leon about the history of the house, a subject the old woman was very happy to talk about.

Among the diaries was an unused black leather book with the words *'le Journal'* printed on the cover, a gift from her mother that she'd never used. Joy had thumbed through the book, the blank pages crackling and clinging to each other, reluctant to be separated. A small card had slid from inside and landed on the carpet. Joy turned the card over to read the inscription:

Ma chérie, Joy,
Écrivez votre propre histoire, Maman xxx

'Write your own story,' Joy had said to the walls of her bedroom. Weighing the journal in her hand, she'd been about to put it back in the wardrobe but had hesitated, then placed it on her bedside table.

To Joy's surprise, she had begun writing in the journal almost immediately, and had kept up the practice since arriving in Brisbane. Somehow putting it all in writing helped her sort out everything she was feeling as so much around her changed.

Joy blinked, aware that the rain had intensified. She wasn't sure how long she had been sitting in the chair as the storm raged around her. She opened the journal, turned to a new page and began writing her favourite verse from a poem she and Henry had often recited together. As her hand moved across the page, the wind rushed onto the veranda and lifted her hair from around her face. The reality of what she'd experienced over the last few months – the finality of finishing school, her relationship with Hugo, moving into her own place and, of course, Henry's death – felt like a weight upon her chest. She closed her eyes.

'*Core of my heart, my country! Her pitiless blue sky,*' she whispered. '*When sick at heart, around us, We see the cattle die – But then the grey clouds gather, And we can bless again, The drumming of an army, The steady, soaking rain.'*

Joy dropped the book and covered her face with her hands. All the grief she'd locked inside since the night of her eighteenth birthday party gave way and she sobbed into the storm.

As a cool mist circled up and under the eaves, Joy let her body sag forward, burying her face in the cushion.

*

Avril was also awake that night.

Her own storm was brewing and gathering momentum.

The clock in the hall chimed eleven as she poured boiling water into the small silver teapot and sat down at the kitchen table. She rested her chin on her hand and stared into her cup, stirring her tea until the milk swirls had disappeared.

How did it come to this? she thought. A daughter she hardly spoke to and a financial mess that should never have occurred. It was the same question James Carmody had asked her over the phone earlier that day. In his predictably calm and systematic manner he'd done more listening than talking during their hour-long conversation, while methodically compiling a list of additional questions.

Despite his retirement from Carmody Meredith Partners some five years earlier, James Carmody had always provided much more than legal advice when it came to Avril. While their romantic relationship had faded after a few years, their friendship had endured. The combination of James's impoverished childhood, his rigorous intellect and an obsession to discover the world beyond the backstreets of Melbourne had been the impetus for all the success that would follow in his life.

'If you can leave this with me for a couple of days, I'll come back to you with a strategy,' he said. 'If what you have here is the misappropriation of funds, then we need to tread carefully. Criminal charges are one thing, but recovering money is another minefield altogether.'

Avril was silent on the other end of the phone as she digested his words.

James sensed her disquiet and said, 'And Joy? How's she getting on in Brisbane?'

'Well,' Avril said, 'I've left messages with her house-mates but she hasn't returned any of my calls.'

'I'll be in Brisbane for a board meeting next week. I'll take her to dinner. Have a good catch-up like we always do. Look, from what I can see, you could both do with some space right now – Joy especially. She's moved out of home, she's starting uni. Let her find her way, Avril.'

'She's always been closer to Tim,' said Avril with a sigh. 'And, of course, her grandfather.'

'In all fairness, you weren't around a lot when she was growing up,' said James, but then he seemed to instantly regret his words. 'I'm sorry. That was unfair and badly phrased.'

'No, you're right,' Avril replied with a sigh. 'I think that's part of the problem. But what she doesn't see is that my work helped give her the life she has – it covered the school fees and Monaghan's upkeep, Tim's plane and the whole shooting match. Where would we have been without it?'

Avril was still thinking about this conversation with James as she sipped her tea in the still of the night. She startled as a voice disturbed her thoughts. Tim was standing in the doorway. 'Can't sleep?' he asked her.

'No,' she said as she refilled her cup.

'Nor me.'

Tim lifted the lid of a cake tin and took out a couple of Anzac biscuits. He sat opposite Avril, poured a cup for himself and dunked a biscuit into the black tea.

'I haven't paid as much attention to the financial aspects of running this place as I should have,' he said quietly. 'I've relied on you to oversee our accounts. You're so good at it and, well, being at a desk in front of a spreadsheet was never my thing. I was so consumed by breeding and selling cattle, trying to keep our herd strong. And you were always so confident, so in control of everything.'

'Obviously not as much as I thought I was,' Avril said with a wry smile. 'I need to analyse every aspect of what I'm doing with the le Chic and jeans stores, the fabric wholesale business and garment factory in Melbourne. I've always been so confident in my decision-making. Ahead of the game, as you used to tell me. But now it feels like I'm treading water. No – not treading water. Floating backwards.'

Tim dunked his second biscuit.

'Do you even want to be in the fashion industry anymore? Why not sell the whole bloody lot and be done with it?'

'And do what exactly?' said Avril. 'I'm only fifty-five. I'm not ready to retire. I can get through this. *We* can get through this. I'll have to sell some assets but at least I have some to sell. The reality is that business is tough and getting tougher.'

This was a moment of reckoning for Avril and she knew it. Weeks of soul-searching had brought her to this point. She thought about how driven she'd always been. How she wouldn't take a break even when she knew she should. And, most importantly, the effect this had had on her relationship, or the lack of one, with Joy.

'What did James say when you spoke to him?' said Tim.

'He'll come back to me in a day or two with his suggestions.'

'And does he agree with your suspicions that Don Whitby's been funnelling our money into his account?'

'He thinks something doesn't add up, but you know James. In the end it's the facts that matter, not just hearsay. We can't accuse anyone of anything until we have proof.'

For some time, neither of them spoke. Avril stared at the ebony handle of the teapot.

'Once you've known hunger, real hunger,' she went on, 'you never forget it. No matter what you achieve, no matter what you own, you never take anything for granted.'

'Is that what drove you to succeed, do you think – living through the war? Or were you always like that?'

But Avril was no longer listening to Tim. It was 1944 and she was pregnant, digging for potatoes in the frozen soil at Chateau de Vinieres, her fingers bloody as the hard ground mocked her efforts, yielding nothing.

When she heard the hall clock chime the half-hour, she pushed her teacup into the centre of the table.

'Avril,' said Tim, his words slowly pulling her back. 'Darling. Are you all right?'

'No. Not really,' she replied.

Tim stood and reached out his hand.

'We'll talk again in the morning. It's time to sleep.'

*

In the days before classes officially started, Joy and Scarlet roamed the Saint Lucia grounds at the university, orientating themselves with the countless faculty buildings and walkways as they worked out where their lectures and tutorials would be held. They browsed the crowded bookshop, flicked through the t-shirts and sorbet-coloured cheesecloth dresses at the Student Co-op store and lolled under the trees on the lush lawn of the Great Court, often meeting up with Hugo and his friends.

Once the semester began in earnest, the campus, with its packed lecture theatres and even busier tavern, was the heart and soul of university life for Joy and Scarlet. A couple of the vet school lecturers, with a passion for the theatrical, enthralled first-year students with a constant stream of notes and diagrams, all courtesy of the overhead projector. Plastic sheets cramped with subject information were whisked on and off the machine as Joy hurried to finish her handwritten lecture notes. Sometimes the projector would overheat, resulting in a shortened presentation and a rush for the exits. Certain academics became known for reciting verbatim quotes from history, anecdotes and statistical information, meant to entertain as much as inform, all of which would be memorised and promptly forgotten once exams were over.

Dealing with the subject workload was one thing. Managing the avalanche of partying was something else altogether.

Friendships and romances blossomed as thousands of Baby Boomers took advantage of higher education in an era when a university degree was fee-free. Relationships developed through social clubs, from rowing to orienteering, chess to tennis, football to amateur theatre. Some connections would fall away as the year closed out, others would last long after the hired graduation gowns were returned, the bar drunk dry and degrees proudly framed and hung.

While the social life at uni was fun, it was Joy's new job at the Crown and Anchor that she found truly educational.

Not considered the most glamorous of establishments, it was nonetheless a well-run money-making machine and Barry O'Brien had every intention of keeping it that way. The Crownie, as the locals called it, was perfectly positioned to capture the sporting enthusiasts who flocked to the Gabba Cricket Ground every summer, the throng of nearby students and the constant stream of tradies and workers who passed through South Brisbane every day. While the all-day menu was limited – steak or chicken – the size and quality of the meals made up for the lack of choice.

In spite of his booming voice and colourful language, Barry treated his staff well, paid wages on time and always gave the band members who provided live music a meal at the end of the night. He had only two rules, and breaking either meant instant dismissal: no drinking on the job; no cheap drinks.

Wherever possible, Joy and Hugo tried to align their shifts. Joy would work a short shift through the week, then longer hours on a Friday night and for the Sunday session.

On her first shift, Joy and Hugo were behind the bar tidying up before the Friday night crowd poured in for the free live music.

'Hey, Barry. Have you ever thought about painting the place?' said Hugo. 'You could replace some of the windows to let in a bit more light.'

'Ya mean doin' a flashy fit-out that costs an arm and a leg? Ha!' Barry laughed. 'Doesn't make the beer any colder.'

'I don't know,' Hugo continued, giving Joy a sly smile. 'I think I could come up with a few aesthetic changes that might double your turnover.'

'Mirrors in the ladies' toilets, for starters,' Joy said under her breath.

'You and yer aesthetic changes,' Barry said, tucking his shirt into the back of his trousers. 'Flamin' architects. Who're ya kidding? I can buy another apartment down at Burleigh Heads for what a paint job and a few sheets of glass would cost me. Come back with yer trendy ideas when ya got more dough than me, son,' and he continued to laugh as he lumbered across the room to speak to one of the bouncers.

*

'Hello,' James called from the front door. 'Anyone home?'

Leo abandoned the cartoon he was watching on television and charged across the room to the doorway.

'Leo,' his mother called, but it was too late. Her son's interrogation had already begun.

'Who are you?' he asked. 'Are you a stranger or a friend?'

'My name's James and I'm a good friend of Joy's. In fact, I'm her godfather.'

'I've got one of those too,' said Leo, his hand still hovering over the lock on the screen door. 'But you can't come in. I have to wait for my mum.'

'It's okay,' Vivienne reassured him as she came down the hallway. 'You can unlock the door. Joy is going out for dinner with a friend, remember?' She turned her attention to their guest. 'Hello, James. I'm Vivienne. We spoke on the phone the other night. Come in. I think Joy might still be getting ready.'

'This place looks terrific,' said James as Vivienne led him into the lounge. 'I haven't been here since Jordy and Duncan finished the renovations.'

'What was it like before?' Vivienne asked.

'Ah. Had great potential. I think that's what the agent

said at the time. And that was being generous.' James smiled.

'Hello, hello,' Joy called as she came around the corner and hugged her godfather.

'I like the new hair,' he said. 'Is Hugo joining us?'

'He can't, I'm afraid, but he said to say hello. He's got a function at the school of architecture and he couldn't get out of it.'

Secretly, Joy was pleased to have James to herself for the night. Although she loved being with Hugo, there were times when she felt he was beginning to play an ever-increasing role in every aspect of her life. Seeing each other during the day on campus. Working together at the pub. There was also the amount of time he was spending at number sixteen in general. Scarlet had even joked a couple of times that Hugo was their 'fourth tenant'. This had all confirmed for Joy something she'd always known but hadn't really thought about: that sometimes she just needed to spend time on her own.

Joy smiled, scooped her denim jacket off the table and smoothed her hair. She was glad James had noticed. New hair. A place of her own. A boyfriend.

'I'll see you guys later,' said Joy as they headed for the door.

'Nice to meet you, Vivienne, and you too, Leo,' said James.

'You too, James,' Vivienne said, and locked the screen door behind them.

*

By the time Joy and James had finished their mains, they'd covered every topic, from the move, to uni life, Joy's job at the pub and Henry's sudden passing.

'So, how are things with you and Hugo? It's a god-father's privilege to ask these sorts of questions,' James said as he refilled their glasses. 'Plenty of partying, I should imagine.'

'Sure. There's always a lot of that. As for Hugo and me – we're great. His final year workload's going to be pretty full-on, so it's not like we'll be in each other's pockets all the time.'

Joy didn't feel like saying much more. They'd only been officially an item a matter of weeks and were still getting to know each other. But already she could tell that Hugo wasn't into the social side of uni in the same way Scarlet was, and to a lesser degree, herself. It seemed to Joy that after four years as a student, he'd seen and done it all. Hugo was nearing the end of his degree and Joy was just beginning uni life. It was all new to her. Between the vet and medical students, there was a constant rota of events and meet-ups on and off campus that Hugo had said he had no interest in going to.

'I've done my fair share of toga parties over the past four years,' Hugo had assured her. Joy wasn't quite sure how she felt about that yet.

The waiter cleared their dinner plates and Joy placed her elbows on the table.

'So. How's all the uni work so far? Have they thrown you straight in the deep end?' asked James.

'Totally. I knew it would be hard, but . . .' Joy toyed with her dessert spoon. 'You know I only just scraped in. Sometimes when I'm sitting in a lecture, I feel like an imposter. Like someone will tap me on the shoulder and say, *What are you doing here?*'

'Getting high marks is only part of it. Initiative. Passion. And an innate understanding of people, or in your case, animals. That's what really matters. If you keep on top of the workload, you'll be all right.'

'What's that look for?' she said in surprise.

Try as he might, the smile on James's face would not subside.

'Sitting there like that,' he said, motioning with his hand as if to outline Joy's posture. 'You remind me of your mother.'

'That's where the similarity starts and ends,' Joy said quietly, keen to move on to another topic. 'Do you and Margot have any travel plans this year? You always seem to be going somewhere interesting.'

'We're off to London in July and then up to Edinburgh to see Margot's mother.'

Although James hadn't planned it, the mention of his mother-in-law provided a gentle segue back to Avril. Ethically, he could never discuss any of Avril's business matters with Joy, even if he did think she could benefit from knowing the full extent of Avril and Tim's financial impasse. But he could encourage contact and that was what he intended to do.

'But not so fast, Joy. There's something I want to say. Firstly, I want to tell you how proud I am of you. The night of your birthday, well, I can't think of a more distressing and difficult situation to find yourself in. You were amazing.'

Joy reached for her glass and took a sip. That night still seemed surreal, and her last words with Henry played constantly in her mind. *Sweet dreams. See you in the morning.* There were days when Joy still couldn't believe he was no longer with them and she longed to speak to him. Wished it was his voice she'd hear on the other end of the line if she called the station.

'And now you've moved into your own place, and you have to deal with everything that goes along with that. Shopping, cooking, taking care of yourself. And starting uni. It's a lot to adjust to.'

'I was ready for it. More than ready,' she said.

'It's important to know who to keep on the outer and who to keep close to you. If I can offer up a small piece of advice,' he paused and looked straight at Joy, 'it's this. Don't push your mother away with silence.'

'You sound like Hugo.'

'Return her phone calls. Let her know you're all right. She loves you more than you could ever imagine. If you've got something you want to say to her, then say it. Talk to her. She'll listen, I assure you.'

Joy sighed. 'That's harder to do than you think,' she said. 'I love Mum and I know she loves me, except there's a big *but* that hovers between us.'

If there was one well-deployed weapon in James Carmody's arsenal, it was his ability to wait. To let whoever was speaking pick their way through the debris. He allowed the silence to develop, and Joy couldn't help but fill it.

'We're so different. You say she'll listen, but that only happens when she's hearing what she wants to hear. Mum's always done what she wants to do. Her life, her businesses. They've always come first.'

'What do you mean?' James asked.

'I've lost count of the number of times Mum said she'd be at the station when I was off school, and then wasn't. She'd come up for a couple of days and then there'd be a problem at the factory in Melbourne or a meeting she had to go to in Sydney. You know, I think a lot of times Dad was really lonely too with Mum working so much.'

'Were *you* lonely?' said James.

'Sometimes during the school holidays. But I had the horses and I was always going somewhere with Dad or Grandpa. I've come to realise I actually enjoy my own company. I don't need to be around people all the time. Animals, yes. People, not so much.'

'All I'm suggesting is that if you get the chance to talk to your mum, really talk, then take it. Better still, instigate it. There's a lot about her life you may not be aware of. If you want to understand yourself then you need to understand your parents and their childhood. Life is one long history lesson passed down through the generations.'

Joy shrugged her shoulders and sat back in her chair. She thought of all the times she'd asked Avril about her past, her life in France, even her work in Melbourne when she'd first arrived in Australia, and Avril had clammed up. After a while, Joy had simply given up.

'I hear what you're saying but it's not always as easy as that, I think.'

She opened the menu and studied the selection, ready to move on to a new topic of conversation.

'More importantly,' she said, 'what will we have for dessert?'

*

Later that night, Joy was sitting up in bed writing in her journal. She noticed just how prominently her conversations with James featured throughout her journal entries. After spending time in James's company, she'd often feel quite reflective. Tonight she replayed their conversation about her relationship with her mother. *He has a point about the phone calls*, she'd conceded at the bottom of the page.

There was a gentle tap on the door. 'Are you still awake?' she heard Hugo say softly. In that instant, Joy wondered if it had been such a good idea to give Hugo his own key. She knew she'd find it difficult to ask for it back, should she ever want to.

She opened the drawer in her bedside table and slid her journal inside.

'I'm awake. Come on in.'

'How was your dinner with James?' said Hugo, coming in and closing the door quietly behind him.

'It was lovely. How was your night?'

Hugo sat on the end of the bed and let himself fall backwards, his arms spread wide.

'The most boring three hours of my life. A presentation at the Guild Hall about structural engineering and some other crap I can't even be bothered talking about.'

'Why did you go?'

'Tony and I thought it might be worthwhile but I can assure you, it wasn't.' Hugo sat up and started removing his shoes.

'Ah, excuse me,' said Joy, 'are you planning on staying the night?'

Hugo crawled over and sat on the bed beside Joy.

'Don't you want me to stay?' He leant over and kissed her.

'Hmm. Let me think about it,' she said, half joking, but half wondering if that was the truth. She admitted to herself that she'd been enjoying her moment of solitude.

Hugo reached over and began tickling her side.

'No! Not the tickling, not the tickling,' she squealed, and she grabbed a pillow and knocked Hugo sideways with an almighty blow.

*

It didn't take Joy long to realise that studying vet science was akin to a full-time job, with her bar work squeezed in around all her study commitments. Monday to Friday her days were packed with back-to-back lectures interspersed with compulsory tutorials. The forty-strong cohort that made up the first-year intake was an eclectic mix of personalities. Some were destined for small or large animal practice, others better suited to research and academia.

Scarlet's timetable for her medical degree was equally taxing. Always on the lookout for how to make some extra money on top of her job at the bakery, she'd placed an ad on one of the noticeboards, advertising her skills as a statistics tutor. She already had three second-year students who were desperate to pass the unit. Sometimes Joy and Scarlet would drive to uni together, but when the weather was fine they rode their bikes, meeting up whenever they could.

Life on campus was a revelation for Joy. For the first time in her life, she started to feel less self-conscious of her height, her physical self. She wasn't the only tall girl at uni. Far from it. And no one seemed to care, let alone pass comment. The closest Joy came to feeling slightly targeted was being regularly asked to play basketball for the university team – a request she politely declined out of sheer lack of interest.

The campus population was a smorgasbord of shapes and sizes, rivalling anything Joy had experienced before. At primary and high school it had been the opposite. There she had always felt like the odd one out, wishing she could simply blend into the crowd. Now, she was just another jeans-wearing, book-carrying student, going from one lecture to another.

The campus grounds provided a plethora of secluded

places she visited regularly, often in the company of her journal. She felt less anxious or uncertain after recording her thoughts; in some ways, it was like talking to Henry. Sometimes a week or more would go by without one word hitting the page, but then she'd find that for a few days at least, she was writing each night before turning out the light.

As the reality of her course workload kicked in, Joy gravitated more and more often to her favourite spot in the main library. From the upstairs corner window she could gaze out over the lawn of the Great Court, watching the passing parade. Life on campus was a world away from moving cattle and checking fences and water pumps, and it was far from easy, but she could feel herself growing into her independence and leaving her childhood behind.

CHAPTER 6

As the weeks passed and the cooler autumn temper-
atures encroached on the steamy summer days, life
at number sixteen settled into a rhythm of its own. The
choice of housemates had worked out well, even if Tony
was not the tidiest person and his rent was always a few
days late. Breakfast was the only mealtime at which the
household came together, and even then it was a scramble
as Joy and Scarlet rushed to make their first lectures and
Vivienne hurried to drop Leo at school before driving over
to the television station. Tony, like Hugo, was focused on
his all-consuming final-year architectural project.

Sunday night was the exception. Joy had suggested they
make it 'House Night'. When possible and on a rotational
basis, one of the four housemates would cook dinner.
Once Leo was in bed, Vivienne would put on some Neil
Young or David Bowie and they'd all sit down to the best
meal they'd eaten all week. It was soon evident that Tony's
supposed love of cooking was more akin to a love of eating.
His two-recipe repertoire, a pasta dish and a chicken
curry, were usually saved by Vivienne's intervention and

a last-minute salad from Scarlet. Nevertheless, the House Night dinner was something they all looked forward to. Hugo would race from the pub as soon as his shift was over, keen to see Joy and share in the home-cooked meal.

After dinner, invariably, Tony would reach for his guitar and a one-man jam session would ensue. One night, as Tony began another song, Vivienne started to sing. The register of her husky voice was soft and hauntingly beautiful.

'You have got to be kidding me,' said Scarlet the moment Vivienne had finished. 'Where did you learn to sing like that?'

'Nowhere.' Vivienne laughed. 'I could always sing in tune, even as a kid.'

'Do you know Fleetwood Mac's "Landslide"?' asked Tony eagerly.

Vivienne nodded and he played the first couple of chords. As a musical duo, Vivienne and Tony were a natural fit.

'I don't know why the two of you don't put your names down for Open Mic Night, at the uni tavern,' said Scarlet. 'You never know, you might get a paid gig for the Sunday session.'

Tony stopped playing and looked across at Vivienne. 'I'm game if you are.'

'Sure. Why not. If Mrs B is free to mind Leo next Tuesday night, why don't we give it a go?'

Joy and Hugo excused themselves to the kitchen to do the washing up, but they could hear Tony and Vivienne chatting.

Hugo flicked Joy with the tea towel.

'Do you think anything might happen with those two?' he said, nodding in the direction of the lounge room. 'You know. Between The Carpenters out there?' And he laughed at his own joke.

'I don't think so. But then, you never can tell. Just look at us. If I hadn't got up the nerve to call you that day, you might not be here now, scrubbing my baking dish.'

'Yes, it was probably lucky your grandpa invited me over first,' said Hugo with amusement. 'I don't think I told you, but I regretted not asking you out the moment we kissed on New Year's Eve,' he added.

'Why didn't you, then?'

'I wasn't sure you'd say yes,' said Hugo.

Joy smiled a little sadly. 'Yes, my grandfather was shrewd, all right. Our family has this motto: *Timing is everything.* I liked the way you turned up the day before my birthday. It sounds like Grandpa and I both timed our invitations perfectly!'

Joy pulled the tea towel from Hugo's hand and dropped it on the benchtop.

'Come on. Let's go and listen to Richard and Karen's performance. We've got front row seats.'

*

Easter came and went, and although Joy had intended to head back to Monaghan for a few days, at the last minute she decided not to. She wasn't sure she was ready to face her mother yet, even though she had been making an effort to talk to her a little more.

'You'll see me in the half-year break,' she reassured her father. 'Besides, the assignments are starting to pile up and mid-semester exams start soon.'

'What about Calypso?' said her father.

'I've asked Kevin if he'd ride him on a regular basis, to help keep him in shape.'

The truth was that Joy was relishing this new life, and the person she felt she was becoming, too much to interrupt it just yet. There was always something new to learn, she found, not only about people, but about herself and what she discovered she liked. There was always a party happening somewhere and, to Joy's surprise, she enjoyed her shifts at the Crown and Anchor more than she'd imagined she would. The work wasn't mentally taxing and it gave her a break from the reams of pathobiology and pharmacology notes she needed to wade through at uni.

In fact, Joy had had a few unexpected wins at work. She found she was a natural, working her way along the bar, taking orders and pouring drinks, sharing a few cheerful words with the customers. Her quick wit and dry sense of humour were similar to Barry's, minus the expletives, and Barry and Joy had both noticed that tips were always up whenever Joy worked a shift.

One Thursday when she went to pick up her pay packet, Joy mentioned a couple of ideas she'd been pondering during her shifts. 'Don't you think we could really do with a big mirror in the ladies' bathroom, Barry? And while you're at it –' she slid a brochure across his desk that read *Customised T-Shirts – Stand out in the crowd*. 'It's just a suggestion, but I think these could make all of us look like,' she hesitated, 'like a team. "Team Crownie". What do you think?'

'A team?' Barry bellowed as he picked up the brochure. 'What for? What are we? A flamin' football club?'

'The Crownie's the *hottest* place in town,' said Joy dryly, as she pocketed the small cash-filled brown envelope. 'But a couple of changes might be good for business.'

'Ya think so, Joyful?' he said.

'Did you just call me Joyful?'

'That's what I'm callin' ya from now on. 'Cause yer so bloody chirpy.'

'Fair enough,' said Joy, unconsciously imitating a phrase Henry had often used. 'Just think about it. A few t-shirts won't send you broke and you'd still have money left over to buy that other place you want down the coast.'

'Very funny. Go on, get out of here, Joyful,' he'd mumbled, dismissing her with a wave of his oversized hand.

'Flamin' t-shirts,' Joy heard Barry say as she headed down the stairs.

But to Joy's surprise, mirrors had been installed the following Monday and the staff, including the bouncers, were each given two black collared t-shirts with the words, *The Crown & Anchor Est. 1883* printed on the back, before the month was out.

*

With the end-of-semester exams only days away, the uni campus took on the appearance of a ghost town. Students hunkered down in the library and at home with only one objective in mind: cramming. The mid-year break would follow and then the whole cycle would start again, semester after semester, year after year, until the degree was completed.

Joy dropped her pen on the kitchen table, rested her chin on her folded hands and gave up trying to study. She couldn't stop thinking about Hugo's reaction to what she'd told him the previous day.

'What are you saying?' he'd replied defensively. 'You don't want us to see each other for the next three weeks? You're only sitting first-year exams. How hard can they be?'

It was a barb that had stung Joy more than it should have and she felt she'd seen a side to Hugo she hadn't experienced before. It was selfish to say the least; was her work not as important as his?

'Well, I'm the one who has to write the papers. I'm just saying that I've worked out my study schedule and it will really throw me if you turn up while I'm working. That's all. I don't think that's unreasonable.'

'Sure,' said Hugo sarcastically. 'Whatever you want. I'll call ahead of time and make an appointment.'

'Now you're being childish,' said Joy.

She was ready to fire back with a quick one-liner she knew she'd regret, but decided instead to bring their 'discussion' to an end.

'I think that's best,' said Joy. 'After all, I'm sure you have a pretty heavy exam load yourself.'

Hugo kissed Joy perfunctorily and left for his afternoon shift at the Crown and Anchor, leaving Joy with the feeling she was somehow in the wrong.

She was still thinking about Hugo when she heard the front door open and looked up from her notes.

'How's the revision going?' said Vivienne as she came into the kitchen.

'Oh, you know. Getting there,' said Joy. 'I can't believe exams start in two days' time. You're home early.'

'My boss told me to take the afternoon off. I think I'm coming down with something. I've had a shocking headache all day and a sore throat.'

'Feel like a cuppa?' said Joy. 'I'll put the kettle on.'

Vivienne dropped her bag on the chair and stretched out on the sofa.

'That would be amazing. A peppermint tea, please. And if I fall asleep, could you wake me at two-thirty? I have to get Leo by three.'

'Are you hungry?' Joy asked. 'Because I'm about to

make a tomato and cheese toasted sandwich if you'd like one.'

'Oh, that's kind. Yes, please.'

Joy set the mugs and plates down on the coffee table and dropped into the chair opposite Vivienne.

'How's Hugo? Did he get an interview with any of the architectual firms he contacted?' asked Vivienne. 'I hear the top companies only take one or two graduates a year.'

Hugo had been speaking of almost nothing but the internship applications he was submitting for weeks now. It was another reason a short respite from seeing him was welcome. 'He's still waiting to hear back,' Joy replied. 'He's hoping to get a job in Sydney rather than Brisbane. But to be honest, he just wants to get his foot in the door with someone so he can get those twelve months under his belt. It's so competitive.' Joy fiddled with the sandwich on her plate. 'Can I ask you something?' she said.

'Sure. Shoot.'

Joy shook her head and started to laugh. 'No. You'll think I'm stupid.'

'Of course I won't,' said Vivienne. 'Wasn't it Carl Sagan who said, "*Every question is a cry to understand the world. There is no such thing as a dumb question*"?'

Joy sat staring at the rug, trying to figure out how to begin.

'Is it about you and Hugo?' Vivienne prompted, taking a sip of tea then cradling the mug in her hands.

Joy sighed. 'You've got it in one,' she said.

'Well, just say what's on your mind. Don't overthink it.'

'Hugo's wonderful. He's a great guy and I know he loves me to bits. But . . .'

'But you're not sure if you love him to bits? Is that how you're feeling?'

'No. Sort of. I don't know.' Joy tucked her feet up under her legs and recounted what had taken place between her and Hugo the previous day.

'He's my first serious boyfriend so, well, there's not a lot I can compare the experience to, if you know what I mean. I guess I was expecting to feel, you know, head over heels, madly in love. The whole "heart pounding every time I see him" kind of thing. I'm sounding like an idiot, aren't I?'

'Ha!' Vivienne laughed but her voice was full of care. 'I'm sorry. I didn't mean to laugh like that and I'm not laughing *at* you. Quite the opposite. Can I be totally honest? And this is only my observation.'

'Please,' said Joy, listening intently.

'From what I've seen – and I've seen quite a bit of you and Hugo together since moving in – you get on very well together. Just enjoy what you have. If he treats you well and you like being with him, then that's all it needs to be.'

'I do love him,' said Joy. 'I mean, sometimes I wish he was a little more spontaneous. A bit more fun. But in the scheme of things, he's great.'

'That's the second time you've told me he's *great*,' said Vivienne. 'But is he great or is the sex great?'

'Both, I guess,' said Joy without hesitation.

'So, what is it you're not sure of? Being an item? Are you not sure if this is more of a physically fulfilling relationship than, say, an emotionally fulfilling one?'

'God, I don't know,' said Joy. 'Maybe I've seen too many romantic movies. I was expecting this big love thing to happen. Some big X factor to exist between us. I mean, he's such a kind person and I can talk to him about anything. But I can't help but think sometimes that something's missing . . .' Joy trailed off.

'Every relationship has its own unique composition.

Some are more physical. Some are more about companionship and shared interests,' Vivienne explained. 'If you enjoy being with him and you're happy with the mutually exclusive thing you've got going on, then fine. Enjoy what the two of you have for what it is. If it's not working for you, then you are in control of what you want to do – keep trying or call it a day. I know it's not an easy decision, but you don't need to overanalyse the situation.'

She reached over and squeezed Joy's arm and Joy smiled. 'Thank you, I think I needed to hear that.'

Vivienne glanced at her watch. 'Is that the time?' she said. 'I'm sorry, I'm going to have to get Leo. But hey –' She put her arms around Joy and hugged her tightly. 'You're going to be fine.'

'You should be studying psychology, not education, if this talk is anything to go by,' said Joy, blinking back tears she felt welling in her eyes.

'Maybe I will eventually. And you're right. Hugo *is* a great guy,' said Vivienne. 'But he has to be right for you, at the end of the day.' She picked up her bag and looped it over her shoulder. 'I'm proof that being madly and passionately in love with someone is no guarantee of a fulfilling relationship. Certainly not the happily-ever-after we see on the big screen.'

*

Icy winter winds rolled up and over Bass Strait, buffeting Melbourne with a grey coldness that blanketed the city. Avril removed her cashmere coat and followed the waitress through the packed restaurant to where James and Reece were seated.

'I have good news, great news and some interesting news,' said James cheerfully after she'd sat down.

'I'll have the great news first,' said Avril.

'Lunch is on me.'

She laughed. 'And the good news?' she asked, tapping her fingers lightly on the white linen tablecloth.

'We've found a buyer for Regency Footwear. It's a little bit of a long-winded deal, but it's a very sound offer and Reece and I think that the sale could be finalised by November.'

'How happy is this deal going to make me?' she asked, and for once Avril broke her *no alcohol at lunch* rule, called the waiter over and ordered a glass of merlot.

'You'll clear your tax liability but there won't be any cash left over,' said Reece.

'At least I'll have that debt off my back. And what about the employees? I said I wouldn't sell to any company who wanted to rip the staffing levels apart.'

'You know that once you sell, those decisions are out of your control. Anyway, from what we've ascertained, Metro Corp wants to expand the business, not reduce it.'

'I knew it was them. Metro has always wanted to get their hands on Regency,' she said. 'Well, good luck to them. I'll be pleased to close this chapter once and for all and get back to focusing on what I do best.'

Once the waiter had taken their orders, Avril leant back in her chair.

'Tell me. What's the interesting news?'

Reece steepled his fingers in front of him. 'Well, it would appear you're not the only one who has their suspicions about Don Whitby,' he said. 'A colleague of mine has a client in a very similar situation to you. It turns out that the forensic accountant he's been working with is the same person who was recommended to me.'

'What was the outcome?' asked Avril.

'He wasn't at liberty to discuss the specifics of his client's case. What he did say was if it's misappropriation of funds we're talking about here, this company will uncover the entire trail.'

'All right. Go ahead. I've given you all the documentation already,' said Avril.

'So tell me,' said James as their meals were placed on the table. 'How's Joy? Have you seen much of each other lately?'

'Seems to be having a wonderful time,' said Avril. 'And the other housemates have worked out well, I think. Well, the young woman and her son have; not so much the other one. Terry? No, Tony. He's nice enough, so Joy tells me, but she's sick of having to chase him for rent money.'

'The trials of living in a shared house,' said Reece.

'It will do her good to have to stand on her own two feet,' said Avril.

'That sounds a bit harsh,' said James. 'I think any success Joy's had since leaving school she's earned.'

'Of course. You're right. That was a little harsh. I just meant that I think it's good for her to have to look after herself, spread her wings a little. Live with other people. Run her own life.'

'It's pretty nice digs she has there in Indooroopilly,' said Reece. 'Not many uni students get to live in such a comfy place.'

'That's true,' said James, 'but then Joy really looks after it. She's quite the homemaker, you know.'

'I could see that,' said Avril. 'Tim and I called in recently to visit her on our way up to Noosa. Joy and Scarlet had a delicious lunch ready for us and we were able to meet Vivienne and her little boy. And Hugo. Talk about an impressive young man. He seems to have the next ten years of his life mapped out. He's just been offered an internship in Brisbane with one of the top architectural firms.' Avril shook her head. 'Which is why I don't see Joy coming home to see us any time soon. She has much more going on in the city.'

'Joy's bound to head up to Monaghan once the semester's finished,' said Reece. 'I couldn't wait to get home once exams were over. Ben's the same. Loves the place. I'm pretty sure he wants to study ag science next year. I've told him, less partying and more time with the books if he wants to get in.'

'Well, hopefully he and Joy can catch up then,' said Avril, 'but I don't know what her plans are. Joy doesn't tell me much these days.'

Avril understood that the little girl who once ran up and down the stairs of the big house playing hide and seek was a little girl no more, and from here on she'd make up her own mind.

She wouldn't be consulting her mother.

*

As Avril had predicted, first semester ended and Joy stayed in Brisbane, working as many shifts at the pub as she could get. During Tim and Avril's surprise visit the second week of August, Joy was still noncommittal about her plans. Even the annual Winter Dance, held in the woolshed at Monaghan, wasn't enticing enough to draw her home.

By the time Joy sat her end-of-year exams, she hadn't been at Monaghan Station for nine months. She hadn't stayed away intentionally, or so she told herself. It was simply the way the year had played out.

But finally she was heading back, excited at the thought

of those early-morning rides she loved so much and seeing everyone again.

Joy was loading the last of her things into her car when Vivienne came through the front gate.

'Almost ready to hit the road?' Vivienne asked.

'Just about,' said Joy. 'Where's Leo?'

'Oh, he's playing over at Mrs B's for a few hours so I can get some Christmas shopping done. You have no idea what I can get through in two hours on my own.'

'I haven't seen Tony for a couple of days,' said Joy, 'so if you see him, will you –'

'He left on Wednesday,' said Vivienne, cutting Joy off. 'He's gone hiking in Tasmania. Didn't he tell you?'

'No. When's he back?'

'Not until the end of January, apparently.'

Scarlet came down the stairs and placed two large shopping bags on the back seat of her car.

'I'll be back in a minute,' said Joy.

She raced up the stairs, charged down the hall to Tony's room and opened the door, which was something she never did. A pile of unwashed clothing sat on top of his unmade bed. The room was littered with empty coffee mugs and plates that looked like they had been there for days, if not weeks. Joy pulled back the half-closed curtains and opened the window to let in some fresh air then went back outside.

'Is everything okay?' said Scarlet.

'Did Tony give either of you his rent money before he took off?' Joy asked, sensing the answer already.

'Not me,' said Vivienne.

'I haven't seen him for at least a week,' said Scarlet. 'But I'd like to. He's owed me a hundred bucks since forever.'

Joy folded her arms and shook her head.

'You're kidding,' said Vivienne. 'He tried to borrow money from me several times but I said no. He's such a user. I figured that out the third time he left me high and dry on Open Mic Night. Didn't show up. No message, nothing. Said, *Something came up.* Three strikes and you're out in my book.'

'Well, this is the third strike. He's out,' said Joy. 'Go and take a look at his room. It's disgusting. When I get back I'll box up all his stuff and stick it on the veranda. And let's get the locks changed. I'll advertise the room after Christmas.'

'Do we even need another housemate?' said Scarlet. 'You know, if the three of us put in an extra ten dollars a week, we can cover the rent and we won't have to take on someone else. Then Leo can have his own bedroom. What do you think?'

'I'm happy to do that if you both are,' said Vivienne.

'Definitely. Boy, that's a relief,' said Joy. 'To know I no longer need to chase him every single fortnight for his rent. I'll happily pay not to have that drama.'

'No more bloody chicken curry either,' said Scarlet as she hugged Joy goodbye.

Joy reached for her sunglasses, started the engine and wound down the driver's side window.

'If either of you changes your mind, you know you'd be very welcome at Monaghan for Christmas and New Year's Eve. I wish I could stay, but I really need to put in an appearance back home. Especially with this being our first Christmas without Grandpa. Have fun.'

As Joy drove away, her hand reached inside her tote, checking for her journal. When her fingers felt the reassuring softness of the leather, she closed the flap on her bag and slid a cassette tape into the player on the dashboard.

By the time she swung onto the Warrego Highway, the midday sun of a Queensland summer was at full strength. As Blondie and Joy sang 'Heart of Glass', the weatherboard houses on their quarter-acre blocks dwindled away until there was nothing but blue sky and undulating paddocks as far as the eye could see.

CHAPTER 7

If Joy considered her first year out of school to be one of freedom and self-discovery, the reality of second year was something else altogether. The practical, hands-on side of veterinary training began to outpace the theory so Joy saw less and less of Scarlet and Vivienne. Scarlet's workload was just as heavy, and often whole days would go by before the three housemates saw each other, let alone spent any time together. As their workloads intensified, the partying fell away, and everything that had felt novel and fresh in first year started to seem run-of-the-mill.

Joy's socialising began to consist mostly of time spent with Hugo and working at the Crown and Anchor, an establishment which, not unlike herself, had gone through something of a transformation since she'd first stood behind the bar.

As Joy and Hugo had discovered, Barry O'Brien was not as averse to change as he liked to make out. When the pub five hundred metres down the road underwent a major renovation and started to attract the young business crowd, Barry began to mull over the ideas Hugo had long been suggesting to him. The stockbrokers and bankers who frequented his nemesis's watering hole, with its large new television screens and modern decor, ordered more rounds, stayed longer and left bigger tips, and Barry wasn't going to miss out on any of the action. He knew his days of catering mainly to the student crowd were over. The Crownie would always be known for its live music and as the place to see a great band, but as the 1980s powered forward, even Barry O'Brien had to admit that appearances were beginning to carry cachet like never before and he could not risk missing the boat.

'Okay, architect,' Barry had said to Hugo shortly after he'd arrived to meet Joy one evening. 'You let me know what ya think my place needs to blow the opposition out of the water, and if I think it's fair, you've got the job.'

'You won't be sorry,' Hugo had assured him. 'You'll earn the costs back in less than a year.'

Hugo, Barry conceded privately, had been right all along. Once the old building was given a fresh coat of paint, the windows enlarged and the bathrooms updated, the Crown and Anchor, while remaining turn-of-the-century on the outside, was a study in rustic simplicity on the inside. Some carefully placed artwork, modern lighting and completely new furniture changed not only the atmosphere of the place but the crowd. Even the menu was given a revamp but, on Barry's insistence, the no-fuss grilled steak and roast chicken remained.

'Hey, Joyful,' Barry had called as he counted out twenty-dollar notes into the hand of the young tiler who'd just finished work in the bathrooms. 'Come and take a look at yer trendy ladies' room.'

Joy had been pulling the protective wrapping from the new chairs. She stood in the doorway of the women's restroom and smiled when she saw the freshly grouted navy and white mosaic floor.

'Hand dryers as well,' she said. 'Everything looks bigger and brighter with those large mirrors. You're going to make a lot of women very happy, Barry. The whole place looks fantastic. You've given the old girl a new lease of life.'

'Well, Joyful, ya can't hide the profits forever.' Barry grinned. 'What's the point of havin' it if ya can't spend it?' He rested his arms on the top of his stomach contentedly.

'You sound like a shearer on payday,' Joy said with a chuckle before returning to finish unpacking the chairs.

The effect of the changes at the Crown and Anchor was almost immediate. Hugo no longer worked there, his shifts having petered out as the demands of his internship grew, but he spent a lot of time there waiting for Joy's shift to end. One evening he was sitting at the bar and he raised his glass towards Joy as he watched her mix three Bacardi and Cokes. With a newly acquired haircut and recently purchased silk shirt and tie, he blended in seamlessly with his work colleagues standing nearby. Having long since decided that contact lenses were not for him, Hugo had ditched the heavy black frames of his student days for a streamlined pair of tortoiseshell reading glasses more in keeping with his profession.

'What does it take to get some service around here?' he joked as Joy served another customer.

She scooped up his empty beer glass and smiled.

'Some manners and a decent tip would be a good start.'

'Look at this place,' said Hugo, glancing around the crowded bar area. 'The Friday afternoon patrons have changed a bit since I started coming here. Full of yuppies now.'

'You realise you're one of them,' said Joy, closing the drawer of the cash register. 'You look every bit the *young urban professional*. If it wasn't for your ideas, this place would still look the same, so I guess yuppies like you come in handy sometimes.'

Joy moved along the bar to the waiting throng.

'Who's next?' she asked.

*

As 1980 rolled into 1981 and Joy embarked on third-year uni, things began to change. The demands of her course load on her time were immense, so that she could barely squeeze in her usual shifts at the pub and also have time left over to take a break now and then. The carefree hours she had once spent with Hugo became fewer and further between, and she found herself beginning to resent the effort it took to maintain the relationship alongside everything else she was juggling. In her quiet moments she began to question what she had with Hugo in a way she hadn't since Vivienne had allayed her fears in first year.

One afternoon at the end of July, Joy was at work in a lull between customers. She hadn't had a break since she'd started earlier that afternoon so she poured herself a glass of water and stood at the end of the bar out of the service area. For midweek, the ground floor was full to bursting, including Hugo, who'd come in after work as he often did.

'What time do you get off?' said Hugo. 'I thought we could go somewhere for dinner.'

Joy glanced at her watch.

'Thanks, but I can't. I'm going home to watch the wedding with Scarlet and Vivienne. You're welcome to join us.'

'The wedding,' said Hugo blankly. 'Whose wedding?'

'Charles and Diana. Live coverage from eight o'clock tonight.'

'Oh. That wedding. No interest,' said Hugo, drumming his fingers on the top of the bar. 'Well, what about this Saturday? Let's go down the coast for the day.'

'I'd love to but Mum's in town and I'm going to the opening of her bridal store in the city, then she's taking me to dinner. You know. It's a mother–daughter thing.'

'I saw the write-ups in the weekend papers about this new business of hers,' said Hugo. 'Impressive. So, what about tomorrow night? Let's at least do something.'

'I'm sorry, Hugo, afraid I can't. I'm not trying to put you off but I'm catching up with James Carmody. The court case against Don Whitby starts next week and he and Reece are confident they can take him to the cleaners.' Joy had been shocked when her parents had sat her down at Christmas and told her about the financial difficulties they had been dealing with. Although it was unfortunate news, in a strange way it had been good: Joy felt it had brought her and her mother closer than they'd been in a long time. 'I might even go and watch some of the proceedings if I can.'

'Well, Friday night then,' said Hugo, a hint of exasperation in his tone. 'Can't you take the night off for once?'

Joy sighed. 'I really can't – you know I always work Friday nights. And besides, that new band Around Midnight is playing this weekend and Friday's their first concert. All three shows are sold out. I thought you really wanted to see them, or did you forget they were playing?'

'Sure. They're a great band. I get it,' he said. 'But you'll be working in the front bar so you're not going to be able to see them play.'

'I'll be able to slip in and see a couple of songs. Someone will cover for me.'

'So, you won't take the night off to be with me,' he said glumly.

'That's not fair,' said Joy. 'I can't let Barry down. Plus it's the best night for tips. What's wrong with catching up tonight? Come and have dinner at my place. It'll be fun.'

'And watch a wedding I couldn't care less about? Forget it.'

Joy began to feel a bit exasperated herself. 'Sunday night then. Let's both see the band's last show. Barry won't mind if we slip in through the back,' she suggested.

'I'll pass. I have to get up early Monday morning. Besides, I find the whole concert scene here's for students. I've kind of moved on from that.'

'Really,' said Joy flatly. 'Meaning what exactly?'

Hugo stood, finishing the last of his beer.

'Here's your tip,' he said, and whacked a ten-dollar note down on the bar. 'I'll see you later.' He pulled his jacket off the back of the chair and slung it over his shoulder. He'd only walked a few steps before he turned back and leant over the bar towards Joy.

'You know, I finally get it. I'm only here to fit into your schedule. I landed a big client today and I wanted to celebrate this milestone with you. I'm simply not a priority for you.'

Joy felt anger spark inside her. 'Hang on, that's not fair. I just have a busy week, that's all. Plus I didn't know about your client and I've fitted into *your* schedule plenty of times.'

Hugo nodded and smiled, but it seemed more like a grimace.

'You're absolutely right. You're all kindness and consideration. Enjoy the wedding.'

'If you walk away now, Hugo, we're done.'

For a moment Joy couldn't quite believe what she'd said. The words had tumbled out so effortlessly it was as if the phrase had been sitting, waiting to be released. And, thinking back on her doubts of the last few months, she conceded that maybe it had.

Hugo stared at Joy but she couldn't read his expression. She wasn't sure if he'd heard what she'd said, and she wasn't sure if she'd meant it.

'Hugo,' she called after him, but he was already shouldering his way through the crowd towards the exit.

*

Avril was in her new bridal boutique on the second floor of the Brisbane Arcade admiring her handiwork. She ran her eyes over the array of white, ivory and champagne-coloured gowns hanging on the pale-pink hangers, checking to see if there was anything she didn't like about the designs. There was nothing. The two sales assistants who were helping set up the store were buried knee-deep in tissue paper as they unpacked satin shoes and diamanté clutch bags.

Over the years, Avril had brought several business ideas to life relatively quickly, but none had overtaken her with such ferocity as had Princess Bridal. Three stores would open the following Saturday simultaneously, in Brisbane, Sydney and Melbourne, with Adelaide and Perth to follow. Her timing could not have been better.

The idea had taken root the previous year, when Avril and Tim were sitting up in bed one Sunday morning reading the papers. Avril had suddenly gone still and touched Tim on the arm.

'I have a feeling about this Lady Diana Spencer – you know, Prince Charles's new girlfriend,' she said, tapping the social pages as she stared into space.

'I know that look. What are you thinking?' Tim asked with a grin.

'It's just a thought,' she said, but she hadn't elaborated, wanting to think it through.

And think she had. Her desire to start a bridalwear business, the likes of which no one had seen before, had kept pace with the press attention and the public's fascination with the nineteen-year-old Lady Diana. Avril was certain that if the fresh-faced willowy blonde was to marry Prince Charles, bridal fashion would enter a new era, or perhaps rekindle the style of over-the-top weddings of the past.

'If these two walk down the aisle, it will be the wedding of the decade, possibly the century,' Avril had said to James when they met to discuss the financial logistics of the business. 'It will bring the big traditional-style wedding day back into fashion.'

'You really think so?' said James, closing the cost analysis document.

'I'm sure of it. If a bride-to-be can walk in and buy her dress, shoes and any other accessories all in the one place, she'll walk out feeling like a princess. "Princess Bridal", I'm thinking of calling it. How does that sound?'

'Well, your business plan certainly ticks all the boxes,' said James. 'You can import material through Lewmont Fabrics. You've already got your own garment factory and you don't need ground-floor shop space, so your rent space will be cheaper.'

'I have such a good feeling about this. If all goes well it might be the answer to our financial prayers,' said Avril.

By the time the royal engagement was announced the

following February, Avril had designed thirty wedding dresses, decided on the fabrics and signed the leases on the rental spaces she'd found. Then she set about assembling a team to help bring her first bridal range together. With the wedding set to take place in St Paul's Cathedral on 29 July, Avril had just five months to fit out her boutiques, hire and train staff, and have her designs completed and on the racks ready for customers.

With only two days to go until the opening of her three new boutiques, Avril hoped that the dramas of the 1970s were far behind her and that the 1980s would be a more prosperous decade.

*

While the front of the Crownie was turn-of-the-century Queensland architecture at its finest, the rear of the building comprised an unassuming old warehouse. In its heyday this was simply a commercial necessity used to house thousands of bales of wool on their way to Europe and the United Kingdom. When Barry O'Brien had first looked at the property, he'd considered the lanolin-scented construction a bonus, but it was really the land he was after. He'd had long-term plans for this flat, two-thousand-square-metre block of land with views across the river.

But then he'd seen inside. Familiar as he was with all the regulations regarding entertainment venues, one look at the lofty height of the ceiling, the four sets of large sliding oak doors and the no-nonsense concrete floor had confirmed for Barry that the old woolshed would make the perfect concert venue. A real money-spinner. He knew that a stage for the band and a bit of gear was all it would take to attract the twenty-somethings who were hungry to see live music on Friday and Saturday nights.

And he'd been right. He'd lost count of the number of bands who'd played in front of the four-hundred-strong crowd since he'd owned the site. A concert at the Woolshed, as it was named, had become a rite of passage for countless rock bands and their fans. A band bumped in on the day of their gig, did their own set-up, sound and sometimes light show, then bumped out the following day.

On this Friday morning, Barry watched as the latest band hefted their gear into the Woolshed and set up in preparation for that night's concert. He didn't care that he'd paid slightly more than usual to secure a three-night commitment; it was money well spent as far as he was concerned. He'd had a feeling about these boys the first time he'd heard them play. He stood in the darkened doorway at the end of the walkway that led from the kitchen to the warehouse and watched the rehearsal, his right hand tapping rhythmically against his leg. The band would soon be headed back down to their hometown of Melbourne for the sellout *Aussie Rock Music Show* to be held at the Myer Music Bowl the first Friday in September. It would be the largest nationally televised fundraiser rock concert ever held in Australia. Barry waited until the song ended, then wandered back the way he'd come, humming.

*

Mick Harris signalled to the guy at the mixing desk that he wanted the band to do one more sound check. As the lead singer of Around Midnight, Mick was a perfectionist, especially when it came to performing live. Before their drummer Simon had joined the band a few years earlier, Mick had worked his way through two bass players and three drummers before he was convinced he'd found the right combination.

Good enough won't cut it, he'd told himself over and over.

There was more to creating a great band than being a talented musician. They were easy to find. He wanted a brotherhood. Solidarity. A loyalty to one another that he thought most bands lacked. With Mick, you were either with him or against him. There was no middle ground.

From the outset Mick had been after a sound that was distinctive – instantly recognisable. A lot like Mick himself. Brash yet sleek, seductive yet enigmatic. Once Mick and his two high school mates had formed their band – the multi-talented Jack Anderson on bass guitar and Dave McCready on lead – finding a drummer of Simon Webber's calibre was like hitting the jackpot. The band was tight, talented, and ready to record their third album.

But it was Mick's voice and his steamy onstage presence that was the backbone of the band. That and his ambition to see the band play large concert venues in the UK and possibly America. He was the engine that drove the whole show. The gig at the Myer Music Bowl was a mere stepping stone to the big league. Having played countless shows up and down the east coast of Australia and in every capital city, Around Midnight had gathered a strong and loyal following, with their last two songs reaching the national top ten. But like all the rock bands that played the pubs, clubs and concert halls across the country, it was international success the group was after, and Mick was determined they'd have it.

Simon counted them in as the lead and bass guitarists followed. Less than a minute later Mick's dominating frame pulled away from the microphone and held up his hand.

'Yeah. Thanks, Angus,' Mick called, his gravelly voice echoing throughout the empty space. 'We're done here.'

He turned to the other members of the band.

'That's great. Let's start with "Shades of Blue" and keep "Don't Look Now" and "Jettison" for any encore. And Jack, let's keep that riff you and Dave have been doing at the end of "Hide Away". It sounded good. Okay, we're show-ready, everyone.'

*

Joy pushed open the squeaky swing door to the Green Room with her back. Although they called it the 'green room', this was really just a large, brightly lit space between the main bar and the Woolshed that served as a dining room cum lounge area for the band members and their entourage. It was totally devoid of the standard green room luxuries found at television stations and upmarket theatres.

Joy hesitated in surprise as she wrestled the tray of drinks onto a nearby table. With two hours to go before the band took to the stage for the first of their three concerts, the room was noticeably empty, except for the band members themselves and a short, heavy-set man in a tan leather jacket that screamed *management*.

'Out!' bellowed a dark-haired man from the opposite corner without bothering to turn around to see who it was.

'Take it easy, Mick, mate,' said another. 'It's only the barmaid.'

A blond man sprang up from the sofa.

'Please, let me give you a hand,' he said, even though Joy didn't need any help.

'Compliments of the owner,' said Joy. 'Here's the menu if anyone's hungry.'

'You're too kind,' he replied.

The man's softly spoken English accent was in keeping with the smooth fair hair that fell across his face and the touch of smoky eyeliner that defined his pale blue eyes.

The man took the menu card from Joy and without consulting anyone else said, 'Some burgers and chips would be delightful.'

'And a salad,' called the dark-haired man from the corner of the room.

Joy glanced at the back of the man's head and shoulders. She recognised him as the lead singer of the band, Mick Harris. His feet rested on a coffee table.

'And no olives,' he added.

'My shift's about to finish, but I'll make sure someone gets your order to you as quickly as possible,' said Joy, familiar with the entitled mentality of many green-room patrons.

Joy signed off on the timesheet, washed her hands and thought about a comment Scarlet had made after reading an article about Mick Harris in *Tracks* magazine. 'Sure, he's hot, but apparently he's a total arsehole.'

Well, she got that right, thought Joy.

CHAPTER 8

Joy applied a thick coat of mascara to her upper lashes.

'Good of Barry to give you the night off.'

'I guess he figured I wouldn't get much work done if I was ducking up and down the walkway all night,' said Joy.

'Have you spoken to Hugo at all since Wednesday night?' asked Scarlet.

'Nope.'

'Are you at least going to call him and work this out?'

'Nope.'

'I think you're being ridiculous. I mean, all he was trying to do by the sounds of it was spend some time with you. You can't break up over that.'

Joy found a lip gloss in her makeup tray and dropped the tube into a small zip-up bag. She turned and stared at her best friend.

'Everyone's got an opinion about the relationships in my life,' said Joy, 'and I'm sick of it. I'm tired of being told what's what. James on Thursday night, like a stuck record – "Make more of an effort with your mother".

Mum and I are doing just fine, even if she did tell me to call my father more often. And now you.'

Joy picked up her bag, stormed out of the bathroom and down the hall.

'Hang on a minute,' shouted Scarlet, running after her. 'It's me you're talking to, so cut the bullshit. No one's telling you what's what, okay? People have disagreements. It happens. Rather than have this stand-off with Hugo, I simply think it would be a good idea to get it sorted. Do it before we go to this concert tonight or you'll end up having a really crappy night.'

Joy glanced at her watch when she heard the car horn.

'Let's go,' she said.

'So, you're not going to call him?' said Scarlet, pulling the front door closed behind them.

'If I haven't heard from him by tomorrow evening, then I'll call,' said Joy.

She stared out the window as they sped through the city. *But do I really want to resolve this?* she thought. *It all feels too hard. Not easy. Not anymore, anyway.*

Ten minutes after the taxi had driven away, Hugo swung his Valiant Charger into the driveway at number sixteen. Though he could see a lamp on in the lounge room and the girls' cars parked on the street, he could tell no one was home. Even so, he knocked just to make sure, the wooden screen door banging beneath his knuckles. Sunday night. The Around Midnight concert. Of course. That's where she'd be.

He slid a card into the large bunch of apology flowers he'd brought and placed them on the doormat. They'd both said things they didn't mean. Hadn't they? He certainly didn't want to break up. The night was clear, the air cold. He slid his hands into the pockets of his jacket and looked at the stars. The new client he'd mentioned to Joy – that was only half the story. Why hadn't he just been honest with her? Told her the truth? Why had he turned something that should have been a celebration into an argument? Was it to soften the blow, to make his decision easier?

There was no point turning up to the concert. It wasn't the place to say he was sorry. *I'll call her tomorrow. We'll sort this out. We'll be fine*, he said to himself.

Behind him, the front gate swung open and Vivienne, a sleeping Leo draped over her shoulder, made her way towards him.

'Hi, Hugo,' Vivienne whispered. 'That's good timing. I just ducked next door. Spiderman here had a date with Mrs B. Want to come in for a drink? Have you eaten?'

'Yes to the drink and no, I haven't eaten.' He paused. 'I'm guessing you know Joy and I haven't spoken for a few days?'

Vivienne passed Hugo her keys and he unlocked the front door.

'So I hear. The merlot's on the kitchen bench. Let me put this one to bed and then we'll talk.'

Two hours later when Hugo reached the end of the street he turned on the radio in time to hear the announcer count down the top ten songs of the week.

'And coming in at number ten this week is Around Midnight with their new release, "Don't Look Now".'

*

Mick knew that smaller seatless venues like the Woolshed created an atmosphere of intimacy between the audience and the band that helped to build a loyal following.

'Better to play a full-capacity show like that than to a

half-filled auditorium,' he'd told the boys right from the start.

With hands in the air the fans danced and sang along to the pulsating beat of the music, while the technicolour light show synchronised with Mick's onstage performance. Voice, guitars and drums surged across the crowd, clear, loud and forceful. It was a slick, well-rehearsed ninety-minute show.

Angus worked the mixing desk like the professional soundie that he was. The band's manager, Robert Flare, hovered in the darkness at the side of the stage wearing his signature tan corduroy jacket, watching his only client. The running joke among the band members was that they'd buy Robert a designer leather jacket the day a song of theirs went to number one. They all hated the safari-style relic he wore. But Robert called it his lucky jacket and was rarely seen without it.

While Barry O'Brien had a reputation for being tough yet fair, Bob Flare was simply tough, a short bulldog of a man who walked in a hurry, studying the footpath, jangling the keys in his jacket pocket. He was always on the hunt for a good band, a sole singer or duo. There wasn't a single aspect of the entertainment industry he hadn't tried, except actors. They were a breed all of their own as far as he was concerned. He'd even had a crack at the 'dinner and show' music hall business that was popular in the 1970s, but that had been too much like hard work.

The moment Robert signed Around Midnight, a month after Simon had joined them, he'd quietly gone about disposing of the other four acts he'd been managing, soon realising that the other artists, as he put it, 'were dogs and always would be'. As soon as he'd met Mick and the boys and heard the type of material Mick and Jack were writing, he knew he was onto a winner. A posh-speaking drummer and the three boys from the 'burbs. Robert could work with that.

'I'll take you boys all the way to the top,' Robert had said the morning the contract was signed. 'All the way. I'm going to turn you into one of the biggest bands in the world.'

And they believed him.

They weren't quite there yet, though. Their bread and butter was still venues like this one with ready-made audiences of local students and would-be rock stars.

Halfway through the concert, the lights went out, and when the stage was lit again, a spotlight fell on a piano that had been waiting patiently to Dave's left. Mick sat at the keys, and as he played the first few notes of a ballad, the crowd erupted.

'I wrote this song some time ago,' Mick said. 'But this is the first time I've performed it live. It's called "Only a Moment". This one's for Bonnie.'

There was only Mick on piano and Jack on lead guitar as the lead singer's husky voice delivered a moving and what appeared to be a highly personal composition. As Mick sang the final chorus, thousands of concert tickets fluttered down from overhead, covering the swaying fans. Once finished, Mick raced back to the mic and Simon's drumming led the charge into the next high-octane, fast-paced forty-five-minute set.

When the band had finished their third encore, Mick gave one final wave, replaced the mic on its stand and strolled from the stage, wrapping a towel around his sweat-soaked neck on his way to the dressing room. The house lights went up, and as security rolled open the giant wooden doors, the four hundred concert-goers spilled out into the wintry night air. Joy grabbed Scarlet by the hand and pulled her through the crowd who were moving in the opposite direction. Joy lifted her hand to the bouncer manning the walkway door.

'Hi, John,' said Joy. 'You don't mind if we take the short cut, do you? Can't be last to the bar.'

The giant hulk of a man grinned and opened the door.

'Good show, wasn't it?' he said. 'If only I could sing like that.'

*

Two Bacardi and Cokes later, Scarlet was on the other side of the room displaying her pool-playing skills. Joy perched on a stool at the end of the bar, rocking her glass back and forth. She poked at the ice cubes with a straw and thought about Hugo, a sense of unease flooding through her. *What the hell do I want?* she asked herself.

There was a time when Joy couldn't have imagined going to a concert without Hugo. *He's not here and I'm not even bothered by it*, she kept thinking. Her gut feeling was that this wasn't a positive sign. It was as if they'd worked their way through a hedge maze only to now be standing at a dead end. No matter how much Joy tried to resist the thought, she knew deep down that the passion she'd once felt for Hugo had drained away. Between the demands of third-year vet science, working at the bar and trying to make it back to Monaghan more often – a commitment she'd made to her father at the beginning of the year – it felt as though her life was all work and no play and she was tired of it.

The previous night, she'd been reading through her journals. She'd filled the pages of the black leather book with the kind of reflections and comments only a naïve eighteen-year-old in the throes of her first love affair could write. She was surprised to read the adjective-loaded, overly emotional entries complete with souvenired coasters and a collection of movie tickets crammed inside the back cover.

She didn't feel like that person anymore.

Joy's more recent journal entries had been predominantly about her relationship with her mother. There were aspects of her mother's life that she and Avril had rarely spoken about. In particular, the death of Avril's fiancé, Guy Leon, just as the war was finishing, and the birth of Avril's first child, a son who had lived only a few hours. This was something Joy had discovered by accident at the age of ten, when she'd overheard her parents talking in the front room of the homestead.

'Who was that baby you and Mum were talking about before?' she had asked her father as he tucked her into bed. 'I wasn't listening in. Honest. But did Mum have a baby before me?'

Tim Meredith was a firm believer in being truthful, so he'd sat down on his daughter's bed and explained to Joy what had happened. As her mother had never mentioned a little boy named Philippe before, Joy thought it might make her sad if she asked her about him and so, she never had.

Joy had asked her about other things, though. And while her mother was quite happy to recall her fortuitous meeting with Henry, and many of her memories of Monaghan in those early days, she circumvented most of the questions Joy asked about her life in France during the Second World War. Joy knew that Avril and her mother, Yvette, had lived at the Chateau de Vinieres with Madame Leon for most of the war. 'They were not happy times,' was all Avril would say, and press her lips together. And yet she'd happily talk about her mother's haberdashery shop and the beautiful dresses and hats her mother would create in her workroom. Sometimes Avril would recall her days at Dior after the war, and the hours spent hand-sewing jetted buttonholes.

It must have been so hard, Joy reflected, leaving your home and everything and everyone you knew for a new country as Avril had in 1950, but Joy had always felt a little hurt that her mother wouldn't talk to her about it.

It's because we're like oil and water, thought Joy. *We're never going to mix.*

Their relationship seemed to take three steps forward on the closeness scale, then five steps back. Their encounters were usually followed by a slew of telephone calls, but inevitably these petered out.

Dinner with her mother the previous evening had left Joy in no doubt that Avril had discovered yet another goldmine with the opening of her bridalwear boutiques. Television, radio, newspapers and magazines were saturated with constant coverage of the Prince of Wales and his newly minted princess. While Joy had watched the royal wedding with fascination for the pageantry and excess, she had little interest in hearing about the plans for the royal-style weddings customers to the bridal boutique were already talking about. There was only so much talk about silk taffeta and jewelled heels Joy could take.

Joy had run her fork over the top of her chocolate mousse and feigned interest while Avril had talked nonstop about how she could grow the business. The conversation changed tempo once Avril started talking about her plans to visit her dear friend, Madame Leon, at Chateau de Vinieres, and for once Joy felt like they were sharing mutual memories, chatting as friends do.

'Remember when we played hide and seek and we hid in that massive wardrobe upstairs?' said Joy, smiling as she recalled their trip to France when she was fourteen years old. 'We scared the bejesus out of Dad.'

'I only wish you could come on this trip with me. We could have rediscovered Paris together,' said Avril, smiling at her.

But that was out of the question; Joy had so much work to do she couldn't have taken a weekend off, let alone flown to France for a holiday. It seemed to Joy that her mother had no idea what she was dealing with. There was little discussion about the two-week prac work Joy had completed at her late grandfather's horse stud and nothing about Joy's relationship with Hugo, apart from a couple of her mother's perfunctory questions about his health and studies.

Then the topic swung back to Avril and her work and an upcoming ad campaign she was developing. Joy was genuinely pleased to see her mother so happy, so animated about her work. But the more Avril spoke, the quieter Joy became.

I think it's always been this way, she thought.

Joy was so deep in her reverie that she hardly noticed when someone dropped a packet of cigarettes and a silver lighter on the bar next to Joy's glass, drawing her back to the present.

'I thought it was you.'

Despite the din from the chatter and music, Joy immediately recognised the smooth, clipped English accent, and was surprised to see the drummer from Around Midnight standing beside her.

'I'm Simon, by the way.'

'Joy.'

140

'Ah. *The pain of parting is nothing to the joy of meeting again*,' he recited slowly, emphasising the word 'joy', and picked up his cigarettes.

'Dickens,' said Joy, and she noticed the hint of a smile on Simon's face. He'd removed his eyeliner and replaced his black t-shirt with a fine wool navy sweater.

'Well done,' he said, and caught the attention of one of the bar staff. 'Can I buy you a drink?'

'Whisky, with a little ice, please.'

'I'll have the same,' he told the bartender. 'Single malt if you have it, and a soda and lime with ice.'

'Your show was fantastic. It's the first time I've seen the band live,' said Joy, shaking her head as Simon offered her a cigarette. He lit one for himself. 'Pleased to get out of the green room for a bit?' she said. 'It can get pretty chaotic back there.'

'Are you speaking from experience?'

Joy placed her empty glass on the bar and laughed.

'God, no. I have no interest in hanging out backstage. I've worked here part-time for quite a while so I know what it can be like, you know, after a concert. Girls clamouring to meet the band.'

'Yes. People. A constant avalanche of strangers,' said Simon. 'It comes with the territory.'

'So, why are you out here and not back there?' said Joy.

Simon rested his forearm on the bar and blew a stream of smoke skywards. The definition of his toned arms was clearly noticeable through the fine knit. He had the most beautiful skin Joy had ever seen on a man, a defined jawline and elongated profile. His thick eyelashes and brows made him look younger than he probably was. Joy already knew he was the senior band member and a year older than Mick Harris. It was as if he'd stepped out of

141

the smoking room in an Evelyn Waugh novel. Pale, slim, refined.

'It's not my thing, I suppose,' he said as he tapped his cigarette on the edge of an ashtray. 'Besides, I like this pub. It's like I'm on the set of *The Summer of the Seventeenth Doll* or *Sunday Too Far Away*.'

Joy knew both the play and the movie he was referring to. But she didn't feel like playing the part of the quiz show contestant all night, so she simply smiled. And as charming as Simon was, Joy sensed he was not trying to pick her up; she suspected his preferences lay elsewhere. Their drinks arrived and Simon raised his glass in such an elegant manner that he smashed any remaining preconceived ideas Joy had about what a drummer should look and sound like.

'To whiskies at the bar,' he said, and they clinked glasses.

*

It was common knowledge among the fans and music fraternity that Mick, Jack and Dave had met at high school, with Jack and Dave both being a year younger than Mick. The garage under the McCreadys' brick veneer house on the outskirts of Melbourne had become the epicentre of late-night jam sessions as the boys dreamed of making a living from their music. Mrs McCready would reassure the neighbours, when the music reached epic proportions on a Saturday night, that 'one day you'll be telling anyone who'll listen that you knew those boys when they were just starting out'.

Joy was interested to know how someone who appeared to be so different from the other band members, especially Mick, had ended up being a drummer in a rock band.

'I know you've been with the band for a few years and you're obviously English, but what brought you to Australia?'

'Are you a reporter?' Simon asked. 'No, can't be, you work here part-time . . . A struggling artist then. Or a model, perhaps. You certainly look like you could be.'

'None of the above, I'm afraid,' said Joy. 'Not even close.'

Joy was enjoying their banter when Scarlet sidled up beside her. In her semi-intoxicated state, Scarlet didn't seem to recognise Simon and after a cursory 'hi', proceeded to tell Joy that she was heading to a party at Toby's place and asked if she wanted to come.

'Thanks, but I'll give it a miss,' said Joy.

'I'll see you later then,' said Scarlet, and she planted a kiss on Joy's cheek as well as Simon's before being hauled away by another girl.

'A friend of yours?'

'My friend and housemate,' said Joy. 'And never a dull moment.'

'Speaking of which,' said Simon, as Mick Harris put his hand on Simon's shoulder and joined them at the bar. He picked up the soda water Simon had ordered and downed half the glass.

'Thanks for that,' he said. 'Don't forget we have a press conference at the Hilton at ten tomorrow and a photo shoot in the afternoon.'

Leaning back against the pillar that buffeted the small alcove behind her, Joy could see she'd gone unnoticed. Or perhaps the front man for the band had seen her and thought she was just a girl sitting on a bar stool having a drink. It was obvious he hadn't realised she and Simon had been talking. Simon gestured in the direction of the darkened corner. It was only then that Mick Harris turned and looked at Joy.

'Mick, this is the lovely Joy,' said Simon. 'Joy, this is Mick, such as he is.'

'Yes. I remember,' she said. 'Doesn't like olives in his salad. Right?'

Mick stepped back and tilted his head to gain a better view of the brunette with the spiral curls. His eyes scrutinised Joy's face.

'You've got it in one,' he replied, still a little perplexed.

Mick offered his open palm to Joy and shook her hand.

In Joy's experience, men sometimes felt uncomfortable shaking a woman's hand – the gesture usually elicited a moment of awkwardness – but not this time. She found his handshake firm and the skin of his palm surprisingly soft. She wasn't expecting his eyes to be a vibrant iridescent green with a touch of mischief about them. In the photos she'd seen of him in magazines, his eyes had seemed dark, almost brooding. Over the peaty notes of the whisky, Joy smelt the woody fragrance of a masculine cologne. The smell reminded her of the scent that lingered in the shearing shed long after the men and their utes had departed for the season.

She startled a little as she realised she was staring at him.

And he was staring at her.

Mick suddenly smiled and shook his head. 'Oh, yes. I remember now. The green room. I'm told I get a little over-focused before a show. Apologies for my rudeness,' he said, holding her gaze.

Simon stubbed out what remained of his cigarette and repositioned his arm on the bar as Mick reached behind him for a stool. Neither of them seemed in a hurry to leave.

Simon ordered two more whiskies as if they were settling in for the night.

'I was trying to guess what Joy does when she's not working here part-time, but I haven't figured it out,' said Simon.

'You could ask her,' said Mick, finishing his soda and signalling for another. 'No need to be so cryptic.'

One of the bar staff called *last round*, a nightly necessity in order to meet the mandatory eleven o'clock closing time.

'You know, I loved the concert, and it's been great to meet you, but I think it's time I called it a night,' said Joy. 'I've got a very early start in the morning.'

'How early is very early?' said Mick.

'Four o'clock.'

'That's not the morning. That's the middle of the night.' Mick smiled.

'What requires you to be out of bed at that ungodly hour?' Simon asked. 'There should be a law against such things.'

'I'm rostered on to help with the delivery of some foals.'

'Aha, so you're studying veterinary science,' said Simon.

'With two years to go. Unfortunately I'll be carrying salads without olives in them for a little while longer. And if you think you're that hard to decipher,' said Joy, 'you've got Eton via Literature at Cambridge written all over you.'

Simon laughed with genuine pleasure. 'Oh, you're good,' he said. 'You got the Cambridge bit right.'

'It takes a lot to surprise me,' said Mick, 'but I would never have picked you for a vet.'

'Really?' said Joy. 'Well, I would never have picked you for a pianist,' she shot back. 'Lovely song, by the way,' she said, trying to soften her retort.

There was something about Mick Harris. An undeniable contrast between masculinity and fragility. She felt his warm smile hovering just below the surface.

'Thank you,' said Mick, and he looked into his glass and rocked the ice cubes backwards and forwards rhythmically.

'That's another thing you and I have in common, Joy,' said Simon. 'Books are obviously the first, and the second is that my brother's a vet. Works with endangered species in Africa. Kenya mainly.'

All thoughts of leaving at a reasonable hour forgotten, Simon and Joy fell into a serious discussion about elephants and the struggle to keep poachers away from the remaining white rhino population. And although he didn't contribute, Mick listened with interest.

The call for last drinks had cleared the room by half and those who were finishing up were spread haphazardly throughout the ground-floor bar area. Looking around, Joy asked, 'Don't the two of you have somewhere you're meant to be? Some wild afterparty? You've just finished three shows.'

'Bit clichéd, wouldn't you say?' said Mick. 'Don't you know you should never judge a book by its cover?'

'Now, *that* is a cliché,' said Joy.

'In our defence,' Simon added, 'we leave the really hard partying to Dave and Jack.'

Mick laughed. 'You can't party hard forever.'

'Do the same rules apply for a rock band?' said Joy.

'Especially for a rock band,' he replied.

Joy stood and pushed away the stool, not sure if they were teasing her or being truthful.

As she reached for her jacket and handbag, Mick gently put a hand on her arm and said, 'Oh, no. Not so fast. One game of pool before you disappear into the night. It's a long-standing end-of-gig tradition.'

Simon picked up his cigarettes and lighter. 'Lead on, my good man,' he said.

Mick scooped up Joy's hand in his and weaved his way through the stragglers towards an empty pool table. Simon racked up the balls, placed the white ball on the marker and handed Joy a cue which she immediately chalked. She tucked her long curls behind her ears.

'Three-man pool. First to sink the black,' she said without hesitation.

Mick and Simon traded glances as Joy stepped up to the end of the table, her left arm extended long and low, her upper body bent to within centimetres of the table's edge. She broke the triangular formation, sending the striped number twelve ball into the back left pocket. She then sank the six dot and the eleven stripe. The hours Joy had spent playing pool at Monaghan Station had been beneficial. She was sure that Henry would have paid anything to see the looks on Simon and Mick's faces.

Simon sank three in a row and then Mick two, then Joy another two, and so it went on until Joy put the black ball in the back right pocket and rested her cue on the ground. Mick smiled and clapped as Simon congratulated Joy on annihilating both of them in less than fourteen minutes. Simon wandered over to the bar to pay the bill, leaving Mick to collect the cues. Despite Joy's height, Mick's imposing frame seemed to tower over her. He took the cue Joy had been using and laid it on the pool table.

'A bit of advice,' she said softly, almost at a whisper. 'Never take a knife to a gunfight.'

Joy couldn't read the expression on Mick's face even though his body was only a hand-width from hers. She did, however, notice a scar that ran from the outside of his right eye to just below his ear. Mick half-sat on the edge of the pool table, gazing at her.

'I'm flat out this month with commitments and this televised concert at the beginning of September. But I'd like to take you to lunch, Saturday the twelfth, if you're free,' he said.

Joy wasn't surprised he'd asked her out. Somewhere between shaking his hand and playing her first pool shot she'd thought it might happen. It was the preciseness of the date that caught her off guard, and as if he could read Joy's look of surprise, he continued.

'I'm not usually so specific. I just know I have that weekend completely free, which is a rarity these days. Could I have your telephone number? I'm between Sydney and Melbourne for the next few weeks, but I'll call you, I promise.'

Joy knew she was going to say yes immediately. Hugo was as far from her mind as possible.

'Sure. But I don't have a pen on me,' said Joy.

'That's okay. What's the number?'

Joy recited the number and Mick listened.

'Thanks,' he said. 'I'll be in touch.'

'Wait. You can remember my number, just like that? No way. What is it?'

Mick repeated Joy's telephone number back to her.

'Do that again,' she said.

This time the numbers Mick recited weren't even close to being correct.

'I knew you were having me on,' she said.

Then he said her number again, perfectly.

'The last time I said your number backwards.'

Joy laughed, intrigued and flattered and curious.

148

When Simon returned, the three of them headed to the door.

While they waited for a taxi, Joy turned to them and said, 'Good luck at the Bowl in Melbourne and with your new album. Oh – and I was wondering, who's Bonnie? Or is it too personal?'

'Oh. You mean "Only a Moment", the song,' replied Mick. He shook his head gently. 'It was just a throwaway line. No one in particular.'

Joy nodded. 'Well, good night,' she said as a taxi pulled up, and she got in, leaving Simon and Mick on the footpath.

'How did the two of you get talking?' asked Mick as he watched the red tail-lights of the taxi glide around the corner.

'I recognised her as the waitress who was in the green room the other day, so I bought her a drink and we got chatting.'

'She's a knockout,' said Mick as another taxi pulled up.

'She sure is,' said Simon as he opened the passenger-side door. 'You want a lift back to the hotel?'

'No. I feel like a walk and it's not that far.'

After the taxi had driven away, Mick pulled up his collar, pushed his hands into the pockets of his leather jacket, crossed the road and strolled in the direction of the city, repeating Joy's telephone number in his head.

*

The following evening Joy and Hugo were sitting on the sofa in the lounge room. Joy had arrived home the previous night to find Hugo's bouquet of flowers and card and had felt more than a little conflicted as she read the apology the card contained. And now Hugo had given her some news that muddied the waters even more. It involved a great opportunity for him, but it also meant that Joy knew she needed to make her position clear.

'When would you start?' she asked, tucking her feet under her legs.

'The beginning of September,' said Hugo.

'That's only a month away. How soon do you have to give them an answer?'

'By the end of the week.' Hugo was quiet a moment. 'I'll hate the humidity. It's worse than a Brisbane summer up there, but a role like this doesn't come along every day. Certainly not to a graduate with less than two years' professional experience.'

'Thanks again for the flowers, by the way,' said Joy. 'And the card.'

'I'm sorry I didn't come to the concert with you. I kind of carried on like a bit of a dickhead, didn't I?' said Hugo.

Joy didn't reply straight away.

'I guess Singapore's not that far away,' she said eventually. 'Don't overthink this. What do you want to do?'

'I want to take the job but, Joy, please, I don't want it to be over between us. Can we talk about how this could work?'

'Well, let's just see how things go, then,' Joy suggested, despite the fact that she'd been thinking about nothing but Mick Harris all day. 'I mean, what if you meet someone else?'

Hugo looked taken aback. 'Why would you say that?'

'We're going to be living in different countries. It's a possibility.' Joy pulled a cushion to her chest. 'Actually, I don't know what I'm saying. I think you should take the job. It sounds amazing. Besides, I'm not going anywhere.

Well, not for the next two years, at least, until I've finished my degree.'

She leant over and kissed him. 'Congratulations, Hugo. It's wonderful news.'

*

A month later, Joy pulled her little red Suzuki into the International Departures bay in front of the QANTAS sign and helped Hugo unload his bags.

'Christmas will be here in no time,' he said. 'And I'll be back for five days.'

They hugged and kissed goodbye, holding each other without speaking.

As Hugo waved and the glass doors closed behind him, Joy suddenly felt winded. Hugo had been in her life for almost three years, and now he had gone.

She held back the tears until she was in the car. Was this an ending? Or a beginning?

And then there was Mick.

True to his word, Mick had phoned Joy, and then continued to phone her regularly throughout August. He'd talked about the gigs they'd played and working on their new album, and Joy loved these glimpses into a world she knew nothing about. Mick seemed similarly keen to hear about the work Joy had been doing with foals and her recent weekend doing prac work at the horse stud. And with each new conversation, Joy could feel Hugo fading into the background of her life as Mick drew nearer.

By the time Joy arrived home from the airport, the Myer Music Bowl Concert was about to start. Scarlet, Vivienne and her new boyfriend Jason, as well as half-a-dozen other friends, were camped out in the lounge room ready for a big night. Joy tossed her jacket and bag on the kitchen table and poured herself a glass of wine.

A feeling of loneliness took her by surprise. As she stared out the window, she heard the cackling kookaburras in the nearby trees and thought about the station. She could picture the late-afternoon sky, the low clouds awash with orange and pink as the last rays of light dipped behind the distant hills. The smell of the bush. The earth. Barking dogs across the yard. Evening, and the emptiness it could sometimes bring.

What the hell are you doing? Stop all this bloody fantasising. Except Joy didn't want to. Her thoughts raced wildly between what was and what could be.

Vivienne stopped in the doorway and tilted her head to the side, as she so often did before giving Joy the unconditional support Joy had come to rely on.

'You okay?' asked Vivienne. 'Are you going to join us?' She opened the oven door and rotated a tray of marinated chicken wings.

Why am I waiting? Joy thought. *I could be there in less than four hours.*

Joy tipped her unfinished glass of wine down the sink and scooped up her car keys.

'Nope,' she said as she filled two bottles of water. 'I'm going home. Just for the weekend. I haven't been back for ages and I'm not really in the mood to watch the concert.'

'Even with Around Midnight playing?'

'You forget,' said Joy. 'I've already seen them live. At the end of the day, they're just another band.'

CHAPTER 9

The labradors barked in excitement at the sound of the tyres on the gravel just before midnight. Henry's pups had grown into handsome dogs and Tim had adopted them as his own.

Joy turned off the engine, sat back in her seat and for a few seconds, closed her eyes. It was good to be home. The great starry sky, the stillness of the land, it was just what she needed.

She was unloading her bag when she heard her father's voice.

'I don't believe it,' he shouted, practically skipping down the steps. 'What a wonderful surprise. Why didn't you tell me you were coming?'

Joy had expected to see her father still awake; he was never one to go to bed early.

'I didn't know I was until this evening. A spur-of-the-moment decision. Easy run. No traffic.'

'You've only missed your mother by a day. She would have stayed if she'd known you were going to be here.'

'Where was she off to?'

'Some fashion awards night in Sydney. A pity. She said she didn't really feel like going. Never mind, you're here now.'

'Have you got much on this weekend, Dad?' Joy asked as they walked up the steps.

'Fortunately not. Only square eyes from watching the US Open. My money's on McEnroe, though Björn Borg's playing brilliantly.'

While Tim made her a sandwich, Joy poured two glasses of red wine and pulled out a chair. They jumped from topic to topic as they caught up on the weeks that had passed – Joy's uni workload, what was happening at the station, the recent birth of Chris Kennedy and his wife's first child, and ongoing family discussions about the viability of Henry's beloved horse stud still operating.

'I'm not looking at one textbook or any lecture notes all weekend,' said Joy. 'I'm having a break. End-of-year exams start in October and I'm dreading them.' She took a deep breath. 'I'll be glad when this year is over. But being involved with the broodmare program was interesting. Especially when the foals were being born.'

'Well, Calypso looks a picture. You've got Kevin to thank for his fitness. He's quite smitten with the animal.'

'That's all I could think about for the last hour of the trip. Getting back in that saddle. Want to ride out with me in the morning?'

'Try to stop me,' said Tim as he took her plate into the kitchen. 'It's so good to have you home, darling.'

*

Joy and Tim cantered the horses to the top of the rise then slowed to a walk, taking in the early-morning light. The cattle were scattered far and wide before them, smudges of amber on the green hills. Everything about Joy's life in Brisbane felt a world away from Monaghan Station.

'Hugo get away okay?' said Tim.

It was time to be honest with everyone. To be honest with herself.

'He flew out yesterday,' she said. 'And I'll save you the trouble of asking your next question, Dad. I'm almost certain it's over with Hugo.'

'Is that why you've come home? To try to make some sort of decision?'

'I think so,' said Joy. 'How did you know Mum was the one? I mean, was it a sudden thing like, *wham*, or did you grow to love her over time?'

'It was both, I guess,' said Tim. 'There was this energy, this chemistry between us right from the start. It's hard to explain except to say, you certainly know when it's there and when it isn't. And all the wishing and hoping in the world can't make two people right for each other if they're not.'

Joy could hear Henry's voice inside her head. *If you ever need to work something out, saddle up and take off for an hour or two across those paddocks. That's where you'll find your answers.* Had she come home to find answers? Maybe. The problem was that deep down, she wasn't quite sure of the questions.

'From the moment I met your mother I thought about no one else,' Tim said. 'She's still my first thought in the morning and my last thought at night. She's my priority and I'm hers. It's that simple.'

'Is it really?' said Joy, with surprise. 'You're her priority? I suppose it's good that one of us has been.'

Tim flicked his horse around so quickly that Calypso shied sideways. Tim moved his gelding up beside Joy swiftly, and looked into her eyes so intently that she was taken aback.

'I know you miss the closeness you had with your grandfather. But don't think for one moment that you haven't been a priority in your mother's life from day one. Our whole family owes her a great deal. More than you could possibly imagine. If you've got something to get off your chest where your mother's concerned, then don't stew on it. Talk to her. Don't use blame. Blame and responsibility can never coexist. Grow up. Behave like an adult.'

Joy looked at her father in surprise. He'd never spoken to her like this and a feeling of regret swept over her. He was right. She'd sounded childish; she knew she had.

'You know we were close to losing the station not that long ago. We survived that by the skin of our teeth thanks to your mother. And if part of how you're feeling relates to the times she wasn't here when you were on school holidays,' Tim shifted in his saddle, 'well, that didn't mean she loved you any less. Being on the land's a tough gig. I don't need to tell you that. You're at the mercy of the weather, the economy, even politics.'

Joy held her father's gaze then dropped her eyes. When she looked back he was still staring at her.

'I'm sorry, Dad. That was a thoughtless comment and I didn't mean it. Not at all.'

She wasn't off the hook yet. Joy could tell she'd touched a raw nerve and that there was more to come.

'You asked me how I knew your mum was the one. Here's the thing about life,' said Tim, staring intently at Joy. 'People are what they do. Not what they say. Talk is cheap. All your mother has ever done is love me, love you and work bloody hard her whole adult life. And the reality is, it's been your mother's foresight, the success she's made of her bridalwear business, that's saved us from possibly going under. I don't think you understand the amount of pressure we've both been under these past couple of years.'

Her father's words hit Joy like a blast of hot wind. Her chest tightened as the reality of what he'd said sank in.

'And as for this matter with Whitby and the bloody court case – well, that's not going as well as we'd hoped. A total nightmare.'

She lowered her head. 'Oh, Dad. I never realised how bad it was.'

'Well, now you do. The way your mother and I run our relationship works for us. Would I like to have my wife here with me at Monaghan a lot more? Of course I would. But Avril working down in Melbourne or in Brisbane and me being up here, that's just geography. It doesn't mean we're not close to one another. Two people can be in the same bed and have an ocean of distance between them.'

An ocean of distance. Joy repeated his words to herself. That was how she felt about Hugo.

Tim moved his horse and came up beside his daughter again. He held the reins in his left hand and rested the other on his thigh.

'When's Hugo back?' he asked.

'Christmas for a few days.'

'That will come around quickly enough,' said Tim. 'Finish off the semester. Get your exams out of the way, then tell Barry you want time off and come home and have a decent break. I'm going to insist on a big family Christmas this year. I want the place full to overflowing. We haven't had the house humming since your grandpa died.'

Joy could picture her grandfather in the ridiculous raggedy red hat he wore every year as he played the role of Santa on Christmas morning.

'Remember the year he gave you and Ben those scooters?' said Tim, as if reading her thoughts. 'He had the two of you racing each other along the veranda, encouraging Reece, Jordy and I to place bets on who'd cross the finish line first.'

They both smiled at the memory.

'One last thing while I've got the floor,' said Tim. 'I don't want to see you beating yourself up over Hugo if you know in your heart it's over. It's a complete waste of time and energy. Believe me, I know.'

They sat for some time and looked westward, listening to the call of the crows. Joy could see the tops of the gum trees that edged the campfire – the place she and Henry had ridden to the day before her eighteenth birthday. She'd been back only twice since his death. And as much as she loved her father, she wanted to keep the campfire, with its mismatched rocks and old billycan, just for her and Henry.

It was her memory. For whenever she needed it.

She turned Calypso's head in the opposite direction.

'Let's go to the big dam and then back along the river,' said Joy.

'Good idea,' said Tim. 'Nothing like riding home with a gentle breeze behind you.'

*

It's only a lunch date, Joy kept telling herself as she tossed one discarded garment after the other onto her bed. 'Bugger,' she said, fumbling with the zip on the dress she finally settled on. She pulled her long dark curls into a loose ponytail, sprayed perfume on her wrists then rotated in front of the mirror. She wasn't going to deny it. Her stomach tumbled with nervous anticipation at the thought of seeing Mick. This was a completely different sensation from anything she'd ever experienced with Hugo. Those early days of her courtship with Hugo seemed like a lifetime ago now and she felt far removed from the inexperienced teenager she'd once been. She had resolved to speak to Hugo at Christmas.

Until then, she was trying not to think about him.

She saw Mick the moment she entered the restaurant. He was seated at the bar, his body turned towards the entrance, staring out over the water. His hair skirted his collar. The jeans and leather jacket he'd worn for the concert were noticeably absent, replaced by a white t-shirt and loose-fitting pants – the latest trend in casual suits. *Very Bowie-like*, she thought.

Joy smiled when Mick turned and saw her. He was tanned for this time of year, clean-shaven with a small stud in his left ear.

'Hi, Joy. It's good to see you,' he said, kissing her on the cheek.

Joy knew she wasn't late but his almost empty glass tumbler suggested he'd arrived well ahead of her – long enough to have had at least one drink while waiting. Mick followed Joy as they were led to a corner table with uninterrupted views down the river.

Joy was a little surprised when Mick had said he'd book a table at the Paradise Room. It was a well-established, upmarket Brisbane restaurant more akin to the type of place her parents liked to go. It was also James Carmody's eatery of choice whenever he took Joy to dinner. Mick had asked her if she liked seafood and when she'd said yes, he'd assured her that the Paradise served the best seafood in the city.

Although Joy and Mick had talked on the phone many

times over the last few weeks, they hadn't seen each other since the Sunday night concert at the Woolshed. But her physical attraction to him was undeniable. Her sticky palms and flushed cheeks gave her away.

He too seemed different. Far removed from the sweaty, stage-strutting Mick Harris who had the fans screaming for more.

'I know this is going to sound really corny,' said Joy, 'but do you come here often?'

'God, that does sound corny.' He laughed. 'A fair bit when I'm in town. And I'm usually on my own.'

'Why's that?'

Mick placed his elbows on the edge of the table and tented his fingers.

'I like eating alone sometimes. I like the quietness of the place. The stillness. And the view's not hard to take.'

An understatement if ever there was one, thought Joy.

Joy and Mick both refused the wine list, each ordering a soda and lime.

'Don't you drink?' Joy asked once the waiter had moved away. 'I noticed you drank something light the night we met.'

'I prefer not to,' he said. 'Not very rock and roll, is it?'

'Simon certainly seems to, though. I'm sure he was ordering doubles.'

As they worked their way through a platter of mud crabs, crayfish and scallops, Joy condensed her monologue about the Meredith family and growing up on Monaghan Station after hearing some of the details about Mick's childhood. His frank recounting of life with a predominantly out-of-work father was not a plea for self-pity – quite the opposite – but it was the polar opposite of Joy's upbringing at Monaghan.

'He was a good dad in lots of ways. Just not the sharpest tool in the shed.'

Mick sang the praises of the neighbours, Mr and Mrs McCready, 'who took me in when Dad died,' he said. 'I lived with them until Dave and I got our first flat in St Kilda.'

Mick didn't mention his mother and Joy didn't ask but the way he spoke about the McCready clan left Joy in no doubt they were very much *his* family.

By the time they were halfway through lunch, Joy had the impression there were many sides to Mick Harris and that the well-crafted, rock-and-roll bad boy image that graced the newspapers and magazines was simply one part of his personality. Sure, his talent was real, but what the fans saw, he told Joy, was the lead vocalist, the performer.

'If you try and play the role of rock singer twenty-four hours a day it will kill you, or at the very least, you'll burn out. Believe me,' he said, as he tossed his head back and laughed slightly, 'I've been there. And it's not all that it's cracked up to be. Well, some of it is, but . . .'

His stare was so intense that Joy could no more look away than leave the room. They were fast moving beyond easy chit-chat to something deeper, and she wanted to know more.

'But that's a conversation we should have another time,' finished Mick.

Joy wasn't looking for a saint and she wasn't about to deceive herself into thinking that Mick had lived his life on the straight and narrow. Yet in the moment of silence that followed, Joy had the feeling Mick wasn't afraid to journey to the more difficult places she knew were inside everyone and she admired him for it.

'Yes, we're in the entertainment industry,' he went on. 'So the band has to put on a good show.'

'Can I ask you something, a little off topic?' said Joy after Mick had explained the recording and promotional side of the music industry. 'Your suit. I mean, I love it. I guess I was expecting you to be in a leather jacket and jeans.'

Mick placed his hand on his heart and feigned a wounded expression.

'And here I am, under the impression that you're a lateral thinker,' he said, lowering his voice without losing any of its intensity. 'That's like me saying you're a vet, so where are your overalls? You look stunning, by the way, in that beautiful blue dress.'

Joy sat back in her chair as Mick's masculinity washed over her. Even the way he sat was seductive. Somehow he'd managed to pay Joy a compliment that sounded sincere, not contrived.

She nodded. 'You're right. That was pretty judgemental of me.'

'Clothing is a form of expression. You of all people should know that, with a fashion icon for a mother.'

Joy's expression must have given away her surprise.

'I'm from Melbourne, I know who Avril Montdidier is,' Mick added.

'Well, I've never known a rock musician before. I have nothing to go on. Back to you.' She smiled. 'Tell me one thing about yourself that's never appeared in print or been said on radio or television, something that your fans would never guess about you.'

Mick looked around then leant forward conspiratorially.

'Here's one you'd never guess,' he whispered. 'I like growing tomatoes.'

Joy leant even closer. 'Serious?'

'Completely.'

'Well, your secret's safe with me. I'm bound by patient confidentiality.'

The waiter hovered momentarily as he refilled their water glasses.

'My terrace house in Sydney has a small courtyard that faces north. It's a real sun trap. Your turn,' he continued. 'Something about you that not too many people would believe.'

Joy hesitated, then said, 'I can fly a single-engine plane. I got my licence when I was seventeen.'

'A handy skill to have,' said Mick. 'Do you have a piece of machinery to go with those credentials?'

She was a bit reluctant to answer, aware that any description of the family's Beechcraft parked in the aircraft hangar at Monaghan Station would sound a bit pretentious, but she could see he was genuinely interested.

'My father does. The use of light aircraft is pretty commonplace on properties these days. And now I'm changing the subject.' She laughed. 'Tell me about Simon. What's the story there? How did you meet?'

'You were right about him going to Cambridge. It was actually four years at Cambridge then two years at Oxford. He's one very talented guy. All he ever wanted to do was play the drums. We met in Melbourne when he was on a bit of a sabbatical. Keith, his long-term partner, had ended their relationship so he headed to Australia to try and get over the breakup. He was working as a session musician and when I heard him play it was like, who *is* this dude?'

'Do you all still live in Melbourne?' said Joy.

'No, we're all in Sydney now. We were spending so

much time there playing clubs and pubs and recording that it made sense to base ourselves there. Simon and I have a place in Paddington and Jack and Dave are a few streets away in Woollahra. Do you know Sydney at all?'

'A little, but not that well. How often are you in Brisbane?' said Joy.

'When I need to be,' Mick said, grinning, and when Joy raised her eyebrows he added, 'No, seriously. Our manager Robert Flare lives here, in Toowong, not that far from where you are. So I'm up and down from Sydney quite a bit. I usually stay with him if it's just a night or two. Any longer and I book a hotel room.'

The platter was cleared away and they both declined dessert. Mick and Joy talked until it became obvious they were the last of the lunch patrons.

'I think we'd better leave before they hand us the dinner menu,' said Joy.

They stood out the front of the restaurant in what was left of the spring daylight.

'Do you have any plans for tonight?' said Mick.

'Only a pile of epidemiology lecture notes to read through. How's that for an exciting Saturday night?'

'Feel like catching a movie?' said Mick. 'That's another one of my guilty pleasures. I love going to the flicks, as my dad used to call them.'

'Great,' said Joy. The reply came easily. She realised she felt completely at ease; she didn't want the day to end. 'I haven't seen a movie in weeks.'

Sitting in the back of the taxi, Mick reached out and took Joy's hand and gave it a gentle squeeze. The gesture felt so natural, so sincere to Joy that she gave a little squeeze back. *A first love has to end sometime*, she thought. *I had no way of knowing I'd meet Mick. What if the roles were reversed? Would Hugo deny himself an attraction as strong as the one I'm feeling? I'm not responsible for Hugo's decisions, only my own. This feels so right.*

Forty minutes later, Joy and Mick were settled in the second-last row of a packed cinema sharing a giant-sized tub of popcorn and waiting for *Raiders of the Lost Ark* to start.

'Do you really grow tomatoes?' Joy whispered as the names 'Harrison Ford' and 'Karen Allen' appeared on the screen. 'Or were you joking?'

'I really do,' Mick whispered back. 'It's rewarding growing your own food. Aren't you supposed to be a country girl?'

Joy dipped her hand into the hot buttered popcorn.

'I guess I should tell you from the outset, I don't like tomatoes.'

Mick placed his arm across the back of Joy's seat. His lips were so close to Joy's ear that she could feel the warmth of his breath and smell his cologne.

'Well, I don't like flying, so I guess we'll both have to compromise a little.'

*

Henry had often told Joy that you hardly ever see the most significant moments in your life coming. He was right. And Mick Harris was one of those significant moments. A beautiful, intoxicating significant moment. A few days after their lunch and movie date, Mick returned to Sydney to start recording the band's new album, which was due for release in April 1982, but not before Joy invited him to her place for a drink so they could see each other before he left. The drink turned into a spontaneous dinner and Mick happily stirred the pasta and talked to Scarlet and Vivienne while Joy grilled some chicken.

After they'd eaten, Joy and Mick took their drinks out onto the veranda and dropped down into the cane chairs. She unfurled a small blanket and wrapped it around her shoulders.

'I've had the strangest feeling all night that there's something you want to talk to me about,' said Mick. 'Should I guess what it is?'

Joy wasn't surprised that Mick had picked up on the vibe. The looks Scarlet and Vivienne had been throwing her had not been subtle. 'No guessing required. And you're right. There is something – or rather, someone.' And as Joy told Mick about her relationship with Hugo – their family connection, how they'd got together just before her eighteenth and their life at uni together – Mick sat expressionless in the moonlight and listened. His composure had made it impossible for Joy to gauge his reaction.

'Deep down, I've known that it's over between the two of us for some time. Then he got the job in Singapore and, well, I should have ended it before he left but I chickened out. I should have been more decisive. I'm sorry. I should have brought things to a head sooner.'

The chair creaked as Mick leant forward and crossed his legs.

'That's a lot of *shoulds* you've got there,' he said, reaching for Joy's hand. 'There's nothing that's happened between you and me to feel guilty about. If you'd been playing Hugo and me off against each other, that would be different. But you haven't, and you're not. We've fallen into each other's lives. It's as simple as that. It's up to you what you do now.'

166

'I'm normally not the kind of person who avoids things. It's just that I don't want to hurt Hugo,' said Joy.

'I'm sure you don't. You'll find the right words. Trust yourself.'

That night, on the steps of the old Queenslander as he was leaving, Mick kissed Joy passionately.

'I can't stop thinking about you,' he said, taking her face in his hands. 'You're like this beautiful breath of fresh air that's swept through my life. I'm ready to see where this goes if you are?'

'I know I am,' she said. 'But you need to know that I've decided to spend all of December and January back at Monaghan. I haven't spent proper time with my parents for ages, and Barry will give me the time off at the pub. I'd love you to come up to the station, if you have the time. I'd like to show you where I grew up and it's a great place to get inspired, creatively.'

'I'd love to,' said Mick.

He wrapped his arms around Joy.

'I have another confession to make,' he said. He suddenly looked very serious. 'And I hope it's not going to cause a problem between us.'

Joy's mind raced. 'What is it?'

Mick let the seconds tick away.

'I'm terrified of horses,' he said finally, and laughed. 'Absolutely petrified of the bloody things. How the hell you ride those creatures, I have no idea.'

Joy grinned. 'Well, I promise you won't have to go near one if you don't want to.'

Then he kissed Joy as the taxi pulled up and they stood for a moment holding hands.

'I have to go or I'll miss my flight. I'll give you a call tomorrow night, if not sooner.'

Joy stood on the footpath and watched the yellow Falcon turn the corner.

Fifty minutes later when the phone rang, Joy lunged off the sofa for the receiver. She knew his flight wouldn't have left and she could see Mick sitting in the VIP lounge making full use of the courtesy phones.

'I knew you'd call. I knew it would be you,' said Joy.

'You must be psychic then. Because I've been thinking about you all day. What have you been up to?' said Hugo. 'What's new?'

*

Joy threw herself into what was left of the semester while dodging calls from Hugo, allowing him to leave messages with her housemates, even when she was home. *Get on and deal with this*, she berated herself. She knew it was gutless of her but every time she tried to find the words, they weren't there. Hugo was always so upbeat each time they spoke, excited to tell her about the projects he was working on. Deep down, Joy knew there was never going to be a right moment. And while she avoided doing what she knew she had to, Mick phoned every other night and flowers began arriving on a regular basis.

Four weeks later, Joy was at home studying when the phone rang. She heard the click of a pay phone and wondered who it could be.

'Hi, babe,' said Mick. 'How's the work going?'

'I'm taking a break. I can't remember another thing.'

'Great, because I've just landed in Brisbane and I'm on my way over, if that's all right with you?'

Joy's heart leapt. 'Oh my god, yes!'

It was one of those rare Friday evenings when Joy had the place to herself. Vivienne, Leo and Jason had gone away camping for the weekend and Scarlet was at her boyfriend's place for the night. Joy raced to the bathroom, had a quick shower and changed into fresh clothes. She lit a couple of scented candles and put a record on – Billy Joel. It was the first album she grabbed.

She charged around repositioning the cushions, tidying the books and magazines on the coffee table while her heart raced. Finally, a moment when they'd be alone. Finally, a night together. She poured herself a glass of wine and turned on the outside lights. She stopped in front of the hallway mirror and ran her fingers through her curls.

'Shit,' she said to her reflection, noticing that she hadn't washed her hair in days. It would have to do.

Get a grip, she told herself. But it was pointless. Joy had never felt such a heightened sense of anticipation before. There had only ever been Hugo, and she saw clearly for the first time that she had never felt for him what she was feeling at this moment. All she could see was Mick. All she wanted was Mick. It was ecstasy on an unknown level. Her mind started swimming. Which Mick would walk through the door? Rock-and-roll Mick? Stylishly suited up Mick?

The short sharp knock drew her from the kitchen to the front door.

'Hi,' she said as he stepped inside and placed his shoulder bag and leather duffel bag on the rug. He smiled at her.

Her heart sang.

*

Joy lay on her side, her head on the pillow, watching Mick sleep in the dim light.

He's so beautiful, she thought. *Free. Uninhibited.* The more she stared at him the closer she felt.

She'd been replaying every second of what had happened from the moment he'd first walked through the door to when he'd drifted off to sleep. The small cheese platter that they'd assembled from the contents of the fridge was still sitting on her bedside table.

The way he'd kissed her lips, face, neck. How his hands had found the buttons on her shirt as she'd pulled his cream sweater over his head.

Joy slid from the bed and carried the platter to the kitchen. She glanced at the clock on the stove. It was just before nine but they'd been in bed for almost two hours. One of the scented candles was still burning and she picked it up and placed it on the windowsill.

Joy didn't hear Mick come up behind her and she jumped slightly as he wrapped his arms across her stomach.

'I was letting you sleep. You seemed exhausted,' she murmured.

'Totally,' he replied. 'Or I was, until I got here.'

Mick gently brushed Joy's mass of tangled hair to one side.

'I knew I was right,' he said, finding her ear with his mouth, gently nipping at her earlobes.

'Oh yeah, and what are you right about?'

'That you're sensational here.' He touched her forehead, 'Here.' He ran his hand across her breast and back down to her stomach. 'And here.' He placed the palm of his hand over her heart and spun her so her back was pressed against the edge of the sink. 'You, Joy Meredith, are a vision.'

CHAPTER 10

By the time Joy waved Mick off on Sunday night, she was in no doubt how they felt about each other. The weekend had been a spontaneous mix of eating, laughing, lovemaking and listening to music, culminating in dinner at the local Chinese restaurant before Mick had to catch his flight back to Sydney.

'I'm trying to instigate some sort of normal working hours with this album. If there can be such a thing,' Mick had said as the Peking duck was delivered to the table.

'Tell me what's involved?'

'We've got a three-record deal with Bachelor Records, but the budget's pretty tight. They pay for the studio time and technicians. But in the end, we still need to earn our production costs, so I want us to be fairly strong when we go into the studio next month.'

'How long will it take to record your ten songs?'

'A week, maybe two. To be honest, so often bands spend too much time dicking around, wasting time on shit they don't need to do. I want us to go in, play, record, done. Leave a couple of weeks for the mixing and mastering to be completed. It's not complicated. There's only four of us and a saxophonist we're bringing in for two of the songs.'

'Has Dave always been your writing partner?'

'I started out writing on my own but then Dave would suggest little things here and there and our collaboration grew.'

'I noticed on the back of both your albums all lyrics are by Around Midnight, not you and Dave.'

'My girlfriend is so observant,' and Mick blew Joy a kiss.

'I like the sound of that,' said Joy.

'And I like saying it.'

Mick wiped his hands on the napkin and passed Joy the rice.

'Once Simon came on board, even before we signed with Robert, Dave and I agreed that the band gets credited with what we produce. It causes too much tension if Dave and I are singled out as the lyricists.'

He signalled for the bill and as they drove back to Joy's place, Mick asked her about the dates of her upcoming exams, which she assured him would all be done by the first week of November.

'The timing couldn't be better. We will have finished recording the album by then. We've got a few concerts to play and some smaller gigs, but I've been thinking I'll try and kick back a fair bit in December and January myself.'

'Are you still keen to come up to the station for Christmas? It will be pretty full-on. Dad's insisting on a big get-together this year.'

When Joy had first mentioned the idea, Mick had told her he'd always found Christmas a depressing time of year. It held little in the way of happy memories for him. Joy hoped that a happy Christmas at Monaghan might help change that, in a small way at least.

'I can't wait to meet your family,' said Mick. 'And I can't wait to visit Monaghan with you.'

Joy smiled, but inside a little voice was admonishing her. Loud and clear.

Hugo, Hugo, Hugo, it said.

*

Vivienne placed her mug of tea on the coffee table.

'I agree with Scarlet. You can't keep going on like this. You have to call Hugo and tell him.'

'Don't put it off any longer,' said Scarlet. 'Imagine if he'd met someone. You'd want to know.'

Joy knew they were right. The whole situation was weighing on her more heavily with each passing day, so she knew that whatever the outcome, it was time. More than time. She was sure if she called Hugo around eleven o'clock her time, he'd be home from work.

'I know. I'm dreading it but I'll call tonight. Any advice? I've never ended a relationship before. How the hell do I do this?'

Scarlet laughed. 'Believe me, in my experience, it's not that hard,' she said. 'Hugo will get over feeling rejected sooner than you think. They always do.'

'Keep it brief,' said Vivienne. 'Something like, "Hugo, it's time we went our separate ways." Or, "Hugo, I don't want to be part of a long-distance relationship anymore. I want my own space." Something along those lines. He's going to be hurt no matter what you say, so don't over-talk it.'

'He'll ask me if there's someone else. I know he will.'

'Then lie,' said Scarlet, flinging a cushion playfully

at Joy. 'Don't you dare mention Mick. That will be like shoving the knife into the poor guy. Besides, I've never seen you so happy. Not ever. There is nothing to feel guilty about. Personally, I've never experienced the sensation,' Scarlet laughed. 'You don't have to justify yourself to Hugo, no matter how much you care about him.'

'Scarlet's right,' said Vivienne. 'Mick's crazy about you and it's obvious you feel the same. There's an energy between the two of you that I never saw with you and Hugo. You can't manufacture these things. But you do have to finish things with Hugo properly. He's a decent guy.'

'You're both right. I'll call him tonight. I just hope he'll understand.'

But I know he won't, she thought. *I know he is going to be so hurt. And I'm the one bringing him all this pain.*

*

With her speech rehearsed and delivered, her heart beating wildly from nerves, the silence between Hugo and Joy was heavier than a dead weight.

She could hear Hugo breathing more quickly as the words formed cold hard facts inside his head.

Finally, he spoke, his tone clipped and sharp. 'Who is he? Do I know him?'

Joy sighed. She had known it would come to this. They had started off with the usual pleasantries as Joy referred to the bullet points on the notepad in front of her. But as Hugo's voice became louder and angrier and more wounded, Joy became defensive and began to over-explain. Her *keep it brief, don't tell him you've got someone else* plan never got off the ground.

'When did it start? Christ, Joy. Have you slept with him?'

And in that split-second between Hugo's interrogation and Joy's desire to be honest, she felt her anxiety fall away. She was no longer eighteeen, sitting on the banks of the river, feeling unattractive and unsure. *You don't have to answer this question. It's none of his business.*

She was suddenly certain that she was in love with Mick, and that what she was doing, however painful, was the right thing to do. She took a deep breath and deliberately lowered the tone of her voice.

'It's time we ended this conversation, Hugo.'

He tried to talk over the top of her but she cut him off.

'Let me finish,' she said firmly. 'If you think this is easy, then you have no idea how much you mean to me. But I won't be belittled and I won't have you speak to me disrespectfully.'

Hugo fell silent as Joy continued.

'If you ever want to see me or speak to me, you know where I am. You're my friend, Hugo, and always will be. I just hope you care for me enough to let me be yours.'

Then she said goodbye before hanging up, her hand trembling slightly as she replaced the receiver. It was done.

She couldn't think of how Hugo was feeling right now. That would finish her completely.

Joy reached for her journal on the bedside table and opened it. Her hand hovered over the paper, waiting for the right words to come.

All of Henry's advice about standing your ground, knowing your own mind and not allowing anyone to bully you rang loud and clear in Joy's ears. *It was time Hugo and I went our separate ways, regardless of whether I'd met Mick or not,* she wrote. *Thank you, Grandpa, for all your wise words. I've never forgotten them and never will.*

She closed the book and lay in the darkness, thinking of the past and what may lie ahead.

*

While Joy buried herself in lecture notes and textbooks in preparation for her end-of-year exams, Mick and the boys were in the studio putting the finishing touches to the album. Mick rang Joy most nights, keen to hear about her day and filling her in on some of the promotional work Robert had arranged for the band.

Joy had never been a big fan of surprises, but when she got home after her last exam, Scarlet met her at the door, her eyes sparkling.

'I've just got off the phone with Mick. You'll never guess what he's planned for you,' she said.

Which is how Joy found herself standing in her bedroom the next morning, doing a quick scan to make sure she'd packed everything for a surpise trip to Sydney.

Suitcase in hand, Joy raced down the front steps. The music blared from the radio as Scarlet whizzed towards the airport. As they pulled up at Departures, Scarlet took Joy's hand.

'I love you, girlfriend,' she said. 'Go have fun with your man.'

Joy turned, smiled and waved madly.

A couple of hours later, Joy gazed out at the uninter-rupted view from the window of the Boeing 727. The city's cluster of high-rise buildings nestled between the Harbour Bridge and the Opera House had been given a front-row seat to the iconic Sydney Harbour, which glimmered dazzlingly in the cloudless late-November sunshine.

Outside the Ansett terminal, Mick left the driver standing beside the car and ran towards Joy the moment she came through the doors. He kissed her, relieved her of a large black case and threw his arm around her shoulders.

'My god you look beautiful,' he said. 'Come on, babe, let's get out of here.'

Joy wrapped her arms around his waist and leaned into the smell of him.

Mick held Joy's hand as the driver weaved his way down the narrow car-lined street to Mick and Simon's terrace in Paddington. In the half-a-dozen times Joy had been to Sydney she'd never ventured much further than her mother's fashion shops and the downtown city area, or the walk from The Rocks around Circular Quay to the Botanic Gardens. She'd seen none of the many bars and nightclubs that thrived in the city. Now, with Mick as her tour guide for the next two weeks, Joy couldn't wait to do all the things they'd talked about. Other than a couple of long-standing engagements the following week, the band's schedule would not pick up again until the new year. And as the band hadn't taken a decent break since they'd first got together, Mick had declared December and January to be *The Summer of Fun*.

Mick occupied the top floor of the hundred-year-old, three-storey building, with Simon comfortably ensconced on the second floor. The rental had come fully furnished with a modern fit-out resembling a *Vogue Interiors* page. Joy hadn't been quite sure what to expect, but yet again, she'd been surprised. The scattering of eclectic items reflected Mick and Simon's distinctive yet contrasting styles. A cow's skull with long horns hung above a fire-place that had been retired long ago. Two well-used acoustic guitars sat facing each other in the corner. Simon was a vintage china collector. His small yet ever-growing number of Clarice Cliff jugs and plates were displayed in a glass-fronted armoire.

'Wow! Look at this place,' said Joy, halfway through the tour. She opened a pair of kitchen cupboards and spied a selection of herb and spice jars neatly arranged in alphabetical order. 'You're like an old married couple.'

'How long is it going to take you to lose your prejudiced, one-dimensional view of me?' chuckled Mick. 'I don't like mess. I need my home environment to be restful.' He folded his arms around Joy. 'I like to keep the chaos outside.'

'Not too restful, I hope,' she teased as he kissed her neck.

'Absolutely not,' he said, taking her hand and leading her upstairs.

*

The next two weeks passed in a daze of happiness as if Joy and Mick couldn't quite believe they'd found each other.

The trip also gave Joy the chance to see a rock star's life up close, and understand the dynamics of the band.

Mick's place was calm and peaceful but they also spent time at Dave McCready and Jack Anderson's place just off Ocean Street, which was all dishes in the sink and bath towels on the landing. It was not uncommon for a stranger to emerge from a bedroom asking, 'Has anyone seen a set of car keys?' Parties were never planned. They just happened. And as the weatherboard cottage – worth the GDP of a small Pacific Island nation – belonged to Jack's uncle, the neighbours had to live with the fact that an eviction was never going to happen. It had acquired the nickname *The Party House*, which everyone who knew the boys used, including the long-suffering neighbours.

On her first night in town, Jack and Dave threw a party to welcome Joy to Sydney.

The revelry was well under way when Mick and Joy arrived, after they'd been to one of Mick's favourite restaurants, a tiny Italian place in The Cross, then stopped briefly at a nearby jazz club. Joy was inhaling it all. Sydney felt like a city on an unstoppable high, a kaleidoscope of lights, heat and traffic – and music. Always music, spilling from the clubs and bars out into the night, where people of all ages and styles meandered along the crowded foot-paths of Kings Cross.

Mick and Joy were barely through the front door of the Party House when Mick was descended upon by half-a-dozen people, as if the messiah had arrived. Once they were through with the hugs and back-slapping and brief introductions, Mick held Joy's hand firmly and they worked their way to the courtyard out the back.

The fashion-conscious crowd, predominantly in their twenties, were a garish cocktail of block-coloured over-sized shirts, teased perms and tight lycra dresses. The music pulsed from the living room out into the body-filled backyard and the kitchen groaned under the weight of beer bottles, cardboard casks of wine and bottles of vodka.

Seeing Mick trapped in a conversation with a photographer, Simon waved Joy over to a corner of the back veranda and settled in for a long chat.

'You can see why the Romantic and I let Jack and Dave hold the parties here and not at our place,' said Simon. 'Heaven forbid. Can you imagine the clean-up tomorrow?'

'Did you just call Mick "the Romantic"?' asked Joy.

'It's an old nickname. It's my little joke.'

'Why?' said Joy, her curiosity piqued.

'Surely you've realised he's a hopeless romantic under

that tough, take-no-prisoners swagger of his? Has he shown you any of his poetry?'

'No,' said Joy. She wondered why, in those moments of intimacy when they'd laid facing each other and she'd told him about her journaling, he'd never shared his love of writing poetry with her.

'You should ask to read some,' said Simon as he tapped his cigarette on the back of his lighter. 'It's seriously good work.'

I will, thought Joy. *I want to know all the layers of Mick Harris.*

*

Each day Joy found something new about the city Mick loved so much and now called home. During the day they visited art galleries or browsed the avant-garde fashion stores along Oxford Street. Mick would point out some of the venues the band had played and some he wished they hadn't. Joy was keen to visit Taronga Zoo, something Mick had only done once, so they took the short ferry ride from the city across to Mosman. It was the ideal way to take in the beauty of the harbour. On another day, Mick dropped the top on the 1968 Ford Mustang Shelby he'd given himself for his birthday the previous year, and the two of them drove up to Palm Beach, laughing as the wind flicked their hair skyward. They swam, lazed on the sand and climbed up to the lighthouse to view the sparkling expanse below. It was the perfect day.

Joy was also discovering that Mick was much more well-known than she'd realised. He was always running into someone he knew – in cafés, bars or just out on the street, someone would call his name or stop mid-stride and tap him on the shoulder. A journalist, another musician.

Sometimes it was a pretty young woman with little to say except, 'Hi'. Mick was quick to introduce Joy, drawing her into any conversation, sometimes adding with a touch of pride that his girlfriend was studying vet science.

On the night before Joy was due to fly home, Around Midnight were playing at the Hordern Pavilion, a five-and-a-half-thousand capacity venue a short distance from the city centre. Robert had jumped at the opportunity to secure the band a one-night-only concert, certain it would be a sellout. He'd been fanning the PR flames for the new album from the moment he'd heard its ten songs, even before the band had stepped into the recording studio. He was calling on every contact he had, from magazines to newspaper editors, radio DJs and the program managers at the three commercial television stations. This was a make-or-break moment for the band, he told the boys. The Hordern gig would help to grease the wheels.

'I wish we didn't have to play this gig tonight, babe,' said Mick as he folded some clothes and placed them in his duffel bag. 'I'd much rather you and I were doing our own thing on your last night.'

'We could go to the pool hall on Oxford Street after the gig, if you want to? But I'm also just as happy to get some takeaway and chill here.'

'Rebecca's picking you up just before eight. That way we will be into our first set by the time you arrive. I'll keep an eye out for you stage-side.'

Although they hadn't met, Mick had mentioned Rebecca Bruce a few times, telling Joy about the work she did as a booking agent for a media and talent agency in Sydney.

'You'll like her,' Mick assured Joy. 'She's funny and honest, and she's a good mate.'

'Really,' said Joy teasingly. 'How good?'

He playfully flicked Joy's leg with a t-shirt.

'Trust me. I'm not her type.'

*

Rebecca Bruce clapped along with Joy as the band said good night to their adoring fans and exited the stage on the other side. She slid her burgundy-painted nails into the back pocket of her jeans and pulled out a business card that contained only her name and telephone number. She tapped the card rhythmically against her palm, fearing she might not get another chance to talk to Joy on her own. She hadn't been able to take her eyes off Joy from the moment she'd picked her up in Paddington. There wasn't a single angle of this girl's face that the camera wouldn't love. Not to mention that skin and her beautiful teeth. *The girl screams magazine cover*, Rebecca thought. *And she doesn't even realise it.*

Joy pulled her hair back and secured it effortlessly into a loose ponytail. She fanned herself with a folded poster of the band as the oppressive humidity closed in around them.

'Oh my god,' said Joy. 'That was incredible. Those last two songs. It was like the whole audience was part of the band.'

Joy's face glowed with delight. Rebecca touched her gently on the arm and guided her back down the metal steps to the backstage ground-floor area.

It's now or never, Rebecca thought.

'Have you ever considered modelling?' said Rebecca.

'Who, me?' said Joy.

'Yes, I know you're still at uni but I book quite a few girls who are studying and modelling part-time. It can be a great gig financially if you're with the right agency.'

'Oh,' said Joy, looking astonished, and she laughed nervously. 'No. It's not something I've ever wanted to do. I've been told plenty of times that I have the height, but it's not for me.'

Rebecca could picture the black and white studio portrait photo of every client on her books: every model she recruited, booked and supervised. The insecure girls she comforted when their boyfriends left them. The anxious girls who were behind in their rent. The bolshie girls who arrived late and held up a shoot. And the half-a-dozen or so she'd let sleep on her sofa when their lives were spiralling out of control. Except these weren't her books, not really. They belonged to the agency and the agency belonged to two men who were never going to give Rebecca a cut of the business, no matter how much money she made them.

'This is my card,' said Rebecca. 'I'd consider it a compliment if you took it.'

Joy accepted the offering gingerly, and her eyes dropped to read what it said. *Go for it*, Rebecca told herself. *What have you got to lose?* She looked up at Joy, shifting in her cowboy boots from one foot to the other.

'I see girls all the time who want to be models. Desperate to find an agent who will take them on,' said Rebecca. 'Every now and again, I meet someone who just has that special something. They usually don't even know they have it, but they do. It's a presence. An energy. And you've got it, Joy. Would you at least consider having a few photos taken?'

Joy didn't say a word. She was processing what Rebecca had said.

'You probably have some sort of part-time job if you're at uni. What is it? Waitressing? Typing pool?'

'Bar work,' said Joy.

'And what do you have, one more year to go?'

'Two,' said Joy.

'Do you realise that for one ad campaign for a magazine or television, you'd be earning more in a day than you do in two months behind the bar? Products need advertising and advertisers need models for all sorts of projects.'

'But I don't know anything about modelling,' Joy said. 'Well, not that much. I mean, my mother suggested it once. I was only about sixteen and I think I stormed off and rode my horse.' She laughed.

Mick had told Rebecca a bit about Joy, so she already knew who Joy's mother was. Avril had even booked some of Rebecca's models for le Chic photo shoots and fashion parades over the past couple of years.

'When do you go back to Brisbane?' asked Rebecca.

'Tomorrow.'

'That's a pity. I would have liked to have taken you to lunch and explained how it all works. I'm serious, Joy, if you'd like to talk some more, please call me.'

'So, you work for a modelling company or agency or whatever they're called?' said Joy.

'Yes. I've worked for an agency here in Sydney for the past six years, but I'd like to go out on my own. The thing is, Joy, I'm really good at what I do. I love working with the models and the clients and getting involved in shaping careers. But in the modelling industry, as with so much else, business management and ownership are dominated by men. There's only so much pie to go around and they don't like sharing.'

'I'll think about it,' said Joy, and she slid the card into her shoulder bag, but Rebecca couldn't tell if she would or not.

Mick came up behind Joy and wrapped his arms around her waist.

'Thanks for looking after my girl, Bec,' he said.

'Any time.'

'I think we'll head off,' said Mick. 'Everyone's planning to kick on back at the Party House, if you're interested.'

'Sure, why not. It's Saturday night, after all,' Rebecca replied.

'Thanks again, Bec. Let's catch up before we take off for Christmas.'

'Where are you headed? Or is it a secret?'

Mick lifted the tattered Akubra hat he was holding in one hand and placed it on his head.

'We're heading bush,' he said, and flashed his trademark smile.

CHAPTER 11

Mick could hear the outbursts of laughter drifting up from the front room where the game of charades was still in progress. Joy's cousin Ben was a natural entertainer, choosing films and books with the most obscure titles and torturing the family and visiting friends with an impossibly difficult challenge.

'Four words . . . first word,' they called in unison.

From the white cane chair on the upstairs veranda, Mick stared at the row of gum trees that chaperoned the bend in the river around to the right. He reached out and patted the panting golden labrador at his side. This one, unlike his brother, had singled Mick out as a companion from the moment he and Joy had arrived, shadowing Mick wherever he was in the big house. However, the dog had drawn the line at the early-morning walks Joy insisted she and Mick take, refusing to leave the mat at the front door.

In five whirlwind months, Joy Meredith had pushed open the shutters of Mick Harris's inner sanctum, blasting sunshine into corners where light had seldom resided. Even so, nothing could have prepared him for the beauty of Monaghan Station the afternoon he and Joy drove through the elaborate iron gates, past the stately jacaranda trees and along the gravel drive to the front of the homestead.

On Christmas Day, the genuine warmth and camaraderie between the members of Joy's family had challenged Mick's emotional repertoire. He tried, without success, not to visualise the limp Christmas trees of his childhood, usually devoid of presents while his father opened his first can of beer for the morning. And as Avril asked everyone to take their seats in the dining room for lunch, Mick could see Mrs McCready, standing at the grey flyscreen door in a floral dress and white sandals. 'Now come on, Frank,' she would say. 'You pull yourself together and come over to our place. Murray's got plenty of coldies in the fridge. You can't sit here all day, the two of you on your own. I've gone all fancy this year and cooked a giant turkey. Never done one before. Mick, love, bring your swimmers. All the kids are in the pool.'

As far as Mick had been concerned, the McCreadys were rich. Carol McCready drove the kids everywhere in the station wagon but kept the red GM Murray had given her when they were first married for her own amusement. Carol did the books at McCready Auto & Repairs, where Murray supervised the six full-time mechanics who serviced everything from cars to motorbikes, trucks and horse floats. No customer was ever turned away. Their backyard was dominated by a rectangular pool with a springboard and inside the house were not one but two colour televisions, the main one in the lounge room and a smaller one in the bedroom that Carol used when the cricket was on.

Mr and Mrs McCready live just like the Queen does,

Mick used to think to himself whenever he stayed over and Carol McCready would let all the kids have three helpings of ice-cream cake on a Saturday night.

But now, seeing the way Joy's family were with each other, and the beauty of his surroundings, the dark reality of his childhood attacked him from every angle. He had known it was only a matter of time before the past found a way to cunningly seep to the surface. His carefully catalogued memories, the facts and fiction he had rearranged and archived, would eventually take up arms against him. How exhausting it had been trying to fend off this formidable foe all these years.

Joy reached around him from behind and folded her arms across his chest.

'I thought I'd find you here. Whatcha thinkin'?' she said playfully, in a musical southern American accent.

'How lucky I am to have you. What an incredible family you have. And if we ever want a fifth member of the band, I'd get Jordy on keyboard. He's seriously talented and self-taught, so he told me.'

Joy pulled over the other chair, placed it next to Mick's and sat down, resting her hand on his arm.

'And that I see what you mean about this place inspiring creativity,' he said.

'What ideas have you come up with? Tell me.'

'The second track on the new album. "Night and Day",' said Mick.

'The one where the saxophone comes in right at the end?'

'That's the one. Dave and I were talking about the big and the small, the light and the darkness we all carry. About contrasts in life. It got me thinking – do you think Tim and Avril would be open to the idea of us shooting the music video for the song at Monaghan? It's perfect. The contrast between wide-open spaces and the detail in the up-close. Those watercolour tones of the sky. The way the fall of the land invites you in. It's really the scenery we're after. The song's mimed and dubbed over during the editing process.'

'Oh, I love that idea. I'm sure Mum and Dad will too. How many in the crew and how many days would it take?'

'Director, cameraman, lights and props guy, someone for hair and makeup. Wardrobe. Five, maybe six? But I'd tell Robert that I want the whole thing shot in two days. He can earn his manager's fee and make it happen.'

'The crew could stay in the shearers' quarters,' said Joy.

'You mean "The Monaghan Hotel"?' Mick smiled. 'They'll think it's luxury compared to some of the places they usually stay.'

They looked down as a shout drifted up to them. It was Duncan, waving to Joy and Mick as he and Jordy walked across the lawn. He lifted the tennis racquets he was carrying as Jordy flicked a tennis ball sideways, sending the other labrador into a chase.

'Six–four, six–two. To the victor go the spoils,' Duncan gloated.

Joy jumped up and leant over the balustrade and Mick ran his eyes down her long, tanned legs.

'Tomorrow morning. Doubles. The four of us,' Joy shouted. 'The city versus the country.'

'Who's who?' said Duncan as Mick joined her at the railing.

'Rock star and Duncan against the vet and the cowboy.' Joy laughed.

'Ha!' scoffed Duncan. 'In your dreams.'

Joy turned to Mick and took hold of his hand.

'Isn't Christmas time always the best?' she said, her face aglow with health and happiness.

'Always the best,' said Mick.

But all Mick could picture was his father passed out in Murray McCready's new plastic deckchair. 'Your dad's just a bit tired. That's all, Mick, love. It's been a big day.' Then Mrs McCready would distribute banana Paddle Pops among the kids, and a longing for the life the McCreadys had would roll through Mick like a wave.

*

Mick had seldom spent two weeks anywhere at Christmas time. And it had never been like the fortnight he'd had at Monaghan. For a few years he'd managed to avoid the mayhem and paper hats altogether. Three days after the fifty-strong crowd had gathered in the woolshed to see in the new year, had danced and drunk and cajoled the lead vocalist of Around Midnight into giving them all a song, Joy and Mick were packed and ready to leave.

They stood on the veranda and said goodbye to Reece and Caroline, Duncan and Jordy. Ben bolted up the steps and play-wrestled his slightly older cousin, quietly teasing her about having such a cool boyfriend.

'I was going to ask him to sign my albums but I chickened out,' whispered Ben. 'You know, he might think I'm a bit of a tosser.'

'Don't be ridiculous. Believe me, the boys never get tired of signing covers.' She grinned. 'And congratulations again, Cous, on topping your year,' said Joy. 'Ag college might make a farmer out of you yet.'

Mick turned to Tim. 'It's been an absolute pleasure getting to know you all. Thank you for your hospitality. It's been amazing.'

'Our pleasure,' Tim reassured him. 'Take good care of our girl.'

'Goodbye, Mick,' said Avril, kissing Mick affectionately on both cheeks. 'We hope to see you soon. I can't wait for your video to be shot. How exciting.'

'Robert Flare will liaise with you both about all the details. We don't want to cause you any disruption.'

'Disruption!' said Tim. 'Geez, that's what we're known for around here. Now, off you go or you'll still be here at lunchtime.'

Joy kissed her mother and father goodbye and opened the passenger-side door.

'When are you back up, darling?' said Tim. 'Are you still planning on making January a holiday?'

'I think so,' said Joy. 'I'm not working at the Crownie. Uni's back on the first of February, but I'm not sure what our plans are.' She smiled at Mick.

Avril and Tim stood arm in arm on the bottom step and waved as the red Suzuki departed. The labradors trotted beside the four-wheel drive like attentive escorts until Joy and Mick passed through the gates and out of view.

'Well, what do you think?' said Tim. 'You've always been spot-on when it comes to judging people.'

'Oh, it's obvious they're made for each other,' said Avril, still looking down the drive.

'And?' said Tim, when the silence that followed suggested she was holding something back. 'Do you have some reservations about him?'

'Not really. But I spoke to James yesterday before he and Margot left. I've asked him to have a subtle look to see if there's any backstory we should know about. He's still got contacts in all the right places. And it never hurts to be ahead of the play, does it?'

'What do you suspect?' said Tim.

'I'm not sure. But there's something. I can sense it. I'm not saying it's bad. But he's a non-drinker, non-smoker, and from what Joy's told me, not into drugs. He's almost too clean. I just want to be on the safe side.'

'Well, if anyone can find out information on someone, it's James. I must admit, I do like Mick and I enjoyed his company. And our girl's certainly in love. More so than she was with Hugo.'

'Yes,' said Avril. 'But Hugo was a boy and Joy's first love. Mick Harris is a man and in the music business. This is the big league.'

*

The band was back on the concert circuit with a schedule Mick classified as 'punishing'. Robert had earned his keep by securing nearly nine months' worth of bookings at medium to large venues, all part of the plan to generate excitement and interest in the band's upcoming new album. Mick had insisted right from the start that Robert furnish him with a monthly cash-flow statement, detailing income and expenditure. In Mick's experience, this was something most band members didn't do – to their financial detriment. He'd seen too many bands work their guts out for nothing. But Mick had made sure this unusual condition was in the fine print of the band's contract. He didn't intend to sit poolside in someone else's plastic deck-chair, like his father had done, without any control over his own affairs.

By mid-January Mick and the boys had gone back to Monaghan Station to shoot the music video.

'When a flock of black cockatoos swooped into frame while we were shooting on the airstrip, the director was ecstatic,' said Mick, recalling the events of the second day of filming. 'He couldn't believe it! You just can't script that sort of thing.'

Joy smiled. Monaghan Station had that effect on people and she was pleased that Mick had also succumbed to it.

'Your mum and dad were asking about your plans for your twenty-first,' said Mick.

'Well, this time,' said Joy, 'I'm saying what happens on my birthday.'

She thought back to her eighteenth, and her last conversation with Henry. She thought of Hugo, and her life in Brisbane and, of course, Mick – all the things Henry would never know about.

'I'm going to have an open house on Saturday the thirteenth, here in Brisbane. Barbeque and salad. BYO drinks,' she said to Avril and Tim on their next call. 'I'm too cash-strapped for anything else.'

'But, darling,' began Avril. 'I –'

'No buts, Mum,' said Joy. 'This is what I want. Please be happy with the plan.'

'If that's what you want,' said Tim, grabbing the phone. 'Then that's what we'll do.'

Joy smiled. She could hear Avril still objecting in the background but she knew her dad would talk her around.

The whole family came to her party. Jordy, Duncan and Anna. James and Margot. Reece, Caroline and Ben. Her parents, of course. Everyone arrived early and left late. Mick had organised the food with the help of Scarlet and Vivienne, while Leo, who had just turned eight, was determined to play drinks waiter, refilling all the water glasses on a regular basis.

Joy silenced the chatter with a fork to the edge of her glass.

'Having all of you here today means the world to me,' she said. 'What a journey these past three years have been for me. I feel so blessed to have such a loving family, and three great housemates.' Joy pointed at Scarlet, Vivienne and Leo, one after the other, and smiled. 'And Mick. Who surprises and inspires me to live life to the fullest, every day.'

There was a spontaneous round of applause as Mick and Joy hugged and kissed.

'Now, I'd like to say a few words,' said Tim, 'but I promise to break with the family tradition and keep this brief, as directed by the birthday girl.'

*

Simon thought it was a good omen to be releasing Around Midnight's third album on the first of April – April Fool's Day.

'If you can't see the irony in that,' he said to the boys, 'then there's no hope for any of you.'

Robert and Mick had also agreed that releasing prior to the Easter break was a wise move. The whole country was about to go on a four-day holiday and were ripe for entertainment. Radio and television exposure, the two largest consumer outlets for the entertainment industry, was the mill that ground the wheat. Leading up to April the band had decided to release two songs from the album: 'Night and Day' and 'What Now'. Robert and the boys had sat around the dining-room table at Mick and Simon's place, trying to figure out the best possible location for the launch event. Half-a-dozen different ideas were suggested, but all were too complicated and costly as far as Mick was concerned.

'Look. We're based in Sydney and considered an iconic

Sydney band, regardless of where we all come from. Let's not overstuff the turkey,' said Mick. 'Let's hold the launch at one of the most iconic locations there is. The steps of the Sydney Opera House.'

'Better still,' said Jack, 'why don't we perform the songs? Hide our instruments behind some sort of screen then pull it away at the right moment and, *voilà*! "Night and Day" and "What Now", live. Press conference, album launch, live gig all in one. What do you think?'

Mick looked at Robert.

'A couple of speakers with a bit of bite. A basic set-up. Power, of course. And approval to use that site. And pray it doesn't rain,' said Robert. 'I like it. Leave it to me.'

*

Joy took the earliest flight she could and caught a taxi straight to Paddington. She knew she'd have a ton of work to make up once she was back in Brisbane. Missing two days of surgical training was frowned upon by the faculty but as she'd explained to her professor, who, thankfully, was a fan herself, she was not going to miss this event.

The one o'clock launch was designed to capture maximum attention from passers-by, tourists and the lunch crowd. Robert had come through with all the arrangements and the Intercontinental Hotel was providing the band with a complimentary suite for the day. They had a film crew with them, capturing footage the band would then use for promotional material.

Mick looked out of the fourth-floor window. So many people had gathered that the police had arrived and were implementing some low-key crowd control. There was a buzz about this event that they hadn't experienced before – they all felt it. Mick took a sip of water, ran his hand through his hair and glanced at his watch. He hated being late to anything.

'Are we ready?' he said.

The boys nodded.

'Nervous?' said Dave.

'Hell yeah.' Mick laughed. 'But we've got this. It's just another day at the office.'

He stretched out his arm as Simon, Jack and Dave's hands layered over one another's.

'All the way to the top,' said Mick.

'All the way to the top,' the boys echoed.

Mick put on his sunglasses.

'Let's go and give them a taste of Around Midnight.'

*

In years to come, friends would often ask each other if they were at the Around Midnight album launch in front of the Opera House in 1982. In Sydney, it was to become a dinner party topic of conversation. While the band knew the media pack and some executives from the record company would be there, they had no way of knowing how many people would actually turn up.

But they needn't have worried.

A three-thousand-strong crowd surged forward as Mick walked up to the microphone, flanked on either side by the rest of the band. The white peaks of the Opera House loomed behind like a ship in full sail, creating a spectacular backdrop to what was hidden under the massive tarp behind them. Up to this point, the name of the album had been kept a secret, with promotional billboards and posters only showing an image of a black record cover with a white question mark in the centre. Underneath the image, just two lines appeared.

The Third Album
Around Midnight

Joy stood with Robert and Rebecca in a roped-off area, shielding her eyes from the sun.

Mick raised his hands and the noise dropped.

'Hello everyone. I'll keep this brief. We're Around Midnight.'

'Around one o'clock, to be exact, Mick,' a male voice called from the crowd, eliciting some laughter.

'Yes, well, that too,' said Mick, smiling. 'This is David McCready, lead guitarist; Jack Anderson on bass guitar; and Simon Webber, drummer. And I'm Mick Harris, lead vocalist.'

The applause was spontaneous and generous, reaching into the glorious blue autumn sky.

'This is our third album. Ten songs and a lot of rock and roll. So, let's do it! Let's launch *An Avalanche of Strangers.*'

The fabric covers dropped from the five-by-five-metre billboards to reveal an album cover showing the silhouette of four hands, intertwined over a bed of sand. There was a momentary pause before a wave of clapping and cheering washed over the steps where the band was standing.

Joy screamed with delight in the wings, and Robert grinned. This was definitely good for business. The crowd was growing rapidly as people noticed something going on and surged down Macquarie Street towards the harbour.

'Do you want to hear some music?' Mick said to the cheering crowd. 'Shall we make some noise here in front of this magnificent building?'

The roadies quickly pulled the black tarps away from

behind the band and the cries became even louder when the audience saw the gear. The boys were handed their guitars and Simon was at the drums as Mick pulled the microphone off the stand. He moved a few paces left and right.

'These are two of the songs we've just released off our new album, *An Avalanche of Strangers*: "Night and Day" and "What Now".'

Joy didn't take her eyes off Mick the whole time he was performing. He was electric, pulsing with the beat and thrilling the crowd as he ranged across the stage. *He is extraordinary*, thought Joy. *This is Mick the performer, the lead vocalist. Only I get to know about the tomato-growing, poetry-writing, art-loving man.* Joy couldn't help but feel a little thrill at the thought. *He's right to keep parts of himself off the stage and out of the press.*

And, as she watched him, it suddenly struck Joy that although she and Mick were very much a couple, they were also individuals. Pursuing her own career was just as important to her as songwriting and creating music was to Mick. *I'm involved in what the band does without being in the band. I'm close to the scene and, yet, somehow I'm apart from it.*

By the time Mick and the boys waved goodbye, the audience had tripled and they had no chance of walking back up to the hotel. Mick came down the steps, took Joy's hand, and along with Simon they bundled into the first waiting car straight back to the hotel where they were holding a press conference.

'How was the quality of the sound?' Mick asked breathlessly as soon as he was in the car.

'Brilliant. So clear. Strong,' said Joy.

Mick reached across Joy's lap and grabbed Simon's hand.

'Well done, mate,' said Mick. 'Well done.'

*

Robert had booked a private dining room at the Royal Hotel for what he hoped would be a fairly orderly night, to celebrate the launch. The last thing he needed was Dave and Jack going on a bender for a week. Once the press conference and the other media commitments had concluded, the plan was for Mick, Joy and the boys to celebrate with Rebecca and those closest to the band.

'Let's try not to turn this into a circus,' Mick had said to Robert. But as it was their one chance to really let their hair down before the band commenced an onslaught of interviews, television appearances, radio station visits and concerts that would last for the rest of the year, Robert was preparing for a big night.

Once word got out that the band were holding a 'launch party' at The Royal, people in the entertainment industry – producers, singers, musicians, journalists and fans – started arriving, keen to join in the celebrations. It wasn't long before the room adjacent was also taken over and a bouncer placed at the entrance to the first floor to regulate the crowd.

'Congratulations, everyone,' called Mick over the top of the chatter and music. 'Here's to *An Avalanche of Strangers.*'

He lifted his glass, saluting everyone in the room. Mick grabbed Joy by the hand and along with Simon, Dave and Jack, they headlined the dancing as the champagne flowed.

'I'm so proud of you. You completely killed it out there,' said Joy.

'Yeah, I think it went well. Let's see how much airtime our first two songs get.'

'Well? I think it's safe to say it exceeded all expectations!' Joy laughed. 'Now go,' she added, placing her hand on Mick's chest. 'Say hi to all the people who are trying to talk to you. Don't worry about me. I'm a big girl. You don't need to hold my hand all night.'

Mick flashed her a grateful smile and then set about working the room as the drinks flowed and the music continued. Joy could see he was good at making everyone he spoke to feel important, valued. People were drawn to his relaxed charm – there was no point denying it. Mick had told Joy all about how opportunities in the music business were built on developing contacts and who knew who. An hour later Mick had more than filled his quota of handshakes and short chats and the sweet smell of dope had begun to choke the air. Joy was still dancing with Bec and Bec's on-again, off-again girlfriend Tracey when Mick came up beside her and took her hand.

'Let's get out of here,' he whispered. 'I've done my thing.'

With only forty-eight hours before Joy had to fly back to Brisbane, Mick and Joy slipped quietly away and strolled the short distance to Mick's place.

'Are you happy?' Joy asked, nestling into him.

'I am now,' he said, kissing the top of her head.

'You really don't like the afterparty scene, do you?' said Joy.

'Let's just say I did my fair share of partying all at once. I'm waiting for everyone to catch up with me,' said Mick. 'You know, I love the fact that you're not in this industry,' he continued. 'That you have your own identity, your own stuff going on.'

Joy stopped and turned to him. 'Oh my god. I was thinking the same thing earlier today when you were singing at the launch. That you're you and I'm me and somehow, as different as we are, we make a whole. Together.'

They reached the front door and Mick hesitated.

'That's probably the most beautiful thing anyone's ever said to me,' he said. 'I'm going to write a song about it. I've got the title already.'

And he opened the door and they entered the tranquillity of the Paddington terrace, leaving the rest of the world outside.

*

Two weeks after the album launch Joy walked in from a shift at the Crownie to find a large white padded envelope addressed to her propped up on the small table inside the front door.

'Hi, Joy,' Scarlet called from the kitchen. 'There's a package there for you.'

'Hiya,' said Joy, picking it up and turning it over to see who the sender was.

Rebecca Bruce's name and address were printed on the back. Joy dropped her things on the kitchen table, knifed open the envelope and pulled out a black folder and a letter.

Hi Joy,

This will give you a little indication as to how much the camera likes you. I'll be in Brisbane for work next Friday and then staying with friends for the weekend. How about we catch up on Saturday morning to continue our discussion? Hope you're free.

Rebecca xx

The folder contained half-a-dozen black and white head shots of Joy, obviously taken on the day the album was released. The candid images, shot in natural light and of professional quality, showed Joy smiling, laughing, and in one photo, staring directly at the camera, her hair blown forward across her cheeks and neck. Joy spread them out on the table. Scarlet appeared beside her and gasped.

'Wow. You look incredible. Who took these?'

'I have no idea,' said Joy.

She'd never seen photos of herself like these before. The background had blurred away, leaving the shape and details of her face clear and smooth. Joy passed Scarlet Rebecca's note.

'What conversation?' said Scarlet, and Joy told her about the night at the Hordern.

'Well, you have to see what she says. You're mad if you don't. What have you got to lose?'

Later that night, Joy looked at the photos again. It was strange how removed she felt from the person captured in these images.

Maybe that's how Mick feels when he's performing, she thought. *How he can be so many different versions of himself. Could I do that too?*

She wasn't so sure.

*

Two hours after Joy and Rebecca had met at a café the following Saturday, they were still talking.

'Look, Bec,' said Joy. 'As interesting as this all sounds, I'm completing a very demanding degree. I can't just not attend lectures to sit around at castings for jobs I might not get. And I wouldn't want to use the agency you work

202

for. From what you've told me, the proprietors don't sound that appealing.'

'Well, the thing is,' said Rebecca, 'I'm finishing up at the end of April to go out on my own. I'd like to build my own business and manage models and possibly television personalities as well. I've got three models on my books already, none of whom have worked for the agency I'm with. I'll be running everything from my apartment for a while. I mean, all I need is a desk, a phone and a diary. I'll be getting my clients photographic work for magazines and TV commercials, fashion parade work and brand alliance. It's all about bringing together the right model for the right kind of work. Some models are great on the catwalk while others suit the camera.' She smiled at Joy. 'I've got big plans and I know it's going to take a lot of work to be successful, but isn't that the case with everything?'

Joy nodded slowly, thinking. 'Okay, I'm not promising anything, but how about I have some studio photos taken as you've suggested. If nothing comes of this at least I'll have some decent photos to give Mick. Where do I go and who do you suggest I get to take the photos?'

Rebecca nodded. 'Her name's Danielle Hogan and her studio's just over the river in Morningside. I'll set it up. How does next Saturday sound, if she's free?'

'Sounds good,' said Joy. 'But can we keep this between ourselves for now? I'm not one for talking about things that might not even happen.'

'Of course,' said Rebecca. 'I never discuss my clients with anyone.'

'Well, we're not there yet,' Joy said, and felt herself blush. 'But, all right, let's see what your photographer thinks.'

They said their goodbyes and Rebecca watched Joy walk to her car, all grace and fluidity. She was a natural, totally unaware of her looks and the effect she had on others. Rebecca had the feeling that something good was going to come of this.

For both of them.

*

After its first week in the Australian charts, 'Night and Day' debuted at number sixteen, with 'What Now' at twenty-two. The next week both songs had climbed higher, to seven and twelve respectively. The following Friday, Joy was stuck in traffic when she heard the radio announcer say, 'And coming in this week at number one and two, Around Midnight with "Night and Day" and "What Now". And here's Mick Harris and the boys from Around Midnight, with their nationwide number one hit, "Night and Day".'

Joy screamed so loudly the guy in the car beside her signalled to see if everything was okay.

When she got home, Joy raced through the front door, phoned her father at Monaghan and her mother, who was in Melbourne, as well as James and anyone else she could think of. Mick called Joy the moment he was back at the hotel after their concert in Adelaide.

'It's happening, babe. This is really happening,' he said. 'Number one and two! We can't quite believe it. God, I wish you were here with me.'

'I know, me too.' She clutched the phone, as if holding it tight would bring him a little closer.

'You know that journo from the States I was telling you about?' said Mick. 'The one who contacted me after we played the Myer Music Bowl concert? Well, listen to this.

It's from *Rolling Stone* – the title of the article is "Rock and Roll Down Under".'

Joy heard Mick riffling through the pages.

'Here it is. *"If the Aussie rock band Around Midnight's ten-track masterpiece,* An Avalanche of Strangers, *isn't already a big enough sensation, Simon Webber's drum fill on their single 'Night and Day' would have to be the most inspiring piece of drumming I've heard in the past five years. The lean blond Englishman brings an added touch of magic to this already impressive and highly original band."'*

'Wow! And that's so great for Simon. You must love seeing him get this recognition!' said Joy.

'I do. Absolutely. But not as much as I love you, babe. Nowhere near as much as I love you.'

*

Life then seemed to take off like a spooked pony.

With the band playing concerts in every capital city right through to October, and Joy's crushing fourth-year workload, Joy and Mick grabbed weekends together where they could. Mick usually flew to Brisbane but sometimes Joy would travel across to Perth or down to Melbourne or Sydney so they could have at least a night together. But the majority of the time it was phone calls and the odd postcard, which Mick had taken to sending as a bit of a joke. A card would arrive with a picture of Rottnest Island and a handwritten comment, *Welcome to the South of France xxx,* or showing a statue of a horse in Melbourne with *Just arrived at Monaghan xxx* scrawled across the bottom.

Why Joy didn't tell anyone about her conversation with Rebecca, she wasn't a hundred per cent sure. There was no doubt that the money she could earn would eclipse that of her bar work, and leave her more time to study. And while she had more of an understanding of the fashion world, advertising and marketing than she thought she'd had, it was still a world that had never held any attraction for her.

Why not? she wondered. *Is it because Mum looms so large in the Australian fashion scene?*

Maybe, she conceded. Or maybe Joy kept quiet about it all because she genuinely thought that the modelling work would last for a couple of months and then peter out. At any rate, Rebecca was the only one who knew about it when she went to Danielle Hogan's studio the Saturday after their meeting.

Danielle Hogan wasn't into small talk and afterwards, Joy thought she'd performed like an amateur in front of the camera. But Rebecca didn't think so when Danielle showed her the proof sheets.

By the time the mid-semester break came around in July, Rebecca had booked Joy for a three-day department store fashion catalogue shoot, as well as a two-day shoot for a jewellery ad campaign, all being shot by Danielle.

A few days before second semester began, Rebecca rang Joy late one night to see if she could be down at Surfers Paradise by eight the next morning for the filming of a shampoo commercial.

'The model they booked is sick, apparently. The ad agency showed your photo to their client and they called me straight away.'

'What would it involve?' asked Joy, her heart racing at the thought of her first actual modelling job.

'Be there by eight for your fake tan. Walk on the beach. Run through the sand. They may want you to dive into the water. You know: hair before using the product, hair after. You'll be done by three o'clock. Every hour costs so they want this shot in a day.'

Joy didn't really fancy diving into the water at this time of year until Rebecca told her the fee she'd be receiving.

'I'm sorry, did you say *two thousand dollars*, for one day of work?' Joy gasped.

'And I'm sure they'll throw in some of their hair products as well.'

The day went pretty much the way Rebecca had described it, including running on the beach and standing in front of a wind machine for close-ups. Joy had even felt she was getting the hang of it, at least until she tripped and landed face first in the sand. She couldn't stop laughing as she apologised to the photographer and cameraman and was ushered over to the makeup chair to repair the damage.

'Don't worry,' the makeup artist assured Joy. 'The shoot's going well and we're way ahead of schedule.'

The photographer was genuinely surprised when, once the dry hair shots had been taken, Joy agreed to have some shots taken in the surf. Again and again, Joy dived under the waves, emerging from the water with her hands pivoting around her head and face.

'That's a wrap, Joy,' the photographer called. 'And thank you. You're braver than me.'

Joy raced out of the water and a junior assistant hurried across the white sand and tossed a beach towel around her shivering shoulders. Joy thought about the backbreaking work the shearers did and the long days the stockmen had in the saddle, driving cattle; freezing in winter, sweltering in summer.

She turned up the car heating and laughed out loud as she headed back to Brisbane. She was thinking about what

Henry would say if she told him how much she was being paid to frolic on a beach for a day, all because she was blessed with the brunette Meredith curls.

Two thousand dollars! I'm in the wrong game, she heard him say.

That night, she decided it was time to tell Mick and her parents what she'd been doing. She explained to them over the phone that she'd had some modelling photos taken and done some minor modelling work, although she didn't elaborate. But once the commercial went to air the following month, showing at prime time, just about everyone Joy had ever known saw it. Mrs B waved from her garden one morning.

'Joy. Oh, Joy,' she called. 'I saw your ad last night. You looked lovely.'

Her mother called her almost immediately. As Avril rarely watched television, Joy was certain someone had told her about it. The moment she heard her mother's voice, she twisted the telephone cord with her fingers, fearing she was about to get an earful.

'I loved the commercial,' said Avril after Joy had spent the first ten minutes giving her the full backstory. 'I also have the latest David Jones catalogue open in front of me, and you're all the way through it! You look wonderful, by the way. Who did the shoot?'

They chatted for hours about the fashion, the logistics of shooting on sand, the wind machine breaking down and Joy's faceplant, and Joy's decision to get into the surf as the photographer had requested.

'It was fun,' Joy admitted to her mother. *We finally have something in common*, she thought, relishing the warmth and delight in their conversation. *Or maybe it's because I'm just letting Mum into my life?*

It was Mick's reaction that surprised her the most.

'I'm a little hurt you didn't tell me about all this – the commercial, the catalogues,' he said when he called later the same night. 'When you told me you were doing some modelling work, I didn't realise it was this big. I thought we told each other everything?'

No couple tells each other everything, Joy thought instinctively. She felt it was a ridiculous assumption, especially coming from Mick. Aspects of Mick's life, his wild days, as he called them, came to mind. This was a topic of conversation they were definitely yet to unpack.

'I'm still getting my head around the whole modelling gig. I didn't want to start talking about something that might not even happen. I wasn't even sure it was something I'd want to do – or keep doing.'

There was a long silence that Mick didn't seem in a hurry to break. Joy felt as if a distance had risen up between them out of nowhere; a coldness that seemed to seep down the line to her.

'Are you still there?' she said finally.

'Yep. I'm still here,' he replied. His tone was dismissive. Abrupt. He'd never spoken to her like this before.

Joy's stomach lurched with uncertainty.

'I don't understand why you're being like this,' she said. 'Okay, I didn't tell you all the details. I didn't tell anyone, actually, not even Scarlet and Viv. I think I just . . . wasn't sure what was going to come of it all. Maybe I felt a bit insecure about the type of work. I've never done anything like it before.'

'Of course. You're right,' he said, sounding, to her relief, like the Mick she knew. 'Well, maybe it's time to give up the bar work. I think you've earned it. Especially if you end up getting regular modelling work until you finish uni.'

'You know, I've been thinking the same thing. I only need one decent-paying modelling job a month and I'm set. Barry's been so good to me but he always knew that one day I'd be moving on. And I have so much reading and prac work to get through. I think it's time.'

*

Robert Flare was hand-carving tall rectangular shapes with a red pen into the lined notebook on his desk as he listened, almost in disbelief, to what the caller was saying. The voice on the other end of the line sounded genuine enough. For a split-second Robert thought it might be one of the blokes he played cards with mucking around. But none of them would be capable of pulling off an English accent like the one he was hearing except Simon, and he was thirty thousand feet up in the air with the rest of the band, and wouldn't be landing in Brisbane until mid-afternoon. *No*, Robert thought. *This guy's the real deal.*

'Terrific. Yes. Of course. I'll get my secretary to process those documents tomorrow.'

Robert had never had a secretary, but Anthony Barber-Linden from Hot Wire Promotions didn't know that. Robert stretched forward and placed the receiver down as if it were a live hand grenade.

'Jesus Christ,' he said to the empty room.

He grabbed the thick black ribbon hanging from his diary that delineated one wishful day from the next, flipped the pages open and circled the day's date.

One for the biography, he thought. When they got off the plane, Mick would head straight to Joy's place and Simon, Jack and Dave to the Hilton. He had to tell them when they were all together.

A few hours later, Robert jangled his keys in his hand

210

as he watched the boys come down the front stairs of the plane and set off across the tarmac. It was Jack who saw Robert first and tapped Mick on the chest.

'I didn't know you were picking us up,' Mick said when they reached him.

'Surprise, surprise,' said Robert.

The members of the band stood before him, perplexed.

'Let's grab your luggage. I've arranged transport for all of you to the hotel,' Robert said. 'I need to talk to you. Right away. All together.'

'What's going on?' said Simon.

'Bugger that!' said Mick. 'I haven't seen Joy in five weeks. I'm not going to any bloody hotel. I'm getting my gear and going straight to her place. Tell us now, Robert. What's this about?'

'Not here,' said Robert. 'I don't want to talk here.'

'Okay then. I'll take the gear in one cab and you can all follow me to Indooroopilly,' said Mick, eyeballing Robert. 'And then the lot of you can clear off.'

Once at Joy's place Mick took her in his arms and kissed her. He slid off his jacket then held her, this time cradling her face in his hands, kissing her neck, her shoulders, her mouth.

'We're not going to be alone for long,' he said. 'The boys and Robert are right behind me. I'm not sure what's going on but Robert was waiting for us when we got off the plane, so something's up.'

Once Joy had hugged and helloed everyone, Mick raised both hands as if to stop the traffic.

'Okay, Robert. What's all this about?' he asked, having never seen their manager look so upbeat before.

'I was contacted earlier today by Bachelor Records and then by their parent company, Hot Wire Promotions, in

England.' Robert stood there, hands on hips, smiling like he'd backed the winner of the Melbourne Cup.

'Congratulations. *An Avalanche of Strangers* is now the number one album in Australia, number five in the UK and number eleven in the States.'

Pandemonium erupted. Joy screamed and Mick lifted her off her feet. Jack and Dave hugged, swinging each other off balance. With Joy still in his arms, Mick's hand reached out for Simon's. Without a word they clamped palms, holding their hands aloft.

'That's the good news,' said Robert over the hubbub. 'Do you want the great news?'

They were all instantly silenced.

'Hot Wire Promotions have booked you for a six-week tour starting the first week of November. Seven-thousand-seat venues, minimum. Flights, accommodation for all band members and immediate personnel. Play four nights with a three-day relocate and set-up.'

'Holy shit,' shouted Dave.

Mick and Joy gazed at each other in amazement.

'London's calling.' Robert grinned. 'Get your passports out, boys. Around Midnight is headed for the UK.'

Later, Joy would come to remember this day for a number of reasons. None of them realised then that the six-week UK tour would end up lasting much longer and would springboard the band to undreamed-of heights. The decision Joy would make about her own life changed its course, too.

It was the moment she realised something funda-mental about life: it never takes you in the direction you expect.

*

Tim sat calmly at the kitchen table, having listened to Avril's side of the argument. He knew one of them had to stay as objective as possible and it wasn't going to be his wife.

'Do you honestly expect us to support this ludicrous idea of leaving uni with only a year left of your degree to go racing off to the UK after some singer in a rock band?' said Avril, her frustration clear in her voice.

Joy had already made up her mind and had no intention of getting into a shouting match with her mother. As far as she was concerned, their conversation was just a necessary formality.

'You really don't like Mick, do you? That's what this is all about,' said Joy. 'You know, Mum, I've sat here for the last hour explaining to you and Dad that I'm not *leaving uni*, as you put it, I'm deferring the fifth year of my degree. Things are moving very fast for the band and they will now be based in the UK for the next twelve months, not just two, to capitalise on the album's popularity. I want to be there with Mick. And he wants me to be there with him, too.'

'And then what?' said Avril.

'I don't know, Mum. I'm planning to come back to finish my degree. It's twelve months I'm talking about, not ten years. I want to see the world. Explore. Find out what I'm capable of. It feels like I've been in this cocoon of a world for too long. Monaghan, Brisbane, back and forth. School, uni. I want to experience new places. New people.'

'And your supervising professor said this is doable?' Tim asked.

'Totally,' said Joy. 'If you want the statistics, around twenty per cent of all students change or defer their degree, in some capacity, at some point. And because my marks have been so strong the past year, my supervisor's parting words were, "*I wish you well, Joy. What a wonderful experience. The vet school will still be here when you get back.*"'

Avril was standing at the window, her back to the room, looking out across to the jacaranda trees she loved so much. A sliver of envy caught in her throat. London. Europe. She suddenly saw her own youth as a distant memory.

'I've made up my mind and I've booked my flight,' said Joy. 'I leave on the fourth of December.'

Avril knew that was a Saturday. She could visualise the dates for each and every Saturday weeks in advance. It was the busiest day for takings in her five bridal boutiques.

'Where will you live?' said Tim.

'The record company has provided Mick and the guys with a flat near the centre of London for the first few months, and then they'll find places of their own. Mick and I are happy for Simon to share with us. Jack and Dave will get their own place.'

'So, you're going to leave Jordy and Duncan high and dry after everything they've done for you,' said Avril tightly.

'No one's leaving anyone high and dry, Mum.' Joy couldn't keep the exasperation out of her voice. 'Vivienne and Jason are taking over the lease and Scarlet has found a cute little one-bedroom place halfway between uni and Saint Anne's Hospital. She was planning on moving out whether I was here or not.'

Avril shrugged her shoulders. 'It's not what I'd be doing.'

'Oh, *Mum*. You're not me. You can't overlay your life onto mine. I'm really happy. And I just want you to be happy for me too.'

'And how do you intend to live? Off a man?'

Joy sighed and shook her head slowly.

'Now, steady on,' said Tim, looking up at Avril. 'That's not fair, and you know it.'

'I'm going to try my hand at modelling over there. You know I've had some success here lately. Rebecca Bruce has given me the name of an agency in London. She's even talking about heading to the UK herself. There are so many Aussies living in London. Did you know they call Earl's Court "Kangaroo Court"?'

Tim lifted his mug of tea. He reached across the table and took hold of his daughter's hand.

'You have my support, Joy,' said Tim. 'Darling,' he said to Avril. 'Come and sit down. This is a milestone in our girl's life. One year out of her studies, to see something of life, won't do any harm. Don't forget, you were a similar age when you travelled halfway across the world.'

Joy smiled at her father. *Touché, Dad*, she thought.

Avril knew it too. She raised an eyebrow at Tim and walked to the table reluctantly.

'Well, I suppose you'll let us visit you,' she said gruffly. 'Or will that cramp your style?'

Joy could see that her mother's eyes were glassy. She stood up and hugged Avril, and Avril wrapped her arms around Joy. They held each other silently.

'*Écrivez vote propre histoire*,' said Joy. 'Remember? It's time I wrote my own story, Mum. That's what you told me to do. I'm really just taking your advice. Finally.'

PART 2

All the world's a stage, and all the men and women merely players. They have their exits and their entrances; and one man in his time plays many parts.

William Shakespeare

PART 2

CHAPTER 12

Joy slipped off her high heels and stepped out of the metallic bubble skirt, handing it to her dresser. She took a seat in a canvas director's chair and closed her eyes while the hairdresser's hands flew over her mountain of teased hair, removing several large plastic lilies. Backstage, beyond the bright lights of the catwalk, Joy didn't feel that there was much difference between her and the other twenty-five or so models who were busily undressing and having their hair and makeup removed. Joy's height was not unique in this company. She was, in fact, shorter than many of the other models.

'Well done, by the way,' said the hairdresser. 'I could tell you were nervous. Your confidence will grow each time you do a parade. Who did you say was repping you?'

Joy was certain that she hadn't said at all, but she was happy to answer.

'The Sullivan Ascher Agency,' she replied.

The hairdresser leant forward as she continued working.

'No one in the industry calls them by their full name,' she said quietly. 'If you say you're with Sully's, it won't sound like you're the new kid on the block. How long have you been in London?'

'Six months.'

'So you either followed a boy, followed the money or followed a dream,' she said with a smile. 'Which one was it?'

'All three,' said Joy, and at the same time she and the petite redhead with the heavy Scottish accent burst out laughing.

'Have you been getting much work? I'm Helen, by the way,' and she slipped a business card onto Joy's lap. 'I do hair and makeup on the side,' she said, 'when I'm not working at Mode Hair. It costs an arm and a leg to live in this town.'

'Thanks, Helen. I'll keep that in mind.'

'There you go, love. All done. Enjoy your weekend,' Helen said. 'Hope to see you again.'

Joy added the business card to her ever-growing pile. London seemed to be full of hardworking, party-loving twenty-somethings, eager to wheel and deal and to make their mark in the world. The city, it seemed, was a nationality all of its own, with fashion its national costume and the live music and club scene providing a national anthem. Around Midnight had jumped from the remoteness of the Antipodes into the epicentre of excess. It was as if everyone was out to shock and they were succeeding brilliantly.

*

The first few months Joy spent in London were magical. Whenever the band was not out of town on a gig, she and Mick walked the streets of London together, whiling away happy hours exploring the shops, restaurants, pubs and department stores, admiring the famous landmarks, and taking countless photos of the obscure and the unexpected. Through the theatre district of Soho, down Oxford Street and into Covent Garden, they discovered a city they were excited to call home – at least for a while. An English winter was a novelty for Joy and the Australian band members and the hallstand in the ground-floor flat Joy, Mick and Simon shared quickly accumulated a fashionable collection of jackets, scarves and hats.

When Joy first arrived, shortly after the band had finished their initial six-week tour, she teased Mick and Simon mercilessly about the neatness of the fridge and the fact that dirty dishes were never left in the sink. Secretly, she loved their tidy house habits and when she and Mick weren't eating dinner at the local pub, Joy was happy to do the cooking. Packages arrived from Avril on a regular basis, containing all of Joy's favourite condiments, and she was never in short supply of Vegemite or Sayo biscuits (two products Simon believed weren't fit for human consumption). Joy's fears that the flat might perhaps prove a little small for the three of them were quickly dispelled. Simon had a strong network of friends in London and was often out.

'I'm like the cat that walks in the night,' said Simon as he made a pot of tea one morning, having just arrived in the door. 'I come home, eventually.'

In any case, Joy began working almost immediately and was often away from the flat herself. Rebecca's introduction had been a good one. Considered a medium-sized agency with a good reputation, Joy's first assignment with Sullivan Ascher had been a Debenhams spring/summer catalogue shoot at the end of February. Still sporting her Australian tan, the booking agent thought Joy would be well suited for the job. A naturally athletic physique was now the preferred look as the aerobics obsession took off. It was all about youth, energy and health, even if smoke still choked pubs and clubs and they operated without patron drinking limits. London was on its way to one big decade-long party, and there was something for everyone. Nobody batted their purple kohl-smudged eyelids or stamped their studded boots or gave a cross-dressing toss about anyone else, as long as they didn't wear beige or look ordinary.

Joy wasn't the only one who was busy. Mick and the band were working like demons. After the success of their November tour, Robert Flare had taken a small office in the fashionable Shepherd's Bush, not far from the offices of Bachelor Records and around the corner from the Black Cauldron, a favourite watering hole for those in the music industry. When the band wasn't working on new material, doing radio interviews or talking to journalists, Robert's office provided them with neutral territory to talk music, business and anything else with their manager. Robert had also hired Mandy. His new secretary came in from nine to one to answer the phone, do the filing and type up any correspondence. This freed Robert to build his list of associates in a city where who you knew was often more important than what you knew. Not only that, he was always on the lookout for the best possible concert venues and booking deals for the band. They were *his* boys, his family, despite the rumours he'd heard about how he and Mick didn't get along, which was tabloid fodder.

Robert had also embarked on a self-instigated make-over, possibly inspired by the Christmas present the boys had given him. As promised, they'd presented their manager with a bespoke leather jacket, taking the advice of the Savile Row craftsman to retain the tan colour Robert loved so much, but replace the safari cut with something more contemporary. The finished article delighted Robert, as it made him look five years younger and ten kilos lighter.

'A well-cut jacket will do that for you,' Simon said as Robert ran his hands down his torso, admiring his own reflection.

When the time came for them to leave the flat the record company had provided, Mick and Joy found a spacious flat in Fulham one street back from the Thames, and only a short walk to Simon's new place. Meanwhile, Jack and Dave had leased a terrace in nearby Putney. It was quickly named *Party House Two*, and almost immediately began living up to its namesake's reputation. The five of them lived close enough to one another to make impromptu visits possible without feeling like they were living in each other's pockets.

As the weeks turned into months and Joy began to get used to this new, fast-paced life, she started to feel less like a tourist and more like a resident. The shops and markets began to take on a familiar feel, as did the layout of London. With all their comings and goings, Joy got to know her neighbours, too, greeting them by name whenever she ran into them in the street.

At night, across the city, pubs and clubs exploded with live music, and dancing was the all-consuming currency. Nightclubs, such as Blast and Cameo Palace, had a strict door policy: only the weird, wonderful and outrageous were allowed in. Those who dressed in the New Romantics style stood shoulder to shoulder with High Camp patrons and those dedicated to King's Road originals dressed in layers of stretchy black fabric. It was all about passion, pushing boundaries, taking risks, and big ideas. Fashion was the universal language of the streets and the youth of London were creating a unique dialect.

Simon had carte blanche entry to most of the clubs and bars and Joy and the rest of the band were frequent visitors to Beats in Chelsea, which had one of the largest dance floors in London. Mick had a fluid, seductive way of moving, but no one loved the dance floor more than Simon.

'All those hours stuck behind the drums,' Joy shouted in Mick's ear over the music one night. 'Simon must relish being able to move.'

Mick nodded, but he seemed distracted, disinterested. Now that she thought about it, he wasn't himself that night, Joy reflected. They'd been burning the candle at both ends for weeks – working hard and playing harder – so she thought he was probably worn out. She saw there were dark circles under his eyes. Taking her hand, Mick led Joy from the dance floor to their private booth. Joy moved close to him and cupped her hand around his ear.

'Is everything all right? You look miles away.'

'I'd like to go,' he said. 'Are you happy to leave?'

'We just got here,' said Joy. 'Whatever's the matter, Mick?'

'Nothing. I'm tired, that's all. It's been a big couple of weeks.'

Joy had been looking forward to the night of dancing and fun, but she figured none of it would be enjoyable if Mick didn't want to be there. Mick squeezed Joy's hand and stared out across the crowded room as Joy collected her bag and they made their way through the pulsing dancers and out into the cool night air.

Joy glanced at Mick's face. He looked tense and unapproachable.

She had started to notice these mood changes in him shortly after she'd arrived in London. At first she'd put his occasional quietness down to the band's punishing schedule of concerts and rehearsals, not to mention the elevated pressure of their growing success, but she wasn't certain that was really the cause. Before, when she'd only seen Mick periodically when he was able to get to Brisbane, there'd been no sign of these mood swings, and so the expressionless silence that now seemed to overtake Mick from time to time – often accompanied by the need to go home, even if they were having a good time – confused Joy. She wasn't sure what set him off.

Something that had happened during the day? she wondered. Or was it memories creeping up on him once again?

Joy knew there was darkness in Mick's past. He often hinted at his chaotic teenage years and the indulgent haze of drugs and drink in his early twenties. His need for organisation and order seemed to stem from those days. 'I'll talk about this sometime,' he'd say whenever Joy touched a raw nerve, but he rarely followed through.

He'll talk when he's ready, Joy had decided. But it irritated and worried her that he couldn't or wouldn't be forthcoming about what was on his mind.

What was he not telling her?

*

Mick paid the cabbie and walked the short distance to the front door of their flat on Carnwath Road. Joy would still be working and Simon was in Paris. He knew he'd have the place to himself for at least a little while. It gave him a chance to process what had just happened. He dropped his keys on the table, made a pot of coffee and sat down at the kitchen table. Then he pulled the business card from his pocket and held it between his thumb and forefinger, turned it over and read the elegant black writing. *Marcus Tan, Attorney*, it read.

Of all the people to run into in London. 'Never in a million years,' murmured Mick to the empty room.

He rotated his coffee cup as he recalled their conversation half an hour earlier. Marcus Tan was well built, well educated and well dressed, a more mature, more polished version of the quiet, bookish kid that Mick remembered from school.

'Mick Harris. I don't believe it,' Mick had heard as he was about to cross Bond Street. 'It's good to see you,' said the stranger.

Mick reached for the man's outstretched hand while asking himself, *Who the hell is this?*

'Marcus Tan,' the stranger said, realising that Mick hadn't worked out who he was.

'Jesus. Marcus. I'm sorry. I had no idea. I didn't recognise you, man.'

'Well, that's understandable. High school feels like a lifetime ago.'

'What brings you to London?' said Mick.

'I got head-hunted by a major media company here in the UK,' said Marcus. 'So I thought, why not? I'd been working in Melbourne since graduating. It was time to spread my wings. I've only been here a month but I love it already.'

'Where are you fixed?' said Mick.

Marcus laughed. 'Earl's Court, of course. Not the most original destination but I was able to get a room with a couple of mates. So far so good. What about you? I've been following the band with interest. How are you finding things since moving here?'

They talked about life in London and the easy access to

cities such as Paris and Barcelona, but Mick deliberately avoided any talk about home and in particular their high school years. If Marcus was aware of Mick's history he made no reference to it.

Eventually Marcus checked his watch and gave Mick his business card. 'I've got to run – but maybe a drink sometime, or if you ever need my professional services? Give me a ring.' And he smiled warmly as he reached for Mick's hand and said goodbye.

They'd spoken for less than ten minutes but it hadn't seemed that way. Seeing Marcus had unleashed something in Mick. Even now that he was home, Mick was still lost in memories; ones that never seemed to leave him and which had risen so easily to the surface despite his years of burying them as deep as they would go. Things he couldn't share. Not even with Joy.

He could hear Carol McCready speaking to him even now, sitting at the kitchen table as the past poured around him. *Mick, love, it's not your fault.*

He took Marcus's card and slid it into his wallet. It would have been just as easy to have tossed it in the bin. Why didn't he? They both knew they were never going to have a beer together. Mick decided there and then that he would forget Marcus's business card, along with his anxiety and the memories their accidental meeting had stirred up. *The bloody past can stay there. I can handle this. I will handle this.*

*

When Joy arrived home later that night, she flicked on the kitchen light.

'Mick,' she called. 'I'm home. Why are you sitting in the dark?'

'Is it dark already?' he said. 'I hadn't noticed.'

Joy came over and ruffled his hair, alarm bells pealing in her head.

'How did it go?' she asked. 'With the guy from *Music Now.*'

Mick looked at her blankly.

'Oh. Yeah. The interview. It was fine. The same sort of questions all journos ask about a new album.'

'Are you okay?' Joy gave Mick a quick kiss and placed her small bag of shopping on the kitchen bench. She turned and looked at him properly. 'You look exhausted.'

'No. I feel great. In fact, let's get changed and go somewhere nice for dinner,' said Mick. 'What about that Indian place we like?'

'Perfect,' said Joy as she put the wine and cheese she'd bought in the fridge. 'So, a pretty uneventful day by the sounds of it.'

'Pretty much,' said Mick, and turned away.

*

When Simon told Joy and Mick that his aunt and uncle had invited the band to a weekend house party in Gloucestershire, it was just the break Joy and Mick had been craving. While they'd stayed in some quaint country hotels in the six months they'd been in the UK, they were yet to experience the beauty and seclusion of a private country estate.

In the days leading up to their trip, Joy felt energised and excited, similar to how she often felt when she'd reach the outer city limits of Brisbane, the open highway calling her home. For Mick, this life of grand houses, land and farming that Joy had shown him was one that appealed to him more and more. The peace, the closeness to nature, felt good for the soul. Not to mention the comfort and lifestyle that often went along with this rural way of life.

Simon had insisted on driving them in his mother's new BMW convertible, playing the part of both chauffeur and tour guide.

'Comfortable back there, m'lady?' he teased.

'Very, my good man,' said Joy, marvelling at yet another majestic view of rolling green hills and summer foliage: the quintessential English countryside.

The BMW came complete with the latest technology: a CD player. Mick had slid the *An Avalanche of Strangers* disc into the player and Simon had cranked up the volume. The three of them sang their hearts out as they drove.

'Mick,' said Joy, leaning forward and placing her hand on Mick's shoulder. 'I've been meaning to ask you. Why don't you think of putting "Only a Moment" on the next album? I know you don't sing it very often, but it's such a beautiful song.'

Mick was quiet for a second before replying, 'It's not one I want to record, babe. I sing it at a live show every now and again when the mood takes me.'

'And speaking of next albums,' said Simon, 'Robert thinks we should go into the studio earlier than we orig-inally planned. By September, October at the latest. Release the fourth album next April to coincide with the second anniversary of the release of *Avalanche*. What do you think?'

Mick nodded. 'Yep. And the title of the album,' he added. 'Have you got any thoughts?'

'Working on it,' Simon said. 'Something brilliant this way will come.'

The car slowed and Simon turned off to the right through

a nondescript gate and down a narrow Gloucestershire lane, the view obscured by a giant hedge on either side.

'Almost there,' said Simon as they crossed a stone bridge then rolled up and over a slight hill.

The hedges fell away and sweeping views revealed the seventeenth-century Brayleedon Manor, bathing peacefully in the afternoon sun.

*

'Simon, my boy. Your timing is matchless.'

Simon and his uncle shook hands then embraced warmly while Mick and Joy retrieved bags from the boot.

'Joy and Mick, I'd like you to meet my uncle, Lord Conbray. Uncle, this is the delightful Joy, Mick's girl-friend, and the man himself, Mick Harris.'

'Welcome to Brayleedon. So wonderful you could make it. We're a pretty big party this weekend. You're the first to arrive. My goodness, Simon, is that your mother's new car? How on earth did you prise that away from her?'

Simon lifted his hands as if to say, *Who knows?*

'The other chaps, Jack and Dave. Where are they? They're each bringing a guest, aren't they?'

'They're on their way, Lord Conbray,' said Mick. 'But if Jack's navigating they might not be here until the morning.'

'Oh. And please, it's Chester, though most people call me Chess. Well, come on in. Let's have some tea in the library. My delightful wife Prue's about somewhere.'

*

The Friday night dinner and socialising was a casual affair, with Prue gliding through the room making intro-ductions. Guests took their drinks out to a courtyard where a firepit had been lit. The beauty of the star-filled sky compensated for the coolness of the evening. Mick and an Irish novelist were sharing a joke when the writer's pretty blonde girlfriend sidled up to Mick, reached over and lifted the cigarette lazily out of her boyfriend's hand, blowing a smoke ring and laughing loudly.

Mick raised his glass at Joy, who was standing on the other side of the fire, and winked, and she toasted him back. She had been with Mick long enough now to trust her instincts. The novelist's girlfriend was not the first female to flirt openly with Mick and she wouldn't be the last.

'Joy,' said Chess, coming up beside her. 'Let me introduce you to the man who is going to rebuild my wine cellar. Joy, this is Dion Beauchamp. Dion, this is Joy Meredith. I'll leave you two to chat. I believe Prue is trying to catch my attention.'

Joy's eyes swept over Dion with his olive complexion, thick fair hair and soft brown eyes. He was slightly taller than Joy and had a solid build.

Dion shook Joy's hand firmly. 'It's lovely to meet you. I was just talking to Simon and he was saying you're from Australia. A university student who is taking a, how do you say it? A sabbatical, and doing some modelling at the same time.'

Joy could tell from Dion's accent that he was French. Although she knew she would probably sound rusty, she decided to reply in her mother's tongue.

'Simon seems to have given you my curriculum vitae,' Joy said. 'So, do you specialise in certain home-building projects?'

'No, no,' Dion laughed, looking delightedly and quizzically at her.

'My mother's French,' Joy explained.

231

'Ah. Your French is excellent. And no, I'm not in that sort of building industry. I am helping Chester rebuild the profile of his wine cellar, not the cellar itself. I advise people on what wines to choose when they want to establish a credible wine collection. To drink and to lay down.'

'I'm sorry,' said Joy. 'I wasn't thinking very laterally, was I?'

'You were thinking literally, I believe. But don't worry. It's not the first time this has happened to me.'

'I don't know much about wine, although I can say that my late grandfather had – how did you describe it? – a "credible" wine collection. And Chateau Margaux was one of his favourites.'

'Oh yes. Chateau Margaux is a renowned wine estate. I know it well.'

'How did you come to do what you're doing?' asked Joy.

Dion motioned to the seat behind him and they sat down.

'I studied and became first a vintner and enologist.'

'A winemaker,' said Joy. Her French was coming back to her more easily than she imagined.

'Yes. To understand the science and chemistry and biology of the wine.'

'We are both scientists, then,' said Joy. 'I am studying to be a vet, although I have deferred my studies while I am over here.'

'Different species,' Dion said with a chuckle. 'But yes. Both scientists.'

Just then Mick appeared in front of Joy and Dion, blocking the light from the fire.

'Darling, this is Dion,' said Joy in English. 'He's helping Chess to restock his wine cellar.'

232

Dion stood and shook Mick's hand.

'Nice to meet you, Mick. What a wonderful time of year to be in such a beautiful place as this.'

'Wonderful,' said Mick. 'We've been looking forward to this weekend, haven't we, babe?' and he rubbed his hand along Joy's shoulder.

'Well, if you'll excuse me,' said Dion, 'this is a work and pleasure trip for me, and the work side of things starts early tomorrow, so I'll bid you good night.'

'Good night,' said Joy as Mick eased himself into the wicker chair Dion had vacated.

As Dion walked away, Mick seemed heavy with silence. A familiar niggle of anxiety leapt up in Joy. It had been happening more and more often the last couple of months. Mick would be full of life one moment, and then withdrawn and touchy the next.

Where does Mick go when he's like this? she wondered. *Maybe I should talk to Simon about it?*

Yes, she resolved. That was what she'd do. Tomorrow.

*

With Cheltenham only a short distance away and a town he knew well, Simon was happy to play tour guide. The following morning while everyone else went for walks, read or disappeared in one direction or another, Simon, Joy and Mick headed off to take in the sights. The highlight of Chess and Prue's weekend house party was to be the dinner that night. The Conbrays were excellent hosts and enjoyed contriving a guest list of 'interesting people' who they thought would mix well and provide stimulating conversation. Guests were expected to dress with flare and personality, as opposed to custom and tradition. The one activity Chess insisted upon was drinks and croquet with all their guests on the lawn at six o'clock, no exceptions.

'Is everything all right with Mick?' Simon asked Joy quietly as they wandered down the aisle of an antique store. 'He seems rather down to me. Has done for a few weeks. He doesn't seem to have that usual upbeat energy of his.'

Joy placed a silver teapot back onto its trivet and checked that Mick wasn't in earshot.

'I'm glad you mentioned it, because I was planning to talk to you. I'm worried. He can be quiet for hours. I think it's a coping strategy to deal with all the pressure he feels, the pressure to be successful. To write the hits and to make it financially worthwhile for the band. You and he are so close – do you think you could ask him? He might open up more to you than he does to me. I feel he might be putting on a brave face for me.'

Simon nodded. 'I will,' he said. 'God knows, we've hit the ground running for the last six months. And you can't rush creativity. It takes the time it takes. And even then it bloody well doesn't show up sometimes.' He gently took her arm. 'These creatives, they're deep thinkers. Moody types. All sunshine – until they're not. Leave it with me.'

He wrapped her in a quick embrace, and, for a moment, she felt the comfort of his words.

*

When they got back to the estate, Joy went in search of Calum, the estate manager, who had shown her where the tack was and had already brought four horses suitable for riding into the stables. She was relieved to have some time to herself and Mick had said he was happy to chill in their bedroom and read.

Several guests had said they were keen to go riding, but when Joy entered the stables, she was the only one.

She selected a snaffle bit bridle, saddlecloth and saddle and tacked up a mare the manager felt would suit her best, having first ascertained Joy's riding ability.

'Looks like the others have bailed,' she said, tightening the girth strap.

'Not everyone,' said a voice behind her, and she turned to see Dion strolling into the stables.

He was kitted out in dark cotton pants, short boots and a t-shirt, very similar to Joy's own attire. Dion pulled what he needed from the pegs on the wall and opened the door to one of the stalls.

'The black gelding. He's not sore anymore?' Dion asked Calum, running his hand down the horse's near-side front leg.

'He hasn't been ridden for a month. Not since you were here last,' the Irishman replied. 'He's been nicely rested.'

'Good,' said Dion as he slipped the bridle onto his mount. 'Joy, shall we ride together?'

The cadence of his words and the way he spoke reminded Joy of her mother's enunciations. She nodded.

'Do you jump?' Dion asked.

Joy swung herself up into the saddle then bent down and adjusted the length of her stirrups. 'Sure. I can jump.'

'Okay. If you know what you're doing, then that's good. We can go where I usually ride whenever I'm here. I think you will love the terrain.'

Dion was right. The lush, rock-free undulating pastures of the estate, with intermittent wooded riding trails and hectares of partially cleared forest, were a rider's dream. Having walked the horses for the first hundred metres or so, Joy shortened up her reins. The mare dropped her nose and transitioned so smoothly to a canter that Joy let out a laugh of surprise.

'You like her?' said Dion. 'This big mare?'

'She's lovely.'

'There's a small hedge up ahead, and once we're over that, we can canter all the way to that rise in the distance and down to the river below.'

Joy urged her horse forward, and for the first time in a long time she felt completely at ease with herself.

*

From the upstairs bedroom window, Mick looked down at the drinks table on the lawn below, and the assortment of white wicker chairs, most of which were already occupied. Jack, Dave and their weekend dates were halfway through a game of croquet with the artist and the theatre director. The new dress Joy had bought for that night's dinner was still waiting on the hanger. She hadn't yet returned from her afternoon ride.

He looked at this watch and frowned. It was unlike her to be late.

He pulled on a fresh paisley pattern shirt and thought of the evening ahead. He could see that Joy felt right at home in a place like this, with people like these and staff who appeared and disappeared with monotonous regularity. They knew what you needed or wanted before you did.

He didn't want to admit it, but he was envious of her ability to know things like which fork to use when. She knew the social etiquette, such as placing her napkin on her chair if she got up during a meal, only on the table once the meal was finished. She could read a wine list without anxiety over the difference between a chardonnay and a sauvignon blanc. There had been a time when Mick would never have noticed such idiosyncrasies. Now he did.

He'd absorbed most of this the first time he'd taken her to lunch, but it was only now that he saw how important this knowledge was to fitting in to this particular world. It was an unspoken yet crucial requirement of a smooth social passage.

Yes, Joy understood all the nuances of this moneyed world and was completely unaware of how it might feel when you didn't.

*

As the summer's day drew to a close and preparations for dinner were in full swing at the manor, Joy was holding the reins of both her horse and Dion's while Dion ran his hand down his horse's leg. He straightened up then held the horses while Joy inspected the leg too.

'He's lame. There's no doubt about it,' said Joy sadly. 'Did you notice how hot his fetlock is?' She patted the regal creature on the neck and looked around.

'I can't walk him. We'll need the trailer,' said Dion.

'I'll ride back and find Calum and tell him,' said Joy. 'We're only a couple of kilometres from the house.'

'I'm sorry. This is likely to make you late for evening drinks,' he said.

'Don't worry about it. Unexpected events happen all the time where I grew up. The health of the horse is more important than a gin and tonic right now.'

*

Joy waved at Mick as she walked wearily across the lawn. He was talking to Simon and the blonde from last night and didn't respond. Perhaps he hadn't seen her, Joy thought.

'What happened to you?' called Simon. 'We were about to send out a search party.'

'I'm sorry I'm so late. Dion's horse went lame a couple of k's away. I rode back to get Calum and the trailer. The leg can hardly take any weight.'

The blonde looked Joy up and down and giggled. Mick didn't say a word. He was wearing his sunglasses so she couldn't read his eyes.

Surely he's not jealous? Or angry at me? Joy thought. She frowned, too tired to think on it any further.

'I'll go and wash up,' she said.

'Wash up.' The blonde giggled again. 'Is that what they call a shower in Australia?'

'I'll have a champagne waiting for you, dearest Joy,' said Simon. 'We really can't start the party without you.'

Joy smiled gratefully at him and set off towards the house, hurt by Mick's coldness. She couldn't be bothered to see if he had registered her departure.

What she really wanted to do was go back to the stable and see if she could provide the animal with some relief. But Calum knew what he was doing and it wasn't for her to interfere.

*

After the plates from the main course were taken away, the wine glasses were refilled and Prue announced that every man was to stand and move three seats along, which they all did. The theatre director ended up on Joy's left while Dion took the seat to her right. Mick had landed between Prue and the artist from Cornwall. Poor Simon had to find common ground with the giggler.

'How's the patient doing?' Joy asked Dion, speaking in French without realising she had.

238

'Calum is doing what he can until the horse is seen by the vet,' said Dion.

'If the horse hasn't been ridden for a month, chances are it's a recurring injury,' said Joy.

She and Dion chatted easily about horses, farming and the delights of visiting other countries.

'I grew up in Limoges, which is only about three hours from Bordeaux, so I think I was always destined to work in the wine industry. Did you always want to study veterinary science?' Dion asked.

'Always. At least, for as long as I can remember.'

'And as your mother is French, I assume you have spent some time in France?'

'A few trips, when I was younger. My mother grew up in Tours so I have a family link to that area.' But as she spoke, Joy was distracted by the sight of Mick asking the waiter for glass of Scotch. Joy looked at him in astonishment. In all the time they'd been together, not once had she seen him drink a drop of alcohol – not even for a celebratory toast. A wave of worry washed over her. Mick had pushed his knife and fork politely around his plate but she saw that he hadn't eaten a thing. Over the next hour, during dessert and cheese, Mick finished a second, third and fourth glass of Scotch, with the fifth spilling partially over the white damask tablecloth and onto Prue's dress.

'Prue,' Mick slurred. 'I'm . . . I'm so, so sorry.'

His head dropped to his chest and then, without warning, he slid from the chair to the floor. Joy jumped up and rushed around to the other side of the table, embarrassed by Mick's drunken performance and concerned that he had hurt himself.

'Simon, help the poor man,' Chess bellowed as Jack and Dave leapt up to assist Joy.

Mick was lying on the floor, his eyes closed and his breathing shallow.

'It's not the alcohol,' said Joy. 'He's having some sort of allergic reaction.'

Simon and Jack worked to sit Mick up. Dave looked at Joy.

'Has he done a test today, do you know?' said Dave.

'What do you mean, test? What sort of test?' said Joy.

Dave looked taken aback. 'A blood glucose test. What other sort of test does Mick need to do?'

It took only a few seconds for Joy to understand the situation they were dealing with. Mick hadn't eaten anything and had been drinking to excess. It would take much, much longer to understand why.

'Oh my god. He's diabetic?' said Joy.

'You didn't know?' said Dave, glancing at Jack and Simon.

'He's having a hypoglycaemic episode. Quick,' said Joy. 'We need something sweet. Some honey. Some sugar cubes.'

The artist scooped up the silver sugar dish and passed it across. Using two fingers Joy pushed the sugar cubes, two at a time, into Mick's mouth.

'I'll get his kit,' said Dave.

'Follow me,' said Prue, and they hurried from the room.

'I think it might be a good idea for the rest of us to move to the sitting room and give Mick some privacy. Do you need us to call an ambulance, or a doctor at the very least?' Chess asked.

Mick was trying to open his eyes and orientate himself by pushing at Simon and Jack as he came around.

'He's coming to. I think we'll be all right,' Simon replied.

Dave returned and handed Joy a zip-up leather bathroom

tote that she'd never seen before. Inside she found a glucose test strip. Familiar with the process from her studies, Joy pricked the tip of Mick's finger with a needle, then allowed the test strip to absorb the drop of blood.

While the test strip went to work, Joy looked carefully through the contents of the bag. The units of insulin were neatly stowed, as were the needles and Mick's injection schedule. Joy could see that Mick had already taken a dose earlier that evening. The time and unit amount were recorded on a card. The last thing Mick needed right now was more insulin.

Within five minutes Mick was sitting in a chair. Thirty minutes later he was talking coherently and asking for some water. He was totally unaware of most of what had just happened. He thought someone had given him a glass of wine, but that was about it. Simon, Jack and Dave helped Joy get him upstairs and into bed. When Joy was certain he was asleep and breathing normally, she went downstairs to reassure everyone that he was all right.

'What can I get you, dear?' said Prue, placing her arm around Joy's shoulders. 'What an evening you've had. Anything. Just name it.'

'I wouldn't mind a cup of tea,' said Joy with a sigh.

'Coming right up.'

*

When Mick opened his eyes the following morning his headache was gone, and so was Joy. He knew where she was. Her riding boots weren't next to the wardrobe.

The black envelope-sized tote containing his insulin lay in full view on the bedside table next to his water glass: the constant companion he'd always been so good at concealing. Until now. Mick blinked at it, the reality of the situation dawning on him. He'd kept his diabetes hidden from Joy, and just about anyone else he'd ever known, since he was seventeen. He wasn't even sure why anymore. Well, that time was clearly past. Mick did a blood glucose test then administered the amount of insulin his body needed. He showered then dressed and ate the plain wholegrain toast and slices of orange that had been left on the dressing table.

Mick felt exhaustion roll over him when he thought of the explaining he had to do.

Pulling on his shoes, he went in search of Joy.

*

Joy had been working the brush gently over the thorough-bred's inky coat for at least half an hour, starting at the withers and moving her way along the back to his strong hindquarters. Then she tackled his mane and tail, chest and legs. She patted the patient each time she completed the groom, then started all over again. In this secluded corner of the stables, Joy had found the stillness she was looking for. She had to get away from the house and the rest of the guests. Away from Mick.

The horse's drooping head lifted slightly and he flared his nostrils in response to the sound of a footfall outside his stall. Disinterested, he closed his eyes.

'I thought I'd find you here,' said Mick, with artificial cheerfulness that wasn't fooling Joy. He rested his arms on the top of the half-door and waited while Joy continued, talking to the gelding as if they were on their own.

'You'll come good,' she said, feathering out the mane with her fingers. 'Some rest, that's what you need.'

Sometime between forcing sugar cubes down Mick's throat and picking up the grooming brush, Joy had been severely disillusioned in her ability to judge people. A window of disbelief had opened and the view was unpredictable. Keeping her hands busy somehow helped her to order her thoughts. Joy gave the horse another pat, then looked at Mick and unlatched the stable door. He came in and touched her tenderly on her arm.

'I'm sorry. I should have told you.'

'You're damn right you should have.'

Mick shook his head, struggling to find words to explain the unexplainable.

'I have so many questions, I don't even know where to start,' said Joy.

'Let's find a quiet place to sit and talk,' said Mick.

'No. Not at the moment. I'm too angry. Too hurt. We'll talk when we get back to London. But tell me this – who *does* know you're a diabetic?'

'Only the boys,' said Mick.

'Not Robert? Rebecca?'

'No. And I didn't want them to know. Don't ask me why, it's just how it is. It's the way it's always been for me.'

'When were you first diagnosed? Type one diabetes, I'm guessing?'

Mick placed one hand in his pocket and ran the other through his hair. He shifted on his feet before looking away.

'I was a teenager,' he said. 'It wasn't long before I left school.'

'Well, that explains why Dave and Jack know.' Joy replaced the brush she was still holding and they walked to the entrance to the stables without speaking.

'Have I cast a dampener over the whole weekend, do you think?' asked Mick. 'I'm really sorry. I remember sitting down to dinner, but not much else.'

'No,' said Joy. 'Everyone was concerned about you. Once I assured the boys and Chess and Prue that you were fine, they all kicked on.'

'Even you? I guess I wrecked your night as well,' said Mick.

Not entirely, Joy thought. Under the circumstances, she didn't feel the need to elaborate about how the rest of the night had gone.

She'd never kept anything from Mick and the moment between her and Dion had been nothing. Really nothing.

She'd just been so hurt. So vulnerable.

And Dion had been there. When Mick hadn't.

CHAPTER 13

As the anniversary of Joy's first year in the UK drew closer, she felt that, unexpectedly, after everything that had happened, she and Mick had become closer too. It had been a year of growth for both of them, and they'd come through it together.

As time passed, Joy become more and more certain she did not want to leave London or Mick. Like a yearling straight from the safety of the round yard into the freedom of the paddocks, she had pushed aside her nerves and lack of experience and made a living out of modelling, had come to love a city and a country she'd never lived in before, and come to terms with the fact that no matter how much you might love someone, you can never know them one hundred per cent. That idea was an illusion.

Robert kept the band's gig schedule as busy as was humanly possible while giving Mick and Dave enough time to work on new material. Joy was modelling practically full-time. She liked the fact that she didn't have to work a nine-to-five job to earn a living, could turn down work she didn't want to do and say no to jobs that interfered with her short trips to Scotland or Ireland and other parts of the British Isles, paid for by the very decent money she was earning. There were some weeks when she was booked solid with photo shoots or parades, and other times when her week consisted of going to a couple of castings, then browsing the antique shops and vintage stores she loved so much, never knowing what she might discover – perhaps a silk-lined jacket or handbag from the 1960s. This lifestyle suited her perfectly.

One night, while looking back through her journal, Joy was surprised to read how sequentially and clearly she'd written about what had happened at the weekend house party in Gloucestershire the previous summer. *A turning point, for several reasons!* she'd written on the top of one page, before detailing what Mick and she had talked about back in London afterwards, the morning they'd sat on a rug in Kensington Gardens and spoken about it properly.

Although there was no reason Mick should feel embarrassed about being a diabetic – the very word Joy remembered Mick using – it was not for Joy, or anyone else for that matter, to tell him how he should feel about a condition he'd have for the rest of his life. Perhaps Mick's desire to be just like his mates growing up, while dealing with the health issue he had no control over, was the reason he liked neatness, order and punctuality – and preferred to keep his diabetes a secret.

The arrival of Rebecca Bruce at the start of Joy's second summer in the UK was a breath of fresh air, and Rebecca was a welcome addition to their Antipodean tribe. She was part of a never-ending stream of Australian and New Zealander twenty-somethings, all keen to work and party, London style. Having tried to get her own agency off the ground and realising that the talent pool was too small and that the 'Big Boys' were never going to let her play in their sandpit, Rebecca had sold her car, packed up her bits and pieces, said a tearful farewell to Tracey and bought a one-way ticket to London. Robert, having long since dispensed with Mandy, who arrived late, left early and made coffee that wasn't fit for human consumption, gave Rebecca a job on the spot. Joy and Mick couldn't stop laughing as Bec retold the story to them over a Sunday afternoon beer at the White Horse Inn.

'I took one look around that pigsty he proudly calls an office and told him how it was going to be,' said Rebecca. '"Robert," I said, "I'll be your PA, not your secretary. We'll get someone part-time for that role. I'll work for you every god-given hour and always have your back. But there's to be no skimping on my expenses when I travel with you. I want a clothing and travel allowance. And I want a month's salary upfront."' Rebecca took a sip of her ale. 'He looked at me and said, "Anything else?"' Rebecca mimicked Robert's broad Aussie accent and they all laughed.

'And?' said Joy, knowing that with Bec there had to be a kicker to the story.

'"And I want our agreement in writing."'

'Ha!' shouted Mick, hitting the table with his fist.

'I know. Sassy of me. If ever there was a man and an office that needed redeeming, Robert Flare Management is it.'

*

The band's fourth album, *Conflict of Interest*, went to number one in Australia after only six weeks and debuted on the UK charts at number nine. It was played on repeat at open-air festivals, pubs, clubs and concert halls. Dance music was a world-wide phenomenon and getting stronger. Records sold in their millions to vinyl devotees who pawed over every artistic detail of an album's front and back cover and the inside sleeve. Printed lyrics that often accompanied an album were analysed for their meaning, talked about and committed to memory.

There was a rhythm to Joy and Mick's relationship that allowed them to be a couple while at the same time pursue their individual passions. During the days they barely saw each other as they went their separate ways to work. But then there were the nights Mick, Joy and their friends were ushered through the door of one of their favourite clubs to dance and party until three or four in the morning. Sometimes Joy felt she could hardly be closer to Mick; their connection was undeniable, electric. But there were still times when she felt him pull away from her; close up and withdraw into his own world. Nothing she did during those times could induce him to talk about what was bothering him. Joy could usually convince herself that this was just Mick, a part of him that was unlikely ever to change, but it worried at her all the same.

If the band was playing somewhere close to London, Joy would go to at least one of the gigs, to show support and because Mick liked to get her take on the show: how the lights looked, the order of the songs. Joy preferred to be among the audience as opposed to side-stage. She told Mick it was a more authentic concert experience than standing backstage or in the wings. Between concert dates, media commitments and working on new material, Around Midnight could almost touch that 'top of the mountain' Robert was always talking about.

And yet, as any mountaineer will confirm, the view on the climb up is not the same as the view from the top.

*

After almost two years abroad Joy felt very much at home in London. Scarlet and James were consistent letter writers, and when one of their bulky envelopes arrived Joy would make herself a mug of tea, curl up on the sofa and devour all the news from home. She could never be sure at what time of day she'd receive a long-distance telephone call from her parents – Tim was not one to worry about the time difference between Australia and the UK – but these came regularly as well.

'This is Australia calling. Can I connect you?' the operator would say. And the moment Joy heard her father's or mother's voice, she was back home again. She could almost smell the gum-scented air. She could picture Tim in his office, his feet up on the desk and one hand behind his head, the window behind slightly open to the breeze. Or Avril, staring down at the Melbourne peak-hour traffic as she began her work day. While Avril detailed all her business dealings and asked after Joy and Mick, Tim was all horses, cattle and the goings-on at Monaghan.

'We got a good price for those steers I was telling you about,' he'd said with delight the last time he called. 'And did I mention Jordy and Duncan are coming up for a couple of weeks?'

'You did, Dad. Give them my love.'

It was during a conversation with Avril, not long before Mick and Joy were due to meet her parents for a holiday in France, that Joy sought her mother's opinion about the subject that was, these days, never far from her thoughts.

'Mum. Can I ask you something?' Joy could hear the hesitant tone of her own voice.

'Of course, darling. Anything.' And, as if she sensed the nature of the question, Avril added, 'Let me close my office door.'

Joy took a deep breath. 'Did you . . . I mean, have you always told Dad everything about your life? You know. Things about your childhood. Events that happened to you. That sort of thing.'

'Well, yes,' said Avril, pausing for a moment. 'Pretty much. I mean, your father doesn't know every single detail of my life, but the significant moments, the monumental events, certainly.'

After all their time together, and although she had tried to comprehend it, Joy had never understood why Mick had not told her he was a diabetic. His aversion to telling her the truth about his medical condition sat at the back of her mind like one big unexplained question and she hated it. It felt like there was a void between them and she wasn't sure how to close the gap. Plus, she couldn't help but wonder what else might be hiding there.

Avril interrupted the long pause.

'It's only a couple of weeks until your father and I see you both. Why don't we pick up this conversation then? Better still, over a cold glass of champagne. How does that sound?'

Joy had always had the most explosive as well as the most productive discussions with her mother face to face. Her mother's suggestion was a good one.

'I'd love that, Mum,' said Joy. 'Let's talk then.'

As she hung up the phone, she burst into tears.

*

Joy put her mother on speaker phone and kept packing – throwing her clothes into the suitcase with fury.

'Mick won't be coming to France with me,' said Joy.

The shouting match she and Mick had had the previous day over the phone from New York was still ringing in her head. 'The band's extended their tour in America so Mick can't get away as planned,' she said. 'They won't be back until just before Christmas. It's going to be even crazier for them next year. They're planning to release their fifth album and Robert's in discussions about their first world tour.'

'That sounds very busy indeed,' Avril replied evenly. 'When do you expect to arrive? Our flight lands at two o'clock.'

'I get into Charles de Gaulle at midday,' said Joy, removing a pair of jeans from her suitcase.

'You'll have a bit of time to kill then,' said Avril.

'That's fine, Mum. Two hours is nothing. I'll get a coffee and read a book while I wait for you. And Madame Leon doesn't know about her surprise birthday party, does she?' Joy picked up the receiver again, muting the speaker.

'Yes, she does,' said Avril. 'There was too much to organise. They had to tell her, which was a good idea. It's given her something to look forward to these past six months.'

'How is she?'

'She's all right, but not great. She's beaten cancer twice, as you know, and the last time I saw her I could see how much she'd slowed down. But she's a fighter and loves life. She has no idea we will all be there. She thinks we're on a cruise to Fiji.'

'Well, I can't wait to see you and Dad on Thursday. Safe travels, Mum.'

*

251

Avril reached across and touched Tim on his arm as they approached the elaborate wrought iron gates of Chateau de Vinieres.

'Pull over please, Tim,' she said, 'and let these other cars behind us go ahead.'

The dark slate roof and pale-grey walls of the chateau were only partially obscured by the heavy branches and remaining russet autumn leaves that clung like paper decorations to the poplar and plane trees lining the driveway.

'Are you all right, Mum?' said Joy from the back seat.

'It doesn't matter how many times I come through these gates,' said Avril, starting to cry, 'sadness overtakes me and then,' she wiped at her eyes with a tissue, 'it's gone, done with, and I'm so happy to be home again.'

Avril had timed their arrival to coincide with the start of Madame Leon's eightieth birthday party, having liaised with Madame Leon's niece for months leading up to the celebration. Despite carrying the heartache of losing both her only child and husband during the Second World War, Madame Leon had surrounded herself with her sister's and brother's children and the relatives of her late husband. She'd lived in Tours her entire life, like her mother and grandmother before her.

'It all looks exactly the same,' said Joy as the trees rolled slowly by. 'Although there seem to be a lot more vines than before. I tried to catch a white pony in this little paddock. Do you remember, Mum?'

'Every time you got close with the headstall in your hand, the little monkey would kick out and run off,' said Avril. 'You told the manager that French horses had much worse tempers than Australian horses and he laughed and agreed with you.'

'Well that white pony certainly did,' said Joy.

Madame Leon was standing in the centre of the large sitting room, greeting the arriving guests. Her black-brown bob – a 'touch of enhancement' she called it, never wanting to be grey – framed her oval face.

Avril, Tim and Joy hung back until there was only Madame Leon and her niece, Charlotte.

When Madame Leon's gaze fell on them, she blinked in astonishment and put her hands to her face. 'Oh! I can't believe it,' she cried, spreading her chiffon-covered arms wide and falling into Avril's embrace. 'You're here! What a wonderful surprise. When? How? Tim. Joy, look at you! So *sophistiquée*.'

She embraced them all – holding the moment for as long as she could.

And then the celebrations began.

'My dear friends have travelled all the way from Australia to celebrate with us all,' Madame Leon explained to everyone as they were all ushered into the grand dining room. 'What an honour it is to have them here.'

As the guests took their seats for dinner, Madame Leon insisted that room be made for Avril, Tim and Joy at her table. Beaming, she whispered in Joy's ear, 'I still can't believe you're here. I'm not letting you or your parents out of my sight.'

Joy was reaching for another glass of champagne when the housekeeper approached.

'Excuse me, *mademoiselle*. There is a phone call for you in the study.'

Joy raced through to the next room, trying to steady her glass.

'Hello?' she said into the receiver. 'Mick, is that you?'

'Babe, how are you? It's so good to hear your voice.'

Joy took a deep breath. She was acutely aware that

their last conversation had descended into an argument and ended with Mick hanging up on her. He'd never been that rude before, and Joy wasn't prepared to tolerate such behaviour in the future.

'Where are you? It's really hard to hear,' she shouted, pressing the phone to her ear.

'We're in Austin, Texas. I'm backstage, on a pay phone. Can you believe it? So much for fame and fortune. That's the warm-up act in the background. We don't go on for another couple of hours. How's France?'

'Great so far. Madame Leon had no idea we were coming and it's been a fabulous night. What time is it there? How was last night's concert?'

'Oh. About six-thirty, and last night was a blast. I'm glad we've got a three-day break after tonight. My voice has taken a hammering.'

The line crackled and Joy barely caught what Mick was saying.

'I'll sign off before this line cuts out. I love you, babe. I'll call you from LA. And I'm sorry. For everything.'

The line went dead and Joy replaced the receiver.

At least tonight it had been Upbeat Mick, which was the one Joy liked the most. When the silent, unpredictable Mick appeared, it was usually after Upbeat Mick, when the band had pulled an all-nighter. While Mick was sworn off wine, he had started drinking whisky during the recording of the last album. Not much and not often, but it was enough for Joy and the boys to need to keep an eye on him when they were out socially. Simon had suggested to Joy that some of Mick's mood swings might be attributed to his diabetes, and Joy agreed.

Joy rejoined the party, but a niggling worry about Mick, so far away, remained with her.

Avril noticed how quiet her daughter had become after the call. 'Everything okay, *chérie?*' she said.

Joy took her mother's hand. 'Let's talk later. Not now. Tonight is for celebrating.'

*

Joy gently flicked the cornflowers as she and Avril walked across the field.

'What a night,' said Avril, spreading her arms wide, closing her eyes and lifting her face to the mid-morning sun.

'Mum.'

Avril dropped her arms and looked at her daughter.

'Are you and Dad okay, financially? I know there was something dodgy going on with your accountant a few years ago. I never asked what happened with your court case in the end. Too absorbed with my own life. Did that get sorted?'

They were walking back towards the chateau, the knee-high grass swishing around their legs.

'Yes,' said Avril. 'That's all been resolved.' They stopped and Avril touched Joy on the arm.

'I should have been more upfront with you about our monetary situation. I regret that now. You're a grown woman and have been for quite a while. It took a while for that to sink in.'

'What happened? Did you get your money back?'

Avril shook her head. 'No. Sometimes in life it's best to cut your losses, as they say. Don Whitby was fired from Parkers and although we initiated legal proceedings, the process of litigation was going to be too long, too costly and simply too draining. In the end, your father and I decided to let it go.'

'What did James have to say about the situation?'

'He agreed with us,' said Avril as she linked arms with Joy. 'Besides, my bridal business changed everything for your father and me. Talk about being in the right place at the right time. I caught the start of that wave and I'll ride it to the end.'

'Kind of like our family motto, isn't it? *Timing is everything*. Go, girl!' said Joy, and she handed her mother the bunch of blue flowers she had gathered. She didn't want to spoil the moment by bringing up her worries about Mick.

*

Chateau de Vinieres was a working farm and vineyard and had been for more than three hundred years. Yves Durand, the estate manager, oversaw every aspect of the wine and crop production, along with four full-time staff. He had helped Madame Leon turn what had essentially been a wholesale wine operation into a cellar door and culinary business, open to visitors from early spring through to late autumn. Yves's partner Camille managed the restaurant and the two worked together like clockwork. Joy noted that this was something she'd often seen on country properties: happy couples made some of the best and most dedicated employees.

In the days after the party, Joy got to know Yves and Camille and marvelled at everything they had accomplished at Chateau de Vinieres. Yves showed her the stables and, upon hearing how much she loved to ride, invited her to saddle up any of the horses they kept for guests.

The next morning Joy and Tim went out riding, leaving Avril and Madame Leon alone in the sunroom to catch up and reminisce.

'And Joy's boyfriend,' said Madame Leon as she replaced her coffee cup. 'Mick Harris. Lead vocalist of Almost Midnight, no? What's he like?'

Avril raised her eyebrow. '*Around* Midnight,' she corrected with a smile.

'Yes, that's what I mean. The young ones keep me informed about these things,' Madame Leon replied.

'They still seem madly in love,' said Avril. 'I was concerned, naturally, when Joy deferred university to go to London, but I think it's been the making of her. She got this modelling career of hers off the ground without any help from me. She earns her own money, so some of my influence has rubbed off.'

Avril refilled both their cups and fiddled with the edge of her cuff.

'The first time Joy brought him home to Monaghan to meet the family, I asked my friend James Carmody to look into Mick's background. The births and deaths records confirmed that Mick's mother died when he was ten and his father when he was sixteen. He has no siblings,' said Avril.

'The poor boy,' said Madame Leon. 'Who took care of him? Where did he live?'

'It seems the parents of Dave McCready, one of the other band members and a school friend of Mick's, took him in until he finished school. Then it all becomes a bit scratchy. James couldn't find any criminal record of any sort. And it seems Mick was always into his music so that became his life.'

'And the veterinary studies? Is Joy going to complete her degree?'

'I hope so. She has a ten-year window to finish her final year, so there's still time. But in the end, of course, we can't make her do anything she doesn't want to.'

Madame Leon patted Avril's hand.

'I consider that independent streak of hers a virtue. You have a curious daughter who wants to experience the world and who's not afraid to go in her own direction. She'll find her way to where she's meant to be. You did,' said Madame Leon, 'and what an adventure that turned out to be!'

*

In the end, the extended American tour had gone better than expected, but by the time the band arrived back in the UK, tempers were short, everyone was exhausted and they all agreed that they'd spend Christmas apart for a change. With the temperature hovering around zero, Joy and Mick were in no rush to leave the warmth of their bed on Christmas morning. And by New Year's Eve, London was covered in a thick coating of fresh snow.

'Happy new year, my love,' said Mick as he placed two coffees on the bedside table.

He climbed back into bed and pulled up the covers.

'Can you believe it, 1985!' said Joy. 'How about we do a surprise trip home sometime this year? Catch up with friends and spend some time at the station? We haven't been away just the two of us in I don't know how long.'

'Maybe,' said Mick, but to Joy he sounded rather noncommittal. 'It depends on our concert and recording schedule.'

'Well, find out what's planned and we can work around it. Carve out some time for ourselves.'

'Sure,' said Mick. 'That's a good idea.'

But his words were lacklustre and Joy wondered if she should simply do a trip back to Australia on her own.

A few weeks later, just as winter was relinquishing its

grasp on London, Joy was painting her toenails in the living room when Mick raced through the door. He'd been to visit Robert and Joy had luxuriated in a rare morning with nothing planned.

He threw his satchel onto a chair, gave Joy a swift kiss and headed to the kitchen, returning with a glass of water. He dropped down on the sofa opposite, his face a picture of excitement.

'What's happened?'

'Tom Henderson – you know, the lead singer of The Crime – is bringing together the biggest live concert ever organised to raise money for world hunger. It'll be here in London at Wembley Stadium. Seventy-five acts, starting at midday, playing for sixteen hours. It will be televised to more than one hundred countries with an estimated one-point-five billion viewers, and we're in! We won't get top billing – there'll be a ranking – but we'll be there. We're likely to go on late in the afternoon, early evening. Each band gets a fifteen-minute set.'

'Oh my god. That's brilliant,' said Joy.

'They've only got ten weeks to pull it all together. They want to hold the event in late June or July.'

'What are they calling it?'

'*Music Live*, and I'm telling you, babe, it is going to be huge.'

Joy was excited for the band, but she couldn't help but notice that Mick hadn't spared a single thought for their potential trip back home.

*

Around Midnight took to the stage at six-thirty and were on for exactly fifteen minutes, with Joy, Rebecca and Scarlet watching excitedly in the wings.

Scarlet had arrived in London the day before for a well-earned holiday and was still congratulating herself for her impeccable timing. It was the concert of the decade and she had the best seat in the house!

Everything on the night was timed to precision. After lengthy discussions, the band had decided to perform their four biggest hits.

'This isn't the time to get all arty and go out with something no one's heard before,' Robert had insisted, and if the crowd's rapturous response to Mick's vocals, Simon's drum work and Jack and Dave on guitars was any indication, he was right.

Off the back of the attention *Music Live* was receiving, the record company decided to bring forward the release date for the band's new album, titled *Make of It What You Will*, from October to August, with a UK tour to follow.

In the whirlwind of activity that the concert, the new album, the tour and the band's growing celebrity was causing, Joy felt she could hardly catch her breath. She and Mick were often ships passing in the night, barely seeing each other for more than a few minutes some days, but she felt they were managing. Just.

Then, a week before the band was about to start five nights performing in Manchester, Mick left the band's rehearsal around seven in the evening but wasn't home when Joy got in later that night.

When he still hadn't appeared by six the next morning, Joy called Simon to see if he'd stayed the night at his place.

He hadn't.

Simon contacted Jack and Dave but no one had seen Mick since the rehearsal the day before. Robert was in Liverpool and hadn't spoken to Mick for a couple of days.

Mick would sometimes go to a certain bar or club on

his own, just to see what other bands were doing, or to meet up with a producer or another musician. But for the last few months, since *Music Live* and the release of the album, he'd started going for long walks at night, returning at three or four in the morning. With a modelling schedule that was getting busier and busier, Joy was usually up and gone by eight, so she often didn't see Mick and hadn't been particularly worried at first.

But when he had still not turned up or called by midday, Joy rang her agency and told them she would not make the in-store parade she was supposed to be doing that afternoon. Feeling increasingly uneasy, she waited at the flat for Mick to ring or to hear from one of the guys. A little after four that afternoon, Joy jumped from the sofa when she heard the key rattling in the door. She unlocked the door from the inside and pulled it open. Rebecca was supporting Mick who was unsteady on his feet and whose clothes stank of whisky.

Rebecca rolled her eyes. 'I'm only the good Samaritan in this situation,' she said as she helped Mick inside. 'Call me later. I'll leave you to sort him out.'

'Where the hell have you been for the last twenty-four hours?' said Joy, feeling a giant cocktail of emotions swirling inside her.

'Out,' slurred Mick. 'I need to do a test,' he said. 'I don't feel that good.'

He staggered to the bedroom and while he sat on the end of the bed, Joy found the glucose test strips and went through the same procedure she'd done with Mick many times since the weekend house party years before.

'Missed me, did you, babe?' he said with his eyes half closed. 'I'm here now.'

Joy knew there was no point replying.

When Mick's test and injection were done and Joy could see he was breathing normally and had gone to sleep, she pulled the bedclothes up over his shoulders and left the room.

She phoned Simon and filled him in. Then, when there was nothing left to say, she burst into tears, covering her mouth as she cried.

'My lovely Joy,' said Simon. 'Go and put the kettle on and make yourself a cup of tea. I know you won't have eaten a thing for ages so I'll be over with some dinner very soon.'

'I'm so sick of this,' said Joy, her voice breaking. 'The high highs, the low lows. The mood swings. And now going off and not telling me where he's been or why. I don't think I can take it anymore.'

'I'm out the door the moment I put down the phone. I'll be with you in no time.'

*

Simon cleared away the cups and saucers and pulled on his jacket.

'I'm going to stay at Bec's for a few days,' said Joy as she hugged him goodbye. 'Can you, Jack and Dave keep an eye on Mick? I can't do this on my own anymore. I'll see Mick before you all leave for this next round of shows, but he needs to start considering someone other than himself.'

Simon nodded sympathetically. 'He's lovable and a nightmare at the same time,' he said. 'You do realise he loves you madly? But I know he has his demons.'

'Well, he needs to sort himself out. And if he won't talk to me about whatever's troubling him, he has to talk to someone.'

*

Mick and Dave sat at the small kitchen table, two mugs featuring an image of the Union Jack between them.

'Do you remember me telling you about the time I ran into Marcus Tan?' said Mick.

'That nerdy guy from school? Vaguely,' said Dave. 'That was like, three years ago. Stockbroker, isn't he?'

'A lawyer. He works for Sun Press Media. Anyway, the other night, I'd just got back from our rehearsal and the phone rang. It was Marcus. I hadn't spoken to him since that day I ran into him on Bond Street. Seems like a lifetime ago now. Anyway, he said he wanted to give me the heads-up about a journalist who had called him. Some guy called Bryce Mitchell, who said he was writing a feature article about Around Midnight and wanted to talk to anyone who'd been to school with Jack, you or me, and who knew us when we were just starting out.'

Dave listened, sensing where this was headed.

'Marcus is no fool so his guard went up straight away,' said Mick. 'You know how these bloodhound journos operate. Then he asked Marcus if he knew any of the details about, as Marcus put it, "Mick Harris and the accident in 1969".'

Mick brought his hands to his forehead, then dropped them to the table.

'What did Marcus say to this guy?' said Dave.

'Played dumb. Said he didn't know about any accident. Marcus told me he tried to get more out of the scumbag – he got his name and contact details and found out as much as he could about this so-called article before hanging up. Marcus said he'd let me know if this guy calls again or if he hears about the article going to print.'

Mick and Dave sat in silence for a moment. Eventually, Mick sipped his tea and leant back in the chair.

'After that, I took off. I just walked and walked. I ended up at Regent's Park, and then some pub in Chelsea,' said Mick.

'Where the hell did you sleep? On a bench?'

'No. I went to Robert's office, banged on the door, and then I remembered he was away but that I had a key. I let myself in and fell asleep on the floor. Rebecca turned up at about, I don't know, three in the afternoon? Something like that. She drove me home.'

'She's a bloody champ, that Bec,' said Dave. 'And you've got an ally in Marcus Tan, by the sounds of it.'

'I knew some bastard would dig this up one day,' said Mick despairingly.

'Mate, it wasn't your fault,' said Dave, trying to process how this could possibly play out. 'And who gives a shit if the story does come out? Our fans are still going to love our music. Jack, Simon and I aren't going anywhere. We're brothers, man. Whose life is it going to impact, really?'

Mick pivoted the mug between his fingers then he looked Dave straight in the eyes.

'Mine, Dave,' he said. 'Every day. Every hour. Mine.'

CHAPTER 14

The band's world tour was going to kick off in the UK in March, then was headed to Japan, with the third and biggest leg to take place during the American late summer and autumn. The final stage would see the boys come home to play a sellout, Australia-wide concert season, finishing in Sydney at the end of November.

When Joy had come home from Bec's a few days after Mick's disappearing act, he had apologised profusely, begging Joy to forgive him. It was the stress, he said, the thought of the album and the tour simply overwhelming him. It wouldn't happen again; he would sort himself out and find better ways to deal with the pressure. And because he seemed so abjectly miserable about what he'd done and determined to turn things around, Joy accepted his apology.

The week before Mick, Joy and the boys headed up to Gloucestershire to celebrate the festive season with Simon and his extended family at Brayleedon Manor, Mick got a late-night call from Marcus Tan. Marcus began by wishing Mick a merry Christmas and telling him what a great night he'd had at the house-warming the previous month. After three years in their small rented flat, Mick had bought a two-storey terrace in Chelsea with a postage stamp–sized courtyard, which had cost him just about every cent he had in the bank. He wanted the two of them to have a real home, he'd told Joy. They were trying to work things out. The house was Mick's idea of a fresh start.

The tenor of Marcus's voice changed from cheerful to grave, suggesting that the pleasantries were over. He cleared his throat.

'I've got a close friend in the publishing world,' he said, 'who's given me some information about Bryce Mitchell.'

'Not this bloody article again?' said Mick, his heart sinking. 'That guy's like a dog with a bone.'

'There's a bit more to it than that, unfortunately. Apparently there's a bidding war going on between three top publishers over a biography Mitchell's written about you and the band. And the word is, whoever publishes will want to release the book to coincide with your Australian tour.'

'Shit,' said Mick. 'I didn't think this scumbag would write a book. Christ! Do you know what's in it?'

'Oh, my source tells me there's plenty of praise and ass-licking, but to be honest, it sounds like it's nothing more than salacious gossip tarted up as a quality biography. This guy's intent on riding on the coat-tails of your band's success. Mitchell goes in sweet then turns the knife on all of you. But particularly on you, your teenage years and early twenties, and Simon's sexuality. Of course, there's a wealth of material about Jack and Dave and they certainly don't come out of it too well either. It's well written, apparently, and he's researched all of you extensively.'

'But why a biography? That's a hell of a lot of work unless he thinks he's got something to say that no one else has,' said Mick.

'That's exactly what his agent said when Mitchell first pitched the idea of a biography to him, according to my source. But here's the kicker. While doing his research, Bryce Mitchell got hold of some amateur footage of a concert you did back in 1981 at the Woolshed in Brisbane, where you played the piano and sang a ballad. That lit the touchpaper, apparently.'

Mick remembered the moment clearly. For a long time afterwards, he'd berated himself for allowing his emotions to get the better of him and he had vowed he'd never play that song live ever again.

'Give me a minute, will you, mate?' said Mick.

Holding the cordless phone tightly to his ear, Mick walked through the kitchen and out into the freezing courtyard. He looked back at Joy who was standing at the kitchen window, her arms hugging her body, imitating someone shivering. He gave her a wave and turned away to speak.

'Go on,' said Mick.

'This Mitchell character has managed to get a lot of his sources to go on the record – direct quotes. Legals have looked at the manuscript and I'm told this guy's work is solid. It's got the green light.'

'Can you give me any specifics? Any details at all?'

There was a long pause on the line.

'Mitchell's used the angle that many of your songs are about your search for redemption – his words – but he's been very careful not to say anything that could land him in court.'

Mick's chest burned as his throat tightened.

'It was something you said just before you played the song that sparked his interest, apparently,' said Marcus. 'I've seen the chapter titles and while they don't mean anything to me I thought you'd likely recognise their significance, if there is any.'

Mick wiped away the sweat that had sprung up on his brow. He listened as Marcus read aloud nine predictable chapter titles for a biography about a rock band.

'. . . "More Money than Sense", "On the Road" . . .' Marcus continued, 'and the final chapter.'

Mick wedged his free hand into the pocket of his jeans. 'What is it? "Just Another Band" or "One Bent Pom and Three Straight Aussies"? Does he stick the boot in?'

'I don't know. The last chapter title sounds quite sweet,' said Marcus. 'He quotes you from that 1981 concert. He's called the final chapter, "This One's for Bonnie".'

*

Robert had kept the entourage for the tour as tight as possible and given all the media and promotions arrangements to Rebecca to coordinate and confirm, leaving the band's manager to do what he loved best: wheel and deal and keep the rock-and-roll juggernaut moving ever forward.

Around Midnight had been taken into the hearts of their UK fans and they broke all their previous ticket sales records on the first leg of their tour. The night before the boys left for Japan, Joy cooked Mick's all-time favourite meal, a roast leg of lamb with potatoes and all the trimmings. Mick had sworn off alcohol, so they toasted with sodas and lime to their love, to each other and the tour, and laughed as they talked about the night they met, their first date and a host of other happy memories. Neither of them brought up any of the darker issues, as if by ignoring them they could will them into the past.

When they'd finished, Mick put down his knife and fork and took hold of Joy's hands.

'I can't wait until November,' he said.

He disappeared into their bedroom and returned to place an unmistakable cherry-red ring box on the table. He swept a lock of Joy's hair from her face and leant forward and kissed her.

'Will you marry me?'

Joy stared at the box for a moment, then reached for it with trembling fingers. She was shocked. Excited. Surprised. Amazed, all at once. Her heart raced. 'Yes, yes, yes,' she said, crying and laughing simultaneously. It was everything she'd wanted.

Wasn't it?

Any doubts soon vanished in the exquisite excitement of the moment and Mick's contagious exuberance. He pulled her into his arms and they fell back against the wall, kissing passionately.

'You'd better open the box, don't you think?' said Mick.

'Oh, yes. I guess there's a ring in there.'

She opened it slowly and gasped as the diamond solitare glistened. Mick slipped it onto Joy's finger and lifted her hand to his lips.

'I wanted to propose when we're both back in Australia but I couldn't wait.'

Joy held up her left hand and stared at the ring.

'It's so beautiful. Oh my god. Have you spoken to Mum and Dad? Did you tell them what you were planning, ask for their blessing or something like that? We don't need anyone's permission, I know that, but –'

Mick brought his fingers up to Joy's lips.

'Of course I was going to talk to Avril and Tim. And I still will. But seeing you sitting opposite me, the two of us together like this . . . It felt like the right time.'

Joy looked down at her hand again, and into Mick's eyes – full of love for her. And a clarity deep inside her framed her words.

'Why don't we keep this just between us until we're back home in November,' she said. 'You leave tomorrow, so we can't celebrate with everyone. I know we're going to meet up in LA, but I don't think that'll be the right time to celebrate either. Let's announce our engagement at the end of the tour. What do you think?'

Mick burst out laughing then wrapped his arms firmly around her waist.

'I know what you're thinking. You'd like the big announcement to happen at Monaghan Station on Christmas Eve, where I'll slide the ring onto your finger with all your family around. Have I got it right?'

'You've got it in one.' Joy smiled as she slipped the ring back into its pretty box.

Back where it belongs, she thought.

*

It was a very strange time. Although she and Mick spoke often on the phone, Joy felt she was living the life of a single woman in London, living by herself and building her own busy social life around work. In fact, she had never been more independent, and despite missing Mick's company dearly, she liked the feeling.

Joy had been right about the so-called seven days together in LA in August. She and Mick were rarely on their own and when they did manage to snatch a few minutes together, there was always someone looking for Mick or somewhere he had to be.

From what Joy observed during her whirlwind visit, Robert had long ago lost control of the manageable entourage once the band touched down in the States. According to Bec, the US record label and their in-house promotions team took over. Mick's rule that there was to be no one in the green room with the band prior to going on stage had become impossible to enforce. His pre-concert agitation was becoming worse and the rest of the band insisted that Rebecca be in the room as well, as she was the only one apart from Joy who was able to calm him down.

Six weeks into the tour of the USA, Rebecca had morphed into a sounding board for Simon, Jack and Dave as they watched Mick transition through some spectacular highs and even more impressive lows that sometimes lasted right up until the moment they took to the stage.

'I have to be honest,' Bec said to Joy as they stood backstage on Joy's second night in LA. 'I'm increasingly unsure which Mick will show up every night.'

Just before they went on stage, Mick would jump up and down on the spot, pumping himself up. He'd shake his head and lead the boys out to the roar of their fans. As the tour had progressed, Rebecca confided to Joy, he had started seeking Rebecca out and opening up to her during late-night conversations in a bar or hotel room. There were times when he felt himself creeping closer and closer to cracking wide open, he'd said. Then the city and venue would change, the temperature would alter and his inner landscape would settle for a while.

'I'm here to dole out the headache tablets to Robert and keep an eye on what goes on backstage,' Rebecca murmured to Joy as they stood at the back of yet another press conference.

It was immediately clear to Joy that the relaxed, excited and enthusiastic person Mick had been before the band had left for Japan had disappeared. She felt a twinge of jealousy that Mick was talking to Rebecca when he hadn't felt he could talk to Joy herself – but she supposed she was glad he was talking to someone. When she took in the heightened activity, the packed schedules, the stress and the pressure of the tour – not to mention all the people who seemed to crowd around the band these days – she sensed things were nearing a breaking point.

'They wanted to go all the way to the top,' said Joy, 'and here they are. But all these hangers-on, the groupies. How manageable are those?'

Rebecca gave Joy a sideways glance.

'You don't want to know,' she said sombrely.

Joy turned to face Rebecca and took her by the arm.

'Yes, I do, Bec. Does Mick fool around? I couldn't stand to be one of those girlfriends who's the last one to know.'

Rebecca looked her in the eye. 'Mick's got his vices, but the Mick I know only has time for one woman, and that's you. Rare in this industry, I know. I just call it as I see it. Yes, he was wild when he was younger. And sure, there were women nonstop for a long, long time back then. But most of that had stopped even before he met you. I think that's why he's so attached to you. You're not overawed by the whole scene. You're your own person. He respects that. Admires you so much.'

Joy nodded. 'If you're my friend, I hope you care about me enough that you'd tell me if there was anything going on behind my back. I know the old adage, "What happens on tour stays on tour", but I promise, I won't shoot the messenger, Bec.'

Rebecca squeezed her arm. 'I know. Now, Jack and Dave. That's another story altogether,' she said, and she and Joy slipped out the door as the questions dragged on.

*

Joy closed her journal and reached for the empty place on her left ring finger. Sometime between her first cup of coffee and the offer of hot hand towels by the flight attendant, she'd managed to fill five pages effortlessly.

Her time in LA had unsettled her in a way nothing else had before. It was as if she was seeing the excesses, the hype, the unreality of the life Mick and the boys were living through fresh eyes. Mick may not be cheating on her, but there had been an unpredictability about him that felt new.

Is this what I really want? she asked herself over and over. *Do I even want to do the marriage thing? Will it bring us closer together?*

If Mick's energy levels had been off the charts while they were in LA together, it was the complete reverse the day Joy left for London. It was a slower, more sombre and secretive fiancé who kissed her goodbye moments before they all piled into the limo for the short drive to another open-air stadium. Everything about the trip had been draining, and it wasn't until Joy was checking in her suitcase that she realised that neither of them had even mentioned their engagement. They had been either too tired, running late for something or Joy was with Rebecca while Mick was doing an interview, rehearsing or asleep.

Touching down at Heathrow, Joy felt nothing but relief.

In the cold light of the London dawn, she could see that something had shifted between her and Mick and it wasn't just because of the pressure of the tour. There had been a distance, a remoteness to the way they'd spoken to each other, touched each other. Or hadn't.

She thought of the night Mick had proposed. High on love. Clutching the ring. Kissing her like he'd never kissed her before. Everything had seemed possible then because Mick made her feel that it was. That the two of them were invincible.

And I wanted to believe it, she thought. *I wanted to believe in the dream of us.*

But now, she was on the countdown to going home to Australia for the first time in almost five years and she couldn't wait. The intended twelve-month sabbatical had turned into a much longer adventure that was starting to feel directionless, despite all the work and travelling she'd done. She felt physically and emotionally wrung out.

She needed to go home.

*

A sun-bathed Sydney was putting on a spectacular welcome home. The iridescent blue of the harbour flecked with white sails was in stark contrast to the dull winter greys of London.

As the captain announced the local time, Joy closed her eyes, already feeling the warmth and light burrowing into her – illuminating her soul.

At customs, the officer flicked through Joy's passport as he checked the photo in the front and located the date-of-departure stamp.

'You've been away for a while,' he said cheerfully. 'Back for long?'

'I'm not sure,' said Joy. 'Maybe.' She surprised herself with her own admission.

The man raised the stamp and brought it down hard on the countertop, closed the passport and slid it under the gap in the glass screen.

'Welcome home,' he said, motioning for the next passenger.

Scarlet was waiting in the arrivals hall but so too were a team of journalists, photographers and a couple of television cameras. The reporters began thrusting microphones at Joy and shouting questions as cameras clicked, recording her stunned reaction. Scarlet elbowed her way through the throng and took Joy's carry-on bag from her shoulder. She took Joy's hand and they bolted for the sliding doors.

'What's your reaction to Bryce Mitchell's revelations in his new book?' someone called.

'Joy. Do you have anything to say about what happened to –'

A black chauffeur-driven car was waiting at the kerb.

'I thought you might need a quick getaway,' smiled Scarlet as she and Joy hugged in the back seat.

Away from the terminal, Joy wound down her window slightly. The air smelt different; a hint of salt with a touch of a late southerly breeze. The two friends held hands as the backstreets of Mascot whizzed by.

'What the hell was that all about?' said Joy when she'd caught her breath.

'Did Mick not warn you?' Scarlet threw her friend a quizzical glance.

'About what?'

'A biography called *Strangers No More – The Around Midnight Story*,' said Scarlet. 'It was released in Australia yesterday. There's been so much press about it. God, I'm sorry. I thought you'd know about it already.'

Joy swallowed, a heavy feeling blooming in the pit of her stomach. 'No, I didn't know . . . Have you read it? What's in it?'

'I think you need to speak to Mick first. Where is he?'

'They arrived here yesterday from New York so I imagine they all have massive jet lag. They've got a week of R&R before they head to Perth and start the final stage of this never-ending world tour.'

'And you're sure you want to come back to my place? You don't want to go straight to the hotel and see Mick?'

Joy looked out the car window at nothing in particular. She thought about the scene she'd just witnessed at the airport.

'No,' she said. 'I want some time with you. I'd like to hear all about the Children's Hospital, this hot cardiologist you're dating and please, please tell me you're cooking chicken parmigiana for the two of us tonight?'

'Followed by crème brûlée,' said Scarlet. 'And accompanied by an obscene amount of red wine.'

CHAPTER 15

By four in the morning Joy had read the biography cover to cover.

She closed the book, placed it on the coffee table, and lay on Scarlet's sofa looking at the ornate plasterwork of the ceiling. Belief and disbelief sparred with each other in her tired mind. Anger and pain shadow-boxed their way around her heart. Where love was lurking right now, she wasn't sure. Sharing a drink with deceit, she imagined. She wasn't going to wait to call Mick. That would be a waste of his time and hers.

She rang Rebecca at dawn.

'The taxi should be here any minute,' Joy said. 'Please make sure he's up, dressed and has had some coffee. This won't take long because all he'll have to do is listen.'

'He'll be ready,' said Rebecca. 'I'll leave your name with reception. He's on the fifteenth floor. Joy, I begged him to tell you about the book. I pleaded with him to talk to you. I really don't understand why he didn't. I think he was frightened. I don't know.'

'It doesn't matter anymore, Bec,' said Joy. 'I'll see you soon.'

'Please, can we talk before you leave?' said Rebecca.

'I can't. I'm going straight to the airport. I've already spoken to Dad and he's flying down in his Beechcraft to pick me up. I'll be back home by early afternoon. I don't want to see anyone right now – I'm sorry but I just can't, so please don't ambush me in the foyer of the hotel because I'll only keep on walking.'

Scarlet was still sleeping when the taxi arrived. Joy left her a note by the kettle. She told the driver the name of the hotel in The Rocks, and twenty minutes later, once she'd been cleared by security, Joy was in the elevator on her way to the fifteenth floor.

*

Mick opened the door.

He tried to pull her into a hug but Joy walked past him as if he were a stranger. The floor-to-ceiling windows faced the Opera House but she was numb to the grandness of the view, her head pounding with tiredness, questions and pain.

Have I always known it would come to this?

Mick looked as though he'd showered and dressed in a hurry. His shoulder-length hair was still wet. She could smell the mix of his deodorant and cologne. So familiar.

The distance between them felt like an uncrossable canyon. Mick's story was a missed opportunity for genuine togetherness. A togetherness Joy now knew would never be.

Joy pulled Scarlet's copy of Bryce Mitchell's biography from her bag and placed it gently on the glass table. She put the cherry-red ring box on top.

'Joy,' Mick said, and started towards her. She held up

her hand. They looked at each other but neither spoke. Joy tried to read Mick's face. There was sadness and fear, possibly regret there too, but who would know?

'It's over,' she said. 'I can't do this anymore. No matter how much I love you.'

Mick reached for her hand but she stepped away.

'I'm a mess,' he said. 'I know I am. Please don't do this. We need to talk. I need you, babe. We're supposed to be together. I can explain –'

Joy held her palm up.

'We don't need to talk anymore, Mick,' she said. 'What's the point now? I've been trying to talk to you for years. Was it really so hard for you to tell me what happened back then? All this time, we've been speaking different languages. I know that now.' Joy took a breath before continuing. 'I don't know how accurate this book is about you, but the saddest thing is that I don't even know if I care anymore. Anyway, it doesn't matter. We're done.'

Joy walked towards the door and Mick blocked her path. Before he could speak she said, 'Please promise me you'll get some professional help about all of this. And I don't mean talking to Bec in a bar at midnight. As much as I know she has your best interests at heart and she's been a good friend to both of us, you need to talk to someone who can help you through this properly.'

'No, Joy, please don't go,' said Mick, standing against the door. 'Not now. Not like this.'

He ran his hand through his hair and grimaced, searching for the right words.

'I love you, Joy. I want to marry you. We're so good together, you're perfect for me,' he said, such desperation in his voice that in spite of all she now knew, it broke Joy's heart. Again.

'You're right, Mick. I *am* perfect for you,' she said. 'I'm faithful, loyal, honest and was madly in love with you for so long. But the thing is, Mick, you're not perfect for me. And that's what will never change. I can't exist on a diet of half-truths, secrets and lies. You talk about the importance of opening up, connecting, going to the deep places in our souls. But you never follow through. I can't make you someone you're not. Finish your tour, Mick, and sometime in the new year, and if and when I'm ready, we can talk, if you want to.' Joy turned for the door.

'Joy, please. At least let me know where you're going, where you'll be.'

She glanced back over her shoulder. 'I'm going where I should have gone a long time ago. I'm going home.'

*

When she arrived at the station, the tiredness hit Joy like a ten-ton truck.

She lay on her bed in the big house, day after day, listening to the cries of the crows and the currawongs. When she wasn't sleeping she lounged on one of the cane day beds that caught the filtered afternoon sun, writing in her journal; trying to find some meaning in her words. Something that made sense of it all.

Sometimes, in the late afternoon, Joy would wander over to Anna's studio and sit and watch her grandmother paint. Now close to eighty, Anna was painting more than ever before.

'Come in, Joy,' Anna would say. 'Sit. Make yourself comfortable. Stay a while.' Then she'd go back to her brushes, and they would sit in companionable silence. 'Talking,' Anna had told Joy on more than one occasion, 'is grossly overrated.'

Avril and Tim hovered quietly around the edges of her pain. Joy knew they were there whenever she wanted to talk. But she didn't. Not yet.

She had come home a shell of herself. Even Ben, who now worked full-time alongside Kevin, noticed the change in his cousin. The humorous banter and playfulness they'd always shared was absent.

When Avril and Tim had asked Joy what she would like to do for Christmas and New Year, they were not surprised by her answer.

'Oh, let's keep it simple,' she said. 'Just the immediate family would be nice.'

So they'd celebrated Christmas with a traditional hot lunch and seen in the new year with a few songs around the piano.

Then the quietness and solitude Joy craved returned to the big house once more. Family members headed off and Joy retreated into lengthy sleep-ins and long walks or rides by herself.

More than anything, Joy felt Henry's absence acutely, more than when he'd first died or when she'd lived in London. As she analysed her relationship with Mick from every single angle, she thought of the way Henry had comforted her as a child. When the world sometimes over-whelmed her, his words would soften her despair.

One of Henry's well-worn Akubras still hung on the hat rack in the mud room, and his brown leather boots were among the footwear lined up below a row of coats.

He was everywhere and nowhere.

Every afternoon, Joy poured herself a small whisky in Henry's favourite glass, and played one of the Stéphane Grappelli records he'd loved so much, invoking the sounds and smells and security of her childhood.

Avril and Tim had read Bryce Mitchell's book and when Joy was ready, she began to talk to them. She spoke openly and honestly, the words finally flowing through her, and Avril and Tim listened. And, soon, Joy began to see her mother in a new light, a less critical light. A less judgemental light. Joy could relate to her mother's drive for financial independence; for accepting nothing less than full and frank disclosure in her relationship with Tim.

Joy began to see that Mick had never trusted her with himself. He had never shown her who he really was.

'And as for our engagement,' Joy said, as they sat on the veranda talking, 'at first I was ecstatic, over the moon. I was so excited at the thought of coming back and announcing the news to the family. But by the time I returned from the States . . . well, something had changed.'

Avril put her hand on her daughter's knee. 'You may not have the correct answer to this question, darling. Well, not yet, anyway,' she said, 'but do you think you and Mick can work your way through this? Could you imagine having a relationship with him that's stronger because of what you've been through?'

Joy sighed. 'I don't know, Mum, and it's what I've been asking myself. I simply don't know and I don't think I will for some time.'

*

January rolled into February and Joy's birthday came and went with as little fanfare as was possible in a family like hers. It was simply not the time for any big celebrations. Scarlet phoned regularly. Sometimes they talked for an hour, other times it was just a quick catch-up. Joy preferred to hear about Scarlet's work on the oncology ward and avoid any references to the charming specialist she was still dating. She didn't have the emotional bandwidth to process anyone else's affairs. Wherever Joy looked, everyone seemed to be loved-up. Even Bec and Tracey had rekindled their on-again, off-again relationship now that Bec was back in Australia for a while, so Joy had heard through the grapevine.

There was no mention of Mick. Joy had read the newspaper articles and caught snippets on the television and the radio about the band's success. Around Midnight's Australian tour had broken all previously held attendance records and their album *Make of It What You Will* had gone platinum in Australia, America and Japan. The release of Bryce Mitchell's biography seemed to have heightened the band's fame, if anything.

'I hope the view from the top was worth the climb,' Joy said to the entertainment page as she folded up the paper and dropped it in the bin.

Reading articles in the papers was one thing. Reading Mick's letters was something Joy was not yet ready to do. Three unopened envelopes were propped against Joy's dressing table mirror. She glanced at Mick's distinctive cursive handwriting as she pulled on her jodhpurs one morning.

As Calypso was recovering from a foot injury, Joy saddled up a young grey stallion called Archie, a three-year-old with a well-proportioned head and a rump that looked like it could run all day. Joy had always liked the character of a grey thoroughbred. Their Arabian ancestry provided the colour, speed and power for which they were renowned. When the decision had been made to retain Henry's stud property outside Melbourne and to lease the facility to an up-and-coming horse trainer, Tim had personally selected the broodmares and a couple of stallions he wanted to be brought to Monaghan. He wasn't as passionate about horseracing as his father had been, although he was keen to improve the quality of the horses at the station.

'Nice morning for a ride,' said Chris, wiping his grease-covered hands on a cloth as he walked from the machinery shed. 'Where you headed?'

'Oh, probably the usual. Up to Bunker's Ridge, over the arboretum of gums by that first lookout and home again. Back in an hour,' said Joy. 'Is that Jordy's old ute you're working on? Don't tell me that piece of junk is still drivable.'

'This baby's got new brakes, had a carburettor overhaul and I'm fitting a reconditioned radiator at the moment. Why? You want to make your uncle an offer? I think this vehicle would suit you.'

'You forget, I know how Jordy drives,' said Joy, and she walked away smiling.

*

Joy gave Archie a pat on the neck and collected up her reins as they passed through the gate and onto the flat. She took her time, gently introducing the silent hand and feet signals she was giving the beautiful grey as they walked and then trotted the length of the airstrip. Archie baulked slightly at entering the river, then pranced through the shallow water and rushed up the bank on the other side, keen to make his exit. On the open ground of the home paddock, Joy gave her horse his head, just enough to make the canter worthwhile – smooth, swift and strong.

Out in the open space the three-year-old was eager to run. Joy jiggled the reins, bringing Archie's nose to a vertical, his neck forming a regal curve, keeping control of both speed and direction. The climb to the top of the ridge, as always, was hard going but worth the effort. Here, London seemed a world away, as did Mick and the life they'd had there together. Joy spent a few minutes at the top of the ridge surveying the vista below, breathing deeply and feeling the calm and quiet of the landscape seep into her. This was what she needed.

Joy walked the descent, remounted at the bottom, and turned in the direction of Henry's campfire. She hadn't ridden there since her return; she hadn't wanted to. But today she did. *A ride-by to say hello then a canter back along the edge of the river*, she thought.

The windless sun warmed her back as she cantered towards a mob of cattle in the distance. The grassy hill was really more of a gradual rise that fell away to the west and joined a fold of similar undulations. Joy spied a pair of honey-coloured calves who seemed to be playing a game of tag behind their mother's back.

It all happened very quickly.

Over the crest of the rise, Joy and Archie surprised two large kangaroos who were head down in the long grass, feeding. Spooked, they sat upright before bounding away as Archie planted his front feet, sending Joy skidding along his neck and mane. Then he reared so suddenly and so vertically that they both hit the ground almost simultaneously. The stallion kicked out his spindly legs and hauled his hulking body up like a staggering drunk. His head bobbed as he oriented himself. He snorted and took a few steps back, then dropped his nose and sniffed at the motionless body that lay twisted in the flattened grass. Joy lay face-down, her right leg bent at a sharp angle. One arm was pinned beneath her chest. The horse lifted his head, looked around and whinnied.

Up ahead, the calves had stopped skipping, having been corralled back into the group by their protective parent.

*

Tim was in his office when he heard the knock at the front door. He was on the phone to a bloodstock agent and when the knock came for the second time, he cupped the mouthpiece of the receiver.

'Patricia, can you answer the door, please?' he called out as the knock came a third time.

'Hang on a minute, will you, Richard. Someone is trying to break down my front door. Better still, how about I call you back once I've made a decision about those heifers.' He rang off and strode down the wide hallway, flinging open the door with irritation.

He would never forget the sight that awaited him.

Chris was standing close to the veranda railing, his hands planted firmly on his hips. Behind him on the gravel driveway, a young stockman called Carl sat astride his sweaty stockhorse, holding the reins of the big grey stallion, Archie.

As a man who had spent his entire life on the land, a saddled, riderless horse rarely brought good news. Tim's breath quickened.

'Joy rode out about two hours ago on Archie here. Headed down the airstrip, said she'd be about an hour,' said Chris.

'Where did you find the horse?' Tim asked as he raced down the steps. Chris was already hurrying to get blankets and the medical kits.

'I was checking the saltpan pump and the grey came up behind me,' Carl said. 'He's definitely gone down. There's a gash on his shoulder and he limped all the way back.'

286

'Kevin,' Tim bellowed, the urgency in his call bringing the station manager from the workshop. 'It looks like Joy's taken a fall somewhere.'

Tim knew his daughter was a creature of habit. Out for an hour's ride, down the airstrip, he mentally formulated the possible routes she could have taken. Clear thinking and staying as calm as possible was what he needed to do now. If anyone was going to fall to pieces, now was not the time.

'Patricia in the flat-bed ute, you in your truck, Kev, and me in mine,' Tim said to Kevin, then turned to Chris who'd reappeared with the first-aid items. 'Chris, you take your ute and drive the airstrip, out to the ridge and weave your way across the home paddock. Carl, who's riding close to home today?'

'Macka, Bart and Bill.'

'Get the walkie-talkies, find the boys and all of you ride the home paddock. Call her name and use some cowbells. And remember, she might be able to hear you but not answer, so stay alert for any sign. Anything. We're all on two-way.'

Chris and Patricia raced to load the blankets and equipment into the utes.

'Where's Avril?' said Kevin as Tim jumped in his four-wheel drive.

'At Channel Nine in Sydney recording an interview,' said Tim. 'She doesn't know yet.' He roared off to find his daughter.

*

Searching for Joy was the hardest thing Tim had ever done.

As he cranked up the four-wheel drive to greater speeds – *faster, faster, faster* pounding through him – he knew time was crucial.

Joy could be severly injured. Bleeding out.

His little girl – all alone.

He was a man possessed as he scoured the country in front of him – the familiar, much-loved landscape suddenly seeming hostile and dangerous.

Then, the radio stuttered to life. Tim grabbed it.

'I've found her, over,' said Patricia. *'We're on the rise north of the river, about five hundred metres from the campsite Joy calls Henry's.'*

'Copy that,' said Tim, his heart turning over in his chest.

He arrived a few minutes later.

Joy was still lying face-down. She had not moved at all.

Patricia was checking her pulse and covering her with a blanket.

'She's alive and semi-conscious,' she said as Tim sprang from his vehicle and raced to his daughter, falling to his knees beside her. He touched her face gently.

'I can't see any blood loss. There's no way of knowing how long she's been here.'

Tim carefully turned over Joy's wrist. The face of her gold watch was cracked and the hands were no longer moving. It had stopped at the time of the accident.

'Nine-twenty this morning. She's been lying here for nearly two hours,' he said.

Kevin picked up the two-way radio and changed the frequency to capture a much larger region.

'Mayday, mayday, mayday. This is Monaghan Station,' he said.

His call was answered quickly.

'Monaghan Station, this is Harper's Creek Station,' came a woman's voice, clear and focused. *'How can we assist, over?'*

While Kevin gave a brief account of what had happened, requested an ambulance, and asked for the Royal Flying Doctor Service to be put on notice, Patricia supported Joy's neck and slid a blanket under her head. Tim and Chris moved her carefully onto her side and into the recovery position. Despite the touch of sunburn to the side of her face, Joy was cold to the touch and Tim placed another lightweight blanket over her and gently stroked her cheek, talking to her constantly, saying her name and telling her what had happened.

'I'm here, my darling girl. And Pat. We're right beside you.'

Chris and Kevin created a canopy of shade by stringing up a tarp between their utes.

When Carl and the other stockmen arrived, they were sent back to the homestead to direct the ambulance.

The next hour and a half waiting for the ambulance to arrive would be the longest ninety minutes of Tim's life. He prayed, pleaded and negotiated with any higher power who might be listening, to spare his daughter. *It can't end this way*, he kept telling himself as he held Joy's hand delicately in his own. *Not like this. Not today, Lord. I won't have it*.

It was only at five that afternoon, once Joy had fully regained consciousness and Tim watched the RFDS aircraft lift up from the airstrip at Monaghan Station, his only child on board bound for the Spinal Trauma Unit in Brisbane, that he allowed himself to collapse into Kevin Lowry's arms.

CHAPTER 16

By the time Avril and Tim arrived at the hospital the surgical team had already been put on standby. Along with a broken leg and arm, they confirmed that Joy had suffered a spinal injury.

'Your daughter has what's called a burst fracture,' the surgeon told Avril and Tim. 'The bone has expanded at the site of injury and is pushing into Joy's spinal column. We need to operate immediately, to decompress the spine so the bone fragments are no longer inhibiting the spinal column.'

'Will she be able to walk normally after surgery?' asked Tim.

'I'm optimistic,' he said. 'But we'll know more once she's had the operation.'

Avril and Tim found a phone and began making calls. It was now early evening and they knew they would not be leaving the hospital anytime soon.

The next few hours passed in a blur. They walked up and down the corridors, jumped at the sound of doors swinging open, and held each other close.

It was a sobering moment when, hours later, the ortho-paedic surgeon walked towards them, still wearing his light blue scrubs.

But then he smiled and said, 'Everything's gone according to plan. She's going to be okay.'

Avril and Tim shook the surgeon's hand and, finally, cried with relief.

*

'Your room's going to resemble a florist's shop before the week's out,' the nurse said brightly as she carried in another bouquet of flowers and checked Joy's chart.

Three days after the operation Joy was still coming to terms with what had happened. Avril and Tim had barely left her side since she'd been wheeled out of surgery.

'I remember riding out,' she said. 'And I remember the view from the top of the ridge, and coming around when I was down on the ground, but the rest is pretty hazy. Can you start from the beginning again, Dad, and tell me exactly what happened?'

While Tim recounted the events of that harrowing day a second time, Avril slipped back to their nearby hotel for a shower and a change of clothes. Jordy and Duncan had driven to Monaghan Station the day after Joy's acci-dent and picked up clothing and personal belongings for all three of them. Reece, Caroline and Ben had all rallied round, too, offering to help in any way they could. And by the end of the first week, Scarlet had flown up to Brisbane and was standing beside her best friend's bed.

'Well, girlfriend. You've really done a job on yourself,' she said wryly as she took Joy's right hand. 'A broken leg and arm. And both on the same side. Viv and Bec send their love. I've had calls from just about everybody: Hugo,

Mrs Banovic. Even Barry O'Brien phoned before I left Sydney. I have no idea how he got my home number.'

'I'm going to be in here for weeks,' said Joy. 'But I'm going to mend, so I'm told.'

'Are you in much pain?'

'More discomfort than pain,' said Joy. 'As long as the painkillers hold out.'

Scarlet couldn't help herself. She picked up Joy's chart, read the pages then replaced the clipboard without making any comment. 'And what about the break to your heart?' She gave Joy a peculiar look.

'Is that how you'd describe it?'

Scarlet sat down on the nearby chair.

'Mick called me yesterday. He wants to come and see you. But he said he didn't want to simply turn up unannounced.'

Joy stared up at the ceiling as tears pooled in her eyes. Her heart told her yes, but her head said no.

'I'm not ready to see him. Maybe sometime soon. But not in here.' Joy wiped her eyes with her good hand. 'I feel so mentally exhausted. More so than I do physically. I feel completely adrift. Aimless. This fall was just the last straw.'

'You've just come out of a long-term relationship. It's going to be three steps forward and one step backwards for a while,' said Scarlet gently.

'You know what the strangest thing was?' said Joy. 'When I was lying out in the paddock, I thought I could hear my grandfather's voice. As though he was standing close by. It calmed me down. Perhaps I was dreaming or hallucinating. Who knows.'

A couple of hours later when Joy opened her eyes, Scarlet had gone and the bright sunshine had all but disappeared. For the first time in days she had her room to herself. Although it was peaceful, she suddenly felt a deep loneliness, as if she were cut off from the world, and her thoughts began to skip from memory to memory like a stone skimming across a pond. Mick and the home they'd created together in London. The first couple of years at uni and the fun she'd had living with Scarlet and Vivienne. Hugo. She thought about Monaghan Station and Calypso; her happy childhood.

For the first time in her life, Joy felt directionless. Without a purpose.

I'll get through this, she said to herself sternly.

Even if she didn't quite believe it.

*

Three months after the accident, once Joy was post-operatively stable and all her vital signs were good, she was moved to a private rehabilitation facility in Brisbane. Here she'd begin the long and arduous process that would allow her broken bones to fully re-knit, her muscles to rebuild and her heart to heal. That part of her body was the most damaged of all. Still unable to bear weight fully, her recovery program would involve walking with a frame, which she jokingly came to call *The Convertible*. There would be weeks of gentle exercises in the pool, sessions with the occupational therapist, and periods of rest in between.

Vivienne and Jason, who had married the previous summer, had bought the house in Indooroopilly from Jordy and Duncan, and were happy to provide Scarlet, Rebecca and Ben with a place to stay whenever they came up to visit Joy. At least once a week, one of the trio would sit with her, entertaining her with what they'd been up to in the outside world. Although they never said so, Joy was positive Scarlet had initiated a visiting roster, all neatly arranged around each of their work commitments.

While Brisbane had once been home to Joy's closest friends, this was no longer the case. When the world tour had ended, the band had headed back Down Under, and Robert and Rebecca had moved back with them. Robert now lived south of the border, and so too did Rebecca and her partner Tracey, who were trying to make a real go of their roller-coaster relationship. The members of the band had long felt more at home in Sydney than Melbourne, and now it was home to all of them.

Whenever Simon visited Joy, she spent the whole time clutching her sides. He'd always made her laugh. They'd reminisce about their London days, talk fashion and music, and he'd impart any news from Brayleedon Manor.

What they didn't talk about was Mick.

Until one day, when Simon said, 'When you're ready, he'd love to see you.'

Joy looked at him. 'I'm sorry, Simon, but I don't want to see him. Nothing's changed.'

'I think you do,' said Simon. 'And I think you need to. You see, Joy darling, I was there right at the start. From our first game of pool to the morning you came and saw Mick at the hotel and told him it was over. My door was the first one he knocked on once you left. But if you're not ready yet, why don't you come and just stay with me in Sydney for a bit?'

'I want to go back to Monaghan as soon as I can,' said Joy.

Simon picked up Joy's hand. 'A country girl through and through. *There is a pleasure in the pathless woods, There is a rapture on the lonely shore, There is society, where none intrudes, By the deep sea, and music in its roar; I love not man the less, but Nature more.'*

'Keats?' said Joy.

Simon rolled his eyes. 'Keats,' he repeated. 'No, it's Byron, darling. Have I taught you nothing? Please, just promise me you'll think about it.'

'I'll think about it,' she said. She could promise that, if nothing else.

*

Being back at Monaghan Station was the tonic Joy needed. She didn't think she could love the place any more than she already did, but as she rediscovered the house, sorting through childhood memorabilia and looking through the books in the library, she grew to love it in a deeper way. To feel a part of its essence, and part of the long line of Merediths who had come before her.

The rhythm of each day was steady, strong, simple.

She liked it. She knew who she was here.

The letter that arrived in the middle of June was unexpected. It brought her life with Mick crashing back into her consciousness.

It was part of the morning post, and Joy was reading on the veranda when Tim delivered it to her. He didn't say anything but his look was quizzical.

Joy took the white Basildon Bond envelope in her hand and turned it over.

Carol McCready's name and home address were written in black pen on the back. A woman she'd never met but had always imagined that one day she would.

The author of the letter introduced herself – even though Joy knew she was Dave's mother – and said she was coming to Queensland and would like to visit, after hearing from Dave so many lovely things about Joy over the years. She didn't mention Mick.

A couple of days later, when Bec was visiting, Joy asked her what she thought about the letter she'd received from Carol. Bec was probably closest to Dave of all the band members, and Joy knew she'd met Carol McCready on several occasions.

'Why would she contact me after all this time?' asked Joy. 'What's that about?'

'I think it's an opportunity to talk. That's what it's about,' said Rebecca. 'You'll like her. She's a really lovely person and she's wanted to meet you for a very long time. I know that for a fact. The McCready family have played a big part in Mick's life, in a positive way. I don't think you'll regret speaking to her. To be honest, Joy, I think it's way overdue.'

And so, two weeks later, Carol McCready arrived at Monaghan Station with a friendly smile, a bunch of flowers and a sponge cake.

If Dolly Parton had a twin sister, it was Carol. She hugged Joy as they greeted each other on the front veranda then moved into the front room where Patricia had prepared morning tea.

'I was a country girl myself,' Carol said. 'I grew up on a sheep farm not far from Bendigo,' she added, slowly stirring her tea. 'I was delighted when Dave and Mick told me all about you. This beautiful girl from the bush on her way to becoming a vet.' Carol dropped Mick's name so easily into the conversation. 'He wrote to me all the time you and he were in London. Did he tell you he used to write?' Carol's soft blue eyes met Joy's.

'No, he didn't,' said Joy, 'but then I discovered there was a lot Mick didn't tell me. I would have loved to have known all sorts of things about him. His parents, his childhood. We were together for almost two years before I found out he was a diabetic. And that was only because he had a hypoglycaemic attack right in front of me.'

Carol nodded her head. 'He told me all about that. He felt ashamed.'

'But why?' said Joy. 'It's a condition, not a crime.'

Carol crossed her legs and tapped the foot of her burgundy stiletto ankle boot up and down.

'I brought some photos with me, if you'd like to see them. Of Mick, Dave and Jack when they were young.'

'I would,' said Joy. 'But first of all, Carol, I'd like you to tell me about Mick. What happened when his father died and, most important of all, why was Mick never prepared to talk about Bonnie and what happened?'

And so Carol McCready began her story and the two of them didn't stop talking for almost three hours. Joy would ask a question and Carol would answer her honestly and without embellishment. Sometimes Carol simply explained events that had occurred over relatively short periods of time, sometimes over months or years. The words flowed and her recollections tumbled forth until Joy had answers she wished she'd known a long time ago.

*

'When Murray and I first built our place,' said Carol, 'we were surrounded by loads of other young couples just like us. Out in the suburbs on a quarter-acre block. Like most people we were establishing our garden, two incomes, waiting for the first baby to arrive.

'Frank and Sandra, Mick's parents, moved in about the same time we did. Frank was driving long-haul trucks for a living across the Nullarbor. The boom was on in WA and he had plenty of work. Then Sandra had Michael and a year later I had Dave, my first. And, well, we all just got on with life. We'd put the pool in when we first built. It was the only one in the area for a while, so there were always kids in our backyard. Swimming, cricket, neighbours dropping by. That's what it was like back then. We were happy. Life was pretty simple.'

Joy could visualise all the skylarking and carrying on between Dave and Mick. A brotherhood that went so far back it could never be broken.

'Then Sandra got cancer and died when Mick had just turned ten. Frank couldn't cope. Drank too much, started missing work, lost his licence. It was a downhill run from there on. And all the while there was this cheeky, mischievous, wild boy called Mick Harris who was desperate to be loved. By now Murray and I had Dave and the three girls, so we just scooped Mick up and made him part of our family as often as we could. Then Frank died suddenly when Mick was sixteen. Thank goodness Frank had had the foresight to name Murray and me Mick's legal guardians in the eventuality of his death. Was that fate? I don't rightly know.'

Joy tried not to interrupt, wanting Carol to maintain her flow of conversation. Then she watched as the carefree expression on Carol's face became serious.

'By the age of sixteen, Mick had the body of a man,' said Carol. 'That, combined with his handsome looks, made him appear much older than he really was. Not long before Mick turned seventeen, in his last year at high school, he met a young woman, not a girl, a woman, called Sarah Todd. The boys – Dave, Jack and Mick – had been to a Bachelor and Spinster ball up in Bendigo and were staying at my sister's property the night before. As I said,

Mick always looked older than he was and Sarah looked a lot younger. She was twenty-four, seven years his senior, but everyone thought she was about eighteen or nineteen. Such a pretty little thing. They started seeing each other and I just knew it would end in tears.'

Carol took a sip of her tea and continued.

'Three months later Sarah was pregnant. Mick was now seventeen and didn't know what to do. Sarah wanted to keep the baby but her father was a member of parliament for the state of Victoria and wanted to move into the big time and try for a federal seat. There was absolutely no way a daughter of Charles Todd was having a baby out of wedlock. That's how people thought in those days. And there was no chance in hell that bully of a man was going to let Mick marry into his family. The only ones who knew Sarah was pregnant were Mick, her parents, Murray and me. Mick didn't want Dave or Jack to know. Well, not at that stage, anyway.'

Joy's eyes didn't leave Carol's face. She sat on the sofa, engrossed in what she was hearing, Mick's image imprinted across her mind.

'Sarah was sent to Sydney to a place for unmarried mothers to have their babies. It would have been too risky to send her anywhere in Melbourne. Charles Todd was always an arrogant, up-himself bastard, but his wife Naomie was a really lovely person. I went to school with her and we were pretty good friends during our last couple of years. But we'd fallen out of touch, because I fell head over heels for Murray, this good-looking mechanic who was going to make his fortune by the time he was thirty-five, and Naomie married into one of the wealthiest families in the district, two years out of high school.'

Carol stopped for a moment and looked at Joy, worried

she was tiring her. 'No, please, go on,' said Joy, absorbed in the unfolding story.

'When the baby was born, Naomie took one look at her granddaughter and told Sarah that if she wanted to keep her baby, she'd support her all the way. Sarah did not have to give her up.'

Joy brought her hands to her face and wiped away tears. 'Bonnie,' she said. 'They called her Bonnie, didn't they?'

'That's right,' said Carol. 'All eight pounds, six ounces of her. A head full of dark hair like her father.'

'What happened?' said Joy.

'Naomie's sister lived on a big property outside Shepparton. Sarah and the baby went there, as did Naomie. I think after twenty-six years of being married to someone like Charles Todd, Naomie had decided enough was enough. It was 1970, for goodness' sake. Two years later every woman I knew was drinking chardonnay out of a cask and singing along with Helen Reddy to "I Am Woman".' Carol chuckled quietly.

'Mick was desperate to see Sarah and his child. So Murray loaned him the station wagon and Mick drove up to see Bonnie when she was three weeks old. He was a good driver. Not a hoon. Sensible.'

Carol reached into her handbag for a tissue and started to dab her eyes.

'He spent the day with Sarah and Bonnie, talking and taking photos. Naomie and her sister were lovely to Mick. And he loved that little girl the moment he held her. You know, I think they could have made a go of it, the pair of them. Later in the afternoon Mick, Sarah and the baby got in the station wagon to go for a drive a few miles away to a spot with a view across the valley. Nothing special. Just a drive.'

Joy waited while Carol smoothed her hand over her wrinkle-free pants.

'Mick hadn't eaten properly for days. He had a hyperglycaemic episode at the wheel. Blacked out, drove off the road, down an embankment, killing Sarah and the baby while he came away with a broken arm and collarbone. It was such a tragic waste of life. A dreadful accident. A truck driver spotted the car on its roof and stopped.'

Joy and Carol were both crying now, wiping away their tears.

Joy could see the young Mick. Inconsolable. So alone.

'Murray and I had no idea what type one diabetes was, and nor did Mick. At around that time, perhaps a month or two before Bonnie was born, Mick had started to have an insatiable appetite and thirst. He drank water all the time. He started saying he felt lethargic but I thought it was because he was so stressed out about Sarah.'

Carol blew her nose and continued.

'Well, we found out about the condition pretty damn quickly after the accident. Murray and I blamed ourselves for a long time. You know, not realising that Mick's symptoms were so serious. It should never have happened, but it did. Of course, Mick was exonerated of any blame and because of his age the police investigation files were sealed. I reckon Charles Todd saw to that. Sarah's death was the final nail in the coffin for Naomie and Charles's marriage. He left politics the following year and Naomie left him for good. Sarah was buried in Bendigo with eight hundred people in attendance while Bonnie was buried in Shepparton with only Mick, me, Murray, Naomie and her sister present. Murray had to virtually carry Mick to the car afterwards.'

'If only Mick had talked to me about this,' said Joy

sadly. 'I can absolutely understand how much this must have affected him.' She sighed. 'How could anyone ever get over this? He's kept it bottled up inside him. The grief. The guilt.'

'He's a complex one, for sure,' said Carol. 'Life threw so much at him. Too much. And then he met you.'

Joy shook her head in frustration. 'It would have helped me make more sense of our relationship; the high highs, when he was full of enthusiasm and boundless energy; and then the times he'd withdraw. From me. From everyone. I put a lot of his behaviour down to being the front man for the band. He was so driven to succeed and, I see now, maybe to try to put the past behind him. In the early days, he rarely drank, and usually only when he was at his lowest ebb. I don't think he did drugs – at least, not in front of me. I used to joke that he was the cleanest rock and roller on the planet.'

'I think he'd got a lot of that out of his system by the time he met you,' said Carol. 'Those boys played dives for years. Made no money. Partied hard. Really hard, but Mick always wanted more. He didn't want to be just another band bumming around. He used to say to me, "Mrs Mac, I'm going to have a house and a pool just like yours one day", god love him. I think he felt he owed it to Dave and Jack. When the boys did finally find out what had happened, they kept it to themselves. Stood by their mate. But Mick's never got over the guilt he feels. And then that stinking book came out and it sent him all the way down the snakes back to the beginning, after all the ladders he's climbed to get where he is.'

Joy could see the cover of the biography, Mick's sultry eyes staring right through her. The book Bryce Mitchell had written had suggested that Mick Harris could *possibly* have fathered a child called Bonnie. The text was vague yet persuasive enough to make Mick sound like the very man he wasn't. The journalist had taken Mick's four-word dedication to his ballad 'Only a Moment' and probed and questioned until he'd decided he might have a scoop. His words were close enough to the truth to entertain his readers but not libellous enough to land him in court.

'What you've told me today, Carol, fills in the blanks I was left with after I read that piece of garbage by Mitchell,' said Joy. 'What an opportunist.'

'Sensationalist rubbish. That's what I'd call it,' said Carol, shaking her head. 'Well. Now you know what really happened. And I'm so relieved you do. I hope it helps you understand.'

Joy and Carol parted with hugs and kisses and a commitment to catch up again soon.

'I can't begin to tell you how pleased I am that you contacted me,' said Joy. 'It's like there's been a big messy jigsaw puzzle sitting in front of me and I could never quite get the pieces to fit together. As close as I thought Mick and I were, there's also that side of Mick that was always remote. Closed off. He wouldn't let me in. Now I know why.'

Later that night, Joy lifted Mick's unopened letters out of her bedside table drawer. She checked the date stamp and opened the one he'd written first. Joy noticed that the letter was several pages thick as she read the first words.

Hi, babe, the letter began.

She could hear Mick's voice as if he was right there beside her.

CHAPTER 17

The decision to go to France for further surgery was not a difficult one. At her most recent check-up, instead of arranging a series of individual appointments, Joy had insisted on a round-table conference with her full medical team – specialists, surgeons, OT, physiotherapist and her psychologist – to ascertain her current condition.

Six months on from her fall, she was still unable to walk long distances or without the use of a stick, and her prospects of ever getting back on a horse were remote, if not non-existent. The thought of this terrified Joy and cycled endlessly through her mind at two in the morning.

'Unfortunately your spine is still unstable, Joy,' the surgeon explained. 'In order to stabilise the spine, which will give you the best possible chance of regaining full and uninhibited movement, you'll need to undergo a spinal fusion operation, and the best place for this, in my opinion, is at a hospital in Paris. The French surgeon who pioneered this technique, Dr Chabert, has had outstanding success with similar cases to yours. That would be my recommendation.'

Joy, Avril and Tim listened to a detailed explanation of what the surgery would involve, and what the post-op period would entail.

'And the actual flight,' said Avril. 'Would I be correct in thinking Joy would need to have access to a bed? She couldn't sit for twenty-plus hours.'

'Most definitely. It would be no different from how things are for you at the moment, Joy,' her surgeon informed her.

'Is Dr Chabert available?' asked Tim. 'And if he were, and if Joy wanted to proceed, when would the operation take place?'

'After I received Joy's consent, I consulted with Dr Chabert and he's available to see her in two months' time. You'd meet with him, have a series of pre-surgery tests and consultations and then a date would be confirmed. You'd be admitted to a private hospital in Paris, but your recovery could take place at home – wherever you'd be staying.'

Joy stared into space, trying to take in all this information. The tick of the wall clock was the only sound in the room as everyone waited for Joy's response.

'Will I be able to ride again?' said Joy eventually, fully aware that her doctor had no way of knowing this for certain. She wanted to ask the question anyway, to allow herself to believe there was hope.

'You're young and in excellent health. There are no absolute guarantees. Every case is unique,' he said. 'However, I have every reason to believe that in your situation, the outcome will be positive.'

As they left the hospital in Brisbane for the last time, Tim threw his arms around Joy and Avril.

'I've booked somewhere special for lunch. Let's go.'

As they waited for their main course, Avril turned to face her daughter.

'I had a phone call from Mick last week and he's asked if he can see you,' said Avril. 'He's leaving for America soon and wants to see you before he goes. It's up to you, of course.'

'Maybe it's time,' said Joy with a sigh. 'Closure, once and for all.'

Avril slid a piece of paper across the table. 'This is the best number to reach him on, apparently. You do what works best for you.'

'Thanks, Mum. I'll think about it.' But Joy had already made her decision.

*

That night Joy called Mick and they agreed to have dinner at the Paradise Room the following Friday. When Joy arrived at the restaurant, Mick was seated at the bar, just like he had been on their first date. They embraced warmly, neither one quite willing to pull away.

In many ways it was like reconnecting with an old friend, Joy thought, a friend she now understood a lot better, irrespective of how much hurt they'd been through.

'Still on the lime and soda I see,' she said.

'Old habits and all that.' He smiled.

He still had that sultry, sexy way about him, but the passion she'd once felt for Mick was no longer there. It was so far in the past that it surprised her. A distant memory of a couple who didn't exist anymore.

'Talk to me,' he said. 'Tell me all or nothing. Berate me or make me laugh.' He reached across the table and took Joy's hand.

'Mick, I'm going to say from the outset –' Joy hesitated,

thinking of how best to express herself. 'That I hope we can always be friends. Good friends. For all our days.'

Mick nodded. 'If we can have that, then I'm a very lucky man.'

They smiled at each other.

'Now, tell me everything that's been going on with you, Joy Meredith.'

'Well, I'm heading to France soon for another operation. One I hope will be my last,' Joy began.

And over the next two hours, Joy and Mick laughed a lot, cried a little and talked until Joy felt they had closed the chapter of their lives they'd written together.

As Mick started to get up Joy touched him on his arm.

'Please, Mick,' she said. 'Why don't you sit for a little while. It's been lovely seeing you again, truly it has, but I'll see myself out. I don't think I can handle a kerbside goodbye.'

'Not even with an offer to see a movie?' he said with a soft smile.

Joy leant forward and kissed him tenderly on both cheeks. 'Thank you, but not this time.'

The show's over, she thought, and she walked towards the door without looking back.

*

Summer had just begun in Paris. The days had started to lengthen and the trees were flush with fresh green foliage.

Joy's surgery and post-operation recovery had gone extremely well. So well, in fact, that she was being released early and was excited at the thought of staying at Chateau de Vinieres once more.

Joy moved slowly to the window of her hospital room and looked across the courtyard at the ivy-covered wishing well. Like so many patients before her, she had tossed many francs into the dark water, praying her dreams wouldn't go unanswered.

Her body was still recovering and she knew she had a long way to go, but she felt strong. Hopeful.

She pulled her hair back into a loose ponytail and added a touch of lip gloss.

At the sound of the door opening, Joy turned and greeted Dr Chabert. He motioned towards the navy chairs and they sat down. They always spoke in French, which Joy now preferred to do, having decided since arriving a month ago that if she was going to be living in France for a while, she might as well speak the language as much as possible.

'How are you feeling, Joy?' said Dr Chabert. He was a softly spoken man with warm brown eyes and a touch of grey around his temples.

'I feel well, happy. And nervous.'

'That's not uncommon when you've been through major surgery such as this. You're now walking unaided, and you tell me that you're pain-free. I see no reason to keep you here any longer. You're well on your way to a full recovery.'

'If I'm being completely honest, I feel a bit emotional,' she added, trying to hold back her tears.

'That is also to be expected,' he said sympathetically. 'Be kind to yourself, won't you? Well, all your discharge paperwork has been completed and the nurse has taken you through your pain management plan, so I will say goodbye, and we will see each other in a month's time.'

'Thank you, Dr Chabert. For everything,' said Joy, and they shook hands and he nodded, holding the door open for her.

*

Madame Leon placed the small vase of lavender on the dressing table and repositioned a silver hand mirror and trinket box so they sat next to each other. The bed had been made up the previous day with brand new sheets, and fresh paper drawer liners had been fixed in place.

Madame Leon walked to the window and watched the car pull up at the front of her chateau.

Here at last, she said to herself.

Marie, the housekeeper, would greet Avril, Tim and Joy and show them upstairs to their rooms. Madame Leon would be waiting for them on the first-floor landing. She surveyed the room once more. It had been a lifetime since anyone had used the lemon-coloured bedroom that over-looked the tall poplar trees lining the driveway. The stately interior had been kept exactly as it was the morning she and Guy had left for Paris in 1944. With Joy coming to convalesce it was time, she'd decided, for this room to be lived in once again. For the walls to hear voices, and for someone to lay their head on the pillow at night.

*

Dr Chabert had told Joy that she could do as much walking, bike riding and swimming as she liked, as long as she didn't overexert herself and ceased if she was in any discomfort. The plan was for Joy, Avril and Tim to stay at the Chateau de Vinieres for the summer, to explore the Loire Valley and surrounding areas, and to possibly make a few small trips to other parts of Europe.

For the first few weeks, Joy explored the town of Tours, wandering the streets and markets, lured down the lane-ways by the aromas from the coffee shops and bakeries. She'd sit and watch the passing parade in the town square and sometimes she'd drive down to the nearby town of

Joué-lès-Tours, stopping to take photos, capturing images of everyday rural life: horses eating the lush feed; a smoky cloud of insects, hovering above the sunflowers, as though suspended in thought.

At her first post-operative check-up with Dr Chabert, he was delighted to see the improvement in Joy's strength and noted that she was walking without any impediment. He arranged to see her again the following month and then possibly six months after that, if she was still in France.

'Let's have lunch in Vendome and celebrate your excellent recovery,' Tim suggested as they reached the outskirts of Paris.

'There's a wonderful little brasserie with a view of the river,' said Avril. 'And quite a few antique and bric-a-brac stores for Joy to browse.'

Joy left her parents chatting with the owner of the restaurant while she went in search of a bookshop she'd spied.

The wide street frontage and bold red-and-white exterior of the shop, named 'Tourne la Page', came into view as Joy turned the corner. The two-storey bookshop was dotted with comfortable chairs and small stools, many of them occupied by late-afternoon customers. Joy browsed for a while, picking up a new novel and an autobiography she'd read about. Written by the renowned French veterinarian Mary Blanchet, it described the author's groundbreaking career in the area of equine medicine.

Joy handed her selection to the friendly redhead at the cash register.

'Would you like to join our "Turn the Page" mailing list?' she asked.

Joy was about to say no when instead she said, 'Sure. Why not.'

She gave her name and the address of the Chateau de Vinieres, paid for the books and waited while the redhead dived under the counter, searching for some complimentary bookmarks and copies of their last two catalogues.

'Oh. And you might like to have this,' she said, handing Joy a program. 'The Vendome Autumn Literary Festival is on here in October and Dr Blanchet will be speaking at it.'

'Thank you. I will definitely be coming to that,' said Joy.

As she neared the exit, Joy noticed that next to the door was a pile of discounted gift cards and she stopped to take a look.

'*Excusez-moi, sil vous plait*, but are you Joy? Joy Meredith?'

The voice was familiar, but when Joy looked at the man in reading glasses, his hair closely shaven and his white linen shirt hanging loosely from his thin frame, she had no idea who he was.

And then she placed him.

'Dion,' said Joy. 'Dion Beauchamp.' Images of the weekend they'd met in Gloucestershire bombarded her. The grand country house. Croquet on the lawn. Mick. 'It must be about six years,' she said.

'Ah! It is you. I thought it was. What a surprise! It is lovely to see you again.'

They kissed swiftly on each cheek then stepped back together to let someone pass.

'What are you doing in Vendome? Do you live here now?' Dion asked.

'Oh, no,' Joy laughed. 'I'm here . . . on holidays. Well, it's a long story. But I'm not staying here in Vendome,

I'm spending some time with an old family friend at Chateau de Vinieres. Outside Tours.'

Then, before she could stop herself, she said, 'What about you? What have you been doing? Are you still in the wine business? Do you live nearby?'

Joy realised that she had rushed to fill the silence, but from the amused look on Dion's face, he didn't mind. He repositioned the package he had under his arm. If he hadn't stopped, she would have passed him in the street and never recognised him.

'Yes, I'm still involved with viticulture,' said Dion. 'I don't work for the same company anymore, though. I live in Orleans now. It's about an hour from here. Not that far.'

'And Chess and Prue – have you kept in touch?' asked Joy.

'I haven't spoken to Chess for a while but I'm going back to Brayleedon Manor in November. More of a private trip than business. And you? Are you still living in London?'

'Not anymore. I had a lovely time there but I moved back to Australia at the end of eighty-seven.'

Dion nodded and smiled, then checked his watch.

'Oh please,' said Joy. 'Don't let me keep you. I should get going as well.'

'I have to be somewhere by five, that's all,' he said.

Outside, the street was busy with a mix of meandering tourists and locals, slowed by the late-afternoon heat that seemed to radiate from the buildings.

'I'm away for the next couple of months,' said Dion. 'If you're still in France when I get back, perhaps we could catch up? At the Autumn Literary Festival?' he added. 'Or will you be gone by then?'

'I'm not sure,' said Joy. 'But if I'm still here, I'd like that very much.'

Dion grinned. 'Great. I'll get in touch when I'm back.'

Joy started to open her bag to fish out pen and paper and exchange contact details, but as if Dion could read what she was thinking, he smiled and adjusted his glasses.

'No conversation is private in a bookshop,' he said. 'Chateau de Vinieres. I know it.'

And as he crossed the street, Dion turned and waved.

*

It wasn't as though it was planned. It began with Joy and Avril taking a walk through the vineyard the day after they'd first arrived and the pattern continued thereafter. Every morning after breakfast they'd put on their sneakers and stroll along the leafy vine rows, down to the river where the erratic swimming habits of the newly arrived ducklings were giving their ever-vigilant mothers grief. Sometimes, the softly winding driveway tempted them to make the one-kilometre walk to the front gate, then they'd climb the railing – carefully – and follow the fence line all the way to the boundary of the estate. There were moments when Joy found herself hesitating to duck through a fence or break into a jog. But as time went on, she worried less and less. In fact, she felt stronger than she had before her accident. Months of no drinking and a healthy diet showed in her glowing skin and boundless energy.

It was in these moments with her mother that Joy and Avril discovered terrain they'd never dared venture to in conversation before. Joy shared the details of Mick's life she'd only recently discovered herself. And Avril opened up about her own life to Joy, inviting her in.

'I may never have left Monaghan Station and created the le Chic chain if your father had known he was not the father of Rachel's child,' said Avril. 'They certainly would

313

never have married. Sometimes it feels like life is one long game of being in the right place at the right time.'

'Or the wrong place,' said Joy.

One morning, as they walked past the back of the stables, Avril stopped, resting her hand on the top of a post. A set of well-worn wooden steps arched over the wire fence to the field on the other side.

'I can't tell you how many times Guy and I went over this fence together,' said Avril. She tilted her head, looking at how the steps had been made. 'These weren't the ones we used. They've been replaced at some point.'

'How do you know?' said Joy. 'They look pretty old to me.'

Avril lifted her foot and stood on the first step.

'Because I took an axe to the original steps in the winter of 1944 when I was nineteen. I'd already cut up all the wood from the railings around the dressage arena. This was all that was left. Except for pulling the barn apart – thank god it never came to that. Although, we came close.'

Towards the end of summer, Simon Webber visited the chateau for five days, an easy hop, skip and a jump from London where he was temporarily based, and this time it was Joy who was tour guide. Together they strolled around the town and visited the local wineries. Their after-dinner conversations were peppered with, 'Remember when' and 'Whatever happened to' as they covered a multitude of memories, from when they'd first met to Joy's most recent operation.

Back at the chateau after a long day of playing tourist, Joy tossed Simon a cushion and he placed it behind his back. She stretched her legs over his knees as he took a sip of wine.

'Have you thought about riding again?' said Simon. 'Didn't I hear Tim say you'd been given the all clear to get back in the saddle?'

Joy swirled the contents of her glass.

'I've thought about it. There's no rush. I'll know when I'm ready.' Feeling slightly uncomfortable with the subject, she moved the conversation swiftly on to her recent unexpected encounter.

'I had a blast from the past a few weeks ago,' she said.

'How so?'

'I ran into a guy, a French guy called Dion. Remember him? He was at Chess and Prue's the first time we all went up to Brayleedon Manor. Boy, did the thought of that weekend bring back some memories.'

'Dion Beauchamp,' said Simon in surprise. 'Yes, I remember. He's become a good friend of Chess and Prue's.'

'I didn't recognise him at first. He didn't look that well to me.'

'He hasn't been,' said Simon. 'He's been fighting some sort of blood disease for the last couple of years. Prue said he was in the clear now but you never know with these things, do you? He stayed up in Gloucestershire with Chess and Prue for a good chunk of summer last year.'

'Well, I hope he's okay. I didn't want to ask. He's lost so much weight. I really didn't know who he was at first, and I never forget a face.'

'When are you all heading back to Australia?' said Simon. 'Did I hear your mother mention the first week of September?'

'I'm not going back yet,' Joy said. 'Not right away. I'm not quite ready to leave. I'm still not sure what I want to do.'

'What about modelling?'

'That was fun for a while but it was never a long-term plan,' said Joy.

'What about your degree? Any thoughts there?'

Joy took a sip of wine while thinking of what to say.

'You little minx,' said Simon. 'I know that look of yours. You've got an idea. What is it?'

'You'll only laugh,' said Joy.

'No, I won't. I promise,' he said, trying to keep the smile off his face.

'I thought I'd see if Yves would give me a job here. There's always work for another pair of hands on a property like this.'

'Shouldn't you be asking Madame Leon?'

'Madame Leon might own the place but Yves runs it. I'm speaking from experience here. You always go to the person who does the hiring and firing,' said Joy. 'And never go behind the manager's back.'

'You sound like Robert. He still wears that leather jacket we bought him when we had our first number one hit.'

The conversation paused as Joy was instantly reminded of Mick. *He shadows every conversation we have*, she thought. She decided to bite the bullet.

'Did you know Mick and I had dinner when I was in Brisbane before I left for France?' said Joy.

'Did you?' said Simon, raising his eyebrows.

'I was pleased we did. He'd written me some letters and I didn't read them for months. Not till after my accident. Then one night I did, and I knew I had to see him. I had to find out if I'd kept him away because I was angry or hurt or confused or just being vindictive, I guess. In the end it was none of those things, or maybe all of them. We talked about everything and cleared the air. But you know, Simon, when it was time to leave I wanted to go. Whatever had drawn us together was gone. I'll always love him in a crazy kind of way. I hope he finds someone he can build a life with. But it isn't going to be with me.'

'He never said a word,' said Simon.

'That doesn't surprise me,' said Joy. 'I know you were eventually told about what happened to Mick when he was seventeen. Carol McCready told me, in the end.'

'Yes, Dave explained everything,' said Simon. 'The secrets we keep.'

'That sounds like the name of an album,' said Joy. 'How is Around Midnight doing these days? What is it now, album number eight?'

'Nine if you count the live album.' Simon refilled their glasses. 'There's no point denying it. Mick lost his shit when we did our first tour in the US. He was stressed out all the time. Layer on top of that the release of that biography and the fact that things weren't great between you two. All his fault, I might add. It was the perfect storm.'

'I don't look at it in terms of fault. I really don't. I was too accommodating of Mick's mood swings. I should have put some lines in the sand long before his behaviour became a pattern.'

'Well, I have no hesitation in saying that he's never going to find anyone like you.'

'Never say never,' said Joy. 'That's one thing I've learnt.'

Simon raised his glass towards Joy.

'Parting is such sweet sorrow,' he said.

'That I shall say good night till it be morrow,' added Joy, clinking glasses, and their heads fell back in laughter.

*

Joy decided it was time to follow through on the idea she'd been thinking about.

The day after Simon left for London, she arranged to speak to Yves in his office. He welcomed her warmly but was curious.

'I'm wondering if you'd consider hiring me on a part-time basis,' she said. 'I really want to learn about viticulture and would love to work on the estate in any way I can.'

She embellished her hospitality experience at the Crown and Anchor a little to include fine-dining waitressing and front-of-house service, but her first-hand knowledge of the running of a rural property and the four years of veterinary studies she'd completed needed no enhancement.

'There's just one thing,' she said. 'I'm afraid I'm not yet able to lift anything too heavy, although, of course, I'm happy to groom and feed the horses and muck out the stables.'

She wasn't ready to try riding again and wouldn't be able to exercise any of the horses – yet.

'Well,' said Yves, grinning at her when she'd finished. 'Your timing is perfect as we are a person down at the moment. I can give you three days a week straight away. One of those days will be a Saturday. I'm sure Camille could do with another pair of hands in the restaurant.'

The news about a part-time job was more of a surprise to Avril and Tim than the fact that Joy wasn't ready to go home. They'd been expecting that. Madame Leon, however, was thrilled.

'Oh. That's wonderful,' she said, beaming. 'Yves wouldn't employ you if he didn't think you'd fit in. You stay with us as long as you want, Joy. There's been nothing but sunshine in this house since you arrived. *Ma maison est ta maison.*'

'Thank you,' said Joy. 'That's a lovely thing to say.'

*

A week before Avril and Tim were due to fly back to
Australia, Yves took Joy and Tim to visit Chateau Margaux
in Bordeaux, something they'd been wanting to do for a
long time. As Avril had visited the famous estate several
times already, she said she'd prefer to spend the time
with Madame Leon. Avril waved the trio goodbye and
returned to the office she'd made her own since arriving
three months earlier.

The modern fax machine meant Avril could receive
weekly sales figures for her le Chic stores and Princess
Bridal boutiques, along with the other retail outlets she
held. Her banker, stockbroker or accountant were able to
send through any document she requested. It had never
been so easy to be on the other side of the world and do
business.

Avril was making herself a cup of coffee when Madame
Leon came into the kitchen.

'May I have one as well, please?' she asked Avril. 'Then
come into the living room. I'd like to talk to you.'

Madame Leon closed the double doors behind Avril,
letting the housekeeper Marie know they were not to
be disturbed. Avril took a sip of her coffee and noticed
a folder on the sofa next to Madame Leon. Otherwise,
the room was as it always was: peaceful with a hint of
gardenia drifting from a single large round candle.

Madame Leon folded her hands in her lap and took a
deep breath. 'Avril. I have loved you like a daughter for so
long, it's hard to believe sometimes that you're not actually my own child. You are all I have left of my past.' She
met Avril's eyes.

'There's something I want to tell you. You may think I should have told you before now, but I hope you will understand why I haven't. Perhaps it's because there's so little of my life left to live. Most of my living's behind me now, not in front of me. I'm not trying to be melodramatic, it's simply the way it is.'

Madame Leon drank some coffee and replaced the cup. Avril sat and listened.

'Two weeks before you sailed on the *Harmony Prince* for Melbourne in 1950, a woman turned up at the chateau with an unbelievable story. It was so outlandish, so cruel, that I shouted at her, told her to leave and slammed the door in her face. Brigette showed the woman to the kitchen and then calmed me down.'

Avril could imagine Madame Leon's loyal housekeeper back then, handling the situation with diplomacy.

'The woman sat in the kitchen with Brigette and told her that Guy Leon was alive. He was apparently in an institution for people with mental problems in Marseille. At first I refused to even speak to the stranger and Brigette was rushing back and forth between the kitchen and the living room, telling me pieces of information as they were revealed. Of course I didn't believe her. I thought this girl must be after money or up to no good in some way. But when I'd calmed down a little and Brigette had convinced me to hear what the woman had to say, I relented and Brigette brought her into this very room.'

Avril was stunned. *Guy? Alive?*

'Her name was Odette, Odette Patou, and she'd grown up in our village. She knew Guy and she knew you, too. After the war, you know what it was like. People were trying to find work wherever they could. Odette and her older sister had lied about their age so they could both get jobs cleaning in what they thought was a hospital.'

Madame Leon took a deep breath and stared across the room.

'It was no hospital. It was an antiquated, cruel place where they shoved the disturbed and often unidentifiable men and women. Odette went to mop a room one day and there he was, sitting on the floor in the corner. They'd shaved his head but she knew it was Guy. She told me she'd always been sweet on him. He didn't or couldn't speak to her but she was certain it was him. Odette and her sister didn't stay in Marseille long. They came back to Tours and that's when Odette came to the house with the news. Not long after, I gave the sisters money for clothes and provisions, and found them work at the bakery. It was the least I could do. I paid for their lodgings. They were both married within a couple of years. They left Tours without a word and I've never seen either of them again.'

'What happened next?' said Avril, her heart in her mouth.

'I still didn't entirely believe them, but I had to find out the truth. I contacted my lawyer, Monsieur Fortin, immediately. We travelled to Marseille and there I discovered that Odette had been right. My son was alive, Guy was alive. We obtained all the necessary documents and he was released at once.'

Avril tried to take in what she was hearing. Her throat was so tight she didn't dare speak.

'We brought Guy home,' Madame Leon continued. 'The doctors were in no doubt that the beating he'd received that night in Paris, a week before you were supposed to be married, had caused irreversible brain damage. How Guy ended up in Marseille, we can't be sure, but it looks as though he was thrown inside a train carriage by his attackers and left to die. Who took him to the institution in Marseille? We'll never know that, either. He didn't speak, he had no papers or anything that could identify who he was.

'Avril.' Madame Leon reached over and took her hands. 'He was no longer the man you knew. He was no longer the son I knew. You are a grown woman. You have lived life. You can imagine his condition. You'd worked so hard and been through so much, and there you were, about to turn twenty-six, setting off for your new life in Australia. Why tell you? What good could have come from it? There are times in life when we all have to make the most difficult of decisions. So I decided for you. I decided to let you get on with your life. It's what Guy would have wanted as well.'

Avril loosened Madame Leon's grip and brought her hands to her head for a moment. Then she pushed herself up out of her seat and moved to sit beside Madame Leon.

'Go on,' said Avril. 'Please tell me.'

'Guy lived, for a while. But his injuries were so severe. We had a nurse, as well as Brigette and me. We cared for him night and day. He didn't know who I was, I don't think, but we made him as comfortable as we could. He died on Sunday the eleventh of June, which was a week after you arrived at Monaghan Station. He went to sleep that afternoon and never woke up. His body gave in. But his pain was over. He was finally free.'

There was nothing for Avril to say. She wrapped her arms around Madame Leon and they cried. After a while, Madame Leon pulled back and held Avril's arms with both hands.

'I have all your letters, still. Every one. Over the years,

I would go to Guy's bedroom and sit and read them aloud and imagine him sitting at the window listening to all your adventures. I could hear your voice as you described the homestead and the people you were getting to know at the station; this incredible world that had opened up for you. And then you fell in love with Tim, and heartache followed. You kept going, though. Believing. Living. Avril, I know I did the right thing. And I've done the right thing today, telling you. I did not want to die with this secret between us.'

'Yes, you did the right thing,' said Avril softly. 'I'm so very pleased you've told me. Where is . . .?'

'Where is Guy buried?' said Madame Leon. 'Is that your question?'

Avril nodded slowly.

'He is all around us. He's riding the fields and swimming in the river. He's grooming the horses and standing by the fire in the courtyard. I stand at his bedroom window and watch him striding along between the rows of the vineyard.'

'You scattered his ashes here?' said Avril.

'I did. And now Guy will always be here. He will never have to leave again. He is home forever.'

CHAPTER 18

Avril and Tim left for Australia in early September, and Joy was already so busy working with Yves on the estate and with Camille in the restaurant that she didn't have time to miss their company too much. And she came to explore the chateau once more, just like she had as a fourteen-year-old. Every corner, every window. Where the light would shine and where the shadows would hide and with each passing day, the place started to feel more and more like home.

Most afternoons she wandered over to the stables and brushed the manes and tails of the horses. The two bay geldings belonged to Yves and Camille, while the chestnut and black mares were kept for staff and visitors to ride. Like her late husband and son, Madame Leon loved horses and had always had them in her life.

In the eighteen months since Joy's accident, not once had she wanted to ride. It wasn't because she was frightened but her desire to sit on a horse, feel the power of its hindquarters and the will of the animal's neck under the control of her hands had gone. In spite of these feelings,

324

she found she was still drawn to the stables. The smell was like an old friend, the brushes and liniments like a rider's makeup kit. Joy found the touch of the leather almost therapeutic as she cleaned the saddles and bridles, working the saddle soap into the leather and polishing it until it was supple and gleamed.

One afternoon when Joy had finished for the day and was walking back to the house, Marie called out from the rose garden. At her feet, a basket of pink Pierre de Ronsard roses overflowed.

'There's some mail for you on the kitchen table,' said Marie.

Joy could see that one letter was from Scarlet and another was from Patricia Lowry, chunky with maybe photos inside. The back of the third letter had no sender's name or address so, curious, she opened that one first. She switched on the kettle, dropped down into a chair and turned to the last page to see who the sender was. *All the best, Dion.*

After his initial greetings, Dion went on to tell Joy that he was travelling in Australia and that he would be 'going across the ditch' to New Zealand in a few weeks, then back home via the United Kingdom. His visit to the Barossa Valley in South Australia, and the Central Otago region of New Zealand's South Island, would wrap up the final stage of the research he'd been doing for his PhD. He mentioned that he'd had a 'few hold-ups along the way to completion' but he never mentioned being unwell.

For the next couple of months, letters flowed between Joy and Dion via fax.

'He writes well,' Joy said to herself as she read Dion's entertaining account of a presentation he'd given and his description of what was involved in collating the last of his data, while waiting out his last day in Christchurch before heading to London. There was humour in the way he wrote and with each exchange, Joy answered his questions as honestly as possible. *And when you're ready, I hope we can go riding together,* he'd written, *this time, perhaps without a horse that goes lame.*

That was the only one of his remarks Joy never responded to.

*

Vendome provided three magical autumn days for the literary festival in October. Joy, along with the rest of the audience, was still on her feet clapping as Dr Mary Blanchet left the stage and headed for the author signing table, which was stacked with her latest release. The panel of winemaking experts Dion had listened to had finished fifteen minutes earlier and he was already sitting at their table in the corner of the restaurant when Joy arrived.

They greeted each other warmly, kissing on both cheeks as Dion signalled for a menu.

'Was she as good as you thought she'd be?' said Dion.

'Oh my god. She's so inspiring. Her surgical knowledge and her whole approach to equine behavioural science is mind-blowing. And yours? Was the panel discussion as lively as you anticipated?'

'Oh, yes. With all those egos sitting at the same table,' said Dion. 'A little heated at one point but I think they were trying to keep us all entertained. By the way, Yves has told me I'm welcome to ride one of the mares whenever I like. I thought I might take up his offer and make a commitment to ride every Sunday morning. Have you any interest in joining me?'

Joy knew Dion wasn't pressuring her. He was only

asking, and yet she could feel herself getting defensive even before she answered him.

'No, thanks. Please don't ask me again,' Joy said tightly. 'If I want to ride, I will. I'm just not ready.'

Dion gave her a concerned look and was about to say something when Joy noticed a woman approaching them. She touched Dion lightly on the shoulder and he turned, smiled and stood, reaching to shake her outstretched hand.

'Congratulations, Dion,' she said in French. 'The dean has just told me the news. I'm looking forward to you joining our faculty.'

'Thank you, Dr Chalamet. So am I. Very much.'

'I can highly recommend the duck,' she said. 'Enjoy.'

Dion sat down again and spread his hands.

'My cover is blown,' he said.

'You've got a job. Where?' said Joy.

'The university in Tours. They must have felt sorry for me,' he joked. 'But yes. I have a lecturing and research position for two years and then I'll see what happens.'

'This calls for some champagne,' said Joy, catching the eye of the waiter.

They ordered, and Dion talked a bit about the scientific area he'd be lecturing on.

'I'll be given first-year students,' he said, 'which is to be expected.' Then he changed the subject, asking Joy more about herself and if she was still enjoying her work at the chateau.

'Three days a week is perfect,' she said.

'And when do you think you'll head home?'

Joy put down her fork and took a sip of water.

'I ask myself the same question every time a new month rolls around,' she said. 'There's no rush. I love living at the chateau. There's a calmness about the place. So as long as

Madame Leon is happy to have me, I'll stay and see where life takes me.'

'And Madame Leon, she's easy to live with?' asked Dion.

'Too easy. She's amazing. Although, since my parents left, she hasn't been that well. She doesn't seem to have the energy she used to and she's sleeping a lot.'

'I imagine she has the best medical help available,' said Dion.

'She does. It's more like she's lost her spark. I don't know. So, to answer your question, you'll have to put up with me for a little bit longer.'

'Hmm. I think I can manage that,' said Dion, and he refilled their glasses.

*

Almost without Joy noticing it, the months rolled from one to the next and the seasons changed. Winter was a quieter time at the chateau but no less beautiful. Spring was simply beautiful and summer glorious, the vines and everything else coming back to life in the warm sunshine.

True to his word, Dion came to the chateau to ride with Yves and sometimes Camille most Sunday mornings, and Joy would watch as they cantered along the fence line that bordered the vineyard and out to the hills beyond. Dion would usually stay for lunch or a coffee with Joy afterwards. He did not mention them riding together again, but they found new common ground around winemaking and the growing of the grapes, which Joy was becoming more and more interested in.

In his own time, Dion also told her about the illness he'd suffered, how frightening and debilitating it had been, but that he had overcome it and, with monitoring, it was now a thing of the past. Indeed, he'd gained a little weight, his hair had grown back and his eyes seemed brighter every time Joy saw him. Their friendship blossomed, and although she didn't feel quite ready to take it any further, Joy could not deny the chemistry she felt between them – had felt, if she were honest, from the very first time they'd met at the weekend party at Brayleedon Manor.

A year to the day after their meeting at the Autumn Festival, Joy and Dion were sitting in the same restaurant in Vendome, having just attended a workshop on playwriting.

Dion broke off a small piece of bread and dipped it into the olive oil.

'When the playwright was talking about the importance of spontaneity, all I could think about was that night at Brayleedon Manor, after your boyfriend had the diabetic attack. Do you ever think of it?'

Joy glanced up quickly. 'Actually, I do,' she said. She had convinced herself long ago that what had happened between her and Dion that night had meant nothing, that it wasn't significant, but now she knew better. She wondered what would have happened if she had paid attention to that instinctual feeling back then instead of burying it.

She recalled how she'd left the house after her cup of tea with Prue, still furious with Mick and needing an outlet. She'd gone to the river, stripped off and dived in.

'You know,' said Dion now, 'there's ten kilometres of river frontage at Brayleedon Manor and you just happened to choose to swim naked where I was swimming. A spontaneous occurrence or a deliberate decision?' he said, gently teasing.

'I think it's called a well-worn pathway down to the water's edge.' Joy smiled. 'I didn't know you were there till I came up for air. I got the shock of my life.' But she remembered the frisson of pleasure she'd felt at finding herself in the river with the kind, handsome Dion; the comfort of a sympathetic ear after the awful events of that evening. She had opened up to him about the secret Mick had kept from her, about how much it had upset her.

They'd come out of the water and dressed in the moonlight, neither of them self-conscious of the other's nakedness. Walking back along the tree-lined path, Joy had stopped and brought her hands up to her face. Dion had come to her, had wrapped his arms around her in comfort. Then his lips had found her face and Joy's lips had found his, and for a brief moment they kissed. A passionate kiss. Then they'd walked to the house and said good night. When she thought about that night now, Joy could see clearly that she and Mick had never been going to last, no matter how much they loved each other.

'I have thought about that night a lot the past few months,' Dion said, and he reached across the table for Joy's hand. 'Sometimes wondering if it was all just a dream. But it wasn't. And I need you to know, Joy Meredith, that I think I've fallen in love with you.'

Joy smiled, took a deep breath and took his hand in hers.

*

Joy was surprised how effortlessly her new relationship with Dion evolved. She was not sure how she had been able to ignore for so long the undeniable attraction she now felt between them. Dion was warm, caring, endlessly supportive. He was also not afraid to challenge Joy, to take her to those corners of her mind she'd rather not visit but knew she needed to. They'd even had a couple of spectacular arguments which they'd ended up laughing about, agreeing that they could both be quite opinionated at times. It felt very different from her relationship with Mick, but somehow more mature, and comfortable on a fundamental level. Like coming home.

One Sunday, as Joy watched Dion, Camille and Yves walk their horses down the rows of grapevines, she felt an unexpected twinge of envy. *You've got to get back in the saddle*, Henry had said the time she fell at the gymkhana in Toowoomba when she was nine years old. *All good riders fall*, he'd told Joy as he gave her a leg up. *But a great rider gets back on.*

Joy hovered in the background until Yves and Camille were almost at their cottage, then she ducked through a side door and into the stables. Dion was hanging up the last of the tack as Joy approached.

'Do you feel like going out again?' she said, keeping her tone casual. 'A walk. Nothing more.'

With an admirable lack of reaction, Dion picked up two bridles and stood so there was barely any space between them. He tilted his head slightly to the right, the way he did sometimes when they were clowning around.

'So, first you swim where I swim, and now you want to ride where I ride,' said Dion. 'Are you stalking me, *Mademoiselle* Joy?'

He was so close she could feel the heat of his body and see the beads of sweat on his neck and forehead.

'I think I might be,' said Joy, noticing just how thick and luscious his eyelashes were.

'Just a walk,' he said. 'We'll walk together,' and he leant forward and kissed her.

331

'Would you like me to tack up a horse for you?' he asked.

Joy lifted the bridle from his hand.

'Thank you. But I think I can figure it out,' she said. 'I'm ready to get back on.'

*

Joy was in the kitchen of the restaurant, getting a pastry-making lesson from the chef, when the phone rang. He picked it up and Joy could tell immediately that something was wrong.

'That was Marie,' he said when he'd hung up. 'You'd better get up to the house straight away. Madame is not well.'

Joy met the housekeeper coming down the staircase.

'What's happened?' said Joy. 'I knew she had a cold. Has it got worse?'

'Madame is in her bed. Unfortunately the cancer has returned; she told me herself. The doctor has just left – he thinks she's in her final days. He'll let us know what to expect and how best to handle the situation. I think you had better call your mother.'

'Of course. Does Madame need to go to hospital?' said Joy.

Marie shook her head slowly.

'No. We are long past that point,' she said. 'She wants to be here, in her own bed. Go and see her. Tell her you have called for Avril. She'll take comfort from that.'

*

Avril had still not spoken to Tim when she boarded her flight in Sydney. He was on a boys' fishing trip in the Dampier Archipelago, forty kilometres off the Western

Australian coast. She'd received Joy's telephone call and was at the airport eight hours later, ready to fly to Singapore and then on to London. It would be tight to make her connecting flight to Paris, but not impossible.

She arrived at Chateau de Vinieres in the early afternoon, hugged Joy and they raced straight up the stairs. Madame Leon was leaning back on her pale-blue pillows and her little record player was playing her favourite music softly in the background. When she was awake, Joy had told Avril, she was as lucid as a healthy woman half her age, and her eyes were clear. Avril kissed her gently on her forehead and stroked the side of her face.

'Oh, Avril,' Madame Leon said, 'I knew you'd come. I knew I'd see you.' Her eyes fluttered closed; her breathing was long and slow. The nurse in attendance touched Joy on the shoulder.

'She's slipping away,' she murmured. 'I'll be outside.'

Avril, Joy, Camille and Marie gathered around the bed. No one could quite recall afterwards how long it was, but eventually they noticed a stillness to Madame Leon that had not been there before.

'She's gone,' said Avril, letting go of Joy's and Marie's hands.

And even though Madame had once said to Avril, 'Don't cry for me when I go. I'll still be here,' Avril's heart broke open and she howled.

*

The morning after Madame Leon's funeral service in Tours, Avril and Joy left the sleeping house and started down the driveway. The wreath Avril carried was composed of pink and white roses, the last of the autumn blooms, which Joy had collected from the garden at first light.

'I'm so pleased I hadn't already left,' said Joy, stirring Avril from her thoughts. 'I was going to surprise you and Dad. I've booked a ticket to come back to Australia in the first week of December.'

'Permanently?' said Avril.

Joy shook her head slowly. 'I'm not sure. But I doubt it, now that Dion and I are in a relationship. Geez, will my life ever be uncomplicated?' And Joy began to laugh. 'It probably sounds a bit weird, but I'd made this agreement with myself when I first came to the chateau after my second operation – a sort of promise that I'd ride a horse in France before I set foot on Aussie soil again.'

'Well, you've achieved your goal. Dion says you're cantering beautifully.'

'No jumps yet,' said Joy.

'Who needs jumps?' said Avril. 'There's enough hurdles in life without looking for more.' And she squeezed Joy's hand.

Joy pulled the giant gates together and dropped the holding bar in place. Avril slid the wreath through the gap in the iron columns and held it in place while Joy secured it tightly at the back with thick white ribbon.

'Not once in my lifetime have these gates ever been closed,' said Avril. 'She was a courageous woman. Kind, fierce, loyal. And she was my friend.' Avril touched the petals of the roses with her fingertips. 'And when the time is right, we'll scatter her ashes just as she's requested.'

Joy pushed her hands into the side pockets of her down jacket. Avril looped her arm through her daughter's and they stood looking back at the elegant house in the early-morning light. The last of the amber leaves were clinging to the plane trees, and the days of sunshine were quietly retreating. Winter was on its way and soon the grass would be covered in frost, a precursor to the snow flurries that would see out one year and welcome in another.

'What happens now?' said Joy. 'Will Yves and Camille and the rest of the staff stay on, and will this place still function as it does now?' She looked at her mother, whose eyes were fixed on a robin's nest in the fork of a branch just above their heads. The industrious little creature was busily poking at the creation, rearranging the twigs to shore up the sides of its home.

'Oh, yes,' said Avril. 'Yves and Camille will stay on. All those decisions were formalised some time ago. Life goes on.'

'And the estate. Who owns Chateau de Vinieres now, Mum?'

A cool wind tossed Avril's hair from her collar as she turned to look at Joy. She ran her hand down Joy's upper arm.

'I do,' said Avril.

CHAPTER 19

Joy stared at her mother in disbelief.

'You own all this now?' she said. 'But . . . how? Why?'

Avril took a deep breath, then told Joy what Madame Leon had confided in her about Guy's death.

'I loved Guy with all my heart. Madame Leon and I have always been connected by that love. After she told me what really happened to him, she showed me some documents she'd had drawn up. She said, "You were to be my daughter-in-law. In the end you became my dearest friend. This house was always meant to be your home." Then she showed me a copy of her will. I could see that she had left the chateau to me.'

They both turned to look again at the stately house and its tranquil grounds that held so many memories for them both and, with tears in their eyes, they embraced.

By the time Joy said goodbye to her mother a week later, her plans had changed completely. She had decided to stay on at the chateau over winter and have a low-key thirtieth birthday with Dion, then head to Australia around March or April the following year instead. Joy's promise of some sort of birthday celebration later that year had appeased Avril and Tim. Seeing her grandmother was one of the many things Joy was looking forward to doing. No longer able to travel long distances, Anna rarely left the station these days. Her health was slowly deteriorating. Her studio was still her sanctuary and she spent the afternoons drawing and painting the surrounding flora and fauna.

Avril assured Yves and Camille that everything would go on as it always had. After a round-table conference with the husband and wife team as well as Joy, it was agreed that Yves would continue to manage the estate and Camille the restaurant.

Two days before Christmas, roads all over the region were closed due to the sheer volume of snow that had fallen. On the morning of Christmas Eve Joy woke to the smell of burning wood in her bedroom fireplace and Dion carrying coffee and warm croissants through the door.

'Merry Christmas Eve, my love,' said Dion. 'I know what you did. You arranged this dump of snow so I couldn't go back to my place. I am captured, like a prisoner in a tower.'

Dion climbed in next to Joy and they snuggled back into the pillows with their coffees.

'How does this feel, just the two of us for Christmas?' he asked.

'It feels beautiful. Restful,' said Joy. 'That is, until Camille and Yves and the others trek through the snow later tonight. It was good that Marie could get to her brother's place before they closed the roads. She looked worn out when she left.'

'She's staying on, yes?'

'She's away for a month, but yes. I can't imagine the place without her.'

That night they were a small yet merry band. The wine flowed as plates of hot food filled the table and Yves carved the turkey. While the chateau was large, somehow it did not seem empty. In the days that followed, for the first time in months, Joy and Dion were forced by the weather to put their usual busyness aside and relax – so they cooked and played music, talked into the night and woke late. Joy was suffused with happiness.

Joy's Australian mates sometimes got the time difference mixed up and it was not uncommon for the phone to ring at five in the morning while it was mid-afternoon back in Sydney. Scarlet was the worst offender.

'You're kidding,' Scarlet shouted down the phone. 'When?'

'I get into Sydney the first week of March. I'll have a few days with you then go up to Brisbane for a week.'

'A week in Brissy,' said Scarlet in surprise. 'To do what?'

'I'll catch up with Viv and Jason, and I'd like to see Mrs B. Then I'll head up to Monaghan.'

'And the new man?' said Scarlet. 'Will he be with you?'

'I don't think so,' said Joy, watching as Dion slowly shook his head. 'He'll be back at work, but I'm sure you'll get to meet before too long.'

'Well, give him a hug from me, even though we haven't met.'

'Hi, Scarlet,' Dion called. 'She is keeping me prisoner here. I cannot move.'

Scarlet chuckled. 'So, Joy, when are you ever coming home for good?'

'I'm not sure. Trust me, you'll be the first to know,' said Joy, then rang off and put down the phone.

She and Dion exchanged a look that contained everything they'd been discussing, everything they were planning.

The ideas were all there: now she just needed to action them.

*

Scarlet's handsome cardiologist hadn't worked out, nor had the radiologist. On Joy's second night in Sydney, Scarlet threw Joy a welcome home party and she finally got to meet Alex, the stockbroker, who Scarlet was convinced was the love of her life.

'A year and a half and still going strong,' reported Scarlet, taking Joy by the hand and leading her out the back in an attempt to locate Rebecca. Although Simon was living in Sydney – he loved the weather – Joy knew he was currently in America.

Scarlet stopped and looked up at Joy.

'I have to tell you because you'll hate me if I don't. I'm not saying they will, but I wouldn't be surprised if Jack and Dave swing by tonight. Bec mentioned you'd be here, and, well . . .'

'It's okay. You don't have to worry. I'd love to see them,' said Joy. 'And Mick. Does he know I'm in town?'

'Mick's engaged,' Scarlet blurted out. 'Shit. I didn't mean to say it like that.'

'I hope you have a better bedside manner with your patients,' said Joy, laughing. 'Scarlet, it's okay. I know Mick's engaged. It's surprising what you discover when you have three hours to kill and a pile of magazines in the flight lounge.'

'Is that how you found out?'

'Not exactly. Simon told me. Please stop worrying.

Anything I felt for Mick has long gone. Now, where's the champagne?'

People kept arriving and by midnight the front and back verandas and everywhere in between was heaving. The fact that Joy only knew a few of the guests didn't matter. Scarlet and Alex knew enough people between them to fill a room at their Federation cottage any night of the week. And they frequently did, apparently. Rebecca shrieked when she saw Joy and embraced her friend, and the pair chatted about Bec's work, Tracey and the people they both knew. Then Bec went to get another drink, leaving Joy standing alone. Through the waffle pattern of the stained-glass window, the lounge room had come alive, and the music was turned up and the dancing began.

The March night air was humid and as Joy looked at the twenty- and thirty-somethings having a good time, all she could think about was Dion, the chateau, and whether someone had checked that the horses had been properly rugged. If she had held any misgivings about what she wanted to do with her future, tonight's party had eradicated them. She was pleased she'd decided to stay in a hotel. As much as Scarlet was her oldest friend, she didn't know Alex at all and she preferred the privacy of a hotel to staying with friends.

Knowing she'd see Scarlet the next day, Joy slipped quietly from the house and waited at the kerb for her taxi to arrive. Then a car pulled up across the street and some new party-goers got out. Even after all the years, Mick's idiosyncratic walk and stature were impossible to miss. He guided the leggy dark-haired woman at his side through the gate then stopped as he caught sight of Joy.

'I'll be there in a minute, Jess,' Joy heard Mick say, and then he came towards her.

'Joy Meredith,' he said. 'As I live and breathe. The girl of my dreams.'

'Mick Harris, I believe.'

Mick hugged Joy with genuine affection and gentleness, yet there was distance in the embrace.

'Are you leaving? I thought tonight was in your honour?' he said.

'It was. But I'm sure the fun will carry on without me.' Joy laughed.

'You look wonderful,' said Mick. 'Radiant. Are you home for long?'

'A few weeks. Catching up with all the family.'

Mick Harris still had the same smouldering good looks, except, Joy thought, he looked tired, and much older than thirty-seven. The truth was, she realised, she didn't want to be standing there talking to Mick Harris, and when her cab pulled up, she was relieved.

'That's my ride,' she said. 'Take care, Mick,' and she stepped away. As she did so, he reached out and took hold of her hand.

'I've never stopped loving you,' he said quietly. 'I think I always will.'

'Always is a very long time,' said Joy. 'I suggest you enjoy the now. I hope you and Jess will be very happy together. I really do, Mick. You deserve it.'

Joy wound the window down as the taxi headed for the city. She checked her watch. It was Saturday, about three in the afternoon in France. Weather permitting, Dion would be out with his cycling friends on at least a two-hour ride. If ever there was a time when Joy felt that the past was well and truly in the past, this was it.

She had moved on. Her life had moved on. She tilted her head out the window and let the Sydney night air rush over her face.

I can't wait to get home, she was thinking. And not to Brisbane, or to Monaghan Station. To Tours, Dion and the Chateau de Vinieres.

*

It had been Dion who'd planted the idea. 'Why not have a birthday celebration here later in the year? Get everyone to come to you,' he'd suggested the day before she'd left for Australia. The thought of having friends and family descend on the chateau en masse had made Joy smile. She could hear the place ringing with laughter already. *Why not?* she thought. And before she returned to France, Joy told her parents, Scarlet, Rebecca, Simon and the rest of her friends that she wanted to have a big party in September, a belated celebration for her milestone birthday, and that anyone who could make it would be welcomed with open arms.

'And I'll be making some announcements on the night,' Joy had added as a teaser.

Avril went into overdrive, rearranging her schedule, making sure James and Margot had all the details. She booked flights, arranged transport and worked on a host of other arrangements for the whole family. Phone calls and faxes were being made right up until the guests were on their way to Paris.

'Do you think they're getting married?' Rebecca had asked Scarlet.

'Maybe. Who knows? Joy's certainly changed a lot since she first left Australia. In a good way,' Scarlet added.

'She's grown up,' said Rebecca. 'That's what's happened.

342

She's completely her own person. Have you booked your flights?'

'Alex and I are taking a month off to travel, finishing up in Tours for Joy's thirtieth. You and Tracey?'

'Just try to stop us,' said Rebecca. 'A week in Greece, a week in Italy and then a week in France. We can't wait.'

*

Avril and Tim could hear the music and laughter from the courtyard as they finished getting dressed. The chateau was lit up like a Christmas tree, all silver sparkles and twinkling lights.

'When will you tell her?' said Tim, pulling on a navy blazer.

'I'm not sure,' said Avril. 'I'll find the right moment.'

'And you're completely sure about this?'

'Absolutely,' said Avril. 'I've never been more sure about anything. Now come on. Let's get down there.'

Tim put his arms around his wife and pulled her close.

'Can you believe our girl is thirty?' he said.

'Not really, no,' said Avril. 'It seems like yesterday she was riding her first pony around the arena at home.' She was pensive for a moment, then smiled and shook her head as if to chase away her nostalgia. 'Let's go down and have a glass of champagne.'

*

The long tables were set with white linen tablecloths, silver and crystal stemware. The buffet table was filled with Camille's finest cuisine. At various times throughout the dinner, those who were closest to Joy stood and made speeches that were heartfelt and entertaining. James Carmody got the proceedings under way, followed by

Scarlet and then Tim, who made special mention of the members of the Meredith clan.

Joy had no idea that Dion was such a natural orator. He recounted how when they'd been introduced Joy had thought he was in the construction business, and how they'd got to know each other over a lame horse and a literary festival or two. He ended by saying, 'And her parents named her well, because being with this woman is pure joy.'

When it was Joy's turn to say a few words, she said that she'd make the majority of her speech in English, but that there were certain things that could only be said in French. This brought on some banging on the tables and whistles and cheers.

Joy gave thanks for good health and friendship and went on to say something about everyone who was seated before her. She started with Jordy and Duncan, then moved on to her aunt, uncle Reece and cousin Ben. Her words about her godfather, James Carmody, were particularly touching, although Joy gave Scarlet and Rebecca a roasting that finished on high notes of praise.

'Simon, your knowledge and love of literature continues to inspire me,' said Joy. Then she turned to her parents and, tears in her eyes, thanked them for a lifetime of love and support. Joy spoke affectionately about Anna, who was now too frail to travel. She asked everyone to raise their glasses and drink to the wonderful Madame Leon, whose home the chateau had been for almost seventy years.

Finally, she turned to Dion.

'Fate has most definitely brought us together,' said Joy. 'From a brief meeting back in Gloucestershire in 1983 to when we ran into each other in a bookshop in rural France a few years ago – a shop which fortuitously enough is called Turn the Page. And that is exactly what I intend to do with my life now.'

Dion playfully raised his glass towards Joy and she raised hers back.

'Some months ago, I told you all that I wanted to make a couple of announcements. So here they are.'

Joy stopped to take a sip of champagne, which made everyone laugh.

'One of the reasons I went back to Australia in March was because I'd been in contact with the school of veterinary science at the University of Queensland, to find out if I was eligible to complete the final year of my degree. To cut a very long story short, I'm returning to Australia in January to commence the fifth and final year of my veterinary degree.'

Scarlet and Ben led the clinking of glasses and the cheering and whistling that followed.

'But once I've graduated, I plan to live in France permanently.'

There was an outburst of applause and more cheering. Once everyone had settled down, Joy continued.

'I know I have an enormous amount to learn, and I'll need to sit some exams to be accredited to practise here in France, which will be a bit of a journey in itself. But I always wanted to be a vet. It simply took a little longer than expected, with a slight detour, to get there. At some point in the future, I'd like to establish a veterinary practice here on the estate for both horses and small animals.'

Joy turned and looked at her mother.

'Mum, our lives have come full circle. A little over forty years ago, you left France, the place of your birth, for a country you knew very little about but grew to love. You made it your home, you've achieved so much, and I'm so proud of you. Now, thirty years after I came kicking and screaming into the world with a set of lungs that would start a stampede, to quote my father, I'm moving from my place of birth to live in a country I love. I'm not leaving Australia and Monaghan Station behind, though. I'm simply creating a second home, here at the chateau.'

With a wave of her hand, Joy signalled to Dion, Avril and Tim to join her. Dion gently slipped his arm around Joy's waist.

'I'm sure those loved ones who are no longer with us are, in fact, among us tonight,' said Joy. Thinking of Henry and Madame Leon, Joy took a moment to steady her voice, then raised her glass. 'To the roads we take. May they always lead us home.'

And as the clink of glasses and the good cheer rang out, Joy noticed that the full moon had begun to peek over the tops of the nearby pine trees.

Yves and Camille were among the first to wish Joy well.

'We are so excited for you, Joy. This is marvellous news,' said Camille as the two of them embraced. 'Your idea to have a practice here is an excellent one.'

'You must have seen the old stone barn on the other side of the field?' said Yves. 'The roof needs work but the walls are solid.'

'And it's right by the road which makes for easy access. I must admit,' said Joy, 'I've got so many ideas I'd like to talk to you both about.'

'We'll be right here,' said Yves. 'We're not going anywhere.'

Once Joy had finished receiving hugs and congratulations from the other guests, Dion steered her back towards the music.

'I was thinking about all those journals of yours,' he

said. 'Are you still keen to transcribe them like you talked about? That would be the perfect thing to do during a long, cold French winter.'

The music slowed as Joy and Dion began to sway.

'You know, I think I might. Perhaps there's a book in those pages somewhere. I've always wanted to write.'

'Then you should. If you get time, that is. You know you're going to be inundated with friends wanting to visit,' said Dion. 'Prue and Chess are likely to be on the next plane.'

'I like the sound of that,' said Joy. 'You, me and a house full of friends.' And Joy couldn't stop smiling as Dion spun her around.

*

While Joy and Dion were on the dance floor, Avril slipped upstairs to fix her hair and freshen up her lipstick. Then she turned out the bathroom light, walked over to the open window and took in the merriment below. Joy and Ben were now dancing together, like they used to do at the Winter Dance when they were growing up.

'She's inherited my dancing skill,' said Avril out loud as she chuckled to herself. She glanced over at the white folder that was sitting on top of the desk.

Back in March, Tim and Avril had sat under the jacaranda trees at the front of the big house and listened in disbelief to Joy's proposal. They had always assumed that one day Joy would return to run Monaghan Station. The news she'd told her parents that day had come completely out of left field.

'The reality is, Ben's been working alongside Kevin for the last five years and doing an outstanding job. We all know he loves this place just as much, if not more, than

I do,' said Joy. 'I don't want to run the property but I'd like it to stay in the family. That's why I think Ben should be the one to inherit Monaghan Station, not me. With a degree in agriculture and a true passion for the rural life, he's got what it takes to keep the place going.'

After several long talks over the following week, Tim and Avril came around to Joy's way of thinking. Ben was young, keen and destined to have a life on the land. Joy wanted to live in France and be with Dion.

Avril walked over to the desk and flipped open the folder, taking out the thick piece of parchment paper.

'How many hands have touched this document over the decades? How many names have been recorded on the bottom right-hand corner?' Avril murmured to herself as she ran her fingers over the elegant old-style script on the title deeds to the Chateau de Vinieres.

As she watched Joy and Ben dance below, Avril looked down at another document on the desk beside her. The document clearly showed that *Joy Yvette Anna Meredith* was now the legal owner of the Chateau de Vinieres. Avril had overseen the transaction two months earlier.

'I can't think of a better thirtieth birthday present,' Avril had said to Tim the morning she'd signed the last of the paperwork.

'She really loves it there, doesn't she?' Tim said. 'Although I can't help but think it feels like we're losing our daughter.'

'No, my love. Think of it as gaining a country,' said Avril. 'We're not going to be here forever, my darling. Monaghan Station will eventually belong to Ben, along with all the responsibility that goes with such an under-taking. He'll make a success of it. You and I know he will.'

'And Joy. How do you think she'll go running Chateau de Vinieres?' said Tim.

'*C'est son destin*,' said Avril. 'It's her destiny.' She couldn't wait to place the precious title deeds in her daughter's hands. What a magical surprise it would be for Joy.

Avril replaced the documents and closed the folder. Joy was now dancing with Dion again. The full moon had slipped under the cover of the clouds and was slowly making its way up among the canopy of stars.

'Yes,' said Avril to the empty room, as she took in the beautiful sight and sounds of the party. 'My darling Joy, you are so right. We have truly come full circle.'

EPILOGUE

Melbourne, August 1994

The death of James Carmody hit the Meredith family hard.

For Reece, James was the mentor and eventual friend who had given a kid from the bush with a newly minted law degree a chance to prove himself. Under James and Reece's stewardship, the legal practice of Carter, Carmody & Wainwright would eventually become Carmody Meredith Partners, a professional partnership lasting over thirty years.

James had considered his role as Joy's godfather both an honour and a vocation, and at James's memorial, Joy had recounted the many times James 'was there for me no matter what'.

While the intimate relationship that had once existed between James and Avril was not to last, their loving friendship had, right to the very end.

Having completed her meeting with Reece, Avril stepped into the lift, knowing this was the last time she'd ever visit these offices. Reece was retiring and so was she. She felt the first flush of excitement at this prospect. Tim and she had so many plans; their 'to do' list was growing by the day. Avril smiled to herself as she thought about the look on Reece's face when he'd realised what Avril and Tim were asking him to do.

'Ben is to inherit the property?' Reece had said in disbelief. 'What about Joy?'

'It was her idea,' Avril replied.

It was only then that Avril told Reece that the chateau had belonged to Joy since 1991.

'Joy would have ended up inheriting it anyway,' she told Reece. 'So I thought, why wait? And look what she's already achieved. Her veterinary practice is up and running, and Dion is working with Yves to produce two new varieties of grapes. This is the perfect arrangement – a property for both Ben and Joy that they each love and call home.'

The rain had stopped but the night air was bitterly cold as Avril's driver Ron opened the car door for her at the kerb. The piano music Avril loved to listen to was already playing as they headed out of the city. She leant her head back against the headrest and closed her eyes.

She was picturing the scene in a week's time, when members of the extended Meredith family, friends, stockmen, jackaroos and the rest of the station staff would gather in the shearing shed for the Winter Dance. It would be a homecoming for Joy and a chance for Dion to experience the natural beauty of Monaghan Station and attend this annual event.

When Henry and Anna were alive, they'd started a black and white photo gallery at the far end of the shed. Avril could see the images of the Meredith family, along with friends and long-time employees, the photographs documenting rural life on the station through the generations – mustering, shearing, parties, campfires, aerial shots and the faces of those whose lives were inextricably linked with the property, staring out from behind the framed glass, watching, ever present.

Before the fun began, Tim would welcome everyone and ask the assembled crowd to raise their glasses in a toast to family and friendship. The music would start and the dancing continue until sun-up. The bonfires would glow orange-red in the darkness and draw the revellers to the warmth. Everyone loved the Winter Dance at Monaghan Station.

It was always a night to remember.

ACKNOWLEDGEMENTS

To the many readers who wrote to me after reading *A Remarkable Woman* saying they hoped there'd be a second book about Avril, Joy and the Meredith family – thank you! This one's for you.

To my publisher, Claire Craig, and the editing, publicity, marketing and sales teams at Pan Macmillan – Brianne Collins, Candice Wyman and Rufus Cuthbert – you really are my *dream team*. A massive thank you for all your support.

Thank you to Kim Annan, Mary Arlington-Watt, Ian Davison, Cindy Jones, Georgi Johnson and Nick Van Mil for your input concerning the initial story concepts, terminology and historical information.

And for Graeme, who listens, laughs and supports my pursuit of creativity, every day.

Jules Van Mil
A Remarkable Woman

**From postwar Paris to Australia to find love, fashion and freedom
One woman's quest to follow her head, and her heart.**

Twenty-six-year-old Frenchwoman Avril Montdidier sails from Paris to Australia with a suitcase and a dream: to start her own fashion business.

1950s Melbourne is very different from the chic atelier of Dior where Avril once worked, but she is determined, courageous and resourceful.

When personal circumstances force her to flee Melbourne, she travels to a cattle station in southern Queensland to work as a governess. It is here Avril meets Tim: the eldest son of her benefactor and heir to Monaghan Station.

Avril must grapple with her twin desires – her love for Tim, who is set to marry someone else, and her yearning for independence.

Praise for A *Remarkable Woman*

'Delightful! Fashion, French culture and sweeping Australian land-scapes – what's not to love! A glorious nod to the strong migrant women who made their mark on the place they chose to call home – Australia. A fascinating look at the burgeoning cultural and fashion scene of Melbourne in the 1950s set against the vast, rugged and magnifi-cent landscapes of Queensland's Darling Downs and the quintessential Australian experience of life on the land.'
– TANIA BLANCHARD

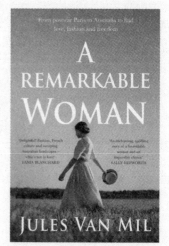

'An enchanting, uplifting story of a formi-dable woman and an impossible choice. A love letter to the pioneering women of the last generation, rich with its historical setting and enticing cast of characters.'
– SALLY HEPWORTH